ALSO BY CAROLYN HOUGAN

Shooting in the Dark

THE ROMEO FLAG

CAROLYN HOUGAN

SIMON AND SCHUSTER
NEW YORK LONDON
TORONTO SYDNEY TOKYO

Simon and Schuster
Simon & Schuster Building
Rockefeller Center
1230 Avenue of the Americas
New York, New York 10020

SIMON AND SCHUSTER and colophon are registered trademarks
of Simon & Schuster Inc.

Designed by Jeanne Joudry
Manufactured in the United States of America

10 9 8 7 6 5 4 3 2 1

Library of Congress Cataloging in Publication Data

Hougan, Carolyn.
   The Romeo flag / Carolyn Hougan.
      p. cm.
   I. Title.
PS3558.O835R6   1989   88-32462
813'.54—dc 19   CIP

ISBN 0-671-61218-2

For Hougan, of course,
and for my sister, Meg

PROLOGUE

Shanghai, 1941

Sergei Borodin had to ask his daughter Anna to help him fasten the straps of the black trunk. His hands had once stitched human flesh together and probed eyes to remove embedded cinders, but now they were arthritic, his huge knuckles and twisted fingers useless for many tasks.

"Pull it very tight," he instructed.

"Yes, Papa," Anna said in her sweet, childish voice.

He'd just finished packing the trunk that morning. He watched Anna pull one strap and push the buckle's prong into the last hole. The leather of the straps was creased and pliable with age. He'd had the trunk for a long time, more than sixty years; it had been his schoolboy footlocker.

Anna pulled the other strap tight. "It's like saddling a horse," she said suddenly. "Tightening the girth. Isn't it?"

"Why, yes, Annie," he said. "It is. How clever of you to see that."

She beamed and her gray curls bounced as she shook her head and blushed with pleasure. Tears welled in Sergei's eyes and he turned his head from her. He worried about what would happen to Anna when he was no longer around. And that time was coming soon. Not only was he an old man of failing vigor, but war was coming, spreading like a virus. Soon, it would infect Shanghai.

The Japanese now occupied all of Manchuria, and eight hundred miles of the Yangtze coast north of Shanghai. It was only because Shanghai was such a strange creature—a city run by Chinese, British, American, and French officials—that the international sections remained free of Japanese control. Still, so many Japanese lived across the Soochow creek in Hongkew that it was now referred to jokingly as the "Japanese Concession."

And once any one of the countries represented in the International Settlement officially went to war with Japan, the Japanese would simply walk in and occupy the defenseless city. That would come soon. Shanghai was running out of time.

When the war did come to Shanghai, stateless Russians could hardly expect an easy time of it. The Japanese were not a merciful people. He rubbed one arthritic hand with the other and looked out the window.

"There," Anna said, patting the trunk. A smile of satisfaction crossed her face. "All done."

He asked her to bring him a glass of vodka and to call Li.

"Yes, Papa."

It was his private theory that Anna's simplemindedness was the result of her long and difficult birth. But although her affliction had been a bitter blow to him and his wife, Marthe, he wouldn't have traded her sweet uncomplaining nature for anything. It was ironic that of his five children, only Anna, the eldest, remained to keep him company now, in his old age.

He sat down with his vodka and his newspapers and watched Li spend the next two hours skillfully encasing the black trunk in a sturdy wooden crate made of pine slats.

"Why are you sending all those papers to the baby?" Anna asked him, pressing her fingertips together and studying the angles they made. "Babies don't like papers, you know. They like dolls." She formed her fingers into circles and held them up to her eyes like spectacles. "They like balls." She frowned, "And sweets," she said. "They like sweets. They don't like papers."

"Yes, Anna, maybe you're right."

"I'm going to cook dinner now."

Anna's talk of papers made Sergei suddenly remember something. And as he listened to her humming and clattering in the kitchen, he took down some sheets of paper and began to write in his shaky, old man's scrawl.

· ·

Tony Sunderland hurried toward the Custom House, where he was to meet his wife, Dasha. As he walked along Bubbling Well Road toward the Bund, he thought that he might be the only man on that busy street to know that it took its name from a naturally carbonated spring discovered in the third century. His bourgeois education made his mind receptive to such frivolous knowledge. And although he considered trivia decadent, a waste of his mental energy, he couldn't stop his mind from noticing and accumulating these trifling facts.

It was unseasonably warm for mid-October and the stench of the ancient city, a putrid smell that newcomers found almost unbelievable, rose heavenward from the ground (and the crowd of humanity that jostled around him) only to be pressed back down by the heavy air of the afternoon.

He was hurrying because he was late and he was frowning because he was annoyed at the whole business. Old Sergei was sending a trunkful of family papers and stuff (probably old sugar bowls, that sort of thing) to the baby! To Nicola! Letters, old photo albums, all that kind of old junk. He and Dasha had promised to take it to the shipping agent and see that it had the proper customs stamps and all that.

Dasha usually got her way with the old man, and she'd done her best to talk him out of this goofy notion, but he was stubborn. Intractable, in fact. So they'd given in. At least they'd persuaded him to send the trunk to Tall Oaks, to England, and not to America, where Hillary and Brian would wonder what on earth they were supposed to do with the stuff in it.

He passed a clutch of beggars sitting in front of the Majestic, opposite the Race Track. A turbaned Sikh policeman, taller than everyone else, surveyed the tumultuous mass of humanity along the busy street, nearly every shred of which seemed to have something to sell.

Those who didn't have goods or services to sell (anything from roasted nuts to silk brocade, silver dollars, shoe shines, letter-writing services) peddled themselves, their own flesh. Shanghai boasted more whores per capita than any other city in the world. Those whose flesh was too unwholesome for that peddled their scars and misfortunes. In Shanghai, beggars were organized into guilds. Some of the wealthiest ones, the most spectacularly deformed, had body-guards. Now the beggars were working the afternoon crowds emerging from the Race Course. Shills for the cabarets kept up a steady, high-pitched barking and pressed leaflets into hands. One ancient Chinese man, dressed up ludicrously as a Dutch girl, tried to hand out flyers for the Amsterdam Café. Foot traffic moved along rather quickly, the pace set by the coolies, who seemed to be propelled forward by the sheer weight on their backs.

Tony was supposed to meet Dasha at the Custom House, under the clock tower, Big Ching, but when he got there, he couldn't find her. Finally he spotted Li coming toward him. Li told him that Dasha had had urgent business at the print shop. She wanted Tony to meet her later, for dinner. He and Li proceeded to the shipping agent's office, where a sweaty little man accepted the crated trunk, the fee, the bribe, and Tony's thanks. Tony pressed the receipt into Li's hand and told him to take it back to Sergei to show him that the trunk had been properly sent. The light was already fading; it was almost six o'clock.

He stood on the embankment for a few moments and looked out on the river. At seven, he had an appointment with Frederich, who would be passing him some photographic negatives which he and Dasha would process and install on the forged identity papers they produced secretly in the back of the print shop.

Crossing the Garden Bridge over Soochow Creek, he watched a couple of corpses float by. One lodged briefly against the pier until it swung free into the current; it rejoined its partner and together they negotiated the curve and floated into the wide brown expanse of the Whangpoo. Some fat drops of rain pelted him and he ran toward the Cathay Hotel. He had an hour to kill, just enough time to have a drink and read the paper.

At seven, he stood in the rain in an alley at the edge of the Place de Candide, trying to decide if the men standing outside Frederich's apartment house were Japanese gangsters or Kempetai, Japanese Secret Police.

There were two of them, one stronger and younger than the other, both wearing sunglasses and ill-fitting business suits. They were standing beside a parked black Mercedes under the building's canopied entrance, while a couple of kids, spitting on rags, polished the hubcaps. The bigger man leaned against one of the canopy's brass supports, hands jammed into the pockets of his trousers, deliberately exposing his shoulder holster. The second man was looking at a newspaper.

If they were gangsters, Tony thought, perhaps waiting for their boss to conclude his business with someone else's wife, it was no concern of Tony's, and he might as well keep his appointment with Frederich.

But if they were Kempetai . . . well, that was a different matter, and it was this possibility that stranded Tony in the alleyway.

Not that the Japanese had any authority inside the French Concession. Not legally, at any rate, and not that it mattered, in any case. Shanghai was theirs for the taking. All of China was. All of the Orient was.

Tony's thoughts were interrupted by the enthusiasm of an approaching beggar. "Mistah! Hey, mistah!" He glanced toward the ground where a small boy with a withered arm pulled himself across the cobblestones on legs cut off below the knees. "I not eat today, mistah."

As a Marxist, Tony did not usually give money to beggars, but it would be impossible to get rid of the boy in any other way. He fumbled in his pockets for some small change, found a coin, and flipped it in the cripple's direction. The boy caught it adroitly, and crabbed off before Tony had to shoo him away.

Tony's eyes returned to the Place de Candide. Whoever their employers might be, the men looked bored, and that was good. But they did not, unfortunately, look as if they were about to leave soon, and that was bad. He wanted to get to the print shop to help Dasha; she had been working so hard lately.

Soaked almost to the skin, Tony was about to stride into the square when a small object shattered a window on the second floor of Frederich's building. Tony heard a hideous scream as the package landed with a dull and sickening clap on the pavement beside the Japanese—who stood, stock-still and appalled, for two long seconds. And then, quite calmly the one man handed the other a part of his newspaper, and both men began to wipe the blood from their shoes.

It was as if a small balloon, filled with red paint, had exploded, and it took Tony a few moments to realize that the window it came from was Frederich's and the package his newborn son.

Tony's breath retreated into his body even as he moved, without conscious direction, away from the spot where the baby had landed. The wet pavement glistened and the murmur of rain seemed to dim the street noise. He passed the neon sign of the American Café—a white neon martini glass, a green neon olive stuffed with a red neon cube of pimiento. Its reflection on the wet street was a surreal, smeary version of the original. He engaged a ricksha. All the way to the print shop, his mind detached, his eyes tracked the splashing progress of the ricksha boy's feet.

Dasha was in the back, in the darkroom, and he knocked and went inside without waiting for her to reply. "It's me," he said. She stood over the developer tray, dragging a submerged print through the fluid with a pair of bamboo tongs. A ghostly face was beginning to emerge, just the smears of eyes and the slash of a mouth. He pulled her outside.

"Tony! What? What's happened? Li said—"

"It's Frederich." He told her what he'd seen and he watched the emotions play on her face—the horror at what had happened to Frederich's baby, the relief that she'd had the foresight and strength to send their own baby, Nicola, away from danger.

The baby was safe in Washington, in the home of Tony's older brother Brian, who was posted to the British Embassy there. Brian's wife Hillary, mournfully barren ("We just can't seem to *hatch*," Brian had written) was delighted to have a little one in the house, and Nicola was reported to be thriving.

Of course, Dasha had suffered torments over the decision of whether to send the baby away or not when the chance came. But conditions in Shanghai continued to grow worse, and the ships departing for safe harbor fewer and fewer, and finally Dasha had decided that she must seize the chance presented by her aunt, Marga. Marga, recently married to an American, was emigrating to the United States and had offered to take the baby on the ship as her own child. Nicola was an infant so young she hadn't required the booking of separate passage. Marga and her husband would take the baby to Washington, to Brian and Hillary.

Tony had steadily refused Brian's insistent invitation that they all come to stay in America but finally he accepted on behalf of Nicola, promising that he and Dasha would join her as soon as conditions permitted. He didn't tell Brian that even if they could have found passage, which was unlikely, the work he and Dasha were doing was of such importance that to leave Shanghai until the task was completed would have amounted to betrayal. They doctored the birth papers themselves to show that Nicola was Marga's child.

But even though it had been her own thoroughly considered decision to send the baby to safety, Dasha had been inconsolable for months, both lovesick for the child and worried, as Tony had been too, for her welfare on such a long and difficult journey. Li had confided in Tony that he had never seen a woman weep so much—and for a female child! For months, no one dared to mention the baby around Dasha for fear of setting her off on a crying jag. Even the anxiously awaited news of the baby's safe arrival had cheered her only slightly. But now, in the face of Frederich's tragedy, her choice to send the baby away could be seen for what it was—not the failure of her maternal instinct, as some had perceived it, but a refinement of it.

He saw that her mind had shifted from thoughts of the baby and its safety to their own predicament. The preoccupied look, the one he thought of as the "Nicola look," left her face and he saw her eyes widen and distort in fear.

She looked quickly around the room. He knew what she was thinking, that maybe they should begin the destruction of incriminating documents. But there was always the chance that Frederich's misfortune was unrelated to them. Maybe it had something to do with a gambling debt, or he'd fooled with someone's woman, or he'd offended one of the powerful Chinese gangs. Anyway, even if it had been Kempetai at Frederich's place, and he had talked, which they had to assume, they still had enough time to hide everything. They gathered up all the blank forms, the papers Dasha was aging with sand and tea, the negatives, the photographs and piled it all into two large portfolio cases. Li would know where to put them for safekeeping, somewhere in Nantao, the old walled Chinese city.

When they were finally finished, they locked the door and went out, walking toward the Rue Père, and Li's house. They'd gone only a few blocks when a black Mercedes cruised past. Tony watched the lights play along the highly polished curves of its surface. Maybe it was a different black Mercedes. He found himself holding his breath as he watched it slide by.

But a few blocks later, when then they turned up Rue Père, there was the car, parked, waiting. It reminded Tony of a large black malevolent beetle. As he and Dasha turned the corner, the two men lounging against the door tossed their cigarettes into the wet gutter.

"Ah," the older of the two said. He removed his sunglasses and put them in his breast pocket. He placed his hand almost gallantly on Dasha's arm and tried to take the portfolio from her. "May I help you with this?"

Her eyes met Tony's. She resisted the man's pulling arm for a moment, struggling against him and then she rushed toward him with such force that he released her in surprise. Tony himself didn't move: the metal mouth of a revolver barrel pressed into his temple.

The older Japanese man quickly overtook Dasha. Tony called out a warning cry. A short, sharp blow was delivered to his collarbone; he knew that it was broken before any pain registered. Dasha did not give up easily, and as the man struggled to restrain her, Tony saw her grind her high pointed heel into his instep. It was enough to make him release his grip but he quickly had her again, and this time he twisted her arm behind her, making her cry out in pain.

They were forced into the car, which smelled strongly of cigarette smoke. The light shining through the rain-spattered windshield fell on the driver's head; his shadow-splotched face was remarkably free of expression.

The gun barrel was pressing into Tony's groin now. Dasha sat back, holding her arm. The driver turned on the wipers and the car nosed into the street. The man who held the gun against Tony spoke. His lips barely moved and his voice was flat and bored: "In case you are interested," he said, "your friend Richard has been arrested in Tokyo."

14

PART ONE

DANTE

January, 1980

CHAPTER

ONE

San Francisco, California

The kid was maybe twenty-one, tops. He had that tidy look some young gay men have—combed, trimmed, everything tucked in. Murray had told him to wait, so he was sitting out in the corridor with his back against the wall. He wasn't happy about it, and every few moments he muttered something, although no one bothered to reply. "Oh, man," he said a few times, each time sounding just a little more annoyed, as if he were an actor trying for the perfect tone.

Murray heard him as a kind of background noise, between the static and chatter of his police radio, the paramedics' radio, and the TV in the apartment, which was turned to "As the World Turns." The volume was up. He would have turned it off, but he didn't want to disturb any fingerprints that might be on the knob. "I guess this is what you get for being a good citizen," the kid said. "I should've just walked away." The actress on the tube was sobbing. An older woman handed the sobbing woman a tissue. There was some portentous music. Murray found himself watching until the screen dissolved into a commercial. He followed the paramedics into the hall.

They stepped carefully over the body and sideways through the door. The dead woman's face was touching the bottom of the door, so it would only open so far. The woman was gagged. The gag was a special contraption—a ball about the size of a golf ball, held in

17

place with leather straps that went around to the back of her head—
a *manufactured* gag. Although he'd never actually seen a gagged
person before, Murray had thought all gags were homemade. Cloth
stuffed in the mouth, cotton and tape. This had an industrial look,
as if it might be used over and over again. The woman had a terrible, startled expression and the one brown eye that was visible
stared in horror. She wore a slinky black dress with a sequined
bodice. Her shoes, silver spike heels, had come off. Murray thought
she had a nice ass. Then he crossed himself surreptitiously because
the thought seemed to him likely to be a sin.

"I don't even *know* about any woman," the kid was saying. "I
only just met the guy who lives here last week. He was a waiter
at the Caspian Sea. We just met, that's all. I don't know his friends.
I don't know about any female friends, that's for *sure*. How can I
possibly be of any help? That's what I want you to tell me."

It was the kid who'd spotted the fingers with their bright red
polished nails sticking out through the gap underneath the door.
The door looked as if someone had once taken it off its hinges and
planed it down so it would close over the thick shag carpet. From
the raggedy surface of the door's lower edge, Murray could tell
that whoever had planed the door down hadn't known what the
hell he was doing. After he'd seen the fingers, the kid had called
911 and made the mistake of hanging around to see what the story
was. Maybe. At least that was the kid's line.

Murray, as one of the arriving officers, wanted to minimize the
disruption of evidence in the room, which was why he'd told the
kid to stay in the hall. Murray was taking down the paramedics'
names and numbers. Now he wanted to quickly establish what
they'd touched. They could be fingerprinted later.

"You can talk to us tonight, man," said the white paramedic in
an impatient voice. "We've got to get back on call. Supervisor will
have a bird."

"Did you go into the bathroom?" Murray asked.

"Come on, man, this dude is dead," the black paramedic said.
"You want to be responsible for someone else checking out while
we stand around here and you take notes?"

It occurred to Murray that he might get hassled about delaying
them and he started to wave them on their way when something
clicked in his head.

"What do you mean . . . *dude?*"

The black paramedic jerked his head back toward the apartment. A weird little grin came over his face. "You know, when we checked the vitals, we could tell, you know. That ain't no lady."

Murray couldn't believe it. "You mean that's a *guy?*"

"You got it," the black paramedic said with a nod. He made a little click in his mouth. "Catch you later."

The kid lurched to his feet. Murray's partner, Olney, was coming down the hall whistling "Let It Be."

"Holy shit," the kid said. "I didn't think Oleg was into that. He didn't give me the impression. . . . I mean . . ."

"Maybe this *is* your friend," Murray said. "Would you take a look at the face? Maybe you can make identification."

"I really wouldn't want to do that," the kid said in a reasonable voice. "I'd really rather not." He tilted his head to appeal to Olney. "The only dead people I've seen have been in caskets, you know? And I don't mess with queens. I mean that's not my scene, you know?"

"That's a guy?" Olney said, inclining his head toward the corpse. Murray nodded.

"*Un*believable," Olney said in an exhausted way. He turned to the kid. "C'mon, take a look." His voice did not offer alternatives.

"I want a lawyer."

"Look, bud," Olney said. "Don't be more of an asshole than you have to be."

"Oh, all right," the kid said.

They filed, sidestepping, through the door. "Don't touch anything," Murray said. The kid squinted, and took a look.

"My God," the kid said. "It's him. It really is him." His eyes flashed up to Murray's. "I swear to God I had no idea this was his scene. I swear to God I—"

Murray reassured the kid. "I believe you. Don't worry." He explained to the kid that he would still have to go down to the station. "There's no way around that. I mean even if you didn't know this guy." He looked at the corpse. "You'd still have to fill in a statement."

"Did they say if he'd been murdered?" the kid asked in a sudden puzzled, upbeat voice. He looked from one to the other. "Or did he just croak?"

Murray shrugged. "Medical examiner will know."

"Oh, man, what a day I have had," the kid said. His voice sounded young and false, like some kid star on a sitcom.

Olney belched. "Poor baby," he said, entirely without sympathy.

CHAPTER
Two

Northern Virginia

Hobart Meredith James, better known as Hobie, sat in the living room of Location #9, an undistinguished split-level set well back from the road on the outskirts of Clifton, Virginia. Hobie—a nickname his wife detested because it seemed better fit for a fast-food restaurant than for a man of what she called "his standing"—was a small, wiry man with a bristle of reddish hair. He reminded the increasingly small number of people whose origin was rural enough for barnyard analogies of a bantam rooster.

Location #9 was one of the safe houses maintained by the CIA's Office of Security, that branch of the Agency responsible for internal security—the secrecy and integrity of Agency property, records, plans, operations and personnel, worldwide. Because of its watchdog role, OS was viewed by Agency personnel with the dislike and fear any population has for its police. Further, Hobie knew that OS was regarded as a haven for sinister and humorless gumshoes, plodding but nasty types, the beat-patrol men of intelligence.

With the exception that is, of its Director: himself.

He had an eager, puppyish manner, the kind of gee-whiz earnestness that made him the object of mild ridicule among his colleagues—even among his friends. He was nosy and restless, a man who couldn't sit still. He considered himself a lucky man because his vocation and his avocation coincided. He was simply fascinated by everything to do with the world of espionage; he had a fan's passion for the clandestine world.

The truth was that he didn't mind being patronized for his some-times gauche exuberance. He didn't mind being taken for a fool. In fact, although his eager-beaver persona was to a large degree genu-ine, he cultivated it some, exaggerated it. He always struck people as an odd choice for the sinister post of OS chief, and that was because his harmless exterior concealed a calculating and complex mind. And this benign facade served him well because people were not *careful* in his presence. Even when they knew better, they couldn't bring themselves to perceive this bumbling cub scout as a threat. It amazed him, the things people told him, the things they let slip.

Hobie got up from the couch and paced the room. He was wait-ing for the arrival of a man named Ronald Peters, who was being driven down from the Federal Correctional Institution in Danbury, Connecticut by Hobie's assistant, Max Lemro. Peters was serving the second of forty years for espionage—which for the fifty-six-year-old man was a life sentence. No doubt he was enjoying the ride.

Hobie was not enthusiastic about the upcoming interview. It was something that had to be done, but he approached it like a man who'd just discovered he'd lost his car keys on a crowded, sandy beach—hoping for a miracle.

When he heard the crunch of tires on the gravel drive, he got up for the third time and stirred the fire. Max Lemro ushered Peters through the front door. Hobie hadn't seen Peters for two years and the change in the man was dramatic. For one thing, although still heavy, Peters had lost about fifty pounds on the prison diet. His formerly pudgy face was handsome without the obscuring fat. But if handsome in form, his face seemed peculiarly inert, devoid of ex-pression. He wore a well-cut suit; a camel-hair coat was draped over his shoulders. His hair had a touch of gray at the temples now. He might have been a professor or a prosperous businessman except for that dead face and the way he walked, with a defeated jailhouse shuffle. His eyes, too, had developed a defensive, shifting focus, as if he would never again be quite sure where to let them come to rest. When Hobie extended his hand, there was an embarrassing moment before he realized that Peters was cuffed.

"Max," he said reproachfully. "I don't think we need those."

Lemro had the artificially thin physique of a heavy smoker. His blond hair was slicked back on the sides, fifties style. He cocked an eyebrow and ducked his chin forward as if to ask Hobie if he was sure. Hobie nodded. "All right," Lemro said in his Boston accent. "It's your call."

When the cuffs were off, Peters flexed his hands a couple of times. But he didn't move.

"Well, Mr. Peters," Hobie said, gesturing toward one of the leather wing chairs that flanked the fireplace, "won't you sit down?" Peters shot a worried glance at Max Lemro, as if he wanted to ask permission first. Then he recovered his composure and sat down. "Would you like anything?" Hobie said. "A drink? What will you have?"

"Bourbon," Peters said in a guarded voice. "On the rocks."

Hobie nodded at Lemro, who left the room. He saw that Peters's eyes kept straying to the manila envelope that lay on the coffee table between them.

"I suppose you're wondering what this is all about," Hobie said.

"Your friend didn't say a word. Not one goddamn word. I think that's rude."

"He's not a talkative guy." Hobie shrugged and tried to meet Peters's eyes. "Max and I are with the CIA's Office of Security." Hobie didn't miss the momentarily sharpened focus in Peters's muddy brown eyes. He looked puzzled rather than alarmed.

Hobie picked up the envelope that lay on the table between them. It was stamped with a red C within a black square—a classification mark for CIA's highest security clearance, C-level. The hierarchy progressed from Secret to Top Secret to Q-clearance to C-clearance. Hobie could never figure out if it was somebody's idea of a joke or not, but the C stood for COSMIC.

Lemro brought out a tray of drinks and set it on the table. A cigarette was suspended between his lips and he drew it down and cupped it in his hand. He always carried his cigarettes that way, a habit he said he'd developed as a parochial schoolboy; he'd grown up in South Boston, hiding various sins from the nuns. Hobie watched him pull the metal top off a can of smoked almonds.

Peters gulped his drink and nervously popped an almond into his mouth. "What would the Office of Security want with me? I don't get it."

Hobie pulled the papers from the envelope and leafed through them. Each page had a white rectangle, which contained the clearance information—in this case the C for COSMIC level and the single cryptonym LUCIFER. He separated the series of police photos from the rest of the papers.

He selected one of the photographs, tugged it free from the bunch, and slid it across the table. It showed the body of a woman in evening dress sprawled on a beige shag carpet. There was a ball gag in her mouth; something about the way the mouth was set around the gag and the one visible eye made the corpse resemble a fish. The meticulous focus and police lighting made the photograph look not just gruesome but grotesque. Peters instinctively reached toward it, then his hand jerked away. "What the hell is that?" he said. He stuffed a handful of almonds in his mouth and swung his big head slowly from side to side. "I really don't know what the hell this is all about."

Hobie picked up the envelope. "This is a report from the Transients Security Bureau."

"Never heard of it."

"It's the part of the Agency that handles the protection and relocation of CIA assets," Hobie said. He stood up and poked the fire. "Defectors usually. They're the usual TSB clients. Oh, once in a while they'll do an agent or officer who's gone way too far and requires a new start as someone else. But your run-of-the-mill TSB client is a defector—someone who's been debriefed by the Agency, someone the Agency is done with. Someone who needs a new identity for the remainder of his life."

Peters had an alert, hopeful look on his face; he thought these services were going to be offered to him, that he was going to be presented with a deal. Hobie sat down again. "TSB does a hell of a job." He ticked off the tasks on his fingers. "They find a new location; they arrange housing, schooling, instruction in English— if necessary. They find . . . or sometimes create . . . a job. In short, they make a new life for someone."

Peters's hand dug in the tin of almonds. "Another drink?" Hobie asked.

Peters licked the salt from his fingers. He sat up in his chair, and crossed his legs. "Sure," he said. He still wasn't sure where any of this was going. "I'll take another drink." Lemro went off.

Hobie took the sheaf of police photographs and scattered them on the coffee table. It was the same subject, just taken from every possible angle. But the spread of images on the table gave Hobie a strange, queasy feeling for a moment, as if his heart was floating free in his chest. He coughed. "Naturally," he went on, "security at TSB is tight. And they get very upset if anything happens to one of their clients. It's their job to protect these folks from retaliation. Potential defectors might think more than twice if too many predecessors got walloped after they told their stories."

Peters continued to look baffled. "I still don't get it."

Hobie held up the sheaf of papers. He found himself on his feet. "Well, it's simple as hell. This dead TSB client"—he gestured at the clutter of photographs—"is your old pal Boris Shokorov."

Peters grabbed one of the photographs and stared at it. "No."

"He was living in San Francisco. He'd taken the name Oleg Uminski. He was working in a restaurant called the Caspian Sea. And his body was found three days ago by one of his friends." Hobie tossed another photograph on the table. This time the victim was laid out on the mortuary slab. It was a shot that was usually taken just prior to autopsy. The body was naked, and even though the makeup had not been removed, without the clothes and wig, Shokorov was immediately recognizable.

Peters gave a little jerk, then tossed the photograph on the table in a casual motion which failed to obscure his agitation. He tried to look at Hobie, but his eyes just wouldn't connect. "How do I know this isn't some kind of trick? He could just be faking it, laying there, pretending. I'm not going to tell you *anything*."

Hobie gathered the papers and tapped the ends together. He pushed the stack into the envelope. "Look, Mr. Peters," he said. "You'd better just hope you've *got* something to tell me."

Lemro spoke from the corner. "You've done two of a mandatory forty in Danbury. You're buried *alive*, mister. We got no interest in tricking you."

"The Soviets might make a trade for me." He dug into the tin of almonds but he'd eaten them all.

Lemro hooted, shaking with inaudible laughter. "Yeah. Right."

"I'm not sure you know what *happened* to you, Mr. Peters. What do you think happened?"

Peters looked worried, as if this was a trick question. "I fell in love," he said dramatically. "I sold secrets to the Russians. I betrayed my country." He sank back into the chair, looking pleased with himself.

Lemro snorted. "More like you got hit by a fucking steamroller."

Hobie James pulled on his lower lip. He stood up and began slowly pacing around as he talked. "Three years ago, in 1977, a team of cryptanalysts at the National Security Agency made a major breakthrough. Never mind how, but they got hold of the specifications for Soviet encryption devices as well as some cryptographic key lists and key cards. For the first time we were able to decipher some of the 'unbreakable' shifting, random, computerized code that Moscow uses to send cables to and from the United States.

"And you know what happened? The Soviets went off the air. We're talking about complete radio silence. It was terrifying. We thought they were about to declare war."

"I don't know what the hell you're talking about," Peters said nervously.

"If you *knew*, you wouldn't be here now, wouldya? You're supposed to be *listening*, Jack," Lemro said.

Hobie looked out the front window. Through the sheer curtains, nothing could be seen but a blurred impression of the landscape. "Of course there was a furor about the leak, a real stink. How had Moscow learned so quickly of NSA's breakthrough? Where was the leak? The National Security Adviser conducted an investigation, which learned absolutely nothing.

"And when the radio silence was over, Moscow had changed their encryption procedures." Hobie's hands fell open like a book. His voice was heavily ironic. "Big surprise. But of course, they couldn't do anything about the years of tapes of cable traffic collected and stored by NSA. Cryptanalysts began wading through the backlog. It was slow going, but one of the interesting bits of information that emerged was news of a source, named DANTE. Let me see if I can get it right. The NSA memo put it this way." He frowned with concentration. " 'A Soviet penetration, code DANTE, in a sensitive, but not necessarily intelligence-related government component.' In other words, a Soviet mole."

Lemro laughed his staccato cackle.

"An investigation was mounted—assigned to the CIA's Soviet Bloc Division. But before the Soviet Bloc investigators actually did much digging, a DANTE candidate fell in their laps. That was you, Mr. Peters."

"But I'm not a Soviet *mole*. I was a GS-14!"

Hobie got to his feet and threw another log on the fire. "A lot of material was held back from discovery for national security reasons. But you did *confess*, Mr. Peters."

"I had to. They told me that if I didn't cooperate, they'd send Boris back to Moscow. The Russians would have killed him."

Hobie knitted his hands together, then stretched them straight out in front of himself. "Not exactly," he said in a low voice. "That's not exactly how it went down. This is what you don't know. What happened was this: just after the DANTE investigation started, a Russian émigré calling himself Boris Shokorov made an emergency appointment with his caseworker at the New York Agency for New Americans. Boris told this young woman that he was a KGB agent who wanted to defect. In return for more money and a better apartment, Boris, identified in reports only as an 'émigré' living in the 'émigré community' of Brighton Beach, was prepared to tell all. Since most émigrés are interested in more money and better apartments, Boris was not, at first, taken seriously. But he persisted and returned with some sensitive State Department documents. He demanded that he talk with someone from the CIA—and we were called. Ordinarily, you see, it would have been an FBI matter, but Boris insisted and he was so adamant that he got his way.

"Boris said that he could identify a mole—at a high level of the U.S. government. He said that the mole's code name was DANTE. That he knew the code name was in itself a telling point. He gave us"—Hobie held up his finger and let it fall, pointing at Peters— "you."

"I don't believe you," Peters said.

Hobie shrugged and continued. "Well, everyone was eager to have you be our Soviet mole—especially the Agency. What were you? A State Department bureaucrat who worked in the Refugee Programs Bureau. Everyone at CIA breathed a sigh of relief. Me too." He pushed his thumb against his chest. "I can't exempt myself. We were relieved on several fronts: we wouldn't be fractured by another mole search like the ones that almost paralyzed the Agency in the sixties. And you were not one of our own. Even more importantly, you were not in a position to have done much damage, to have passed much information of value. In short—you made our day."

• •

Hobie remembered when Ronald Peters was arrested and charged with espionage. Peters confessed instantly. Alcoholic and unstable, he seemed to relish confessing his sins, volunteering details that interested no one. He gushed the news that he'd betrayed his country for just five thousand dollars ("It wasn't the money; that was just change. I didn't do it for the money.") and the sexual favors of Boris Shokorov. Confessing seemed to soothe him. "I don't expect anyone to understand. It's a great relief to me not to have this secret anymore." Ronald Peters's grim-faced wife stood next to him, smiling an odd, beatific smile. She, too, seemed to be enjoying herself, as if she'd been waiting for her chance to stand up for her man all her life. "Whatever he's done, whatever he does, I will still be his loving wife."

There was extensive media coverage. Hobie had been amazed by the Peters—who seemed to find a sleazy fulfillment in their notoriety. Peters described his seduction by Boris Shokorov in one television interview: "He cooked blinis for me and served vodka. I was charmed. When he first began to hug me, I took it for a virile Russian expression of friendship. It took me a while to realize it was a caress. I think I've always been a homosexual without knowing it. Perhaps a bisexual (a glance at his wife, who offered a buck-up smile). Possibly that is the source of my alcoholism," he speculated. "Ronald Peters is one of the finest men I've ever known," Mrs. Peters said. At the height of their brief celebrity, Hobie had heard there was a book deal in the works.

"So," Hobie said to Ronald Peters, "the mole investigation came to an official end. You were sent to Danbury. Shokorov went to San Francisco." He shrugged. "Not the best outcome for you, but the rest of us were living happily ever after. Until last week."

"I still don't know why I should believe you."

Lemro made a noise like the sound of a closing bus door. One of his ears was red, a sign of anger. "We're not trying to *convince* you of anything. We could give a fuck what you believe."

"Let me explain why you're here, Mr. Peters. As the NSA team waded through more Soviet intercepts, it eventually became clear that data from Source DANTE couldn't possibly have come from Ronald Peters."

Peters's face went through some interesting changes.

"If you think somehow you're going to get off the hook here, be *exonerated* or some such crap," Lemro said, "forget it. You sold what you had. If you'd of had better stuff you woulda sold that too."

"The point is," Hobie said, "that a reopening of the DANTE investigation was ordered. And it was reassigned to us. That was one week ago. After reviewing the files, it seemed that the first logical step was to interview Boris Shokorov." Hobie stood up. "But before Max could even get out to San Francisco, the man was found dead." Peters opened his mouth to say something but Hobie cut him off. "*Boris is dead.* Our investigation is less than one week old and we get this." He made a loose gesture toward the spread of photos on the table. "Mr. Peters, we don't believe in coincidence."

Peters looked wide awake for the first time, as if his brain was whirring away behind his eyes, working out the best angle. "So?"

"So," Lemro said. "The next logical step was to interview you, buddy. The fact that you're still alive to *be* interviewed probably makes this whole session a waste. You probably don't know squat that can help us."

"Wait a minute," Peters said with a desperate edge in his voice. "I might."

Hobie leaned forward, palms on his knees. "You're going to spend the next couple of weeks *thinking*, Mr. Peters. Thinking out loud. Right here. You're going to remember everything you can about Boris Shokorov. And if you can help us, maybe we can help you."

"If I go along with this, how do I know you'll come through?"

Hobie sighed. His voice got lower in volume, but harder in tone. He sounded weary, almost bored. "I want you to have a clear picture, Mr. Peters. We are not making a deal with you here. If we have positive feelings toward you after the time you spend here, we may be able to recommend some relief—some reduction in sentence, perhaps. If we have negative feelings, it is within our power and, I hasten to point out, *perfectly legal*, for us to recommend your transfer from Danbury to another prison." His hand waggled in the air. "For security reasons. You could do a lot worse than Danbury, as I'm sure you know. In fact"—he cocked his head to the side as if considering the notion—"much, much worse."

CHAPTER

THREE

Bath, Maine

On the morning of January 9, 1980, which happened to be her fortieth birthday, Nicola Ward knew nothing about a dead man in San Francisco or a Soviet mole called DANTE. If anyone had told her that within a few months, the identity of that Soviet mole would be a life-and-death matter to her, she would have drawn back her head and given that person a deep sideways look.

It was a look that was characteristic of her, good-natured but suspicious. She taught the fifth grade. It was a look that let children know when she didn't believe the outrageous excuses they invented.

But Nicola Ward would have thought it a luxury, anyway, to worry about something months in the future. She had more pressing problems. Right now, she was sleeping. And even in sleep, concern showed in the slight frown on her face and the almost fetal clench of her body. Her hands were tensed into fists.

When the alarm went off, she slapped the snooze-bar with a practiced left-handed jab and settled back into that dreamy cocoon between sleep and wakefulness. The lulling sound of rain on the roof tempted her to stay there in her warm and comfortable bed. But when the alarm beeped a second time, a strict interior voice commanded: *get up*. And she rolled over and out of bed.

Expecting the lost, gray light of a rainy day, she stood in the bright sunlight, disoriented, squinting like a moviegoer coming out from a matinee.

30

Then she smelled the bacon.

Of course.

Kate was cooking breakfast. She squeezed her eyes shut. Bacon sputtering in the pan *did* sound exactly like rain. She wondered if, in radio plays . . .

Still, the smell of the bacon, the density of the light—she should have known it was bacon cooking, not rain. She got out of bed and pulled on her old chenille robe. It was not the first time she'd doubted the integrity of her perceptions.

"Mom?" Kate's trembly voice came through the door. "Are you up? I'm making breakfast."

"I'm getting up."

She went into the bathroom and splashed water on her face. The moment she looked in the mirror, she remembered that today was January 9—her birthday.

Forty.

She stood back and appraised herself in the mirror. Her hair was black and poker straight. "Like oriental hair," said Brenda, at Headhunter, who cut it for her. She'd always worn it in the same style—bangs straight across her forehead and the rest of the hair blunt cut at chin level, a China chop. Her eyes were a light, almost milky blue. She pulled her hair back to see what she'd look like with it away from her face. She turned her head to the right and then to the left, studying her face from different angles. She thought: I don't look forty. She released her hair and watched it fall into place. Of course she looked forty. She looked *exactly* forty.

She spotted a gray hair spiraling out from the rest and reached up to yank it out. Her hand fell away. She couldn't pull them out forever. Besides, these gray hairs were so different from the rest, so wiry and energetic. Maybe she would become springy and resilient along with her hair.

Forty, she thought.

Of course Kate remembered that it was her birthday. Kate was cooking her a birthday breakfast. Kate was enthusiastic about occasions; she looked forward to them with an unhealthy fervor. Sometimes, it seemed to Nicola that notations on the calendar were the only things dragging Kate into the future.

When she stepped into the kitchen, she saw that the round table beyond the counter was meticulously set with their best china and silver. Balloon glasses held yellow linen napkins pleated into the shape of fans.

"Happy birthday, Mom!" Kate said brightly.

"It looks wonderful. The table looks so pretty."

"I'm making bacon, and mushroom omelets. And mimosas."

"Fantastic." Kate would now require a constant stream of compliments until the meal was finished. "What a treat."

Nicola sighed and deliberately unclenched her jaw. She looked at her daughter. Kate was dressed, somewhat garishly, in a bright blue sweater and yellow slacks. This was a good sign. More and more often, she didn't bother to dress. She lay in bed all day in her nightgown, bedraggled, unkempt, the invalid she really was. But this morning Kate had put on makeup, another good sign though a disconcerting sight. Bright spots of blusher shone on her skeletal cheeks. Metallic blue eyeshadow glittered above her exhausted eyes; mascara weighed down her eyelashes.

"You look nice," Nicola said enthusiastically. "Can I help?"

"Oh no, it's your birthday. You relax. Read the paper."

"You're terrific."

"Aw shucks," Kate said in a bright voice. "Ain't nothin'."

The paper previewed an eclipse of the sun the next day, despite the fact that it would be barely noticeable in Maine. Nicola supposed it was a slow news day. She read the article anyway and somewhere in her mind the information lodged: Baily's beads, burned retinas, smoked glass, pinhole techniques.

Kate served the mimosas.

"Delicious," Nicola pronounced after a sip.

"You don't think I used too much orange juice?"

"It's perfect, just perfect."

"For the perfect mom," Kate gushed. "Happy birthday."

They touched glasses. Nicola couldn't help noticing that Kate's hand trembled. Kate brought the glass to her lips, and it fluttered there for a moment, but Nicola could see that she only pretended to drink.

Kate bustled back into the kitchen.

Nicola looked out the window. The snow had melted slightly since yesterday and refrozen into a hard crust overnight. The harsh light of the morning glinted off the mounded white contours, giving the yard a sculpted sheen. The snow had a permanent look, as if it would never melt.

She paged through the newspaper. There were mudslides on the West Coast—illustrated by a photograph of three expensive, glassy houses in various states of splintered disintegration, the very ground beneath them skidding down a treeless hillside. On another page there was a photograph of Leo Adler, the National Security Adviser, his heavy features congealed in a frown. Underneath his scowl was a story about unrest in Iran, flanked by a piece detailing the administration's peacemaking efforts in the Middle East. Nicola scanned the articles. Key words in the headlines filtered through, the smiles or frowns of administration spokesmen, the bent of the editorial cartoons.

She leafed forward to the feature section, stopping to read her horoscope. *If January 9 is your birthday, you are sensitive, passionate, forgiving to a fault . . . attracted to Libra, Sagittarius persons . . . financial situation . . . June, July . . . Major domestic adjustments may occur.* What did that mean? While she didn't believe that the machinations of the stars, or even God, controlled her fate, she remained stubbornly superstitious. *Major domestic adjustments may occur.*

She passed up an article on "Keeping Your Poinsettia Healthy After the Holiday," and her eyes fixed on a square-bordered ad for *Evergreen: A Center for the Treatment of Eating Disorders.* She held up the paper vertically, so Kate wouldn't be able to see what she was reading. *Anorexia, Bulimia, Obesity: a new start for the New Year.* A Portland address and telephone number.

Nicola sighed. If she so much as left the paper open to the page the ad was on, Kate would take it as a rebuke. Kate seemed to be past the point where anyone could help her. Kate was in control and Kate seemed intent on self-destruction. Nicola folded the paper carefully, and without thinking about it, cradled her head in her hands. *Major domestic adjustment*, she thought. *Kate will die.*

"Mom! What's the matter?"

"Oh, I don't know." She lied easily; she'd developed a flawless internal censor. "I just don't feel like teaching today."

"Call in sick," Kate said. "After all, it's your birthday."

"No, I can't. It's too late. They wouldn't be able to get a sub."

"Want some more omelet?"

"No, I shouldn't. I'm full."

"Just a tiny bit?"

Nicola gave in. "It really is delicious."

Nicola was good at giving in. It sometimes seemed to her that her entire life had been a series of concessions, of giving ground.

Kate beamed, a bony grin. *Why don't you have some?* Nicola thought. But she didn't say it out loud. To make any suggestion or take any notice of Kate's eating was to risk a daylong stony silence, a retreat to Kate's room, a locked door. That was "pressure," that was "forcing." That just made it "worse." The paper fell open to the op-ed page. The cartoonist had drawn Uncle Sam standing on a map of the Middle East. Little exploding stars showed the hot spots: Lebanon, Cairo, Teheran, Baghdad, Damascus, Kabul. Uncle Sam was tossing bullet-shaped handfuls of birdseed from a bag labeled "U.S. AID" toward the various targets. Nicola took two more bites of omelet, feeling like a surrogate eater, and got up.

"Thanks for the breakfast, sweetheart." She leaned over to give Kate a hug. Kate's body was grotesque in the same way that an extremely obese person's body is grotesque: a hideous, unnatural deviation. And it produced in Nicola the same physical revulsion. Kate's emaciation had progressed to the stage where her body had begun to exhibit the last pathetic signs of self-preservation. Long, furry hair was growing on her arms and legs, her body's last-ditch effort to keep itself warm. The hair on her head was lifeless and thin, falling out in clumps. Nicola retreated to her room, suddenly stiff with fear. Her thoughts dissolved into a worried incantation: *do something, do something.* She hoped some new strategy might unfold in her mind, that some thought would crystallize—a thought so powerful and so correct, it would catapult her to a new plane where she would *know* what to do. But her mind produced nothing more than blank fear. She sat on her bed, on her birthday, taking stock.

Aunt Hillary, who'd brought her up, had encouraged this habit—of taking five minutes on her birthday. She could summon Aunt Hillary's precise British voice now, her sweet, dimpled smile: "You must try to look ahead, Nicola, don't you know? Pretend you're coming to a corner. Try to see around the bend. Imagine what you hope to accomplish this year, what alleys and side streets should be avoided, which ones should be explored."

But Nicola was afraid to look ahead. Instead, she thought back. A year ago, on her birthday, things had been different. A year ago, she'd bought an expensive new dress and had gone out to share an elaborate and romantic dinner with Jack Alaric. Jack wasn't the first "boyfriend" (as Kate called them) that Nicola had had since Stan had left her, but their relationship had been the most enjoyable and the most serious.

A year ago, things had been going well with Kate, too. Her first semester at Bowdoin College, she'd made the Dean's List. She'd begun to diet, too, and Nicola had been happy about that. Kate had gotten a little bit pudgy at puberty and just stayed that way, about fifteen pounds overweight. Nicola remembered painfully how pleased she'd been by Kate's diet, how proud of her self-discipline.

And then she'd also been delighted when Kate found her first real boyfriend—a Bowdoin sophomore named Charlie Dils. The two things she'd worried about—Kate's weight and her seeming indifference to boys—had disappeared.

Nicola had always blamed herself for Kate's tendency to overeat, for Kate's shyness with the opposite sex.

But then Nicola always took the blame; she always knew things were her fault. Right before he left them, she remembered Stan screaming at her: "It's not your fault! It's mine! *This is my fault!*" But she retained the belief that there were remote and tenuous links between herself and disastrous events in the world, invisible, powerful links. She saw the world as a vast interlocking network. If she picked a daisy, or threw a rock in the water, a man in Seattle might trip on the sidewalk, a girl in Little Rock might begin to weep.

As a child, Nicola was "good," she was "never a bit of trouble." As an adult, she'd led the same kind of good life, free of nasty compulsions and dark secrets. How was she to know it would be her very goodness that would end up driving Stan crazy, driving him away from her? He'd called her a tin angel and although she'd recoiled when he shouted that, she knew what he meant. She was good because she lacked the vision or the courage to be bad; she was in the form of something good, but she was made of baser stuff.

She began to button up her blouse, wondering when it was, exactly, that things began to deteriorate. Everything had been steadily improving and then just as steadily and gradually, everything began to disintegrate. It was now possible to see it as a parabolic curve, only at the time, Nicola had failed to recognize the apex. She'd thought they were still going up when in fact she and Kate had begun a perilous descent. Kate had lost the right amount of weight and looked thin and wonderful, but she continued to lose weight. She kept getting sick, with one thing and another—strep throat, the flu, bronchitis. Eventually, she missed so much school that she dropped out in the middle of the spring semester and came back home to live. After a number of physicals and a series of costly and painful tests—including an exploratory operation to see if there was some hormonal problem—it became obvious that Kate had been lying to Nicola and to the doctors, that Kate was suffering from an "eating disorder"—some lethal combination of bulimia and anorexia. Nicola remembered invading Kate's room, Kate trying to bar her way, screaming and pleading. The evidence was there in every form—towels fouled with vomit under Kate's bed, drawers littered with empty syrup of ipecac bottles, empty boxes of laxatives. Nicola thought that Kate had been accumulating evidence for months, waiting for her mother to overcome her polite respect for privacy.

At first, Nicola wasn't that worried. There was a problem; they'd solve it. She took Kate to psychiatrists, to group-therapy sessions, to family therapy. They stammered out intimate details of their lives in rooms full of strangers, compared compulsions. But nothing had the slightest effect on Kate.

At first, Nicola's friends were sympathetic too. Anorexia was a "fashionable" disease, one of them told her; it was popular now. They seemed to think it was a phase Kate was going through, something transient and optional—as if she'd chosen to take ballet lessons, or learn the flute. They clipped out magazine stories for her, newspaper articles. Nicola clung to these clippings as if they were life preservers. If so many young girls were afflicted with this disorder, there would be ways of dealing with it, established treatments. But as Kate's emaciation progressed, Nicola watched her friends begin to blame her. They'd say that Nicola should *do* something and implicit in that attitude was the sense that it must be Nicola's fault, an opinion she shared. A *mother* ought to be able to do something. She had failed somewhere along the line; her ability to nurture was fatally flawed.

So she did everything she could think of; the problem was that nothing helped. Kate had been through every "eating disorder program," even enduring a "crisis intervention action"—a three-week stay in a hospital, where nutrients were delivered to her inert and hostile body by a feeding tube. The doctors hoped that once Kate's

36

body was forced out of acute starvation, her mind would clear and function properly, and her appetite mechanism would be restored. But when Nicola went for her one allowed visit (more and more, she was being seen as part of the problem), Kate greeted her with cold, reptilian eyes and said, "This isn't going to work, Mother." She spoke with such absolute assurance that Nicola's pathetic optimism—Kate looked good! It *was* working!—was crushed instantly and she left the room, unable to speak. Once out of the hospital, Kate quickly lost the weight so painfully gained. She remained implacable, trapped in the ruthless logic of the disease.

Nicola even thought she understood it—at least in crude psychological terms. Kate was reverting to a prepubescent state. Maybe it was because Stan had left them when Kate was twelve—the books and doctors agreed that that was a bad time, the worst time. Maybe it was jealousy—Stan had written a thoughtlessly graphic letter describing his new baby's birth. Maybe Kate was afraid of her sexuality. Maybe it was Kate's boyfriend, or something Nicola had done or failed to do at some crucial juncture. Maybe this, maybe that. It didn't matter. Kate looked exactly like a concentration-camp victim, systematically starved by ruthless captors. Nicola was watching her daughter disappear.

She finished dressing and pulled on her Bean boots, remembering to put her shoes in the tote bag along with her books and corrected test papers. Yesterday, she'd forgotten her shoes; she'd been forced to clump around all day in the heavy, rubber-soled boots. She took a final, assessing look at herself in the mirror over her dresser. She had to be careful these days—she was liable to put on something inside out, button up her blouse incorrectly. She gave herself a good front smile. A good front was better than nothing; it meant you had some kind of grip on things.

Her eyes slipped down from her own image to the array of photographs on top of her dresser. There were several of Kate, taken at different ages, one of Aunt Hillary, and a silver-framed photograph of her parents. When Nicola thought of Tony and Dasha, it was this photograph she saw—she had no memory of them and this was the only image of them she'd ever seen.

As a child, when things weren't going well, she'd almost prayed to the photograph. She'd had the usual fantasies that Aunt Hillary was wrong, that the reports were wrong, that everyone was wrong.

Her parents weren't really dead and they would return one day to sweep her up in a gush of love and tears. It was always these formally dressed, smiling young people that Nicola visualized returning and showering love upon her.

The photograph was taken at the time of their marriage, Aunt Hillary said, although it wasn't obviously a wedding photograph. They both wore suits and faced the camera squarely, smiling at the photographer. When she was little, she had liked to study her parents' faces. To see how she resembled them. She had one dimple—in her left cheek—just like her mother, and they shared the same straight black hair and even the China-boy haircut. Maybe, she thought now, that was why she'd chosen the hair style. Her cheekbones were prominent, like her mother's, and her eyes, similarly almond-shaped, but pale like her father's. In the sepia-toned photograph, Tony's eyes stared at her, opaque, almost white. She had eyebrows like his also, arched and strong, while her mother's were rounded, quizzical semicircles, plucked thin.

She frowned. The woman in the photograph was a girl in her twenties, much closer to Kate's age than her own. Had she lived, Dasha would now be sixty-one or sixty-two. Her hair would be gray, or streaked with gray. Nicola herself was much older than her mother ever got to be.

The thought made her feel lonely. She picked the photograph up and ran her finger along the top of the heavy frame, pushing off a film of dust, and then put it back on the dresser amidst the crowd of young, healthy Kates. She sighed and went to get her gym bag out of the closet. She had an aerobics class after school.

"I'm going now," she called.

"Don't forget," Kate said. "We have reservations at the Stowe House at seven-thirty for dinner."

Nicola gave a little wave.

"Bye," Kate said. "Happy birthday."

Routine propelled Nicola out the door.

She turned on the ignition of her red Subaru and then began the laborious process of scraping the hard ice off the windshield. It was very cold; the snow squeaked underfoot and the frigid air pinched her nostrils. When she had gotten most of the ice off, she sat in the car and waited for the defroster to melt the rest. As she sat there, a cavern, something dark and deep, opened in her mind. And from it crawled that thought again: *Kate will die.* It was a corporeal thought this time, stiff with reality. It forced everything else out of her mind. A shocked breath caught in her throat. She shut her eyes and banged her forehead against the steering wheel. She shook her head wildly, as if she could shake the thought loose. The terror subsided. She turned on the radio.

She backed out of the driveway and drove down Willow Street; she turned up Washington and merged onto the approach ramp for the Carlton Bridge. Below the line of traffic on the bridge, the Kennebec River was tufted with whitecaps. She drove a little fast and recklessly toward the Thomas Point School, where her class of fifth-graders would see her through the next few hours with their energetic innocence.

CHAPTER

FOUR

As Nicola crossed the Kennebec River, which separates the city of Bath, Maine, from the town of Woolwich, Neil Walker was six hundred miles to the south, still sleeping. Now that he was self-employed, now that he lived alone, he often slept until nine or ten. A twenty-year habit of waking at six-thirty had loosened its grip with surprising ease.

The strong morning sun had penetrated the borders of his light-blocking shades and a sharp diagonal stripe of light crept toward his face. When the light reached his eyelids, he rolled over and away from it.

In a way that he could never explain, he knew that he was dreaming. He was detached from the images, but he couldn't summon the burst of energy required to shake himself free from the nightmare and wake up.

The Agency shrinks had told him that most recurrent nightmares were fantasy dreams. His was unusual because it was a dream about a real event. They seemed to think the reason he had the dream was simple: since he had never understood what happened that morning in Rabat, his unconscious played it back for him so that he could puzzle it out, so that he could come to terms with it. He was sure they were right. It was a pivotal event in his life, the demarcation between the man he used to be and the man he was now. But if he dreamed about Rabat because he was trying to understand something mysterious to him, so far he had learned nothing from the constant nightmares. Not one thing.

The dream started the way it always did: the night of the phone call. Walker was doing the dishes at the time, a generous gesture, a surprise for Diana. But when she came down from putting Andy to bed, she didn't even come into the kitchen. She went right by into the living room and turned on the TV. He was pissed. He didn't do the dishes very often, and when he did, he expected her company, her gratitude. When the phone rang, he let it keep on ringing until she finally came in to answer it. He knew that he was being childish, but when *she* was doing the dishes, he always answered the phone. When she said, "It's for you," he knew from the way she said it that it was not just a call, but a Minuteman summons.

What he didn't know at the time was that it would be the last one he'd ever get.

The voice on the telephone said: "ZX, standard." Then the connection was severed.

Z meant that he was needed for an operation, X, that it was beginning immediately, a car already on the way to pick him up. "Standard" referred to the weather conditions of his destination. He dialed a number and waited for the voice to give him the confirmation code.

"I have to go," he said, but then he returned to the sink to finish the dishes. Diana came up behind him, put her arms around his waist, resting her head between his shoulder blades in such a gentle and tender way that he didn't want to move.

But his mind had already leapt forward into a rehearsed, automatic progression. He took his wallet and keys out of his pocket and put them on the top of his bureau. He went to the hall closet. There were three nearly identical suitcases on the big shelf to the left, one with a Hawaii sticker on it, one with a label that read SKI ASPEN, and a plain one. He heard the car outside give a honk. He picked up the plain one and his raincoat.

"Be careful," Diana said in a tight voice.

As he went out the door, Neil heard Andy upstairs beginning to cry. The car's horn probably woke him up. From the car, he could see Diana through the storm door, her hand half-raised in a wave. Motherhood had turned her into a worrier and he knew she was starting to worry already. They pulled away from the curb.

Walker didn't bother to talk to the driver because he knew that the driver wasn't supposed to talk. It was against regulations. Like the guards in certain CIA parking lots, the drivers were picked according to a few rigid criteria—a driver's license and unquestioning obedience.

Once, in his early days at the Agency, he'd borrowed a car to drive to CIA headquarters at Langley when his own wouldn't start. And he'd learned that you could be the Director himself and talk like Johnny Carson and the guards would remain uninterested. You couldn't talk your way past them because they didn't talk. They didn't listen. They *checked*.

Drivers on Minuteman assignments didn't talk either—they just drove. All they knew was where to pick you up and the airfield that was your destination. Walker himself wouldn't know any more until he was on the plane, though one thing was certain— wherever he was going, he knew there would be a disaster.

It was a miserable night, cold and rainy, the temperature at just about freezing. The driver had the defroster cranked all the way up to keep ice from forming on the windshield. They turned onto the approach ramp for the beltway. He cracked his window open. The rush of air seemed to drain the tension from his shoulders and he relaxed, letting his head loll back against the seat.

He thought of the word "Minuteman." Of course they didn't call themselves "Minutemen." It was a name that smacked of some cute Washington mind. But like their Revolutionary War namesakes, they had to be ready at a minute's notice. And like the huge, outdated Minuteman ICBM missiles, standing ready in their silos along the DEW line, they were a strike force launched into the unknown. Walker had heard that the Minuteman missiles—now the dinosaurs of strategic weapons—were being phased out. They were to be replaced by the Cruise, the MX, and something smaller and sleeker called (this was not a joke) the Midgetman. He laughed out loud, a kind of muffled chuckle, and the driver surprised him by speaking: "It ain't funny. It's goddamn slippery out here."

There were about thirty Minutemen in all, but they had never operated as a big group. They operated as small units—in groups of three or four. Walker's unit consisted of himself, Dan Pisarczyk, and Mike Hale. He now imagined Pisarczyk and Hale, somewhere in the Washington burbs, getting into cars with silent drivers, heading for Andrews. The Agency even had a service for unmarried men—to clean up after them, to stop mail, take out garbage, stop newspaper delivery.

• •

Walker had joined the Agency straight out of college and for years he'd progressed steadily up the ranks of analysts in the Soviet Bloc Division. His one outstanding talent was linguistic: he spoke five languages fluently, and was competent in many more. It was a talent, rather than an accomplishment, and as an undergraduate, he'd worried that being able to slip from tongue to tongue so easily indicated some shifty, chameleon quality to his soul.

The Agency had no need for a general linguist, so he was channeled into Soviet Bloc. It was a big division, and they could utilize his fluency in Russian, and his proficiency in Polish and Czech. Like many analysts, he'd always been anxious to go into the "field," to see action. He became an occasional member of the team that debriefed Warsaw Pact defectors, and then was asked to join the new Director's brainchild, the Minutemen.

He was flattered, and he didn't hesitate to say yes. The Minutemen were the ultimate field men, an elite among the elect. They made up a task force of highly trained troubleshooters attached to the Clandestine Services Division. Their assignments were always the toughest, if only because they entered an operation only after it had already failed.

They led schizophrenic lives—one minute dining in Georgetown with a girlfriend, an hour later flying on a military transport bound for Prague or JoBurg or Djakarta. They all kept the three suitcases ready: one for tropical climates, one for temperate, and one for severe cold. Airborne, they would speed-read unfamiliar dossiers and situation reports, swill endless cups of coffee, and memorize their new cryptos.

In his three years as a Minuteman, including a year in training, Walker had accumulated forty-five cryptos, code words giving him access to data from as many operations.

Walker was old for a Minuteman when he started—almost thirty-four—and his athletic body had begun the soft slide toward middle age. A year of training put an end to that. Most CIA officers went through a dozen courses at the Farm in Camp Peary, Virginia. The Minuteman, if he lasted long enough, would eventually attend most of the sixty classes taught there. Walker, for instance, had black belts in Tae Kwan Do *and* Akido, and had gone through Recondo, Ranger, and SEAL training. It seemed to him that each new belt, degree, and certificate put a distance between himself and his own mortality, although lately, he'd started to see his endless acquisition of skills as juvenile and pointlessly macho.

The driver turned off the beltway onto 295. Shortly afterwards, they turned up the road for Andrews Air Force Base. The driver negotiated several checkpoints and finally let Walker out on the tarmac, right next to the plane, a small Learjet.

Dan Pisarczyk, who was already on board, handed him a fat brown envelope that contained the briefing papers, the dossiers, the currency, the false ID.

"Hale coming?"

"If they can find him."

Although some of them had skills that others lacked—Walker's linguistic ability, Hale's photographic memory—speed of response was essential. If they couldn't find Hale, they'd get someone else.

"Where are we going?" Walker asked.

"Rabat, Morocco."

"Rabat, Morocco," Walker repeated without enthusiasm. He sat back and closed his eyes. The envelope remained in his lap, unopened. He was thinking about Diana.

She had changed after the baby was born. At first, he was like her, totally wrapped up in the baby, dazzled, amazed, in love. But Diana hadn't let up. The baby was over a year old now, starting to walk and talk, and Diana still hovered over him as if he were an infant. Walker knew she must miss her old job at Justice, miss the friends who'd stopped coming around, bored by her litany of baby stories. He'd even caught her watching soap operas; she was turning into a real suburban mommy, a pastime she herself had denigrated for years. When he told her she seemed depressed and moody, she said she was "just tired." He worried that when he was away on assignment she had no adult company at all.

He finally tore open the envelope, breaking the seal. He took out a sheaf of papers and set it aside. He removed the worn wallet and examined its contents: a wad of currency—dollars as well as Moroccan dirham—and the false ID, which, unlike the flash ID used for some purposes, had been backstopped several times. He read his operational name from the Maryland driver's license: Mitchell A. Billings. "Mitch," he said aloud, softly, to attune his ear. "Mitch Billings." A small supply of business cards occupied one leather slot. They identified Mitchell A. Billings as the Vice-President,

Sales, of Global Exports, Ltd. There was a Rabat street address, a cable code, a telephone number. He concentrated, memorized them, memorized Mitch Billings's birthdate. He put the wallet in his pocket and opened the passport. His face confronted him. He leafed through, looking at the visas, the entry and exit stamps. England, Amsterdam, the United States, Algeria, Morocco, Tunis. He put the passport in his breast pocket and picked up the sheaf of papers. He read over the cryptos: PHOTO BULLY DREAD TIMER. Then he read the situation report.

Global Exports was a CIA proprietary. Its major function was as a conduit—to run arms and supplies to dissident forces in Chad. As a cover, it exported Moroccan leather goods and textiles. Global had also been running a double—an agent involved in one of Qaddafi's operations. The briefing paper speculated that either the double got caught and got sweated by the Libyans, or else he never was a double. First he missed two consecutive meetings with his case officer, then the case officer himself disappeared, then a Global delivery truck ferrying an innocent load of rugs got blown up, the driver killed. Global had a staff of sixteen—three Americans, all CIA officers under cover, the rest locals. Of the locals, only two had been aware of Global's true purpose; the rest were actually involved in the export of leather and textiles. Global had a small suburban office building and a separate warehouse. The problem—and this was surprising—was not at the warehouse, which was stuffed with arms, ammunition, medical supplies, and machine parts. The problem was at the office.

Walker left his seat to get a cup of coffee. He wished Hale would hurry up. He didn't feel like working with someone new.

The situation report got fuzzier. An anonymous caller told the Rabat cops that Global's president could be found at a construction site near the airport. In a conduit pipe. And that "we took out the office, too." The conduit pipe was checked. The body was there. A preliminary investigation of Global's office and warehouse was made by the Moroccan police. A booby trap was considered possible, so no entry was attempted.

But the Agency had an asset in the Rabat police department and he rang the alarms. Rabat station called Langley; the decision was made to send a team of Minutemen.

Meanwhile, Rabat station was "containing" the situation. The report noted that Global's closed-circuit camera had been sabotaged, but the phone lines were intact. Possible hostage situation? Missing-persons reports had been filed on several Global employees who had failed to return home from their jobs. The Global office had been incommunicado for nearly twenty-four hours.

The local police were staying out of it for now, but they wouldn't be able to keep away for long. The relatives of the missing Global employees were temporarily put off with a story about sensitive ransom negotiations. But they were becoming increasingly hysteri-cal. Someone from the Rabat CIA station would be meeting the plane to provide an update.

Walker finished the summary and started on the PHOTO file. He thought he recognized a name—Omar Salit—and he marked it with his pencil. He wrote the words "Harry Winston?" in the margin.

Mike Hale's curly head peered through the cabin door. "This my flight?"

Pisarczyk laughed. "About time."

"Hey, I'm never *home* when these calls come. *Never.* It's like they *wait* for me to go out. I didn't even get a shower. He flipped open the clasps on his suitcase, tossed his coat on a seat, and began undressing. He was wearing sweat pants and a sodden T-shirt. He shivered.

"There I was, into my fourth racquetball game when this mus-clebound geek in a club uniform starts knocking on the door. I ignore him for a while, because I think he's telling us to get off the court, you know, time's up, but finally he comes in through the door. I catch the ball and tell him I'm two points from game, does he mind? But it turns out my beeper's going off in the locker room, do *I* mind, the noise is irritating the patrons."

Hale paused to pull the T-shirt over his head and stood in the aisle in his jockey shorts, pulling clothes out of his suitcase. He stepped into his blue jeans, then lifted each leg high, bending it at the knee. "Jesus Christ, these things are *starched.* What kind of chick starches your blue jeans?"

"That's the new way of doing things," Pisarczyk said. "You wear blue jeans, but with a knife crease. It's the Robert Redford look. Outdoorsy, but *tailored.*"

"Fuck. I don't think I can sit down. If I wanted to be this un-

46

comfortable, I'd wear a suit and tie. In fact, I *am* going to wear my suit and tie.

The pilot came into the cabin and told them they were ready for takeoff.

Mike Hale fell down into the seat across the aisle from Walker and kicked his suitcase under the seat in front. The plane started rolling.

All of them were trained in speed reading, but Hale read twice as fast as anyone else, and despite his late start, he finished first. He also had a photographic memory, a useful asset because they could rely on him to remember names and numbers; the printed data would be shredded before they left the plane.

Pisarczyk finished last, tapping his papers together to announce that he was ready.

"So," Hale said. "What do you think?"

Walker hummed the theme from "The Twilight Zone."

Pisarczyk let out a high, artificial laugh.

"You got no cable traffic," Hale said, "no radio traffic. The phones work and ring but no one answers them. You can't see anything from outside. The local cops are on hold but not for long; the relatives are nervous."

"But you also have no hostage demands," Walker pointed out. "You've got a warehouse full of illegal arms and it hasn't been touched." He felt his stomach gurgle, the churn of acid. "One name rang a bell," he continued. "Omar Salit. Used to work for Harry Winston, I think." Harry Winston was a so-called "bad man," a rogue, an ex-Agency officer who'd quit and become an arms dealer. He did a lot of work for Qaddafi and the Libyans.

"*Salit*," Pisarczyk said. "Didn't the brief list him as legit? Didn't he work for Global as a legit salesman—rugs and leather jackets? I can't imagine Global taking on one of Winston's boys—they wouldn't be that stupid."

Walker shrugged. "Maybe it's not the same guy."

"Wait a minute," Hale said. "Tunis, right? Omar Salit. Little guy. Wore those safari suits and a couple of gold chains around his neck? Bad teeth?"

Walker nodded and leaned back against the wall. "You got it." The aircraft went through some turbulence and then steadied.

Hale lit a cigarette, then offered one to Walker, who declined. He was trying to quit. The plane lurched again and Walker felt the liquid slosh in his gut. Just the thought of his stomach as a container for liquid made him feel queasy. Sweat oozed from his pores; his palms and his upper lips were wet. ". . . thing I heard about Harry Winston," Hale was saying. "He bought an old minesweeper off someone and sold it to the Iraqis. Then he sank it, with all hands on board. He got the money from the Iraqis *and* when the fucker sank, he got a bundle from the insurance. His own guys went down—*his own fucking guys.* Harry Winston would do anything. I mean *anything.* He's got the moral fiber of a slug."

Walker was thinking about Diana—that little half wave at the door. He could imagine her standing there until the mist crept up the door slowly from the bottom and then obscured her. He'd seen her standing at the door many, many times—different doors, different weather. Diana had a superstitious need to watch him until he was out of sight; he loved her for it. Tonight, as he'd reached the car, and heard Andy crying, he hadn't been able to suppress a twinge of pleasure. Because Andy was crying and yet Diana didn't leave her post.

Half listening to Mike Hale, trying to ignore his nausea, Neil Walker had a startling thought. *I am jealous of my own son.* And although defensive mental gyrations began immediately, to confuse and obscure the truth of that realization, the thought stuck with him. Diana wasn't some overprotective, doting mother; Andy wasn't a spoiled brat; Diana wasn't bored or moody. He was the one who was out of step, who ought to fucking grow up. Now he understood that look he'd been catching on Diana's face—a formal appraising gaze, as if she was trying to guess his hat size or read his mind.

"Hey, Neil, you all right?"

"I want to go home," Walker said. He was trying for an ironic tone but he didn't quite make it. Hale shot him a glance; Walker managed to volley a smile.

"Just keep telling yourself it's a glamour job," Hale said.

They discussed their operational plans and the cover story they would prepare for the Moroccan police—if in fact the Global Exports office was the tomb they suspected.

"Drugs," one of them said in a tired voice.

Pisarczyk sighed. "I guess so. The old standby. Rival drug gangs. Someone got burned. Vengeance, yatta, yatta. The police like the old standbys—they still play."

"They still play in Rabat," Hale said.

"You'll have to get all the files out of there, whatever telltale equipment is there. . . . Let me know right away how much there is. We're going to have to move all those guns out of the warehouse, too. I'll try to round up some trucks. But *first*, find out if the ciphers are missing."

Hale was up, straddling the aisle. "Harry goddamned Winston," he muttered.

"What kind of manpower are we looking at?" Walker asked. "Just us and the two Global guys that worked the warehouse? Is that it? You think Rabat will give us anything?"

"They ain't gonna give us a bite of couscous, the way I see it. But whatever, we can't leave anything in that office but invoices and lading orders."

When he tried to remember it later, the last thing Walker could recall anyone saying on the plane was Dan Pisarcyzk complaining that he had a headache and blaming it on the quality of the Agency's printer.

"You'd think they could afford something that didn't make those fucking little dots."

"Dot-matrix," Hale supplied.

Pisarczyk massaged his forehead. "Reading anything more than twenty pages of those dots gives me a headache."

Although this conversation was without importance, Walker recalled it whenever he saw a dot-matrix printout, as if every syllable had the vibrancy of revelation.

Midway through the descent, Hale finally sat down. He wiggled his eyebrows at Walker; his eyebrows had an unusually acute arch, which gave him a crazed, demonic look.

Walker smiled reflexively and then looked out the window at the lights of Rabat, which lost their cohesive, gridlike appearance as the plane got closer to the ground. It was still dark in Rabat. When the plane touched down, Walker closed his eyes and enjoyed the rush of air produced by the reverse thrust of the engines. He liked wind.

As a child, he'd insisted on having a fan in his room, even in winter. When he opened his eyes, his stomachache was gone.

The Agency man, Tom Coolidge, didn't meet them at the airport after all. He was waiting for them at the Intercon. Even his smile kept its distance.

The Global operation had been part of a regional anti-Qaddafi action and not directly under Rabat station's control. Despite this, and despite the fact that Rabat didn't want to deal with the Global mess itself, Coolidge displayed the usual dislike stations showed to arriving Minutemen. It was a territorial thing, Walker supposed.

Coolidge did provide them with two cars, a map, directions to Global's office and warehouse, and the name and number of the police contact.

"If that's it," he said, looking at his watch.

"We'll have to dismantle Global's communications," Pisarczyk said. "We'll need access to your code room. We'll probably have something ready in three hours—maybe less."

Coolidge looked annoyed.

"Shit," Hale said, and Coolidge left.

It took them a little more than a half hour to get their technical gear together. When they left, Pisarczyk was eating a granola bar; he never traveled without them.

They had some trouble finding Global's office. The directions were wrong and failed to take into account some one-way streets. When they finally found it, it was almost dawn.

The building was a generic commercial structure of a certain sort in an expensive, nondescript suburban neighborhood. They could have been in the outskirts of any medium-sized city in the world. The buildings had a bland, landscaped look. They could have been anything—doctors' or dentists' offices, weight-reduction clubs, import-export firms, birth-control clinics, foundations, obscure consulates. The Global building was a clumsy marriage of cement-block office building to Moorish palace. It was surrounded by a low stucco wall that existed for decoration and not security.

They spent an hour at the kind of mind-numbing surveillance that makes each minute seem like fifteen. During the hour, not a car passed. Not a pedestrian. Walker did some calculations in his head to force his mind to keep working. Finally, Hale stepped out of the car.

50

"Nothing," Hale said when he returned. "There's a closed-circuit camera on the front dor. The lens has been sprayed with white paint. It's still scanning, but . . ."

They called Pisarczyk. "We're going, Dan."

"You sure?"

"If you hear a big explosion, you'll know we fucked up."

Walker's heartbeat began to accelerate the moment he stepped out of the car.

While the early, preparatory stages of an operation were characterized by a joking, almost adolescent, camaraderie, at some point there was always a crude mood swing, and it happened now as he and Hale approached the front door.

Hale shone a tiny light up to where the closed-circuit camera whirred and tracked in the night; its blinded lens gave it a wounded, stupid look—a machine eye with a cataract.

They made their way around to the side of the building, and set up behind the low stucco wall, which might provide some degree of protection if the building exploded. Walker, who was the better shot, took the silenced Ingram submachine gun from his backpack and fired a single round dead center in the upper center pane of the window. The bullet itself made no sound, but they could hear it smack into the window, and the glass crack.

They waited again. There seemed to be no sound at all: no wind, no insects, no traffic, no planes overhead. Nothing. Only their own breathing. They approached the building in a crouch. Hale stretched up and cut around the perimeter of the pane of glass with his glass cutter, then punched the glass in with his gloved hand. Even the glass shattering made very little noise, breaking as it did along the stress lines Hale had cut. It fell in against the heavy draperies and slid down to what must be a carpeted floor.

They stepped aside from the window and leaned against the wall with their backs against each other. It was a defensive rather than a predatory stance. They stood absolutely still, like herd animals testing the leading edge of the air for the hint of fatal intent, the disruption of grass, the whiff of the tiger. A long way overhead, Walker heard the drone of a jet passing over Africa.

They stood there for a minute or two, only their eyes moving, and then they went in. Walker went through the window first, and then held the draperies away to make Hale's entry easier. Although this was the point of maximum danger if there was a trap waiting for them inside, Walker felt no fear. It was almost comical, the trouble they had getting through the draperies and into the room. Standing in the dark and waiting had flattened his emotions.

And even before he got through the draperies, he smelled the blood. They stood motionless one more time, listening. Walker could hear a faint electronic whirr from several parts of the room—a computer, maybe a clock—and the louder insistent hum of what sounded like the motor of an electric typewriter. The weak light from the streetlamps and the brightening sky did not penetrate the heavy drapes but his eyes were already accustomed to the dark. He could make out shapes, but his brain made no attempt to identify them. He was trying to detect motion, life. He was listening for a human noise—a rustle, a breath, a cough. But there was nothing, nothing at all.

Finally, Hale said, in a voice that sounded explosively loud, "Let's go." Hale flicked on a small powerful flashlight before Walker even got his out of the knapsack. Hale played it quickly around the room.

Walker was expecting to see bodies and he did. It was an abattoir.

The flashlight played over the room, illuminating the bodies, one grisly revelation after another, like a horrific slide show. He'd read somewhere that bodies seemed smaller when they were dead, as if the life force itself took up some space, but these bodies were huge. They seemed to take up the whole room.

Hale began walking toward the light switch he'd been searching for with his flashlight; Walker stumbled after him, walking through the bloody rug. The blood in the thick carpet had become tacky and his feet stuck slightly at each step. Each time he lifted his foot, it seemed to require more and more energy, and by the time Hale reached the light switch and turned it on, Walker had stopped moving entirely. He stood next to the reception desk, where a woman with a pretty face was still partially seated in her yellow typing chair. Around her neck was a pearl necklace that disappeared into the gore of her cut throat.

Walker began to tally the dead in a meticulous voice that resonated inside his skull. Some portion of his brain was conducting a quick postmortem: one female, one male—throats cut; one male—multiple stab wounds in chest; one female, one male—gunshot wounds, large caliber. . . .

"Let's check the other rooms," Hale said. This time, Walker perceived his voice as coming from a great distance; he strained to catch the words.

"Okay," Walker said. He felt his lips move, but he couldn't hear any sound over what now seemed to be the roar of a small hurricane, with gale-force winds, taking place inside his skull. He watched Hale begin walking toward the back of the room where a hall and two doors were visible.

Walker had the impression that his shoes were permanently attached to the lime-green carpet by the sticky adhesion of coagulated blood and that to move, he would have to untie his shoes and step out of them. He was looking at the blood on the walls and a detached part of his mind was trying to calculate the range—from the two examples available—how far blood would spurt when the carotid artery was severed. Hale finally noticed that he hadn't moved and said, "You all right, Neil?"

Walker heard himself say it: "No."

"Hey," Hale said and began walking toward him. Walker could see a look forming in Hale's eyes that he recognized as a mixture of compassion and contempt. He could almost hear Hale's voice, projected into some future anecdote: "Well, Neil *freaked*, you know. Neil wasn't having any more." What he really said was, "Go outside, get a little air."

"Don't give me that fucking look."

"You'll be all right, man, just give it a minute."

Now Walker could see a different look in Hale's eyes. He couldn't read it.

"No." The word fell out of his mouth. He was surprised by the simple decision in his voice. "I'm leaving."

"Go outside," Hale said. Now his voice had the forcefulness of an order.

"Give me the keys. Tell Dan I'm going home; he knows where he can reach me." This struck him as funny and a little laugh came out.

"Come on, man."

"Give me the keys."

"I'll drive you to the hotel."

"No!" His voice seemed to fill up the whole room. He saw that he had the Ingram in his right hand. "Give me the goddamn keys."

Walker watched his left arm wave in a beckoning gesture; in no sense did he feel in control of it. The arcing motion of his hand seemed to leave an afterimage in the air, like light caught by a long camera exposure.

Hale shrugged and tossed the keys. It was a bad throw. Walker watched the keys tumble through the air. He had to lunge for them. He had to make a tricky catch with his left hand. It seemed very important that they not touch the floor and get blood on them.

"I think you're making a mistake, man," Hale said.

"You're right," Walker said. "I can't leave you here without a car." He tossed the keys back, a shaky, wild throw. Hale made a diving catch.

" 'He makes a diving catch, he pivots, he throws to first,' " Hale chanted in falsetto. "*Not* in time," he said, pointing to the dead man sprawled against the wall. His laugh rattled around the ghastly room. Walker felt unbearably cold. His body began to quake. "I can't believe I'm giving you my 'you're making a mistake' speech," Hale said. "Fuck it. Maybe you're not making a mistake." He tossed the keys back to Walker. "*Adios, ameeeego*," he said in a Speedy Gonzalez voice. "But, hey, Ceeesco, leave your gun here, okay?" He raised his hand in a parting wave. Walker began to say something, but no words formed. Some heavy inarticulate sounds came out. *Struck dumb*, he thought. He felt that if he didn't leave the room in the next minute, he would die. He saw that Hale already had the telephone receiver to his ear; he was dialing. "*Hasta la vista*," Hale said in his chirpy cartoon Spanish.

Outside, the air was heavy, dense as a liquid, and Walker struggled through it toward the car. He sat there for a few moments breathing heavily—big, greedy breaths that were unbelievably noisy.

Later, he was never sure how he was able to find the airport so quickly; they hadn't landed at the commercial airport but at a military strip. Even so, he drove straight to it like a lifelong resident of Rabat.

He'd taken the first flight out of Rabat. It happened to be going to Rome. He shared the first-class compartment with a tour group of multinational executives who drank a lot of Jack Daniel's and talked about a dam in Pakistan. Walker avoided eye contact and read the flight magazine.

He spent two hours in the airport in Rome, finally getting a standby seat on a flight to New York. He was jumpy and tired; he tried to keep moving, half afraid Pisarczyk would have put some kind of alert out on his false passport. His plans did not extend past getting home.

He kept thinking he heard his operational name—Mitch Billings—over the PA system, but the seductive female voice seemed to be filtered through water and eventually he realized all the names sounded identical. He also had the feeling people were staring at him; every time he looked up, he seemed to catch someone's eyes flickering away. He fought off paranoia by trying to meditate, but he found it impossible to sit still enough to do it.

He called Diana from JFK and told her he would be on the next shuttle home.

"Are you all right?" Her voice was alarmed and relieved at the same time.

"Yeah, I'm all right." His voice lacked conviction so he said it again. "I'm all right."

When the taxi pulled up in front of their house, Diana was standing at the storm door with her hand against the glass. It gave him the uneasy feeling she'd been there the entire time he'd been gone. Once again, the baby was crying upstairs.

They embraced. "They've been calling and calling." The baby's crying reached a new pitch of hysteria.

"Go get Andy. I'll call in."

He slumped against the wall in the kitchen, looking at the clock while he dialed. It amazed him to see that he'd been gone less than twenty-four hours. While he waited for someone with the correct clearance to come on the line, he thought about all the rules he'd broken. Apart from abandoning the team, he'd flown, unauthorized, on a foreign flag-carrier, using his false ID. He'd abandoned the car at the airport. He'd . . . but before he could add to the mental list of his crimes, a voice spoke to him.

He couldn't remember what was said. The voice was soothing and reassuring: "Get a good night's sleep," it recommended. "And call in the morning." He asked about Hale, about Pisarczyk and the voice reassured him that they were fine. He didn't believe that everything would be fine, as the voice promised, but he was too tired to care. He expected them to arrive at any moment to take him away for debriefing.

He fixed himself a drink, something he hadn't allowed himself on the airplane. His hands were trembling. He didn't kid himself that it was fatigue; he watched them in a detached way and hoped that they would stop.

After Diana had given Andy a bottle and put him back to bed, they went into the living room. Walker started to stretch out on the couch.

"God, Neil," Diana said. "*God*. Your shoes. What's that on your shoes?"

He was wearing dark blue running shoes, covered halfway up the ankles in what even now was recognizable as blood. An ugly gulping laugh came out of his mouth. It sounded like something ripped out of his stomach.

He'd walked through three airports and passed three security checks with these gory shoes on his feet. He looked at his feet as if they belonged to someone else; maybe from a distance, it could look like mud. Green fibers from the carpet at Global Exports were stuck to the blood like feathers to tar. He tried to untie the shoelaces but they were stiff and hard with blood and his fingers shook too much.

"I didn't," he started, "I didn't . . ." He wanted to tell Diana that he hadn't killed anyone, but it seemed beside the point.

Diana finally got a pair of scissors and cut the laces. He pried the shoes off, then the socks. He began to put them in the kitchen garbage, but the thought of those shoes in there—next to the orange peels, the eggshells, the Pampers, the ordinary detritus of human life—made him stop. He put them in a separate garbage bag, twisting the metal tie until its ends disappeared and put the garbage bag in the garage. When he sat back down on the couch, he felt exhausted in a way he'd never felt before. He felt as if his brain was shrinking away from the sides of his skull.

Diana sat next to him. "Do you want to talk about it?"

He shook his head. The last thing he remembered before falling asleep was Diana's hand stroking his head. His scalp was supersensitive. He could feel the tracks of her fingers as if they were engraving grooves into his skull.

As always, when he woke up *in* the dream, the next morning, still on the couch, he woke up *from* the dream, too. He always experienced a rush of relief to find himself in bed, to realize he'd been dreaming, that Rabat had happened a long time ago, that there were no shoes encrusted with blood in the garbage.

It wasn't always morning when he finished the dream, but this time it was and he went downstairs to make himself some coffee. It seemed a long time ago that the Rabat dream had represented the worst thing he thought would ever happen to him. He caught his head in his hands and took a number of deep breaths. He'd been dreaming about Rabat, fine; it was better to think about that.

CHAPTER

FIVE

Hobie James left Location #9 at about eight-thirty in the morning. Lemro and another one of his assistants, who'd arrived late the previous night, stayed behind. They would continue questioning Ronald Peters. Hobie didn't have much hope about their prospects of learning anything useful. Still, you never knew.

He thought he'd waited long enough to avoid the worst of the rush hour—but a snowfall, a mere dusting during the night, had prolonged the mess. People kept moving farther from the District to avoid the skyrocketing cost of close-in housing. Town houses marched straight out into this old Virginia farming country. Flextime helped. Carpooling helped. Metro helped. But the traffic was still appalling. On the two-lane, no-shoulder country highways of outer Fairfax County, a stalled car, a flat tire—anything could cause a huge backup. An hour's commute was nothing now. Hobie couldn't imagine spending two hours a day in his car, although this morning he didn't really mind being stuck. He inched along behind an old Toyota with a Reagan/Bush sticker on its bumper. He was thinking.

About LUCIFER.

CIA Director Paul Childress had called him into the office last week following the Fifty-four Committee meeting. The Fifty-four Committee, named after Room Fifty-four in the Old Executive Office Building, where it met, coordinated the various components of the federal intelligence community (CIA, FBI, Naval and Army Intelligence, DIA, NSA).

It had been created following some disastrous foul-ups—FBI agents arresting CIA officers, DIA surveilling an FBI sting operation, and allegations of "inadvertent" deaths. Fifty-four tracked covert operations with an eye to avoiding that sort of thing, and sometimes launched interagency efforts.

At the January 2 meeting, the need for reinvestigation of the DANTE matter was discussed. OS was selected as the most secure base from which to launch the investigation, which was to be called LUCIFER.

LUCIFER was the most limited-access investigation Hobie had ever run. At most, there were twenty-four people who knew about it. There were the members of Fifty-four, the President, himself, and his three assistants. That was it.

That was about as tight as it got. Most operations, even highly classified ones, involved scores of individuals. There were specified procedures to observe and those procedures generated paper and paper required typists, filing clerks, routing clerks, classification processing. There were accounting guidelines to follow (large "discretionary funds" being frowned upon, post-Watergate), requisitions for funding and technical support, expense sheets.

LUCIFER was different. LUCIFER was being run out of his own head. Some emergency Fifty-four fund had been tapped for financing.

And all the people who knew about LUCIFER had C-clearance.

He thought about that. His knee started to hurt.

The car was steaming up. He flicked on the rear-window defroster. Traffic had been at a standstill for five minutes. Some jerk a few cars back was losing it, honking his horn, a futile wail.

Childress had said that eventually NSA would be able to determine DANTE's identity through a statistical analysis of the leaks—who knew what, when, etc. The leaks would leave a pattern that would pinpoint the source. "That kind of tracking is being done," Childress had said, "but it could take years. Judging by the level this guy seems to be operating from, we can't afford to wait."

In front of him, the driver of the Toyota stepped outside his car to peer ahead. Apparently he didn't see anything. His eyes met Hobie's and he shrugged. He got back into his car.

Hobie knew that the murder of "Boris Shokorov" was only the first shot in what promised to be a long war. His part would be to lay siege to the enigma of DANTE's identity. He usually loved the beginning of an investigation, was invigorated by the assembling of evidence, finding the strands of truth in a duplicitous weave. But just now he felt tired, unequal to the task. The murder of Shokorov had raised the stakes. Obviously the KGB wasn't taking any chances. He took his hands off the wheel and cracked his knuckles.

Presuming the siege on DANTE's identity was successful, success itself might contain the seeds of disaster. Shokorov's murder meant that DANTE knew about operation LUCIFER, knew already that the investigation into his identity had been revived. Suppose DANTE felt him closing in. Anyone with the kind of access DANTE had would be in a position to inflict heavy damage in a scorched-earth retreat. Hobie pinched the bridge of his nose.

He saw that he would have to obscure the progress he made, invent a shadow investigation, expend energy on false leads. He would have to create a whole shadow LUCIFER investigation—and report on *its* progress to Fifty-four.

The levels of duplicity required of him were going to be exhausting. His knee was really starting to ache.

And while it would have been nice to start his investigation with a few givens—like trusting the Fifty-four members, trusting his own assistants, trusting Paul Childress—in fact, now that Shokorov had been killed, no one could be exempted from suspicion.

The impatient driver behind him had succumbed to temptation and tried to pass the paralyzed line of cars on the nonexistent shoulder. He made it about a hundred yards past Hobie and then his wheels lost their purchase. Hobie watched the car slide down the embankment. As traffic inched forward, he watched the man rock his car back and forth, trying to get out of the half-frozen mud.

It wasn't going to work.

Interrogating Ronald Peters was likely to be as futile. But it was something he had to try, even though he was all but certain that Peters had been an unwitting player in a Soviet disinformation operation.

It was a crisp, clear day; huge, puffy clouds sailed across the blue sky. Hobie's mood was in exact opposition to the weather. He felt a deep edginess, a heavy fatigue. He pinched the bridge of his nose again, this time hard enough to make a pulse of light flash into his head. He remembered that in three days, he was scheduled for knee surgery.

He watched the impatient man get out of his car and look at the deep wells of mud his tires had churned out. The man was actually removing the floor mats from his car, nice carpeted ones, and putting them under his rear wheels when the traffic suddenly began to move. Hobie didn't see whether it worked or not.

When he reached his office, he put in calls to the members of the team who'd originally debriefed Shokorov. It was a Soviet Bloc team: Val Zamatin, John Sanger, and Neil Walker.

A good team. Even a good team could be fooled by a false defector, of course. He just hoped that he would find the team had done a solid job, put a full-court press on Shokorov when they'd debriefed him. He frowned. Otherwise, it would be painful. Zamatin and Walker were two men he counted as friends.

CHAPTER

SIX

As Hobie James continued the tedious drive from Clifton to Langley, Val Zamatin, who would soon be heading for Langley himself, stepped out of his shower. He stood under the heat lamp for a few moments, dripping onto the new bath mat from the Vermont Country Store. He'd ordered it from a catalog—something he generally avoided because it often led to disappointment, the thing itself seeming smaller, duller, and paler than its depiction.

He wrapped a white Turkish towel around his waist like a sarong and stepped toward the bank of mirrors, giving himself a critical once-over. He was in good shape for a sixty-five-year-old man who liked food. Even his abdomen (of course he was sucking it in, but he believed every person looking in the mirror did so) betrayed little loss of tone. But he worked at it; he deserved his fitness. He played golf and tennis, did sit-ups, push-ups, and stretching exercises regularly (if not religiously) and every morning he walked three miles—fast, swinging his arms like an idiot.

Suddenly, his shoulders slumped a little and his buoyant mood sank. He remembered that it was Thursday, time for his weekly lunch/chess game with the man he always thought of as Dante.

It had been a nickname first, before it became a code name. When Zamatin and Dante first met—in Shanghai—the latter was still a teenager, a refugee from Hitler's Austria. His family had been a prosperous one in Vienna, his father an industrialist who owned several factories. The boy and his family were lucky to have escaped with their lives; they hadn't escaped with much else.

Their life in Shanghai was a far cry from the comfortable existence they'd left behind in Austria. They were poor; they lived in the Hongkew ghetto. In the ordinary course of things, a bright young man like Dante would have received a fine education in Austria, probably finishing at the University of Vienna. But like most of the refugee children in Shanghai, his education was a patched-together effort. The parents taught what they could and supplemented their efforts with instruction from whatever tutors they could find—and afford.

Dante's favorite tutor was a transplanted German named Strasser who had once taught classics at Heidelberg. Strasser, a strange old man with a huge, snowy beard, tutored the boy in classics in exchange for food and candles. For almost a year, the boy was rarely seen without his battered copy of the *Divine Comedy*. The great poet's hierarchy of the damned was a source of endless discussion. What did they think? Was a soothsayer, for instance, really worse than a *tyrant?* There would follow a discussion about the influence of religion on the poet's thinking. Soothsaying involved magic; it implied mucking about with God's given time frame. The only acceptable divination for a fourteenth-century Italian would be revelation. The boy also enjoyed launching comparative discussions about how his hero Lenin would rank the damned: surely avarice would have to be a more serious counterrevolutionary offense than blasphemy; surely heresy—to Marxist tenets—would be worse than seduction.

Eventually the boy's copy became so worn he had to keep it wrapped up in a cloth. Somehow they started calling him Dante and the nickname stuck.

Zamatin remembered the way Dante had looked then—a distinct and somewhat comical figure, a gangly, earnest boy with protruding ears. Dante had tortured himself about those ears, certain that no girl could possibly be attracted to a boy with such big ears.

Later, when a code name was required for the boy, it was simplest to use the nickname. Somewhere along the line, Zamatin thought, Dante had had his ears fixed, because now they lay flat against his head.

Dante's identity was now hidden behind a wall and Vassily Zamatin had done much to construct and maintain that wall. He had mixed the mortar, as it were, done the brickwork, embedded in the top the metalwork spears that discouraged intruders from scaling it. Moscow Center, of course, had *designed* the wall, and continued to dissuade explorers from locating it.

Zamatin worked at the CIA and was a Soviet mole himself, although his access (and therefore, importance) did not compare to that of Dante. He was Dante's contact. A delivery boy. In the trade they had a word for this role: babysitter. Zamatin grimaced at his face in the mirror, checking his teeth.

He trimmed a hair from his nostril.

He did not look forward to these chess matches with Dante, although he was certainly used to them: the two men had been playing a game a week now for almost thirty years. Their weekly chess game was a device which allowed their friendship to drift along on its well-laid tracks with a minimum of arrangement. It saved them from the trouble of trying to maintain a less focused "friendship" and never aroused the slightest interest or suspicion. Chess had proved to be the perfect cover for meetings: a game for only two, and spectators, at least in the States, were easily bored by it.

And that was a good thing, Zamatin reflected, because Dante was a terrible chess player. His mind was brilliant but undisciplined. He hadn't put in the required time to learn traditional defenses and move clusters. His only victories came off wild games when he made a lucky combination or was playing against an experimental game of Zamatin's. Had a true student of the game observed their decades-long competition, he would have wondered why Zamatin bothered to play Dante—although now that Dante was so powerful and famous, the assumption would be that he did it for that most pervasive of Washington reasons—to be close to the ear of power.

Dante himself got plenty of mileage out of their weekly bouts. It was part of the standard thumbnail sketch of him—"chess player," "chess enthusiast," "chess aficionado," even "chess fanatic." Dante got points on two fronts: first for playing the game at all ("the brainy" man, "who plays chess as a hobby") and again for keeping up with his old friend ("'Once a week, a thirty-year war,' he said of his regular games with old pal Val Zamatin.").

The games continued to serve their original purpose—providing a steady connection between the two men. And of course, he and Dante *were* friends of a sort, although more as a result of the length of their acquaintance than from any mutual affection. Dante in private was vastly different than his charming and witty public self.

As Zamatin dressed, he thought about the persona that Dante had created. It had taken consultation with the best in the business to mold the creature that now graced the front pages and "Faced the Nation." Those with long memories might remember the stumbling, awkward professor that Dante used to be, the bright man whose thick accent made him all but unintelligible. But that person, having gone largely unfilmed and unrecorded, had disappeared from public history. Even private memories tended to replace that old Dante with a younger, only *slightly* less polished version of the new, urbane one.

The Dante the world knew, the so-called "man of the seventies," had really surfaced in 1974.

Dante had accomplished the transformation in the six months between his departure from Harvard (as a full-time professor) and his assumption of the editor's chair at *Foreign Affairs*. He'd hired a speech expert—to teach him to cover a slight speech impediment, modify his accent, and instruct him in public and private speaking. In the meantime he'd enrolled in his own sort of finishing school—a program of tennis lessons, backgammon, a course in French cooking, dance lessons. These days he even had a press agent—although the man's title was "research assistant." This creature called in bits to the gossip columns, alerted the press for Dante's ramblings about town, and did everything he could to keep Dante's public image favorable and his profile high. Nearly every press release contained a comparison of Dante to Metternich, to Kissinger, to Adenauer. The word "statesman" was never far from Dante's name in print. And Dante's staff was the best in town—he had a Pulitzer prize winner writing his speeches.

But when Dante was with his "old friend," Zamatin, it was different. He didn't have to charm Zamatin and he didn't bother. And consequently, the Dante that Zamatin knew was a different man, a man whose driving characteristics were not the famed intelligence and wit but instead arrogance and a sadistic penchant for manipulation.

Dante enjoyed throwing his weight around.

Of course their relationship was an odd one anyway: Zamatin believed he was the only person in Dante's life who *knew* the man's true political affiliation, just as Dante was the only person in his life aware of his secret role. While one might think they would be able to truly relax in each other's presence, it wasn't the case. Their secret knowledge of each other made them wary instead of comfortable. For one thing, each had the power to reveal the other. To destroy the other. And Zamatin thought that perhaps they were so used to hiding their true colors, they were ill at ease without their pretense.

But as Dante's stature—and the importance of the intelligence he provided—had grown, far outstripping any information originating from Zamatin himself, there had been a shift in their relationship. Where once there had existed a symbiosis, and a kind of father/son support and deference, now there was more of a sense that Zamatin was Dante's creature, that Dante was his boss. Certainly Zamatin's present value to Moscow Center was mostly as Dante's handler, and as his retirement from his analyst's post in the CIA's Soviet Bloc Division neared, he began to feel uneasy.

He was to be allowed to actually retire, go to Florida, something which pleased and offended him at the same time. When he'd informed Center that the great paring down of the Agency that followed the Watergate scandal included the mandatory retirement of old folk like himself, he'd expected them to insist that he get some sort of consultant's slot lined up, remain in Washington to continue in his role as Dante's handler. But they seemed perfectly willing to let him go. He was not even to be replaced. It made him feel that what he did was of no importance. The current plan was that Dante would handle himself—learn the telephone numbers, the brush contacts, the coding procedures. While this would expose Dante slightly, it was considered less dangerous than bringing in a new man.

Zamatin got his Burberry overcoat out of the closet and meticulously brushed the shoulders. He wished Dante would start handling himself *now*. Within the past few months handling Dante had become dangerous, and now that it did pose a risk, Zamatin, a kind of lame duck, disliked the notion of taking it. He locked up and went to the garage, sliding into the comfortable leather seat of his BMW. He headed toward Memorial Bridge. The bright day was becoming overcast, puffy clouds massing together suddenly, the air growing heavy with threatened precipitation.

· ·

For most of his life, Zamatin had operated as a double agent, first within German military intelligence and then within the United States intelligence service. It was a precarious life, both actually and emotionally, and now that he was close to getting out, he realized just how tired he was of its schizophrenic demands.

Only six months from retirement (he'd already purchased his "golf" villa in Florida) he looked forward to his leisure. Unlike many Americans, he had a cluster of interests (he refused to think of them as "hobbies," a word which seemed to trivialize one's passions) and relished the prospect of having time to pursue them.

He sighed. He rarely thought of himself as a Russian anymore. His devotion to Mother Russia was not the clear ardor of his youth. Most of his pleasures and virtually all of his friends were American. Center had asked, when retirement loomed, if he wanted to come home, but he'd declined—probably to their relief. Moscow held no attraction for him beyond the mild curiosity one felt for a place one had not seen in decades, a place where one had been young.

He crossed the river. The Potomac was frozen over and under the heavy sky had a sullen, brutal look. Zamatin headed up GW parkway toward CIA headquarters in Langley, listening to a tape of Handel's *Water Music*, which did not succeed in freeing his mind from thinking about Dante.

Born in Austria, not Russia, Dante had never worked for Moscow, had never "defected," had never been even suspected of Soviet sympathies. He'd been recruited as a teenager and it was just a matter of luck, Dante's own ambition and ability, and a little help from Center—that he'd ended up as Center's most highly placed mole. As Dante's handler, Zamatin had never worried about exposure, just because it seemed so unlikely that suspicion would ever fall on Dante. Then, three years ago, the NSA made their quantum leap in decrypting Moscow's cable code.

He remembered the night Dante broke the news to him about it, remembered it well. They'd been at one of those Georgetown parties that Dante's second wife, Alana, was fond of giving. Zamatin was uncomfortable, because Dante had invited him at the last minute, which had clearly (from the puzzled and rather hostile glances she cast his way) annoyed Alana. It had wrecked her seating plan, unbalanced the numbers.

Dante had been animated to the point of mania, making Zamatin worry that he was drunk. He was, of course, the star of the party, and since every guest wanted to be seen talking to him, it was late in the evening when he managed to maneuver Zamatin into a private conversation. Zamatin had been intensely curious as to what it was all about. Their scheduled meeting, their chess game, was just two days away. He knew it must be something that couldn't wait. They'd made their way to the chilly sun porch where a neglected spread of pastry provided an excuse. "Val," Dante said, his eyes bright with excitement, "the go-go boys at NSA have busted Center's cable code."

At first he'd thought it was a joke but when he'd raised his eyebrows, Dante had grabbed his arm with sufficient force to obtain his full attention.

"I'm not kidding, Val." Dante said through his clenched-teeth smile. "It's not a perfect break, but they can decrypt—it's mechanical, I don't quite understand it."

Zamatin almost dropped his glass of cognac. "How did they manage. . . . What else do you have? Anything else? I mean—"

"I'll keep you posted," Dante said and then he stuffed some Black Forest cake into his mouth, as if he could swallow his anxiety. A chatting group drifted toward them and soon absorbed them, Dante once again holding court. Zamatin had left as soon as he could and made an emergency contact with Center.

The response was almost immediate: radio silence, then a change in code. There was a high-level furor about the leak. Apparently, no one shouted louder about it than its source, Dante, who immediately demanded an investigation. This ancient device for deflecting suspicion would not have been effective at any but the highest level of government—where, happily for Moscow, some people remained above suspicion.

The code break had been the beginning of the problem. Dante's code name had surfaced in the decoded material and an investigation had been ordered. Moscow had thrown up a patsy and all was quiet for a while. But now, according to Dante, the Fifty-four Committee had recognized the patsy as a patsy. A new investigation had been ordered. Even worse: it was to be run by OS.

They'd been sitting in Dante's ludicrously luxe office when he'd dropped this latest bombshell. They'd been playing chess with a hand-carved set Zamatin specifically disliked, because the pieces toppled over at scarcely a touch. Dante had been holding a knight in his hand when he'd brought the matter up. He was amused. "They decided there was too much access to the crypto DANTE, so they changed it. LUCIFER—that's the new crypto." His laugh boomed around the ostentatious room. "Don't you love it? They must be up on their classics, don't you think?"

"What?" Zamatin said dully.

"Well, the ninth circle of Dante's hell is reserved for traitors, you know, to be perpetually frozen in ice. The only creature below the traitors is—you guessed it—*Lu-ci-fer* himself. I guess I should consider it a kind of promotion." His laugh bounced around the room again.

Still smirking, he took a pawn with his knight, as Zamatin had wished him to do.

"I don't see anything amusing in this."

"I think it's kind of thrilling," Dante said coyly. "It gives me a *frisson.*"

Zamatin had passed the message about the reopening of the investigation. He wondered what Center would do. Throw up another patsy?

He turned up Dolley Madison Boulevard and shook his head, remembering that last chess game. Dante's arrogance was as annoying as it was dangerous.

He was still frowning a few minutes later as he walked into his office.

"Good mornin' Va-a-al," said his secretary, Dottie. Her Georgia accent transformed his nickname into at least three syllables. "If you don't look like someone who just stepped in some you-know-what."

He tried a smile.

"Why don't I get you some coffee?"

"Why don't we run away to Jamaica?" he asked. "You and me. Leave all this behind. *Grow* coffee."

All two hundred pounds of Dottie seemed to giggle. He hung up his coat. Dottie chugged in with his coffee. "I've got to walk a requisition form through," she said. "Somehow I let us run totally out of file folders. I'll be back in about ten minutes."

He cleared his mind and started reading over the final draft of a memo he'd written about population shifts in the Urals.

CHAPTER

SEVEN

Alexandria, Virginia

While he waited for the water to boil, Neil Walker forced his mind back to the dream, to Rabat. He didn't think he'd ever understand why he'd walked out like that, although he'd certainly been given every opportunity to think it through.

The next morning, he'd felt guilty, degraded, as if he'd been arrested for pissing in public. Nothing in his life had prepared him for failing in such an abrupt way. He couldn't understand it—the really dangerous part had been over with; he didn't like to think it was that, that he'd just chickened out. It was hard for him to bring to mind the way he'd felt, standing in that room in Rabat. He couldn't explain it to Diana; he couldn't explain it to himself. He thought he could detect, even in Diana, a certain lessening of regard. He was not entirely trustworthy any more.

His handlers at the Agency were sympathetic and supportive. This sort of thing happened all the time; the burnout rate was fantastic. Walker's team had been lucky, they told him; one of the few small teams that was still intact. The attrition rate for Minutemen was close to forty percent. Given the amount of training Minutemen required, it was a serious problem.

Because it was a problem, Walker found himself a participant in a prolonged study. The Agency was taking a new look at the Minuteman program. They were considering making Minuteman duty a limited thing—like fighter pilots, a certain number of missions and your tour was over. Another look was being taken at the training program itself. Perhaps the problem was that the training procedure did not allow for failure. Failure at any point along the way meant expulsion. Instead of sifting out the unstable, perhaps this process tended to select a specific kind of strength, strength over flexibility.

Walker took part in encounter groups, group therapy for active Minutemen, counseling efforts of every variety. He filled out endless questionnaires, dutifully answering trivial, arcane, and quite personal questions.

"Do you put your right or left shoe on first?"

"Do you have any specific attitudes toward the Hindu deity Ganesha?"

"What is your preferred position for intercourse?"

As far as Walker knew, nothing had helped: there were still Minutemen burning out, some quietly, as he had done, and some far more dramatically.

He began to have the feeling, working with the Agency shrinks, that the true aim of their testing and profiling was to find a way to identify those who might flip in a destructive way.

Less than three months after Rabat, Walker was back at his desk in Soviet Bloc. Despite his violations, he retained his high security clearance, his burnout diagnosed as a stress-related fluke. Too many consecutive missions without enough recovery time. His therapist, Carl Becker, likened Walker's collapse to a runner's muscle failure. "If you're out on the track, running intervals, you have to gauge the recovery time to the intensity of the effort." Walker had nodded, trying to adopt this notion that his psyche was a kind of muscle, his breakdown a mere cramp.

Becker always referred to Rabat as "the episode" during their sessions. He asked questions like, "During the episode, did you notice any unusual physical manifestations—shaking hands, blurred vision, anything like that?" "After the episode . . . before the episode . . ."

Walker tried hard to see it that way, as something outside of the normal time and progression of his life. Although eventually he did come to think of his crack-up as "the episode," a linguistic distancing for which he was grateful to Carl Becker, he knew that it was more than that. He knew that he'd suffered some crucial failure

71

of nerve in Rabat. He'd felt something inside of himself give way; there was some slippage, or something, in his internal structure. And he knew that he would never be the same again.

Carl Becker was vehemently, professionally neutral. Through the months of therapy, Walker began to wonder what it was like spending hours a day without offering an opinion or making a judgment. He thought it violated some basic human law, the way people link to each other. One day, he said as much to Becker.

"Don't you think your attitude—I mean the way you are so *neutral*, professionally neutral . . . Don't you think that eventually that will erode your ability to talk to people? You never say what you think. You never have an opinion. I won't say it drives me crazy, but . . ." He laughed.

Becker didn't budge. "Let's talk about why you're interested in my personality," he replied.

The water boiled. Walker poured it into his Melitta coffeepot.

It wasn't the blood, or just the blood. He'd seen plenty of blood before. At the Saigon embassy, for instance, when the entire CIA station had gone out with a single bomb. Walker's team and four others had replaced the suddenly blinded secretaries, the paralyzed case officers, the dead and the wounded—replaced them overnight without a hitch in either operations or analysis. There was blood on the floor in Saigon, brains on the walls, and while it wasn't true that it hadn't bothered him, he'd stayed. And done his job.

A couple of years after "the episode," Diana had confided, in her quiet way, that she'd considered leaving him while he was a Minuteman. If it hadn't been for the baby, she thought she would have gone off, left him. He'd been turning into someone she didn't like. Diana was like that; she didn't deliver ultimatums. She made up her mind and then . . .

The phone rang, but Walker didn't move to answer it. The answering machine cut in after two rings and he turned up the volume, but the caller hung up. He looked outside. The snow had almost melted away but it persisted in shady spots. The asphalt street was white with the residue of salt. He poured himself a cup of coffee.

Maybe the reason he'd walked out of Rabat was simple. Maybe he'd sensed that one more walk through a blown operation, one

72

more bloodstained attempt to carry on business as usual, one more setup, one more deal, one more look over his shoulder, one more *phone call* might turn him into something not quite human.

Walker glanced at the front page of the *Post*. Leo Adler's eyes stared at him from above the fold, the powerful eyebrows creased into a frown over his trademark glasses. He flipped the paper open. Adler's photo was above a story about the administration's response to the latest Soviet aggression in Afghanistan. Another photograph showed a startled looking Paul Childress, the CIA Director, blinking into the camera. Under the photograph was a story containing Childress's denials of Soviet allegations that there were U.S. "advisers" in Afghanistan. The State Department also made the front page—the Secretary of State had met with a group of relatives and friends of the Iran hostages. He, too, made promises, denials, and threats.

To the left, Jimmy Carter and Rosalynn strolled away from a helicopter. Carter looked suddenly old, his face pinched, the skin under his neck gone crepey—as if he hadn't slept for months. He put the newspaper aside after glancing at the sports section (Georgetown won; the Bullets lost) and took his second cup of coffee up to the large room that served as his office.

He pulled out the yellow pad he used as a telephone log and pressed the play button on his answering machine.

"Hey, Neil," said a voice he immediately recognized as belonging to Hobie James. "Give me a call, okay? Got something I need to talk to you about."

CHAPTER

EIGHT

At lunchtime, Nicola Ward was in the teachers' lounge, enduring a detailed recitation of Betty Feldon's gynecological problems. Between the saga of Betty's recent D & C and the room's dingy decor with its discouraging collection of half-dead plants, she didn't have much appetite. She excused herself to correct papers. As she walked back to her classroom, she was preoccupied, thinking about money. Kate's illness was expensive; the fees for therapy and treatment centers, only partially covered by Nicola's insurance, had devoured most of her savings. Then, too, the diversions Kate found most soothing—shopping, and eating out in restaurants—were extravagant for Nicola's means. Kate could shop all day. Every shopkeeper in town knew her by now. They thought that perhaps she was dying of cancer, and were unfailingly kind to this wraith—who might spend half an hour choosing between a pink and a red bandana, fifteen minutes selecting a quarter pound of mushrooms.

It was the only social contact Kate had and Nicola couldn't bring herself to curtail it. As for eating out, she encouraged that, too. Kate actually seemed to eat in restaurants (and she was reluctant to throw up in public restrooms). Nicola would linger over coffee, over dessert, prolonging the meal, hoping some nutrition would seep into Kate's system. Still, money was so tight that she'd have to do something soon—maybe mortgage the house, or sell the cabin. Something.

The fourth-graders were lined up outside Arlene Stern's room.

The squirming line steadied for a moment as she passed. Several children called out to her: "Hello, Mrs. Ward!" competing for her attention. She was a popular teacher—nice, but strong enough to keep order. She'd been approached—and even courted—by several private schools over the years, but she'd never been tempted. She liked the challenge, the variety—the poor kids from the fishing village who were lucky to have one book in the house, and the upper-middle-class town kids, who took lessons in everything and skied in Switzerland.

She passed the wall where she'd arranged a display of fifth-grade artwork. WINTER TREES was spelled out in black block letters. Some of the trees looked quite realistic, complete with shadows, a few convincing dead leaves clinging to their branches. On the other hand, there were hasty little inverted green cones, the crudest representations of pine trees.

As she opened the door, the sound rushed out to meet her: "SURPRISE!!!"

She took her place behind her desk. The faces of the kids shone up at her, so bright with pleasure they almost seemed to emit heat. She should have guessed—they'd been giggling and whispering all morning. They looked totally pleased with themselves now, and she stood there with her mouth deliberately agape, admiring their efforts. Streamers of red and green extended from the corners of the room to the center where they met under the cover of a large bouquet of balloons. HAPPY BIRTHDAY MRS. WARD was written in huge, three-dimensional-looking candy-striped letters on the board. Elaine Mudge had done the lettering, Nicola knew, because all year she'd been perfecting the style on her classroom papers.

"*Wow*," she said. "You really, *really* surprised me."

They all laughed in unison, a surprisingly hearty sound that seemed to penetrate to the very center of her head.

"What's the occasion?"

They laughed again, in perfect unison. The sound struck her as slightly sinister, as if the class were a creature with a mass mind. She sat down and smiled at them. Their proud happiness, their simple delight in the break from routine lifted her heart.

Emily Rider popped up.

Emily had a nose that was so snubbed, it presented to the world

75

the flat ovals of her nostrils. There was a style of drawing faces, popular in about the third or fourth grade, in which the nostrils, eyelashes and fingernails were particularly prominent; Emily Rider might have served as the model for those faces. ". . . the *best* fifth-grade teacher in the *world*," Emily was saying in a surprisingly good imitation of an announcer's hucksterish pitch: "Nicola Ward, *this is your life*."

She gasped like a quiz-show contestant, a little wail coming out of her mouth as she covered her face with her hands. "I don't believe it." The class bounced and squealed with delight. Some adult had put them up to this. Even she hadn't thought of the ancient TV show in years, although she retained a clear memory of it: families stashed behind stage, then dragged out for corny reunions. The person whose life was being nationally televised sat in a thronish chair, reduced to gasping while the moderator tried to squeeze in his or her autobiography between commercial breaks.

Scott Paisley, one of Nicola's favorites, stood up and rattled some sheets of paper in his hands, pretending to be nervous. He cleared his throat and reached into his desk, pulling out a cassette tape recorder. Some vaguely oriental music, scratchy and indistinct, began to play. "We don't know what kind of day it was because it was so long ago," Scott began, "but on January 9, 1939, a child was born in Shanghai, China." Billy Wade appeared, dressed in a sheet, with a toy stethoscope bouncing on his chest. At arm's length, he held a doll wrapped in a baby blanket. "It's a girl," he boomed.

Nicola laughed out loud and then hid her mouth behind her hand. Billy Wade blushed. "It's wonderful," she said. "Fantastic."

In fact, she herself knew little more than that about her early life. The most exotic fact about her—that she had been born in Shanghai—was information she'd managed, as a college student, to work into almost every conversation with new acquaintances. Usually the glamour of her birthplace failed to make an impression because in the next moment she'd be forced to admit that she didn't exactly "remember" Shanghai, having been sent to the United States as a baby. Then she would brazenly mention that she was an orphan.

"War broke out in Shanghai," Scott Paisley read. The room exploded in mock gunfire. After she restored order, things rolled along quickly. There was a naturalization ceremony, her high school graduation (Elaine Mudge in a mortarboard made out of poster paper, holding aloft a copy of her yearbook, the Morse *Shipbuilder*), followed a minute later by her college graduation. Scott had taped appropriate music for each event and there were pauses while each cut was located. After "Pomp and Circumstance," she was married (the *Lohengrin* "Wedding March") and then had a baby (the Brahms "Lullaby"). That was the end of her life, as far as the kids were concerned.

She was grateful they hadn't thought to include the divorce.

After Nicola's prolonged applause and effusive praise, the self-satisfied group gorged on chocolate cake. The frosting of the cake was embedded with colored sugar crystals (red and green), multi-colored balls, coconut flakes, and chocolate sprinkles.

While Scott Paisley ably parceled out second helpings of cake, and Vanessa Handley poured the bright red Hawaiian Punch, Nicola looked through the yearbook. She had no idea where her own yearbook was—this one belonged to Art Burleigh, the principal of Thomas Point. He'd been a high school classmate. She found her picture easily and read the inscription, frowning at the rounded, childish handwriting. It hadn't changed much. It seemed to her that most teachers had juvenile handwriting—there was a need to be aggressively legible.

> To Art,
> It's been a riot sitting next to you in English. I'm sure
> you'll be a success. Good luck.
> Love ya, Nikki

Amazing that this banal nugget had been preserved for over twenty years. And there, under her picture, the italics read: NI-COLA ALETTA SUNDERLAND *"Nikki"* . . . *"Oh, sugar!"* . . . *beautiful eyes . . . one dimple . . . Stan's her man . . . that turquoise Merc . . . witty and smart . . . college in her future.*

Nikki. All her life, she'd been called Nicola except for the last two years in high school and the first year in college when she'd insisted on *Nikki.* She'd taken enormous pleasure in signing her name, turning the dots over the "i"s into little open circles, perfecting the hard, angular shapes of the "k"s. It was this shameless Nikki who had openly bragged of being an orphan, elaborating in a breathless way that her parents had been killed "in China," "during the war."

Learning that she was an orphan hadn't been the powerful blow anyone might assume. She was seven years old at the time and she'd been living in Washington, D.C., with her Aunt Hillary and Uncle Brian, since she was a baby. Aunt Hillary delivered the news as gently as possible, and she remembered her attempts at grief, trying to squeeze tears from her eyes. She did miss the *idea* of her parents' being alive; it was as if an opening into the future, a window that looked out on a different life, had closed forever. But it was hard to actually miss parents you didn't remember. She could even remember the little nut of relief she'd felt, learning that her parents were dead. It meant that she'd stay with Aunt Hillary and Uncle Brian, that her parents wouldn't come and take her away from the only home she'd ever known.

After the mess in the room was straightened up, and Nicola had thanked the kids for the party, she got the class prepared to go—lining up the bus riders, the walkers, making sure they had their coats and hats and mittens. She solemnly shook Scott Paisley's hand, thanking him for an excellent job. He confessed that part of the idea came from his mother, the "This Is Your Life" part. His honesty touched her, his modesty. She had a sudden impulse to tell him all her troubles, as if he could solve them.

When the class had filed out, she stayed for about half an hour, correcting papers. Then she grabbed her gym bag, hurrying. She'd lost track of the time; she'd be late for her exercise class. But when she got to the parking lot, she couldn't find her car. She doggedly circled the parking lot again. It was small—it held fewer than thirty cars—but still, she didn't see hers. She stopped next to the ugly, dirt-streaked pile of snow heaped up by the plow at the end of the parking lot. It seemed so unlikely that someone would steal her car. Still: *Where was it?*

Betty Feldon came out, talking to James Mackenzie, the P.E. teacher.

"*Rectus abdominus,*" James was saying.

"That doesn't sound quite nice," Betty said. She had a harsh braying laugh, which issued vigorously from her mouth and then stopped abruptly. She put down her tote bag. "Right *here*," she insisted, placing James Mackenzie's hand against her abdomen. "Right here."

"Sit-ups," James Mackenzie said in a distracted voice, looking at Nicola. "Still the best. Without anchoring the feet," he added in a strict voice.

"Sit-ups give me heartburn," Betty Feldon said.

"Is something wrong, Nicola?" James asked.

"I can't find my car," she said weakly. "I actually think," she laughed nervously, "I think someone stole my car."

A frown settled on James Mackenzie's face. "*Nicola*, are you all right?"

"Apart from losing my car and having to walk home, you mean?" She laughed. "Fine, I'm just fine."

"Nicola, your car is *right there*." Not ten yards from them was her red Subaru.

She laughed, covering: "I must be losing my mind. It's old age, I guess. I was looking for my old blue Pinto."

James gave her a look and let the corner of his mouth curl up. "Talk about the absentminded professor," he said in his Bill Murray impersonation. "Get outa here."

Nicola laughed and got into her car, embarrassed. In fact, it wasn't so funny. She'd traded in the Pinto three years ago. She took it as evidence that her mind was becoming unreliable, that the simplest mental connections were getting difficult, that her brain was a mass of jumbled synapses, the linkage wrecked by stress.

While she rummaged in her purse for her keys, James drove off in his black TransAm. He had vanity plates that read MUSCLE. She thought about James Mac while she drove toward the Grace Episcopal Church. He was twenty-seven years old, a jock with a master's degree in exercise physiology. Religiously devoted to his body, he followed a diet humbling in its austerity. He came from a "good" Boston family, which he claimed made its fortune selling sanitary napkins to institutions.

When he'd first joined the faculty at Thomas Point, someone had incorrectly identified Nicola to him as a "fitness enthusiast," and he asked her if he could go running with her sometime. They ran a few times, and played tennis a couple of Saturdays. One day he'd stopped while pointing out the nuances of the Continental grip, grazed her breast with his hand, and with amazing speed had his tongue in her ear and his hands under her tennis skirt.

It happened less than a year after Stan had left her, and she had not thought of herself in sexual terms for so long that she'd stood there, shocked, letting him kiss her, until she recovered herself and pulled away from him. Then she'd told him to forget it, she couldn't manage a romantic relationship with him.

"Who's talking romantic?" he'd insisted. "I'm talking physical." He then sermonized a bit about the effects of accumulated tension. "And social. If we eat dinner together at the Harbor Light, you know, a taco platter and a couple of beers, we're not actually talking romance." She remembered saying: "Look, James, we can run together every now and then, that might be nice, but I can't *date* you—that's just not going to happen. I'm more than ten years older than you are. I'd feel ridiculous."

"Well, I didn't know you were so worried about your self-*image*." He imitated an old biddy: "Who does she think she *is*, running around with a younger *man*. She ought to be *ashamed*. . . ."

Nicola laughed. "Well, you know." She waved her hand in the air. "It's a small town."

"Well, yes, I *know*. And you're what? The little schoolteacher. The widow Ward—oh, excuse me, he's not dead, is he?—the wronged woman, left in the lurch." He held his tennis racket as if it were a violin and sawed away at it with an imaginary bow. Before resuming his tennis instruction, though, he looked her straight in the eyes and then kissed her again, deeply, expertly. "If you ever change your mind," he said.

She'd stepped away from him, flushed, her body aroused, wishing she *didn't* care what people thought. She and James had remained friends and soon after that she'd begun going out with men for the first time since Stan left. She'd always been grateful to James Mac for reminding her of her sexuality.

She parked the Subaru next to a maroon Ford Galaxie that was losing its chassis to rust. She changed her clothes in the ladies' room. The aerobics class was held in a large room on the second floor of the church annex and from the hall she could hear Dolly Parton singing the warm-up tune, a sad ballad.

"Step together step," said the instructor. "Houlihan hands. Flat back stretch."

Nicola took her place and looked up at the portrait of Jesus looming over them. It was El Greco–inspired—slightly insane eyes rolled up toward the heavens—a passive, suffering Jesus. It always made her think of Stan.

She'd married Stan Ward when she was twenty-one years old, shortly after Aunt Hillary died. Aunt Hillary's death had truly made her feel orphaned. Sometimes she thought she'd married Stan just to feel connected to someone else.

The marriage lasted until 1973, when Stan abruptly left—left her, Kate, and his job at the Bath Iron Works to "find himself" in Los Angeles.

She could recall some of their bitter phone exchanges. She'd developed a certain edgy sarcasm:

"Hello, Nicola."
"Who's this?"
"Come on."
"Oh, you found yourself."
"How's Kate."
"Found himself in the City of Angels."
"Can I speak to her?"
"Just a sec. I'll see if I can pry her loose from the television."
Nicola put her hand over the receiver. "She wants to know if you can wait for a commercial."
"Nicola, this isn't like you."
"I've changed. I had a makeover. I'm fond of slingback shoes and dangling earrings."
"Nicola."
"Here's Kate."

After a year of exploring the single lifestyle so fully documented for him on television and on the pages of the slick men's magazines he liked to read, Stan found . . . not himself . . . but God and a twenty-two-year-old woman named Consuela.

Stan and Consuela had married in a mass ceremony of their religious sect, the Lambs of God. Real estate prices in Southern California being what they were, the Lambs soon moved to a commune in New Mexico. A year after their marriage, Stan and Consuela had a son. They called him Jesus.

"Floor work," the instructor said. "Get your mats."

Spanish pronounciation. Give Stan credit. He'd pointed that out to Kate when he'd sent her the needlessly graphic and ecstatic description of his son's birth. "Your half brother's name is Jesus," he'd written. "Pronounced *HAY-ZOOZ*."

Nicola prepared to execute the opening combination. "Heel toe, heel toe, *rocking* horse," yelled the instructor.

When Stan first left them, Nicola had been paralyzed. She was a dependent person with no one left to depend on; she was numb, stunned. The first year was a poisonous blend of helplessness and anger. She'd done her best to hide her hysteria from Kate, pretending to cope; she even cried in the bathroom at night, with the water running, so Kate wouldn't know. Gradually, real competence had displaced her bravado; their life lost its gritty, desperate edge and even achieved a kind of graceful rhythm of its own.

She had continued to teach, a job she'd taken when Kate had entered the first grade. Though her salary was small, she and Kate were able to manage financially because they were free of rent or mortgage payments. Stan, in his zeal to divest himself of his worldly goods, had signed over to Nicola (in lieu of further child support and alimony payments, impossible because the Lambs had a barter economy) both the house in Bath that had been in his family for almost a hundred years, and the summer cabin on Langan's Cove.

Stan. *Stan.* Stan had actually dared to mention "God's will" the last time she'd tried to explain to him how sick Kate was, and how worried she was. His moronic serenity infuriated her; everything got chalked up to "God's will." She'd told him it was an abdication of responsibility; he'd smiled and observed that the Lord moved in mysterious ways.

CHAPTER NINE

Dante was so hyper that Zamatin wondered if he was doing cocaine. Between moves, Dante got up and prowled around the room—he seemed unable to sit still. Zamatin wasn't enjoying himself and wasn't in the mood to be merciful—he wanted the game over as soon as possible. It didn't take long until they were in the endgame.

Zamatin had learned that it wasn't wise to *ask* Dante if he had any information to pass along to Center. That just led to teasing. Dante enjoyed telling lies, seeing if he could get Zamatin to believe some outrageous invention and then laughing at him. He also liked to bring up business matters in the endgame because it wrecked Zamatin's concentration.

"Oh, by the way," Dante said finally, when Zamatin had him in check. "I have something for you." He reached into his back pocket, took out his wallet, and withdrew a tiny square of paper, much folded. "It's a diagram, something to do with Extra Long Frequency transmissions, subs. I don't know whether it's anything new or not, but what the hell, send it on. By the *way*, the coaches (this was the way he always referred to Moscow Center) took care of our little problem, you know—*Boris*." He flicked Zamatin's remaining bishop down with his fingernail. "Departed."

Zamatin picked up the bishop and replaced it in its correct position. "Really," he said in a neutral voice. He sounded calm but his heart squirmed in his chest. Last week, after Dante had dropped the bombshell about the reopening of the investigation into his identity, about project LUCIFER, Zamatin had immediately arranged a brush contact to pass the information. He'd had the dismal feeling, when he and the blond man had exchanged their rolled-up newspapers, of giving the initial nudge to some well-greased engine of destruction. It was unpleasant to have that premonition confirmed, to learn so quickly of the first dark product of his encounter. "That was quick. I'm not so sure that was wise."

Dante shrugged. "Ours not to question why, you know." His manicured hands seesawed in the air. He stood up and recited:

> "Theirs but to do and die . . .
> Into the jaws of death
> Into the mouth of hell . . ."

His big laugh ricocheted around the room.

Zamatin said nothing.

"But because Boris's demise *was* so quick," Dante continued, "you can probably expect to be questioned by the Office of Security. I mean you *were* on the debriefing team, weren't you?"

Zamatin nodded and looked at the board, which seemed to quiver before his eyes. He could feel fear rising in his chest. He forced himself to calm down. He would be questioned about the debriefing, that was all. He thought back to it to see if he'd behaved in any suspicious way. He reviewed it in his mind.

He had to hand it to Center, Shokorov had been well prepared. His knowledge of his legend had been solid, and no nagging inconsistencies had turned up. The one glitch had been something Neil Walker had noticed, some discrepancies in Shokorov's speech patterns. Walker was famous for his so-called "magic ears," an uncanny ability to detect regional speech patterns. He could do it in English and he could do it in Russian and French. It came in handy during debriefings—if a defector said he was from Tbilsi, or Georgia, or Moscow, Walker could pretty much tell if that claim was true. Zamatin himself had warned Moscow about Walker's unusual talent years ago.

Sometime toward the end of the debriefing session, Zamatin remembered Walker suddenly saying, "Everything checks out, but you know, Val, something bothers me."

"What's that, Neil? What do you mean?"

Walker had a puzzled look. "I don't know. Everything checks out—his legend matches the facts. It's—well, his story is that he came originally from Leningrad and then moved to Moscow. But certain words and phrases he uses—not many—are right out of the Ukraine. According to him, he's *never been* in the Ukraine." Walker's hands flew up.

Zamatin wondered if Moscow had been in such a hurry as to send a Ukrainian to pose as a Russian. Add to that Shokorov's sloppy tradecraft when he'd first defected (it was Shokorov who'd raised the matter of Dante and Shokorov who'd insisted that the FBI bring in the Agency), and you could conclude that standards were slipping at Center.

Zamatin did what he'd been trained to do: changed the subject. "I didn't notice that you were growing a mustache, Neil. All day, it has seemed to me you looked different and I am asking myself: has he lost weight? Has he got a new haircut? Just this second, I see it is your mustache. I think I like it."

Walker smiled. "I used to have one, you know. My wife doesn't like it, but I'll keep it for my vacation, anyway."

Zamatin pretended to return to the subject of Shokorov. "Ukrainian phrases, eh?" But now he'd remembered that Walker had tried to avoid being assigned to this debriefing effort, that Walker was leaving for a vacation in a few days and no doubt didn't want his plans disrupted. "Is it possible, Neil, that he had a friend or a baba or something, an influential teacher, perhaps? Could this account for it?"

Walker didn't look enthusiastic. "It's possible. That happens with some people. Their speech patterns are corrupted because they emulate someone they like or admire. It can happen."

"You tell me," Zamatin said. "What should we do?" He put down the HOME SWEET HOME trivet he was fiddling with and got up to get a glass of water. "Put him through again? Go deeper? Go another level?"

Walker's eyes narrowed and Zamatin knew that he was totaling the extra time another level of interrogation would require and how it would affect his vacation plans. "If we find *anything* else, I think we'll have to run another level. But as it stands now, let's play him. I'll do it; I'll sneak in some questions and see if he trips."

Zamatin couldn't risk warning Shokorov. So he simply hoped for the best, assuming that Shokorov's training and indoctrination would be thorough enough to get him past some halfhearted probes by Walker. And it did. The training had stood.

A few days later, they'd been in the kitchen again. Walker's lanky body leaned against the doorway. Zamatin was drinking some terrible decaffeinated instant coffee. He made a face.

"What's the matter, Val?"

"This is the worst coffee I've ever tasted. During wartime, I had coffee made out of acorns that was better than this."

"You Eastern Bloc types," Walker said in a teasing voice, "especially you Ivans—you have a touching faith in capitalism. You think it provides a good product. You forget what *advertising* can do—the power of the coupon, the *free sample*." Walker picked up the jar. "Have you noticed that in the last year or two, they've begun to stock these safe houses with house brands instead of name brands? It's insane. One time, they even had generic cigarettes. The subjects looked at them like they were rolled up turds. They wanted *Marlboros*. Or *Parliaments*. *Kools*. I mean, wouldn't you? Defectors want name brands; hell, they're not coming over to the West for generic equivalents. They want the real thing. It's not the place to cut corners, you know?"

Zamatin nodded and poured the rest of the coffee in the sink. "Did you . . . did you . . ." he began. He had trouble thinking of a way to phrase his question. "How did it go with Shokorov?"

"The Ukrainianisms? I think we can relax. I baited some hooks for him, but he didn't bite. He didn't nibble. Not a twitch. He had a Ukrainian lover—here, in New York—it usually doesn't work that way, but maybe speech is more vulnerable when you're off your own turf." Walker lit a cigarette.

"I thought you quit."

"Yeah."

And that had been the end of the close call with Walker.

Thinking about the debriefing of Shokorov, Zamatin concluded that his own behavior had been blameless. If anyone got hassled, it would be Walker.

Zamatin watched Dante make another stupid move. He couldn't shake a certain uneasiness. It was because he was so close to getting free of the whole thing. Once he retired, once Dante handled his own stuff, Zamatin would be out of danger. In the meantime, if he were to be exposed now, as a double agent of forty years' standing, he could expect to remain in debriefing sessions for . . . the rest of his life. And if he came in from the cold and went back to Moscow, it would just be the same thing from another set of inquisitors. They would have endless questions about CIA operations; they would suck his brain dry. He stared at the board, trying to concentrate.

The worst thing about the reopening of the investigation was that it had been moved to OS. If it had remained in his own backyard, Soviet Bloc Division, he'd have been able to keep an eye on it, and he knew the Bloc's plodding exactitude well enough to be sure that the probe would take a long time. An investigation by the Office of Security was an unknown quantity. He sighed and made a move with his knight. "Are you concerned?" he asked Dante.

"Not yet. It would take a real leap of imagination for them to think of me. *Me? A Russian spy?*" He shook his big head. "No way." He moved his pawn. "*Unthinkable.*"

Zamatin tapped the floor with his foot. Dante thought he was invulnerable. Like a child or an adolescent who can't imagine certain catastrophes happening to him, Dante felt immune. Maybe immortal. He repositioned his rook. "Checkmate."

"Damn. I thought I might get you today."

"As I've said before, chess requires a methodical approach with flashes of brilliance, not just the occasional blaze of insight."

"I'm sure I could beat you regularly if I applied myself."

"Perhaps if we took up backgammon you might."

Dante turned his big head and glared at him. "No, I mean it."

The man's competitive arrogance was irritating. "There's no chance of that," Zamatin snapped.

"Of what? That I would apply myself? You're probably right."

"You would never be able to beat me regularly, no matter how much you 'applied' yourself. Never."

Dante's face colored. "Is that a challenge?"

Zamatin recovered. "Certainly not," he joked. "I am teasing you." He smiled, but he knew that soon he would have to throw a game.

CHAPTER

TEN

Dante showed the little Russian to the door, smiling. He wagged his finger: "I'm going to get you next time, Val. I can feel it." He clapped his arm around the man's shoulder and then stepped aside. He watched Zamatin's compact form trudge through his outer office, a slightly defeated shrug disturbing his otherwise militantly good posture. He thought of Val as a man who followed orders well—a kind of worker bee.

He knew in fact that "next time," the Russian would let him win. He'd caught the wary, defensive look in Zamatin's eyes at his faked anger and knew he could look forward to a victory. It was always fun watching Val throw a game. It was so obviously painful for him—he cogitated more about how to undercut his own position than he ever did about a winning strategy.

He went back into his office and asked Alice to hold his calls for a while. He wanted to think.

He'd seen the fear in Zamatin's face today when he'd dropped the news about Shokorov's demise. But while Zamatin was frightened, he himself was exhilarated.

For a long, long time, it had amused him to know that he was playing a gigantic joke on the world, holding the positions he did, and being a Soviet agent. It was a great game and the higher his ambition and ability took him, the more diverting it was. But sometime in the last couple of years, it had suddenly stopped being quite enough. Maybe because he knew that even if he was found out, he'd never be exposed now. They'd never risk that—it would be too humiliating. No, if the Agency found him out now, he'd suffer some sort of accident, they'd see to it that he left the picture quietly, without the fanfare that he deserved, without the colossal nose-thumbing that he looked forward to. It was almost enough to make a fellow defect. Not quite, because he wanted the game to continue; he still had so much to do.

Which was all the more reason to stop taking the risks he'd been taking. Stupid risks. Whatever the reason, he had gradually become addicted to the feeling of putting himself in peril. The diffuse danger inherent in his position was not enough anymore. He craved the surge of energy that he got from direct risk, the hum of tension that burned through him like current on a high-voltage wire.

Maybe he'd be able to stop now that the DANTE investigation was heating up and he was in actual danger of exposure. Especially now that he thought exposure meant not a scandal but a potential death sentence.

He was sure a therapist would have it all figured out, his compulsion to take risks—like a man who cheated on his wife, he wanted to get caught. A self-destructive reflex, a death wish. Here was a laugh: his mid-life crisis! He didn't know. He propped his big feet up on his fine desk, mashing down a draft of a White Paper on the clergy in Iran.

The risks took different forms—sometimes physical, sometimes social, sometimes professional. Usually, all three. It had started a couple of years ago. At first, the risks were small: driving for a few seconds with his eyes closed, seeing how long he could drive with his hands off the wheel. He made jokes, like saying to the President, "Actually, I work for the Russians." He made obscene phone calls to cabinet members' wives (from pay phones: he hadn't been entirely deranged). It was that kind of thing. Soon, however, it wasn't enough and he began to tune up the danger.

Now he might drive his car at ninety miles an hour down the parkway for five minutes. A month ago he'd walked the railing on a balcony at an apartment building in Rosslyn (twentieth floor), à la Norman Mailer. It was during a party and no one saw him do it. Once he embraced a Significant Lady at a White House gathering. Instead of the air kiss on the cheek, he'd nuzzled her ear and fondled her ass. She never said a word.

Lately, there was a sexual component to his risk taking. When the flush of adrenaline was combined with orgasm, the feeling was really spectacular, the best thing he'd ever felt in his life. Two weeks ago, he'd picked up a prostitute on 14th Street and had her give him a blow job in the car. Ever since then, he'd been tempted to repeat the experience—this time in broad daylight.

He thought about the Russian. He was glad Val was retiring. For one thing, the man was a bore. For another, he was looking forward to taking over, himself, the task of making actual contact with Center. He wondered what they would do now to deflect attention from him. Would they throw up another dupe, some kind of smokescreen? Would it be better than the Ronald Peters show? Or would they decide to bring him in? He'd be a fucking hero in the Soviet Union. They'd have a parade.

Just thinking about picking up a prostitute made his prick begin to stir and assert itself. He could drive while she did it, although his attention to traffic patterns might fade while he came. He lifted the Iran paper and tried to read it, but the pressure in his groin destroyed his concentration. Finally, he went to the door and stuck his head out and asked Alice to come in. "Sure thing," she said with the characteristic toss of her head that flung the curtain of her smooth brown hair back out of her eyes.

"What can I do?" she said in her perky voice as she came through the door with her steno pad.

"C'mere," he said from his desk.

Her smiled deepened and the dimples showed in her cheeks. He stood up and embraced her, his hands quickly diving under her sweater to caress her breasts. She pressed her hand against the hard knot of his erection. "What do we have here?"

She was so thrilled by their affair, she'd do anything he wanted, anytime, an adolescent's dream come true. She'd even confessed to him once that having sex with him made her feel she was doing something for "our country." The notion had delighted him; he found the combination of her earnestness and her wanton behavior enchanting. "My little patriot," he'd said. "Well, most people wouldn't understand," she'd said, "but I do feel it's patriotic, you know?" Now she began to lift off her sweater but as she did so, some remnant of modesty made her turn her back to him. "Oh sugar," she squeaked. "The door's not shut."

An indescribable thrill flashed through him as he looked over her shoulder at the door, which was about six inches ajar. "Don't worry about it," he said in a strangled voice as he unbuttoned his pants and fumbled with his zipper. "They'll knock." He kissed her deeply. "You're fantastic," he said, putting his hands on her shoulders. He pushed her gently down so she would understand he wanted her to go down on him. "Fabulous," he said. Her head bobbed below him and except for a very few moments, he never took his eyes off the seam of light that marked the open door.

CHAPTER

ELEVEN

Neil Walker stopped the machine after Hobie James's message and picked out a sharp pencil from the lumpy clay container Andy had given him last year for Father's Day. Now that he didn't have a secretary, he was trying to develop new and orderly work habits, doing everything the same way each day, inventing a workable one-person system for his new business as a genealogist.

An early riser who now slept late, a born slob who now kept meticulous records—it seemed to him that his whole personality had radically changed. The subtle shifting of habits, like the small motions of tectonic plates that cause earthquakes, had resulted in an upheaval which had turned him into a different person.

He looked out the window.

The bare branch of the oak tree rocked up and down, rattled by the wind. He wrote on the yellow legal pad in his large clear hand, *January 9, 1980.* Below that he noted Hobie's name and number, then resumed playing back his messages.

"My name is Jan Kulik. You can reach me at 387-5333." The voice was accented but sure of itself. A man used to leaving messages and fluent in English. He wrote *Jan Kulik*, followed by the telephone number. Maybe this was the guy his friend Steve Wisner at the National Archives had told him might call.

The tape continued: a familiar, congenial voice said, "Hey, Neil, Mike Hale. Interested in finding out if I'm related to Nathan. Heh

heh. I'm out in the country, 998-8712, give me a call before noon if you have time." Even though Hale was his best friend and he'd called the number hundreds of times, Walker wrote it down. He found it best to write everything down; it seemed that his secretary had *been* his memory.

There were several beeps—calls made but no messages left—and then Andy, calling from the clinic. "Dad, are you *there?* Answer the phone if you are, okay?" There was a pause. "I guess you're not there." Sadly. "Call me back tonight, okay?" Another pause. "This is Andy," he added, as if his father might possibly confuse him with someone else.

There was one more call, from Lou Graves, confirming their appointment for dinner.

Ever since Walker had quit the Agency, there'd been a steady supply of invitations from former colleagues who thought they ought to make a social gesture—drinks, lunch, dinner. But each invitation carried the heavy freight of solace or advice and mostly, he declined. Lou was a little different; he and Lou had worked closely together and considered each other friends. When Lou first suggested dinner, he'd hinted around that perhaps Neil would like a "date," another woman to round out the table: "I don't know if it's too *soon*, or what, but . . ." "It is, Lou," he'd said. "It's too soon."

It had happened just six months before.

The Volvo was packed. He and Diana and Andy were going to leave early the next morning for their annual stay at Walker's old family cottage in Maine. He was almost looking forward to the Norman Rockwellesque ride: the songs, the traveling games. . . . "I packed my suitcase and in it I put . . ." Their trips were usually preceded by a certain preparational frenzy, and this time they were proud of their organization. When the phone rang, Diana made a joke about how it was probably the Boy Scouts, wanting to schedule an award dinner. But when she answered it, the jokiness drained from her face. She handed it to him without a word.

It turned out that the CIA chief of station in Helsinki had returned home from a party to find a KGB major sitting on his doorstep, a little drunk, but determined to defect. Walker was booked on the next flight.

"It's the magic ears, right?" Diana said from the couch after he'd hung up. "They need your magic ears somewhere."

"Helsinki."

"Oh well, Helsinki." She sighed, resigned. "Their timing sucks." She refused to consider postponing the trip; she and Andy would just drive up on their own.

"You can meet us up there," she said.

"Down there, Di. *Down* East."

She didn't laugh.

He knew that she wanted to leave on schedule because she couldn't stand to disappoint Andy.

The cabin had been built by his own grandfather in 1915. Over the years, it had become more comfortable and less rustic but it was still something special. His father had brought in electricity and installed the septic system, a huge improvement over the old smelly outhouse. He and Diana had refurnished it—with the antiques, wicker, and pine that Diana loved to shop for—and built a new dock and a driveway. But it still was a country place, a place in the woods.

When he'd been a boy, there was nothing as wonderful to him as the weeks he spent in Maine. It was time set apart—he was often alone, and his unstructured days flew by in the same pursuits that would involve any kid around the ocean—fishing, clamming, exploring, sailing, kicking around the bay in Billy Tuttle's motorboat. There was something special in the fresh salt air and the fact that the rhythm of his days rose and fell with the tide. You could swim at high tide, clam at low tide, fish on the incoming tide. He'd gained a sense of his own strength and self-sufficiency there. He thought Maine's attraction for Andy was much the same as it had been for him. It was a different environment, where Andy had more independence, more freedom. He didn't need his parents to drive him to this lesson or that—he was on his own.

Andy had been marking the days off on the calendar since school got out. He wouldn't tolerate a postponement well. He didn't have the sunny, flexible disposition one wished for a child. He was intense and moody like Diana, and like her, too, he was incredibly smart and perceptive. Sometimes, it was hard to remember that he was only ten years old. When he did have a childish enthusiasm for something, like the trip, it was hard to let him down.

94

"You'll probably only beat me there by one day," Walker had said.

In fact, they never made it at all.

When he'd gone through passport control in Helsinki, a small, colorless man came up to him. "Mr. Walker?" he asked in a confirming tone. It made Walker nervous because the arrangement had been that someone would meet him at the hotel. Was he going to be arrested? For espionage? It happened sometimes—some Russian or American spook would get popped into jail. ("A member of the Soviet trade delegation was arrested today in London . . . an American businessman held in Cairo . . . a risk assessment analyst detained in Cyprus . . .") This would be a lesson for the parent country, a gimmick bust, a public relations move, a ploy in the endless battle for positional strength.

"Come this way," the colorless man suggested, and led him to a deserted waiting area. They sat down in a place that could have been anywhere people were forced to wait: overflowing ashtrays, half-filled paper cups, discarded newspapers. Although the man was so nondescript as to be almost invisible, his voice still lingered in Walker's head months later, the voice that told him his wife and son had been in a traffic accident on the Connecticut Turnpike.

"What?"

It was not a scene he'd ever envisioned; he'd imagined himself injured, even dead, but never Andy, never Diana.

"How bad?" he insisted. "How bad?"

A hole opened up in the world and through the hole he heard the little man say, "Your wife is dead." The man paused for a second, and Walker seemed to balance there, agonized, on a fulcrum of possibility. "Your son is alive, but he's critically injured."

"I see," he said mechanically.

"I'm a doctor," he heard the man saying, "and I'm going to give you an injection to make you a little sleepy. I recommend that."

"Are you sure?"

"That it's your wife and son?" The man's eyes stayed away from his. "Yes, I'm sorry; they're sure."

"Let me say that you're booked on a flight in," he flipped his wrist up and looked at his watch, "thirty-five minutes. And your father-in-law will meet you at the airport in Hartford. Your son has been taken to the Shock Trauma Unit of the Connecticut Hospital in New Haven. It's one of the finest facilities of its kind in the world, and everything that could possibly have gone right for your son, following the head-on collision, has gone right."

Head-on collision, Walker thought.

"What's gone right?" he demanded in a loud voice.

"The first car that stopped to assist was driven by an orthopedist. The boy was protected from inadvertent damage and was promptly helicoptered to the best facility on the East Coast."

"I thought it was the best facility in the world," Walker heard himself correct the man, "one of the best in the world."

"It is," the man said. "How about that injection, Mr. Walker? You're in mild shock—this will counter the physiological effects. No, please don't stand up."

Walker wanted to touch him, but the man was so nondescript, so insubstantial that he was afraid, afraid his hand might pass through the flesh. He watched the needle penetrate his skin.

Diana's father, Delmore Holt, who had seldom in his life been called anything but Del, met Walker at the airport. The two men had never liked each other and they embraced awkwardly.

"The sonafabitch was drunk, he didn't even put on his brakes, Neil, she never had a chance."

"Del. God."

"You look at that wreck, you're never gonna believe anybody got out of it alive. I would say, *don't*, don't look at it. Still, he's hanging in there, Andy's a tough one, but Neil, Neil, NEIL . . ."

Del started sobbing. The crowd at the baggage-claim area pulled away from them and left them in a little island of space. Like a child, Del gulped air, trying to control his breathing. Neil put his arms around him. Del's body felt small and extraordinarily dense. The phrase "specific gravity" rolled through his mind. They left the airport without speaking. The air outside seemed to calm them both down.

Later, as they approached the intensive care unit and looked at Andy, who was unconscious and nearly invisible, surrounded by huge machines, with tubes in him everywhere, Del had seized his arm and looked him in the eyes.

"Where were you, Neil?" Walker saw Del's eyes bearing down

96

on him. "What the fuck were you doing in Helsinki when you were supposed to be driving up to Maine?"

Neil was silent, and a moment later Del said, "I'm sorry, I didn't mean that, Neil. I'm way out of line."

It turned out that Andy was paralyzed from the waist down. The doctors hoped the paralysis was not permanent. They said that his spinal column was massively bruised, but intact. Eventually, he would regain some lower-body function, but they weren't sure how much and they weren't sure when. The more Walker pressed them for guarantees, the less hopeful they sounded. "We're guessing, Mr. Walker, but we think he was very lucky."

Lucky. Walker looked at his paralyzed son, who seemed so tiny in his bed, still dependent on massive intervention, on almost industrial processes to perform his bodily functions. He couldn't think of Andy as "lucky," and he couldn't shake the futile guilt that compounded his grief—that if he'd been driving the car, or even if he'd just been *in* the car, it never would have happened.

At first he took a leave of absence from work. But a month after the accident, he quit entirely. Everyone tried to talk him out of it—they'd extend his leave of absence, he'd feel differently in a while, work was the best medicine, etc. etc. But quitting his job was an atonement, a sacrifice to Andy and Diana. Somewhere behind his conscious action was this equation: quit the job or he'll never walk again.

Andy's progress was frustratingly slow. He was shuttled in and out of intensive care for six weeks. He had several fractured vertebrae which were not discovered until he'd stabilized enough to be moved for X ray. Eventually, he was put into a full body cast. Somehow, Neil found it reassuring, as if the hard white casing might protect his son.

He spent hours each day in Andy's room. Del flew in for weekends.

Eventually, he returned to the Agency to quit formally. There were papers to sign, rituals of departure, accompanied by new attempts to persuade him that he was making the wrong decision. He couldn't explain to them why he felt compelled to quit. He talked about it in terms that made everyone comfortable. He needed more flexibility; he didn't want to travel; he wanted less demanding work.

About six weeks after the accident, one of Andy's doctors had taken him aside in the hospital cafeteria. In this basement room, Walker had developed a strange bond with the relatives of other critical cases. Their conversations sounded like medical conferences. They traded news and diagnoses over tuna sandwiches. There was a truck driver from Milford, Mr. Kotzbeck, who had an astonishingly complete knowledge of the spinal column. Kotzbeck, who told Neil he'd quit high school in the tenth grade, had a daughter who'd been run over by a school bus. Kotzbeck was now an expert on spinal-cord injuries. He read articles in *The Lancet*, in the *Journal of the American Medical Association*, in obscure orthopedic journals. He rattled off the names of sophisticated therapists, the big guns in back surgery; facts shot out of him like ammunition. He didn't stumble over Latin phrases. He'd become a reference librarian for the rest of them.

The doctor had included Mr. Kotzbeck in the conversation. While they talked, they ate Salisbury steak. The plastic surroundings and the texture of the meat reminded Walker powerfully of his high school cafeteria.

"In my opinion," Dr. Schenk confided, "very soon, Andy will be better off in a private clinic." Kotzbeck agreed, nodding his heavy, bearlike head.

Dr. Schenk explained that the therapeutic atmosphere in a clinic was better. "We're not geared for rehabilitation here. What we do here is intervene in a crisis. We *rescue*." He stopped to probe his teeth with his tongue.

He handed over a list of possible clinics which Walker began to investigate, relieved to finally have a task to accomplish. He was assiduous in his effort: interviewing physicians, directors, patients, staff, observing rehabilitation procedures, comparing equipment.

In October, Andy was moved to the Wessinger Clinic near Philadelphia. He was out of the body cast and beginning to recover some function in his lower body. His therapy was slow, painful, exhausting. Still, soon he was able to take a few staggering steps on his metal braces.

Walker wanted his son to be the kind of patient who has a boundless will, defiant in the face of adversity, the one who can always do "one more" leg lift. But Andy wasn't like that. Andy would look at his father dully and say, "I can't do one more, Dad, I really can't."

Helping with Andy's therapy, Walker got angry, disappointed, and enthusiastic by turns. He couldn't seem to find the right emotional stance. Was he making excessive demands? Was he pushing? Or was he giving Andy the friendly nudge the therapists said he needed? His whole relationship with Andy seemed unstable and treacherous.

Andy was coming home this weekend—he was permitted weekends at home now. Walker worried that he was inflicting pain on his son—emotional pain—by demanding things; but then he also worried about the opposite, that he sheltered him too much, babied him, that worry would make Andy weak. He frowned and drummed his fingers on the yellow pad.

He looked outside. Tiny flakes of snow were sifting down. He needed to get to work, stop daydreaming. He wanted the desk clear this weekend and he had a lot to do. He had to be careful that working for himself didn't become even more time-consuming than working at the Agency. Work was piling up; he needed to learn to turn a job down—that, or get some help.

He'd only really started working full time a month before. At first, he'd seen the work as a stopgap, something to do while Andy recovered, work he could do on his own terms. A friend of his, an archivist, had suggested it. His Agency work, investigating defectors' legends, had made Walker a skilled genealogist and genealogy was a big business in Washington. The Archives and the Library of Congress were overrun in summer with earnest tourists tracking down their roots and legions of Mormons whose faith required a genealogical search. Friendly archivists had steered a little business his way and he'd even had two referrals from one of the big genealogical concerns, although both of the referrals were Poles who could barely communicate in English. Despite the fact that he was just getting started, word had spread that he could do "iron curtain" research.

He glanced at his clock. Ten-thirty already. God. He looked down at the list of names and numbers on the yellow pad. He dialed Jan Kulik.

Later that night, Walker was in the Adams Dining Room at the Hay Adams Hotel, having dinner with Lou Graves and his wife, Margaret. Lou and he had often worked together closely. Poring over the minutiae of the lives of strangers, they had become friends.

But dinner was going badly. Several times, Lou had leaned forward with that glint in his eye that meant he'd made an interesting connection. Then he'd remember that he couldn't talk shop with Neil, at least not current shop talk. For a while they resorted to the comfortable territory of past cases, and talked about Carter, Reagan, cabinet appointments. The real conversation took place in the pauses and silences that threatened to engulf them. By the time they reached dessert, it was clear that they wouldn't be seeing much of each other in the future.

Margaret, if anything, was more ill at ease than Lou. All evening, she tiptoed around the risky subjects—wives, children, cars, marriage, vacation—not wanting to mention Andy or Diana, not wanting to introduce tragedy between bites of veal piccata. Her self-censorship turned her conversation choppy and tense, like that of an actress who couldn't quite remember her lines. After drinking a martini, her share of two bottles of wine, and then sipping her way through two cognacs, Margaret finally rested her manicured hand on Walker's and clamped her eyes to his. He could almost hear her think: *eye contact.* Her malevolent red fingernails dug into his skin in what he supposed was a reassuring squeeze.

"Do you miss her very much?" she intoned with numbing sincerity.

"Yes," he said.

"Of course," Margaret said, borrowing a British accent. She gave her head a little shake and lowered her eyes. "Of course. We're dreadfully sorry," she continued in her borrowed voice. She gave his hand another squeeze. "If there's *anything* . . ."

He thought Margaret had been watching too much "Masterpiece Theatre."

But the truth was that he did miss Diana, and in a way so pervasive and desperate that at times her absence from the world struck him almost senseless. It was a feeling that reminded him of an experience he'd had as a child. Once he'd been in an accident on his bike and had been thrown ten or fifteen feet through the air. When he landed, the impact seemed powerful enough to stop every process of his body and detach all the muscles from his bones. He felt entirely numb and the world seemed pale and weak, as if he were seeing everything through a membrane. A short time later, when the driver of the car that had hit him arrived at his side and asked, "Are you all right?" he had almost cried aloud out of happiness because his impression had been that he was dead.

Lou Graves was saying something, but Walker was having trouble following. Distracted: that was how he categorized this feeling. He wasn't quite meshed into the world. Lou Graves might have been speaking Swahili. Walker excused himself to go to the men's room.

His pinched white face in the mirror reminded him that he'd lost quite a bit of weight. In that way, too, he missed Diana. There were vast regions of his life where he operated as a complete novice: buying food, cooking it, keeping house, keeping in touch with relatives, setting up doctor's and dentist's appointments, doing laundry, buying presents, Christmas.

Their pathetic little Christmas in the clinic—even that he'd fucked up. As a treat, he'd bundled up all the Christmas cards and let Andy open them. And Andy had found the notes: *Dear Neil and Diana and Andy*. Andy had fallen apart over those cards: "They don't even *know*, Dad. They don't even know she's dead."

Dinner staggered to a close and he was grateful to pull free of Lou and Margaret Graves and return home.

After he had shut up the big house for the night, turned the heat down, the lights off, fastened the deadbolt locks, he went into their bedroom. He lay down on top of the queen-sized bed, on top of the messy bedspread, facedown, with his shoes on, fully dressed.

He could hear the faint and steady hum of traffic on the beltway, the deeper and more pervasive clacking of a long freight train passing at speed. It was a sound he used to think romantic; now he worried about hazardous cargo. Outside, on the street, he heard a car door slam; a woman's laugh spilled into the night air. He tipped off his shoes, suffused with a languor that made even that exhausting.

CHAPTER
Twelve

When Nicola got home from her aerobics class, all the lights in the house were on, every window a bright square. Not just the lights were on. The television pulsed away in the living room. The radio whined faintly from Kate's bedroom. As Nicola went around turning things off, a melodious radio voice ran through possibilities of weather: "Snow flurries," the voice purred, "warmer tomorrow." The TV and radio were always going. Like an elderly lady, Kate used them as companions.

Dinner at the Stowe House went well until Nicola started talking about her day at school.

"The kids gave me a surprise party," she said. "I could tell they'd been talking to you, getting the bio straight. You could have given me a hint, you devil."

Kate smiled shyly. "Well . . . a little person named Elaine Mudge called me."

"Do you remember Scott Paisley?"

Kate frowned: "Wait a sec. Is he one of the kids or is he a teacher?"

Nicola looked down at her lobster.

"He's one of the kids," she said evenly. A twist of fear tightened her stomach. Kate had met Scott Paisley four or five times; Nicola had also talked about him often. It was impossible to ignore the fact that Kate's intelligence and memory were deteriorating. Malnutrition? She didn't know. Maybe Kate was like an Alzheimer's patient and her memories were slowly detaching from the cerebral cortex. Maybe her memories were drifting into oblivion. Nicola wondered at what point you stopped being yourself. If you forgot everything about yourself, did you remain yourself? She could picture Kate's mind, decaying like a tooth.

She watched her daughter chew; it was like an anatomy lesson, watching the muscles work.

"Oh Jeez, I *forgot*," Kate said. "*Dad* called to say happy birthday." She looked down at her plate. "He still wants me to come out for a visit."

"Maybe you should," Nicola said lightly. "Maybe a trip would be good for you."

Nicola tried to linger over coffee, but Kate seemed anxious to leave, so she called for the bill.

They drove home in a building snowstorm. The roads were tricky and driving required Nicola's full attention. When they pulled up in front of the house, there was a huge, glowing white sign set up on a trailer on the front lawn. The sign had stars and flashing arrows and it said, in the kind of letters motels put on marquees to welcome large contingents of guests: LORDY, LORDY, NICOLA WARD IS FORTY! ! ! ! ! ! !

She screamed and started laughing. "I can't believe it, I can't believe it."

"I thought we ought to let the world know," Kate said in a chummy voice, vibrating with pleasure.

Nicola felt like a contestant on a radio call-in show, just told she'd won an unexpected prize. "Oh my Gaaad," she shrieked again and hugged Kate. "I don't believe it."

Kate was laughing too. "I really surprised you, didn't I?"

They went inside. Nicola was pleased with Kate's pleasure, embarrassed, impressed that Kate had the energy to arrange for such an elaborate present, and worried that it must have been expensive.

Kate had another present for her, and Nicola was about to open it, when the phone rang. She held up one finger to Kate as she picked up the receiver.

"So what's it like, being forty?" asked a voice, followed by a stutter of static.

"Joanne?"

It was her best friend from college, calling from Germany, where her husband was stationed. Her oldest, deepest, most uncritical friend.

"Yep. Frau Santorini."

"But it must be the middle of the night there!"

"It *is* the middle of the night. I thought just for your *fortieth*, I'd stay up and rub it in a little."

After she finished talking to Joanne, she opened Kate's present. It was one of those picture frames designed to hold a collection of snapshots. Kate had burrowed through the box of photographs and the twelve openings displayed a collection of shots. Most of them were of Kate and Nicola, but Aunt Hillary and Uncle Brian were represented, Joanne and herself as teenagers, mugging for the camera, a shot of the cabin, and one of Stan, too, holding a baby Kate.

"You don't, you don't mind that Dad's in one of them, do you?" Kate asked. The hesitancy in her voice seemed faked.

"Stanuelo? No, I don't mind. You might have put that little black strip over his eyes, but . . ."

"Mom."

"I'm sorry." She looked at the snapshot. Stan was wearing a plaid shirt. "There's nothing in this photograph to indicate that the man would one day join the God Squad and name a child Hay-zooz."

"*Mom*." Kate giggled and Nicola felt guilty. She shouldn't be making Kate laugh at her father.

But when she looked at it again, her heart contracted, her mind bubbled with hate. Stan's all-American-boy face looked out from the photograph, so pure and without guile. She remembered the moment he told her he was leaving and the way his face looked, unmarked, unconcerned, his beautiful eyebrows knitting earnestly together. She remembered herself: "*You can't do this to me.*" And his measured reply: "I'm not doing it *to you*, Nicola; I'm doing it *for me*. Surely even you can see the difference."

Even you. Even you.

"What about him?" Kate said, pointing to Brian Sunderland. "What ever happened to him? He's still alive, isn't he?"

Nicola looked at the snapshot of Brian Sunderland: a handsome man with thinning hair, he looked uncomfortable holding the one-year-old Nicola. She had a bonnet on, and a forced smile that was almost a grimace. Brian Sunderland looked off into the distance with a concerned, dignified expression.

Which was not the way she remembered him.

Although she hadn't seen or heard from Uncle Brian since she was eight years old, she still remembered him with his face contorted in rage. She still remembered not *him* so much as her own fear of him. "As far as I know," she said, "he's still alive."

"Don't you wonder about him? Or don't you remember him at all?"

"Oh yes, I remember him very well; I lived with him until I was eight."

The funny thing was that *he* was her blood relative, not Aunt Hillary. He was her father's brother. The family legend was that when it got too dangerous in Shanghai, the baby Nicola was sent to stay with Uncle Brian. His wife, Hillary, was depressed because she couldn't have children and he hoped having a baby to care for would lift her spirits.

"What was he like?" Kate asked.

"He was nice until he started drinking." She was remembering his transformation from a busy but nice man into an abusive drunk. She was remembering the bruises that discolored Aunt Hillary's arms, and twice, black eyes.

Every once in a while, Nicola would forget Kate's affliction, and holding a mental image of the old, pudgy Kate, would look at her daughter and be shocked anew. It happened now as she looked up at Kate's skeletal face.

"What's the matter? *Mom.* What's the matter?"

The air was still, tomblike. The house often felt like this to Nicola lately. She had to keep it so hot, to keep Kate—who had no body fat to keep her warm—from shivering; it was suffocating, a bell jar. Nicola seemed to see Kate through heat distortion—she wiped her hand across her forehead. The air shimmered in front of her eyes and the room seemed too bright, devoid of shadows, the clarity surreal.

She heard herself say, "I'm afraid you're going to die." Immediately, she was sorry; the tone of her voice seemed to accept the eventuality of death, almost to welcome it. Kate made a horrible yelp, the sound a cat makes when its tail gets stepped on. "When you die, I don't think I can stand that, you know." Her voice was beginning to flutter, to rise, to dissolve. "You know?" she asked. "You know? I think I'll lose my mind, and if I don't, I think I'll wish I lost my mind."

"I don't want to talk about it," Kate said in a strangled, enraged voice.

"Talk," she said, as if the word was foreign to her. "I don't want to talk about it either. I can't make you get better. I can't even make you *want* to get better."

Suddenly she was so tired it took conscious control to make her feet move. They started toward her room, stumbling. From the living room window, she could see the white glow of the sign outside, the spill of light on the lawn.

"Happy birthday!" Kate yelled in an angry voice, a voice full of tears.

Nicola didn't reply.

It took her a long time to calm down. It must have been three or four in the morning before she stopped tossing and turning, before her breathing took on the smooth involuntary cadence of sleep.

She dreamed about Brian Sunderland, but not the drink-glazed Uncle Brian whom she remembered with the blank fear of a terrified child. In her dream, Uncle Brian sent her on a sled down a snow-covered hill with a cheery: "Off you go." The wind was cold on her face, and the fear that was generated by zipping down the hill was the kind of fear that is delicious because it will soon end.

106

CHAPTER

THIRTEEN

Once again, Val Zamatin stood dripping onto his bath mat, looking at himself in the mirror. This time he had no jaunty thoughts about his physique. He was in too much of a hurry for that.

He brushed his teeth vigorously, spat into the sink, and studied the results for traces of blood. His vigilance about his gums was powered by a memory of his mother, a woman who then must have been much younger than his present age. Her ill-fitting false teeth stayed in a water tumbler most of the time. Like her good shoes, she put them on for shopping and social occasions. Without them, her face crumpled, her mouth the central implosion in a landscape of collapsed skin. He smiled at himself in the mirror, and then rinsed with mouthwash.

He ought to pick up Moira at seven if they were to make the eight o'clock curtain at the Kennedy Center Concert Hall with time to spare for a drink. He opened the louvered doors in his dressing room and pulled out some clean underwear. He'd wear the pin-striped suit. He didn't much like it anymore; he'd gravitated to a less somber style. But it had the most commodious slash pockets, and tonight, he would need them. He'd arranged a brush contact—at the KenCen, during intermission—to pass on the data Dante had given him earlier that day.

He always arranged contacts so that they dovetailed with his normal life, avoiding any detour from routine. The Kennedy Center was one of his favorite places for these encounters. Really, it was ideal—crowded, chaotic, and this time he'd have Moira for camouflage.

His routine for setting up contact was simple. He preferred it that way, not sharing the popular opinion that complexity itself provided security. He called one of two memorized phone numbers, always from a public booth. It was part of good tradecraft; any telephone might be bugged and there were devices called phone traps that recorded the numbers of incoming calls. He avoided using the same booth repeatedly, and tried to call from different locations in the metopolitan area.

Going out to find a public phone was the most annoying part of the whole procedure—they were so often vandalized or defective. Today, for instance, the first telephone didn't work; it ate two of his quarters. The second one was occupied by a fat blonde smoking a cigarette. The way she lounged in the booth, her cigarette and lighter ready on the shelf, made it seem likely that she'd be talking for some time. He didn't want to draw attention to himself by asking her to let him make a call, so he drove to yet another booth.

He called three hours before the time he wanted a meeting to occur. If he called at five-thirty, he wanted to meet at eight-thirty, and so on. When the Kennedy Center was the site of the meet, the contact always occurred at the first intermission. The day of the meeting was also determined without using words. (A voice print might provide evidence if the conversation was being monitored.) When the receiver was picked up at the other end, he pressed one Touch-tone button for a meeting the next day; two buttons for two days, and so on. No tones meant the same day. There was no need to speak. There was a preestablished rotation of meeting places. Saturday was the Kennedy Center—either the concert hall or the opera house.

The contacts didn't make him nervous, exactly; they made him . . . careful. The moment of transmission was his point of maximum vulnerability, the point at which he could be caught red-handed. He winced at the pun. He could too easily imagine it: a clutch of men subtly detaching themselves from the convivial crowd at the Kennedy Center, the firm hands clasping his elbow, steering him with discreet ferocity to another room, into an elevator, into a car . . . and eventually to a soundproof room in a house in Virginia or Maryland, where he would be asked the same questions, over and over again, until his mind was pulp. He could envision the deeply puzzled look on Moira's studious face as the men came for him, how she would flinch at the implied violence of their hands on his arm, their hard faces. . . . He shook his head and patted some Trumper's aftershave on his cheeks, slapping his face with open palms. He recognized that this was one of the few "Russian" mannerisms to have survived from his youth, probably because it had always been done in private. He refixed the top to his Trumper's—the top was a little metal crown which spun smoothly on its threads.

Zamatin lifted his shoulders up to his ears and let them drop. His teeth were clenched with tension. He took a few deep breaths and massaged the hinge of his jaw.

No matter how secure one might feel (and if anyone had a right to feel secure, it was probably himself), it was not possible to have cipher machines or burst transmitters or copying cameras stashed around the town house. He had to rely on the old techniques. A brush contact, where hand-prepared, book-coded data was passed was so antique it seemed almost quaint. Technology should have overcome the need for such things, but in fact something like the opposite was true. In a world where lasers could "read" voice vibrations off windows, the old ways, those that required no telltale equipment, were sometimes the least detectable, the least vulnerable to discovery.

He twirled the circular rack that held his collection of ties and selected a specific, muted regimental stripe. There was nothing remarkable about the tie except its colors, which were a bit unusual: thin mauve and yellow diagonal stripes against a field of brown. He had several of them. He'd purchased the material in Hong Kong in 1969; a tailor had made the ties. Fortunately, ties had been wide at the time; he'd been able to keep in fashion by having them thinned, sending them to a firm that advertised in *The New Yorker*.

At intermission, he would find a man wearing the same tie, also carrying his concert program curled into a tight baton. It never took Zamatin any time at all to spot his contact, despite the plethora of similarly dressed men. His eyes homed to the fabric of the tie like a heat-seeking missile. Eye contact would be established. They would merge into the crowd around the drinks stand and then find each other.

His hands automatically went through the motions of knotting the tie. Years ago, he'd constructed his brush contacts in a romantic way—he might insist on red carnations, copies of a particular spy thriller. For a time, he'd insisted on a female counterpart; he would kiss her lavishly and the pass would be made. His theory then was that people automatically averted their eyes from lovers, unconsciously granting them privacy for their passion.

He found nothing romantic about espionage now; at best it was routine, and during procedures like the one facing him this evening, the boredom was dense with dread. Years ago, in the days when he'd still been passing bulky documents, he'd practiced the time-honored methods of transferring data: the dead drops, the chalk marks on sidewalks, the country rambles. He'd always felt terribly exposed when required to stroll in the country. He was an urban man, a man who would never walk if he could drive or ride. A smile came to his face: now he was out there at 7:00 A.M. churning out the healthful miles in his unbelievably comfortable shoes.

The romance of espionage had come to an early end for him in Shanghai, when he'd been a young man. His superiors at Moscow Center had ordered him to do something so hardhearted, it had immediately plunged him from idealism into a pragmatism so complete as to be indistinguishable from cynicism. He'd been ordered— just at a point when he was a youthful stalwart, his fantasy of glory pure and selfless—to betray a whole network of agents, his comrades. His betrayal had served as his passport to acceptance as a double agent; he'd climbed to his position on the broken trust of people he admired, people he liked, people who liked him. Some of those people had died. *Were hanged.* Why Center had sacrificed so many to provide him his *bona fides* as a double agent had mystified him at first. He was young and relatively untested. He'd been flattered, in a grim way, until he saw the real truth of the matter. The network he'd betrayed had quite simply outlived its usefulness. Moscow Center had utilized it in the best available way. It wasn't a measure of their faith in him, as he'd first thought, or of his high promise. It was more a measure of their ruthless pragmatism, their farsighted, absolute focus. He'd never come to terms with that; he'd never been able to rid his mind of the bourgeois notion that duty should be rewarded, that justice should prevail.

Since then, since the first betrayal, his whole career had been a series of betrayals. Betrayal is the double agent's stock in trade.

But he liked to think his *life* had held a secret consistency.

He picked up the flimsy onionskin sheet from his antique secretary, and folded it lengthwise, like an accordion, pressing down the pleats one by one with his fingers. The finished product was a thin, flat baton of paper which he pushed into the roomy pocket of his suit. He put on his overcoat and scarf, armed his burglar alarm, and went down the steps to the garage. His BMW coughed once and then started, just as the garage door responded to its electronic cue and rolled up behind him. He'd installed the device for his wife, Lisa, dead now for seven years, but he loved not having to get out and open and shut the door, especially in the cold. He flicked the radio on and drove down Rock Creek Parkway toward Memorial Bridge. A few flakes of snow swirled and shot around haphazardly in the lights. Nothing that required the wipers. He hoped it wouldn't snow. He could remember a time when he'd missed the snow, when he'd thought the cold provided camaraderie, when he'd missed the long dreary Moscow winters. He'd been that young once.

Now he hated the stuff. Its beauty did not compensate for its messy inconvenience. And he no longer found cold refreshing or invigorating—just cold. Being so protected from it all the time—by the excellent heating and insulation in the buildings, even in his automobile—he almost found the cold an affront. He patted his pocket ritualistically and heard the tiny reassuring crinkle of the onionskin sheet.

He was worried. He hadn't been so worried for a long time. There was something wrong with the way Dante was behaving. That, coupled with the new investigation and the consequent danger to himself, was destroying his peace of mind. He liked to think he could ride out any storm, that he would never *panic*, but he knew it wasn't true. After forty-five years of practice, you don't panic easily but panic is far from out of the question. He'd always had steady nerves and they had served him well, but his military service and his early work for Soviet military intelligence had brought him many opportunities to witness panic. It was never pleasant to watch someone lose control, to watch desperation accelerate until a personality lost its attachments and dissipated into a destructive gush of reflexes.

The bumper sticker on the car in front of him read: I BRAKE FOR HALLUCINATIONS.

He hadn't panicked when he'd found out they were reopening

the DANTE investigation because, for one thing, he'd *expected* it. He'd known all along that it was only a matter of time until the decryption process turned up information from Dante that couldn't possibly have come from Ronald Peters. Only a matter of time until the Dante investigation was revived. And he wasn't surprised that they'd moved the investigation from Soviet Bloc to the Office of Security. OS was where it had really belonged from the beginning. The transfer had, however, removed it from his sphere of observation. Zamatin was very friendly with Hobie James, but it wasn't likely Hobie would tell him anything about an investigation as sensitive as this.

A few months ago, Center had managed to infiltrate the decoding team at NSA. But although, through that penetration, Center knew what was being decoded, there was no *stopping* the team. Every day, as the analysts plowed through that old, encoded material, the danger increased that information that only could have come from one man would show up or that a pattern of information would emerge pointing to Dante. By now Center had undoubtedly reconstructed their own cable archive to see just what NSA was learning.

He braked sharply to avoid colliding with a car merging blindly into his lane at high speed. The BMW held the road reassuringly well and the brief surge of adrenaline subsided, leaving a momentary prickling feeling in his hands. Snow was beginning to stick along the shoulders of the road and visibility was decreasing. He crossed Memorial Bridge and headed down Shirley Highway toward Moira's town house.

The snow had turned hard and granular and it stung his cheeks as he walked toward Moira's door. Before he reached it, she came out. She smelled good, and the rustle of material as she settled into the seat pleased him. He kissed her cheek. She waited until they reached the highway to buckle her seatbelt, an act she always performed surreptitiously, as if afraid it might offend him. As they passed the Pentagon, he reflexively studied the parking lot. Quite a few cars. It was one gauge of international tension—the number of cars in the Pentagon lot on nights and weekends. He wondered what part of the world was heating up.

Moira was saying something about a dream but he wasn't paying attention; he was thinking about Dante. As long as Center protected Dante, they protected him as well.

"What do you think it means?" Moira asked.

"I'm sorry, my dear," he said. "I was concentrating on the road. It's hard to see."

"What do you think it means that I dreamed I discovered buried treasure?"

"Sounds like a good omen to me. I envy you. I have very tedious dreams."

"Like what? What do you dream about?"

"Driving in rush-hour traffic. Doing the laundry."

Moira's robust laugh cheered him. It made him so happy, just to be in the small car, warm, with the snow falling outside. He felt he could drive on forever. "I don't believe you," she said. "You don't dream of doing the laundry."

They whizzed by Arlington Cemetery. The white gravestones, which always reminded him of teeth, had disappeared into the snow.

"Or perhaps it works that way," Moira went on, as they crossed the river. Usually the city was quite beautiful at night—the lit-up actual city made romantic by its rippling reflection in the water. But tonight the frozen river was white with snow and that blank surface, plus the haze of white flakes in the air seemed to absorb the brilliance of the light, leaving the city dull and pale, ghostly. "Maybe if you have an exciting life," Moira said, "you have dull dreams and vice-versa."

They pulled up behind a huge old Cadillac; its tailfins looked like rockets. They waited to drive under the Kennedy Center, directed by a frozen-looking man wearing a striped, Day-Glo orange vest. There were plenty of parking spaces. Zamatin was careful to lock the car. His golf clubs were in the trunk; someone had once told him that it was possible to get access to a car's trunk through the back seat.

He and Moira rode the escalator up toward the splendor of the Grand Foyer. He thought that Moscow Center certainly had some kind of scenario worked out. They'd acted quickly to remove Shokorov—obviously that was part of a contingency plan. He checked the coats and fetched Moira a sherry.

People paraded down the Hall of States, happily shaking snow from their hair. Melted snowflakes nestled in the lacquered hair of the women, glittering like jewels. Snow was not so common here;

people were still charmed by it. Despite his distaste for snow, it suited a performance of Prokofiev that there should be a storm outside. He took the program from the usher and they went in to enjoy the concert.

Two days later, Zamatin was sitting across the table from Hobie James. They had lunch together every couple of weeks. Usually, when they weren't talking food or golf, they were talking shop— in the broadest sense of the phrase—and that's what they were doing now. They shared an intellectual interest in the clandestine world—although Hobie was more than interested. He had a fan's passion for espionage.

Once Zamatin had been conducted through what amounted to a small espionage museum in the study of Hobie's apartment. It contained a select collection of spy memorabilia, including letters to and from and photographs of and by famous spooks. There was also an array of ingenious secret devices (tiny cameras, exploding lipsticks, microphones made to look like olives), and a choice sampling of spy literature (most of the books inscribed by the authors). Hobie's wife, Ellen, had gently poked fun at her husband's assemblage of spy paraphernalia. "Hobart's Folly," she'd called it. "I'm the curator. I dust the stuff."

Suddenly the harmless shop talk took a sharp turn from the general to the dangerously specific. One minute they were talking about the new crypto-ciph B machines, and the next minute Hobie looked over the tray of sushi, forked a wedge of California roll into his mouth and said casually, without glancing at his lunch companion, "Val, do you remember Oleg Uminski?"

Zamatin felt that familiar squirm of fear in his chest. He cocked his head, as if the name might roll into its proper slot in his memory, then worried a slice of preserved ginger apart from the tangle on the board in front of him. He always took his time when answering an unexpected question. Oleg Uminski was the new name the Transients Security Bureau had given to Boris Shokorov when he'd been resettled to the West Coast. But he, Zamatin, wasn't supposed to know that. Transients Security was deliberately isolated from the rest of the Agency. He'd learned of Shokorov's new identity from Dante. And Dante had just been showing off.

•   •   •

114

"The Agency is subject to *oversight* now, Val. I can find out any fucking thing I want."

"I don't think so. You're dreaming."

"Tell me something to find out and we'll see. Make it kind of hard."

He'd asked Dante to find out Boris Shokorov's placement because he'd thought it would be too risky, even for Dante, and because he'd thought that Dante would fail. But at their next chess game, Dante held a pawn in the air and waggled it: "Boris is Oleg now. Oleg Uminski," he said. "Works at a fancy Russian restaurant, the Caspian Sea, in San Francisco."

What Zamatin replied to Hobie's question about knowing Oleg Uminski was: "I don't think so," in a voice careful to hint that the speaker wasn't completely sure. Then he stuffed a piece of sushi in his mouth. Hobie peered at him from under his bushy brows.

"Hmmm. Well, actually, you knew him all right, but I guess it was under another name: Boris Shokorov. You helped debrief him, didn't you? You and, let's see, Walker and Sanger."

It worried Zamatin that Hobie had asked him if he remembered Oleg Uminski. It was a deliberate, if clumsy, test. Why?

"I remember Boris," he said evenly. "Of course. The Ronald Peters case."

"Boris was resettled in San Francisco where he seemed to be working very happily as a maître d' in a Russian restaurant."

"And?"

Hobie composed a tricky little smile. "Liz McInally, his handler, was quite pleased. Shokorov was settled in, happy, well-adjusted. He was gay, San Francisco was congenial, and such a pleasant city anyway. He was a social guy, not one of those dour drinkers who end up hating it here. So when he was found dead, eyebrows were raised."

"I should hope so. I hope more than eyebrows are raised when I buy the farm. What happened to him? How did it happen?" His voice was neutral.

"Overdose of heroin."

Zamatin took a sip of water. "Well, I'm always amazed when defectors do well. A terrible word, really. Defector. Sounds like 'defective,' flawed. It seems to me that nobody really understands these people. Even the handlers at the Agency tend to think of them negatively, as traitors to a country, rather than as"—his hands made a circular rolling motion—"defectors to a dream. We think of them more or less like stool pigeons, informers. No wonder they don't do so well—a new life might sound beguiling, but—"

"Well, I agree, actually, but I'm not so sure about Boris. Seems to me Boris was a guy who was pretty nifty at transitions." He paused. "Of course, Liz is wringing her hands. The handlers take it so personally, when someone doesn't make it. It's particularly bad when they fall to some 'Western' malady, like drug use."

"It's too bad." Zamatin said. "The KGB uses any defector's death as a warning to others."

"Well, that does make one wonder, doesn't it. And also it was just as I wanted to have a word with Boris that he turned up full of smack. And he didn't seem to be habituated to the drug. I *hate* coincidence, don't you?" Hobie touched a napkin to his mouth and folded it carefully. "Anyway, I wondered if there was anything special you remember from the debriefing, anything that might help?"

Zamatin remembered Walker. He wondered if Hobie had talked to Neil Walker yet. "I just remember that he checked out; everything checked out." He dabbed his chopstick into the wasabi and touched it to his tongue. "You might try Neil."

"I've seen Neil already," Hobie said.

"Oh."

PART TWO

THE
TRUNK

June, 1980

CHAPTER

FOURTEEN

Alexandria, Virginia

Neil Walker leaned forward toward the bank of mirrors in his bathroom and bared his teeth. He'd been to the dentist the day before to get his teeth cleaned; the hygienist had been glum and fervent about the state of his gums. For the first time, she wore rubber gloves on her hands. This made him worry. It worried him each time there was some innovation to protect dental workers. He supposed he'd been thirty the first time a dental hygienist had thrown a lead apron over his genitals, muttering the phrase "gonad shield." This had made him concerned for the dozens of previous times his gonads had gone unshielded. Now it seemed there must be lethal germs in his mouth, or dangerous chemicals, forcing the hygienist to protect herself.

She mentioned several dismal possibilities: "pockets," "bone loss," "deep scaling." The vocabulary alone was depressing.

"You'll have to do better," she'd said finally, shrugging in a way that implied his periodontal fate was certainly not her problem. Then she'd wrapped his tongue in gauze, "checking for oral cancer." She'd seemed vaguely disappointed at not finding anything.

"You smoke, don't you," she'd said ominously.

He went outside and rolled down the windows of the Saab, revved it up, and waited for the air conditioning to kick in. He was on his way to Adams-Morgan, where he was going to have lunch with Jim Jacobsen. The hygienist's voice stayed with him as he

119

cruised down Shirley Highway. *Gingivitis. Bone loss. Root canal. Dental appliance.* He turned onto Rock Creek Parkway. *Deep scaling.*

Jim Jacobsen was an old friend from school—a fellow Badger from the University of Wisconsin. Walker could distinctly recall Jim telling him, over a pitcher of beer in the Rathskeller, the definition of a badger (which he had subsequently memorized): "It's a plantigrade quadruped that digs for itself a burrow which it defends fiercely against attack. Hell of a thing, huh? Is that what they want us to emulate?" Walker told him that he understood from an uncle that when a badger was frightened, it flattened itself out on the ground. "What a role model!" Jacobsen had yelled. "We want a new mascot, Bucky Badger. I'm calling for elections."

Although they'd been friends at school, after a couple of years of postcards, and one reunion, they'd lost touch until last December, when Walker ran into Jacobsen at a Christmas party in Cleveland Park. Jacobsen worked for Allenby's, the art and antique auction house and had just moved to Washington, where Allenby's was opening a new branch. Walker had gone through the two-minute version of his life, described his new business as a genealogist, and a few days after the party, Jacobsen had called to see if Walker was interested in trying his hand at some provenance work—specifically some work on a couple of Russian icons. Walker had protested that his artistic knowledge was very limited. But Jacobsen had insisted that research skills were what was required—and the linguistic ability to read foreign shipping records. So Walker had agreed to try it. It would be a change of pace from genealogical work and it was fairly lucrative. Tracing the history of an object was similar to tracing that of a person, so he'd been reasonably equipped for the task.

He'd enjoyed it. The first assignment had led to two more and today they were lunching to celebrate the fact that Walker had completed his work on the "Meissner icon," a sixteenth-century virgin on ivory. This particular icon had logged more miles than the vice-president of a multinational. Being four hundred years old, of course, it had had more time to do so.

Walker turned off 16th Street and headed down Columbia Road.

120

Jacobsen had wanted to try Ethiopian food. Parking in Adams-Morgan was always a challenge and he gave up looking for a meter and parked in the lot. The attendant was watching a tiny television set in his cubicle and spoke to his friend in a language Walker didn't recognize, although he thought it might be Farsi. He walked past a shop with a neon crescent moon in the window, and a Spanish-language newsstand, and crossed the street to the Ethiopian place. A beautiful woman in a long white dress led him to a table in the back where Jacobsen sat.

"You wish a drink?" she asked Walker.

"No, thanks. Maybe later."

Jacobsen looked pained and raised his glass. "I'll have another one of these."

By the time the food arrived, Jacobsen was into his third scotch and they'd stopped talking about icons. Jacobsen was getting looped and telling him why he'd been transferred from New York.

"Hell, it was the whole New York"—Walker watched his hands work hard in the air, trying to squeeze out the right word—"*thing*." Jacobsen settled for thing. "I was too midwestern for them, you know? You *know*? I was too midwestern but I wasn't the right kind of New Yorker–Midwesterner that everybody finds charming and refreshing." Walker was hoping Jacobsen wouldn't get too carried away, too confessional, but his attempts to angle the conversation in a less personal direction failed, and by the time the waitress brought the food, Jacobsen was telling him about the affair he'd had with his secretary.

Walker signaled the waitress and asked for coffee, hoping Jacobsen would take the cue, but Jacobsen ordered another scotch. As the waitress left, he leaned forward: "I know I'm drinking too much," he said.

Walker shrugged reflexively.

"It's the only thing that keeps me going, Neil. I'm so fucking tired. That's why I had the affair, really; I was just so fucking tired, I thought it might rev me up. And it did." He chuckled, and for a fraction of a second, Walker had a glimpse of the college boy Jacobsen had been—his quick-witted, endlessly enthusiastic friend.

"I don't know what to say."

"The thing is, everybody *expects* so much. I'm trying to scale down, you know, on the expectation front. I was telling my daughter—she's thirteen—I was telling her, Wendy, don't *expect* too much. And don't expect to be *happy*. No one's *happy*. All I did was scare her; she looked at me like I had gangrene. I was trying to tell her—all this searching around, the"—he made quotes in the air with his fingers—" 'finding yourself' . . ." He stopped suddenly and leaned back in his chair. Air burst out between his lips in an explosive way that only loosely could have been construed as a laugh. He began pushing the air in front of him as if clearing branches while walking through jungle.

"Maybe you need to cut yourself some slack, Jim. I mean . . . I don't know how to say this without sounding like an asshole, but maybe if you cut back on the drinking, sometimes . . ."

"If only that was it," Jacobsen said in an urgent voice. "That's not it, I don't even feel—" He leaned back and looked at the ceiling. Walker saw the waitress consulting with the manager. Jacobsen continued to look at the ceiling. "I think if I didn't drink, I'd die. I think drinking is the only thing that's keeping me . . ." He sat back farther and inhaled sharply through his nose.

Walker tried to create a sentence in his mind that would mean something, that would somehow alleviate Jacobsen's stress, but the truth was, he didn't want to know any more about Jim's problems. He didn't have time in his life to be more than a casual friend to Jacobsen. What he wanted was to leave. He frowned and drained his coffee. It was wrong—he ought to have room in his heart, some room for someone in such distress. His mind was rattling off time management clichés. He actually thought the word: *prioritize*. But it was true that Andy's problems consumed all of his emotional energy. "If there's anything I can do," he heard himself say. He hated himself for saying it. It wasn't even a gesture. It was an exit line.

Jacobsen recovered enough to shake his hand, thank him for his excellent and prompt work on the Meissner icon. "We'll probably have something else for you soon." At the last moment, Walker relented and invited Jacobsen and his family over for dinner.

But then, when they were outside on the sidewalk, saying goodbye, he thought Jacobsen looked deranged, dangerous. He wasn't sure he wanted the man to know where he lived. It was easy at that moment to imagine Jacobsen pulling a gun from his pocket and killing everyone within range.

As he went toward the car, Walker passed a woman in a nautical-style dress. Speaking intently to the man with her, Walker heard her say: "It's ridiculous. Over ninety-five percent of the blacks in California . . ." She strode out of range and her words were swallowed up by street noise. Walker tried to imagine the end of her sentence but couldn't. He had an impulse to sprint after her, but this wasn't really a neighborhood where running fast in street clothes seemed like a smart idea.

Back at his desk, Walker felt gloomy, infected by Jacobsen's despair. While things were going well with his work, they weren't going so well with Andy, who had returned home six weeks before, just after Easter. While he was at the clinic, Andy had been a star, a star patient. While rapidly improving himself, he was surrounded by people who would never get better and by people who were getting worse. He felt like the luckiest of the bunch.

But at home, away from the carefully supportive environment of the clinic, Andy felt truly handicapped. For the first time, he'd confronted the ghost of his former existence. Not only was his mother dead, he couldn't even walk up his own front steps. Steps he used to bound up in one leap now left him defeated at the curb. He couldn't play tag, let alone soccer or basketball. He couldn't even go to a movie, or *anywhere* without becoming the centerpiece of an elaborate effort. Neil Walker had watched his son's elation over returning home gradually turn into sadness and depression.

He'd done everything he could to make the transition easier. He'd interviewed dozens of housekeepers before finding Lavinia Bradshaw. Lavinia Bradshaw's good humor was obvious within five minutes of meeting her. Other qualities had now become apparent: she was intelligent, good-natured, honorable, and wise, a fine person in every way. She was fifty-two years old and black and had an independence of mind that allowed her to stare down her college-educated son and daughter who'd been annoyed that she'd take a job as a housekeeper, a "servant's role." Lavinia, or Mrs. Bradshaw as Neil and Andy called her (they all seemed to find this formality reassuring), was endlessly patient, but never patronizing to Andy. She refused to baby him: "Come on, Andrew, you're not *trying*," she would say. If Neil said that, Andy got defensive, sulked, whined about how hard everything was.

The other real brick in Andy's life was Mike Hale. After the accident, Hale had materialized at the hospital in Connecticut, an appearance which had marked something of a turning point in Andy's recovery. Since that time, he'd been a devoted friend to Andy—who, after all, as he was fond of pointing out, was his godson. It was a rare week when Hale didn't plan something for Andy, or appear with some silly present.

Mike Hale had lasted a year longer than Walker as a Minuteman, but when he'd burned out, he'd gone out flaming. He'd been on a solo mission to Nicaragua at the time—probably he'd been waiting for a solo job to do what he did—which was to abandon the two field men he'd been sent to bail out and steal the operational funds (reportedly over half a million dollars) he'd been given to spring them. The Agency, wary of discovery proceedings, never prosecuted and Hale became a private spook, on the Harry Winston model, dealing in arms and covert action for hire.

Walker's friendship with Hale had survived Rabat, and had even survived Hale's colorful exit from the Agency. Hale had forgiven him for his bolt from the Global Exports office in Rabat with easy grace ("Think of it as a movie—you faded out a little early. I'm not forgetting the other times you saved my ass."). And shortly after Hale's "retirement," he'd appeared on Walker's doorstep one night and told him not to believe what he was hearing, that the operation in Nicaragua had been a trap, "well, more like a *play*. I was being sacrificed for the greater good, Neil—not *my* greater good, naturally. The money—that was one of their stage props, and frankly, I don't feel too guilty about taking it."

As a private spook, Hale had proved a brilliant success. It turned out that demand for clandestine services and technical assistance was brisk, a "seller's market," as Hale put it, particularly in the Third World. Hale began spending most of his time out of the country in cities whose names frequently appeared on the World News pages.

At one point, the CIA's Office of Security had summoned Walker and officially frowned on his friendship with Hale. "I felt like a teenager," he remembered telling Hale, "warned of evil companions. It was like being called into the principal's office, you know. But when I asked if they were ordering me not to see you, they backed down."

"Well, I burned them, they're not going to forget that in a hurry," Hale had said. "Give 'em a few years, a couple of new faces at the top—they'll be *cultivating* me."

Hale had parlayed that purloined operational money first into a small fortune, and then into a larger one. Initially, he'd been the traditional Paladin, the kind of guy you'd see if you were in the market for a Zodiac raft or two, a limpet mine, a quantity of plastic explosive, a shipment of AKs. That was in the beginning. Now, Mike Hale was one of the wealthiest men in Fauquier County, Virginia, a gunrunner *cum* gentleman farmer. He owned a chain of fast-food restaurants. His photograph and name appeared often in the Style section of the *Post*. He was a patron of the Kennedy Center; he raised funds for the National Symphony; he sponsored a series of road races to benefit halfway houses for drug abusers. His money came to him now through such a complicated paper shuffle that even the best IRS and SEC hounds couldn't make a case against him. Still, although Hale had become quasi-respectable, he'd been wrong about one thing. He remained on the Agency shit list.

Hale had even organized a small marching band and a houseful of banners and balloons for Andy's homecoming, but after that first burst of excitement, they soon realized just how far their life had veered from its normal course. Watching Andy struggle up to the corner to mail a letter, Walker saw in his mind the way Andy used to walk—a bouncy, sure-of-himself jock's walk. And now he dragged each foot painfully forward. His metal crutches with the circular loops for his arms looked functional, long term, lacking the rakish temporary glamour of the wooden crutches a kid with a broken leg might use.

The one thing motivating Andy now was a promised trip to Maine in the summer. But even that prospect was not always enough to alleviate his depression. Walker pulled into the driveway and loped up the steps, rapping on the door once to let Mrs. Bradshaw know he was home. Her voice floated down from the second floor: "I'm up here ironing."

He stopped off to see her on his way up to his office.

"Your phone's been going crazy," she said.

On the television screen a woman in a red plaid shirt fondled some fabric and said in an amazed tone, "Final Touch! If that's Final Touch, then Final Touch is for me!" She was replaced by a smarmy-looking weatherman who used precise, rehearsed gestures to amplify the computerized graphic display that seethed through violent color changes behind him. Seeming to cup Florida and the Caribbean in his hands, he thrust up violently toward the Northeast to demonstrate airflow patterns.

"He says it's going to rain," Mrs. Bradshaw said, "and I hope he's right. I put in all those seedlings and I'm tired of watering."

CHAPTER

FIFTEEN

Lyme Regis, England

At that very moment, across the ocean in the town of Lyme Regis, in Dorset, England, another housekeeper was hoping the opposite: that it wouldn't rain.

It was evening in Dorset, and Etta Sainforth, Brian Sunderland's housekeeper, was listening to the weather forecast on the radio. They had no telly—Mister wouldn't have one in the house. She flicked the radio off now with an angry gesture. A clipped, smug voice had just announced the forecast for the next day: rain likely. Tomorrow was her day off and she'd hoped it would be fine because it was the day of the church fete. And they'd worked so hard. She sighed and walked toward the kitchen to check on Mr. Sunderland's dinner.

Very few people in the picturesque village of Lyme Regis had ever laid eyes on Brian Sunderland. For years a source of irritation because of the way he let his gardens go wild (and his house one of the finest in town), he had attained a certain status as the village recluse. He was the subject of much gossip, although in recent years interest in him had dwindled.

Brian Sunderland had, in fact, come to think of himself as "the recluse." It was gratifying, in a strange way, to be something with a name, some identifiable entity. He didn't know how it was with others, but he hadn't set out to be a recluse. He hadn't suddenly turned his back on the world. There just seemed less and less reason to go out until, finally, there was *no* reason to go out.

He still blamed it on Tony. Oh, it was ironic enough to think about it now—how he'd been chased out of the foreign service because Tony got caught at his Communist shenanigans. Once the anti-Communist fervor really began to get its grip on Washington, someone somehow dug out an ancient article about Tony's career, his arrest in Shanghai, all that. The security office at the embassy had checked over his past ("just routine, Sunderland, you *do* understand") and found, of course, that he'd been in the same clubs at Cambridge as his brother, had the same "Communist cronies and professors." His lips curled. He hadn't been accused of any malfeasance, just guilt by association. He could still remember Dicky Rutherford calling him into his rooms at the embassy: "It won't do, Sunderland. We'll have to let you go. Surely you see that."

He'd had to laugh, later, when Burgess and Maclean and Philby finally got caught. They'd got rid of him, Brian Sunderland—no threat at all—and let those three waltz around, compromising secrets for the better part of a decade. Typical British bureaucratic efficiency.

Tony had been a real Communist, a believer, but for him, it had just been a social thing. He'd just been hanging on with Tony, the way he always had. And that was the worst of it. If he'd gone down for a *cause*, something he'd believed in, suffering for it wouldn't have been so terrible. But it was just his weak, toadying nature—to do what Tony did, to join what Tony joined—that had undone him. He'd never cared for politics; he didn't care a whit about Communism.

But it had ruined his life, all the same. When the embassy had revoked his security clearance, and "let him go," some flaw in his nature had caused him to give in to the wash of wronged self-pity that swept over him. In fact, he'd embraced his ruin like a long awaited lover, drinking himself into a spiteful enjoyment of his state. Most of all, he relished the fact that it was Tony who had wrecked his life. Tony was his younger brother, and in a cruel reversal, the leader to his own follower. "Oh," Tony would say in his offhand way, "this is my brother Brian." And Tony's brat, Nicola, living there in the house with them in Washington—it was more than he could stand. It only increased his rage that Hillary,

128

his lovely, sweet Hillary, had in the end chosen Tony's brat over him. When it came right down to it, she'd abandoned him, sneaking away with Tony's child. And it was his idea, he'd gotten Tony to send the child to them! To please Hillary! He saw in the crushing irony yet another dark design, another triumph of his golden younger brother—who from the grave managed to steal both his career and his woman. Of course, Hillary was dead now. The brat had written him a letter to tell him—not that he cared.

It was a few weeks after Hillary had run off from him that he'd returned to Tall Oaks. And now, it had been over twenty years since he'd left the grounds. At first, he'd had visitors, of course, but gradually, he'd stopped seeing the people who came to visit. He was always making excuses why he couldn't receive guests. One day he realized he couldn't think of anyone he really wanted to see. And why should he do anything he didn't want to do? Of course, he still saw staff: he was a recluse, not a hermit. And the staff did all the work.

He checked his watch. It was almost time for him to come down from the library for his nightly predinner glass of sherry. He was working on a 1/32-scale replica of *The Golden Hind*. His large hands were ill suited to the task of model building, but he compensated for his lack of delicacy with patience. The truth was he had nothing else to do, and his model collection was, consequently, large and impressive.

He reached for the tube of cement and a pain rippled up his left arm. The pain was thrilling, voluptuous, absolute. He yielded himself to it almost gratefully. And now, he thought, the end of a meaningless life.

Etta Sainforth started up the stairs. She didn't approve of the models. It surprised her that Mr. Sunderland spent his time with foolish, childish things like models. Although she had the common human delight in the miniature, she knew just how long each model took to build—a truly staggering amount of time that surely would have been better spent otherwise. On the other hand, she supposed the replicas did no harm, and since they kept Mr. Sunderland occupied, perhaps that was the best that could be hoped for. He was a man with an evil temper.

She hesitated slightly before knocking on the door to the library and then she rapped lightly. He disliked being interrupted, although, heaven knows, food remained one of the few pleasures in his life. He hadn't followed the doctor's orders after his heart attack. As usual, he did exactly as he pleased. Doctor didn't even bother to chide him anymore. No one liked him well enough to nag him. She herself had tried to keep him to the doctor's diet in the beginning, but he'd bullied her out of it: "Cream!" he'd demanded. "Butter!" His temper was feared; when she'd first arrived, the rumor had been that he'd killed a man, that's why he was a recluse.

She put her hand to the doorknob, but then took it away. Possibly he was in the middle of some intricate task—he'd been working on the mainmast rigging, she'd seen that earlier in the day when calling him for lunch. She weighed the two alternatives in her mind. He would bite her head off if he was in the midst of some detail work; on the other hand, he'd be furious to have his food held too long in the warming oven. She decided to wait a moment before rapping again and moved back into the hall toward the window that overlooked the garden.

The gardener was working in the perennial bed, digging in fertilizer around the phlox. He was a new man, a Geordie—seemed nice enough. Etta Sainforth undid the button of her skirt and tucked in the flaps of the waistband. It had been pinching her all day: she must have put on a pound or two. She watched the gardener rise from his knees and stroll over toward the old stone wall that provided a nice gray background for the bed of oriental poppies. They were just passing their prime, their papery orange petals frayed and losing color. She assumed the gardener was admiring their subtle coloration—she herself was fond of them at this point, when their garish orange faded to translucence. But when he stepped back, she saw a dark stain on the wall and putting that together with the motions of his hands, she suddenly realized he'd just urinated. Her hand flew up to her face; although he had no reason to believe he was under observation, still, she was shocked and disturbed by this casual response to nature's call. She turned abruptly and strode right up to Mr. Sunderland's door. She rapped sharply.

When he failed to respond with the angry "What is it?" that she expected, she raised her hand slowly and knocked again.

"Mr. Sunderland?" A fluttery agitation rose in her: she had a feeling. . . . She sucked in her breath and turned the knob.

130

She was not really surprised to find Brian Sunderland sprawled in his wing chair, dead of his second heart attack.

"And no wonder," Etta Sainforth told everyone who would listen. "He didn't do a thing the doctor said; he did exactly as he pleased, same as ever."

She called his solicitor promptly, and that night, the two of them labored to arrange the funeral. As far as the solicitor knew, there were no kin, but Miss Sainforth begged to correct him. Some years ago, she explained, a letter had come informing Mr. Sunderland of his ex-wife's death. " 'Didn't know I had a wife, hey, Miss Sainforth?' he said. 'But she's been dead to me for years.' She managed to capture something of Brian Sunderland's imperious tone. 'Well, who sent the letter?' I asked him. 'My little niece,' he said, 'my bloody niece.'

"It wasn't like him to swear. Then he tore it in half. I picked it up, though." Her voice took on a defensive turn. "Anyone might have—knowing Mr. Sunderland. I was curious, like. I saved it, too." She looked at her feet. "I thought to myself that someday he might change his mind, and then he'd be grateful when I could fetch the letter out. He didn't have any people, you know, and I thought, maybe someday, this niece . . ."

"Did he?" Mr. Fulton asked without interest. "Did he change his mind?"

"No." Miss Sainforth excused herself and then returned, bearing the letter with an air of triumph. After all, it had been years since she'd put it in the soup tureen in the china cupboard. In all the time she'd been with Mr. Sunderland, there had never been a need for the soup tureen, a massive piece of Royal Doulton.

Mr. Fulton took the envelope from her and peered at the return address. "It's from the States," she explained further.

"I see, yes, Maine." Fulton looked at the corner: *Nicola Sunderland Ward*. "Thank you, Miss Sainforth," Fulton said, "I'll see that a notice is sent."

CHAPTER

SIXTEEN

Bath, Maine

Kate was lounging on the couch, half watching television and half reading a cookbook called *Good Food from Mexico*. Nicola came in from putting a bag of odds and ends in the car and stopped working for a moment to watch television. Phil Donahue was stalking through the audience, gesturing and occasionally shaking his silver hair. Nicola got the feeling that most of the audience trusted him. It was his earnestness, the frowning concentration, the glasses. She admired his energy, and the passion he brought to bear on such disparate issues as penile implants and nuclear war. How was it possible to get so stirred up about every single issue?

Today's guest was a woman who claimed to be a lesbian nun. She was hidden from the view of the studio audience by a partition on wheels, the sort of thing used in hospitals to isolate your bed from prying eyes while embarrassing tests are performed on you. Donahue lurched through the introduction in his agitated, engaged way. There was scattered applause from the audience and then the nun spoke. Her voice was electronically altered so that it would not be recognizable.

Nicola thought the woman's notion of privacy was askew. Why write a book and appear on television if you're concerned about privacy to this extent? Why write a book and go on the Donahue show if you're then going to become invisible?

The electronically altered voice was saying something about "woman love."

"They shouldn't do that to her," Kate said. "Her voice is driving me crazy. It makes you hate her."

"What's her message?" Nicola asked with Donahue-like intensity. "What does she want to get across to the American people?"

"Take it easy, Mom."

"*Phil*," Nicola implored. "You're reaching. America can't worry about lesbian nuns right now. Right, Kate?"

On the screen, Phil Donahue looked deeply concerned by something the woman had just said. Kate pushed the off button and the images on the screen immediately shrank into a tiny bright dot. "I think he should be talking about nuns *per se*," Kate said. "I mean, you used to see nuns all the time and now I can't remember the last time I saw a nun."

"I think you're right," Nicola said. "What *has* happened to all the nuns?"

Kate unfolded her body from the couch and stood up. "Can we stop at the One Stop on the way down? I need some cheese for the enchiladas."

It was a sign of improvement that Nicola could joke with Kate. They'd taken to joking a lot: it was a deliberate, positional shift. Maybe if we become ironical, Nicola thought. Maybe if we just lighten up around here.

For quite a while, Kate had lost her sense of humor. Nicola was always saying: "That was a joke, Katie." And Kate would say, "Oh," not getting it, uncomprehending, dulled out.

Today, they were going to finish moving down to the summer cabin on Langan's Cove. Usually, she waited until school was out, both because the commute to school was fifteen minutes longer and because the nights were still cold and the poorly insulated cabin was expensive to heat. This year, a warm spring had tempted them to move early. Nicola was glad; being on the water seemed to cheer them both up.

She asked Kate to take the frozen food out of the freezer and bag it up for the trip to the cabin. That was the one chore they hadn't finished—cleaning out the refrigerator and turning it off for the season. Nicola carried two spider plants out to the car and tried to put them in the back without crushing their dangling parts. When she went back inside, Kate was hopping around on one foot: she'd dropped a box of brussels sprouts on it. It couldn't possibly have hurt enough to make her carry on the way she did, Nicola thought. Kate's threshold of pain was as low as a baby's. She was annoyed and she went to the freezer and began tossing frozen food in a brown bag. Kate whimpered from the table. "It really hurts," she said in a defensive, tremulous voice.

"I'm sure it does."

Nicola's patience was gone, worn as thin as Kate's resistance to pain. The continuing worry about Kate—while she hadn't gotten "worse" (she hadn't lost weight) since Christmas, neither had she gotten "better." Nicola sighed and discarded some ancient frozen chicken.

"I'll finish this," she said to Kate. "Can you take the small plants out to the car?"

"Uh-huh."

While Kate's condition had stabilized, their financial situation had not, and Nicola was hurrying now because she had an appointment to see the real estate agent that afternoon to talk about renting the Willow Street house for the summer.

Kate came back in, looking fatigued from the small chore of going out to the car. She was limping.

"I think I broke my toe."

"On a box of brussels sprouts? I don't think that's possible. It would be a medical first."

"Well, it feels like it," Kate said defiantly and plopped herself down on the couch. She removed her shoe and sock and said, in a small voice, "Mom, would you look at it?"

Nicola was sickened by the sight of Kate's sticklike leg, the calf muscle atrophied, the two bones of her leg clearly articulated through the skin. The ankle looked gigantic and distended in comparison.

"Well? Look at that bump."

"Kate, everyone has that. That's part of your toe, your—I don't know, your knuckle."

"Are you sure? It hurts."

"I'm sorry it hurts."

Nicola flicked on the radio. The announcer was delivering the "News at Noon." She wiped down the inside of the refrigerator with a solution of baking soda and water, listening not so much to the news but to the announcer's curious style. There was a pronounced pause between each item of news, as if he were digesting the information, as if he, too, were hearing it for the first time. The long pauses made her nervous. She felt he was stalling for time before delivering some disastrous, horrific news, that he couldn't quite bring himself to do it, and kept retreating to banal fillers. Nicola knelt on the floor and reached way into the back of the refrigerator. There were some disgusting leftovers back there. She threw them away, good Tupperware containers and all, afraid of what might be evolving inside the hermetically sealed plastic. Through one translucent plastic bowl, some ancient fettucine was visible, growing a bulbous, lethal-looking pink mold.

Earlier that month, when she'd been cleaning the house in preparation for their move to the cabin, she'd found bowls of dried-out cake batter under Kate's bed. Her daughter's favorite food was not pizza or hamburgers but raw angel-food batter. Even stranger: Nicola bought it for her. Half-eaten cookies, banana peels, animal crackers, lollipop sticks littered Kate's room. Nicola tried to consider these things signs of progress.

Just as she was on her way out the back door, she heard the mail plop through the letter slot in the front door. She picked it up and tossed it on the dashboard.

The letter caught her attention immediately—the heavy cream envelope with its little row of Queen Elizabeth stamps. The letter was from a firm called Fulton and Shears. There was an address in Lyme Regis, England. She couldn't imagine what it might be and opened it at the red light on Washington Street.

> Dear Mrs. Ward,
> I'm sorry to inform you of the death of your uncle, Brian Adair Sunderland, who suffered a fatal coronary on May 15, 1980, at his home, Tall Oaks, in the town of Lyme Regis, Dorset.

This statement was followed by the details of the funeral and a strange little paragraph which, without actually stating it, made her understand that although she was Brian Sunderland's "closest living relative," she had not been "acknowledged" in his will. It was signed Nigel Fulton.

The driver in the car behind her tapped his horn and she lurched away from the now green light, tossing the letter into Kate's lap.

"What's this, Mom?" Kate asked.

135

"Remember my Uncle Brian?"

"Sure."

"He died."

In the seat next to her, Kate shrugged. "Well, that answers the question about whether he was still alive. He was pretty old, wasn't he?"

"Maybe seventy-two or -three."

Kate yawned.

Nicola drove the eight miles out to the cabin almost automatically. It was a trip she'd made so often that each bump and bend, each hill and curve, was permanently imprinted on her brain. She drove quickly and skillfully, at a speed which would have alarmed anyone but Kate. She passed the bridge at the New Meadows, noted that it was low tide, and ascended the long hill on Berry's Mill Road. She slowed slightly at the DeHaviland Farm, in case the tractor was around the blind curve, and honked her horn once on Chatham Hill, in case a car was careening toward her from the opposite direction. While she drove, she thought about Brian Sunderland, dead.

She felt a certain satisfaction in that. She couldn't deny it.

One of the worst years of her life had been the year of Brian Sunderland's "nervous breakdown." What she'd witnessed had lacked the reassuring blandness of that phrase: watching a pleasant, somewhat distracted man who enjoyed instructing her on the identification of North American trees, and helping her learn to ride a bicycle, turn into a shambling, abusive drunk.

She remembered the night it started, the first big scene.

It was the noise that had awakened her. She crept down the stairs, just a few steps. She saw Aunt Hillary standing in the middle of the living room shrieking, with her hands to her ears, while Uncle Brian systematically tossed the contents of the china cupboard into the fireplace. This shocked Nicola so much that she stopped where she was, frozen. Then, when Aunt Hillary tried to stop him from setting into a new batch of glasses, from the sideboard, he flung her to the ground. Aunt Hillary began backing out of the room, on her hands and knees. Brian Sunderland was not a strong man, and Nicola had watched, terrified by his apparent strength, as he completed his demolition of the living room. He'd picked up a heavy leather wing chair and tossed it toward the fireplace. Aunt Hillary began to whimper and pull at her hair, hysterical, a response which frightened Nicola almost as much as Uncle Brian's violence.

Shortly after that night—the night he'd torn up the living room—Uncle Brian had become cruel to Nicola, flying into rages at the slightest provocation. Once he'd locked her in the basement for three hours; once he'd hung her by the heels and dangled her over the banister in the center hall, threatening to let her go. Aunt Hillary had beat futilely on his back with her fists and he'd just laughed. "Look! I'm going to drop her." He'd pretend to do so and then laugh and catch her. Even now it made her sick to think of it, the swooping dives of her heart. As the weeks went on, he began to develop a sadist's fine-tuned ability to orchestrate fear.

When she remembered it now, the night they left, the night Aunt Hillary finally got up the nerve to take off, it seemed like a long-ago adventure, something that happened to some fictional child—the Bobbsey Twins, Anne of Green Gables. Not that she herself had done anything brave or clever. At the time, sitting in the taxi, during the first leg of their escape from Washington to Boston, she'd been blank, numbed-out, almost sick with fear.

What she knew was this: she was an orphaned immigrant, in the care of a hysterical and passive aunt, also a foreigner. They were running away, going to Boston, a city where the hysterical aunt had one friend, a friend (Nicola knew this because she'd listened in on the telephone conversation) not so happy to have them as house guests, and not willing to have them for long. Nicola could easily imagine Aunt Hillary collapsing too, breaking down. She might end up in a foster home, an orphanage. . . .

It took a month for Uncle Brian to find them. When he did, he shouted and pleaded outside the door to no avail. Nicola held her breath as her uncle banged on the door, remembering the wing chair flying across the room: would Uncle Brian be able to kick the door in, as the cops did on TV? She and Aunt Hillary pushed the sofa up against the door; Aunt Hillary called the police. Now that her plan was in motion—she was attending classes to qualify for a nursing certificate in the United States—Aunt Hillary had grown stronger-minded. Brian gave up pounding and began pleading, telling Hillary he'd quit drinking, he'd changed. Aunt Hillary never said a word, just stood there with her eyes squeezed shut.

The police came and forced him to leave. And that was the last Nicola had heard of Brian Sunderland.

She wrote to him when Aunt Hillary died, but there'd been nothing back from him—no flowers, no acknowledgment at all. She'd half supposed he was dead.

She turned down the private road; it was washed out near Joe Fayva's driveway, and despite her care, the Subaru bottomed out.

Kate was tired and went into her room to take a nap. Nicola put away the food and then lugged the plants in from the back of the car. She made some coffee and took a cup out onto the deck. It was so quiet on the bay. Not many tourists arrived until July, really. There were only three boats—one was hers—in the cove. Later in the summer, it would be crammed with sailboats and small power boats. She heard the harsh call of a blue heron and saw him light on the point of the island. He stood motionless, fishing.

She couldn't help feeling a little sad, learning that Uncle Brian had died. She'd never entirely given up on him. Someday he might reverse himself, return to being the nice man with candy in his pockets, the giver of piggyback rides. She frowned. Now her circle of relatives had narrowed to just one: Kate.

Her mind compressed into an urgent but short wish, almost a prayer, for Kate's well-being; she hoped that Kate's upcoming visit to Stan might make a significant difference. This reflex was so short, a fraction of a second, the mental equivalent of crossing oneself—because she believed that if you hoped for something too hard, the urgency of your desires counted against you. But no matter how much she told herself not to count on anything, she couldn't keep from hoping that somehow Kate's reunion with her father, or the clean hot southwestern air, or the arid, sparse landscape, or meeting her half-brother, or the "real life" (as Stan called it, which meant that water needed to be fetched from a well, and that there was no plumbing) of the desert, would restore Kate to her senses.

Nicola had even managed to control her cynicism toward Stan and his motives, biting her lips when she started digging at him or at born-again Christianity. Kate was excited and she tried to be very careful not to undermine that mood. They'd be leaving June 10—both of them. They were flying together to New York. Kate would change planes and go on to Santa Fe. Nicola planned to spend a weekend in the city with Joanne—who was in the States for a month visiting her mom in New Jersey. Joanne had found some summer weekend deal—a room at the St. Moritz and tickets to *Evita*.

She jogged around the "circle," a mile-and-a-half circuit formed by two private roads that led to cottages on the shore. She didn't run the way she supposed other people did—by planning to go a certain distance. After a mile or two, she held out to herself the possibility of stopping every hundred yards or so. *I'll stop when I get to that clump of ferns*, she told herself. *I'll run as far as that birch tree. I'll definitely walk when I get to the pond*. She continually broke her promises; each stride was a moral victory. A small, aggressive dog came out from one of the homesites on the Brigham's Cove Road and yipped its annoyance at her. A fly got caught in her hair and she shook it free with her hand.

That morning, at the house in town, she'd come across two large cardboard boxes marked MODEL HORSES. Without opening them, she could picture the contents—Kate's model horses, careful plastic Breyer replicas, packed away in newspaper cocoons. Kate had begun collecting them when she was eight or nine—when the horse mania hit her. Eventually, she'd had dozens of them. The ten-, eleven-, twelve-year-old Kate had created entire biographies for these plastic horses, bloodlines, racing histories. They had specific jockeys, trainers, owners. There were different farms and stables: Meadowbrook Acres, Thistledown Farms. Kate bred the plastic stallions to the plastic mares, and bought a new one to be the foal. She photographed them, entered them in horse shows, gave them ribbons. Kate had been a stern judge, a fair judge: the best horse always won.

Nicola wondered how it was that a child who could invent elaborate histories for plastic horses could now think of nothing but food: nothing but food and the resistance against food. But Nicola didn't want to think. She ran faster and faster. When she reached the driveway to the cabin, even though she'd promised herself she would stop, she went on, starting another circuit.

The names of the model horses floated in her mind as she ran: Potluck, Cinnamon, Sandman, Thursday, Oreo (a pinto), Fury, Dandelion, The Hobbit, Shooting Star. The names buzzed in her head like the flies that kept getting caught in her hair.

When she got home, she could smell the acrid fumes of marijuana smoke seeping out from Kate's room. They'd had one confrontation about this, Kate insisting that the marijuana calmed her stomach, that she was able to ride its languorous calm and resist the impulse to vomit. And Nicola half remembered something about cancer patients: THC, the active cannabis ingredient, antinausea, chemotherapy. Still, when she smelled the marijuana, she was annoyed with Kate. Not so much for smoking it, but for making her mother officially *allow* it, for making her the partner in crime. It seemed to violate some generational divide that ought to remain a chasm. She didn't want to know all Kate's secrets.

CHAPTER

SEVENTEEN

It was a couple of weeks after she'd learned of Brian Sunderland's death that Nicola received the second cream-colored envelope from Nigel Fulton. She'd read it in the car outside Shaw's, waiting for Kate to emerge with the groceries.

Dear Mrs. Ward,

The agents responsible for liquidating the estate of your late uncle, Brian Adair Sunderland, have discovered a shipping crate addressed to yourself in the attic of Mr. Sunderland's house, Tall Oaks. The agents were compiling an inventory of the contents of the estate for the purposes of conducting an auction when they came upon this crate bearing your (maiden) name. The crate was apparently shipped to Tall Oaks during the Second World War, from Shanghai, China. Having arrived there during Mr. and Mrs. Sunderland's absence, it appears to have been stored in the attic and never opened. It therefore cannot properly be considered to belong to the estate, but to its addressee, yourself.

Since it does not seem certain that you still reside at the address to which this notice is being sent, please write to me or telephone at your earliest convenience so that your instructions for shipping the crate can be followed.

Sincerely,
Nigel Fulton

She began to read it over again. A crate? Sent during World War II. She would have been just a baby—or a very small child. She'd been living in Washington at that time. She told Kate about it as they loaded grocery bags into the back of the car.

"But that's *exciting*," Kate said. "What do you think it could be?"

"No idea," Nicola said. "I mean zero. Family papers, maybe? Who knows?"

"Just think," Kate said. "From *Shanghai*. I can't wait." And then her animation turned to its usual subject: food. "I'm making shrimp curry for dinner," she said.

"Mmmm," Nicola said automatically, "fabulous."

She called Nigel Fulton the next morning. His clipped voice assured her that the crate would be sent "straight off." She asked how long it might take to reach her. She and Kate were leaving in a few days for a short trip. He offered "an educated guess" that "in the ordinary run of things," she might get it in a month or so, although, he warned, "it could well be longer."

On June 10, she and Kate left for their trip.

It felt good to be up in the air, above the power lines. It seemed all too soon that the plane touched down at Kennedy. The wheels made contact with the runway with a sound that reminded Nicola of fingernails running over corduroy.

She went with Kate to the Braniff terminal—where Kate was to catch a connecting flight to New Mexico. She watched her daughter hand her ticket to the attendant, then carefully place her purse and carry-on bag on the conveyor belt at the security gate. The grave concentration she brought to this task reminded Nicola of Kate as a child, arranging toys on her shelf, or utensils on the dinner table. Kate stepped through the scanner. Nicola was ashamed of the rush of relief she experienced watching Kate's emaciated body retreat from her vision until it merged with the crowd, until the little swatch of khaki that she knew was Kate might have been anyone boarding a plane for anywhere else. *And not*, she thought, *my crazed daughter traveling toward my loony ex-husband.*

She pushed out the doors and waited for the airport limo with impatience, caught up in an exhilaration doubly fueled—by her

142

release from Kate and by the fractious power of the city. Even the dirty air, brutal with exhaust fumes, seemed charged with energy.

Nicola had a great time in New York with Joanne, a weekend of pure indulgence, and returned to Maine with new energy. She compiled a list of kids who wanted tutoring for the summer—to earn some extra money—called them, and set up some lessons. Then she started in on the huge list of household chores she'd been neglecting. The two houses needed continual maintenance and they were beginning to get away from her. She couldn't afford to hire anyone to do the chores; she really had to take advantage of the summer to get most of the work done.

First she wallpapered the dining room at Willow Street. Then she gave the deck at the cabin a new coat of stain. She cleaned out the kitchen cabinets at both places. She took a certain amount of pleasure in these chores, in her self-sufficiency.

She was starting in on another one—giving the front door of the Willow Street house a new coat of paint, when a big truck wheezed up in front. The driver, a young man with long hair pulled back into a ponytail, jumped out of the cab and sauntered up the walk. He had a handsome face, with strong eyebrows and white teeth, and she felt a quick, sexual spark. He looked her up and down and she flushed, looking away from him.

"Are you Mrs. Nicola Ward?" He had a lazy Maine voice that stretched out her last name: Wawwwwhhhd.

She nodded.

"Got a big crate for you. Where do you want it?"

She unconsciously leaned against the door. Feeling the warm, sticky paint on her hand, she recoiled. Her hand was smeared with red. "Damn! Well," she said. "I guess you'd better come around the back."

"Yes, ma'am." She watched him manhandle the crate—which was about the size of a large steamer trunk—from the van onto a dolly. He rolled it up the driveway and, with some difficulty, maneuvered it through the kitchen and into the living room, as she directed. "Heavy sucker," he said. Then he snugged it up against the wall and squared it in a way that made Nicola like him. He was sweaty with the effort and she offered him a glass of water. When he took it, his hand brushed her leg and he gave her another frank appraising glance. "You a runner?" he asked. "You sure got pretty legs."

This is how it could happen, she thought. *How I could make love to a complete stranger.* The thought shocked her and she stood up and crossed her arms in front of her protectively. "As a matter of fact, yes," she said, in a bright schoolteacher voice. "And thank you." She watched his eyes lose interest as she marched toward the back door. "I better get back to my painting," she chirped. "Thanks a lot."

"You take care now," he said, and sauntered up the walk, whistling.

As soon as he drove off, she rushed back in to study the crate. It was carefully made of closely fitted slats of wood. She had seen lots of "rustic" furniture not as well made. She pulled off the typed packing ticket, which bore her name and address. Underneath it, the original address was written straight onto the wood in what seemed to be black crayon or grease pencil: the medium had skidded and skipped over the raised grain. Nicola could not have pinpointed why she thought this, but the letters were formed in a "foreign," old-fashioned way. She read:

NICOLA SUNDERLAND
(in care of)
BRIAN SUNDERLAND
TALL OAKS
LYME REGIS, DORSET
GREAT BRITAIN

The return address was also clear:

BORODIN
23 RUE PÈRE
SHANGHAI, CHINA

She worked very carefully taking apart the top of the fine old packing crate. She had the idea that she might use it for something—make it into a coffee table or whatever. It was so well put together that it took half an hour before she'd made much progress. Eventually, she could see the trunk itself. It was black, varnished wood and had a curved top. It gave off a powerful musty smell. Not the fetid odor of damp decay, but the stale nose-twitching smell of attics. Splotches of mold had once flourished along the leather patches which protected the corners and on the leather straps which secured the top; circular tracings remained on the stiff black leather.

She tried to lift the trunk free of the crate, but it was too heavy and she set to work to pry off the slats on one of the sides. Finally, with a lot of maneuvering, she was able to slide it out of the crate. First she unbuckled the straps. Even this was hard, because the buckles were crusty with corrosion. Then she worked at the equally unyielding rusty metal clasps.

She was nervous; the trunk had an ominous fairy-tale look to it. It gleamed dully, too big, too dark for the room. It might contain anything: a body, an ancient curse, a . . . The top pulled free with a slight shriek and the odor intensified: powdery, dessicated, mummified. The trunk was only half full and she reached down into it.

The next few minutes were lost in an orgy of discovery that reminded Nicola of the last happy Christmas she'd had as a child. The top layer consisted of documents and a leather-bound book, which seemed to be a diary. All of these were unintelligible to her since they were written either in Chinese characters or Cyrillic letters.

But then she found an old photo album. She settled back against the wall, opened the stiff cover, and began going through the book, which had perhaps thirty pages, each one a stiff black board thicker than posterboard. The prints, astonishing in clarity, were held in place on the crumbling black pages by gummed corners. The glue had long since dried out, so that each photograph was actually loose, held in place only by an adhesion caused by time. She wondered who had compiled this album—her mother? Aunt Hillary had told her that her mother was a photographer.

Whoever had put it together had written the notations to the pictures in Russian—sometimes on the backs of the pictures, sometimes on little labels glued underneath. She tried to be careful, turning the pages, but some of the corners crumbled away in her fingers.

She recognized her father—he was in a lot of the photographs—his handsome face, his pale eyes. There were several formal group shots, collections of unfamiliar, stern faces. There were brown shreds, the ancient remnants of pressed flowers. Then she turned a page and came upon a photograph of her mother proudly showing her pregnant belly. Her mother had a goofy, cross-eyed look on her face and was pointing down with one finger toward her bulging middle.

Tears pricked at her eyes: for the first time, she had a glimpse of her mother as a person, rather than as that formal distant figure in the wedding photograph. All of a sudden, it seemed unfair not to have known her. She felt cheated. A plush drift of sorrow settled on her and tears fell over her lower lids onto her cheeks. It seemed unbearably sad that this happy-looking person with apple cheeks, who looked down at her distended belly in such a goofy way, had died so young.

When she'd looked through all the pictures twice, she put the book aside, on top of the stack of Russian and Chinese papers and turned to see what else was in the trunk. Sadness made her throat feel swollen; and the loss of her parents struck her with a new ache. She cleared her throat and picked up a flat rectangular object covered with a nubby gray cloth. Pulling the cloth down, she exposed an exquisite Byzantine face, painted on what looked like ivory. For a moment the cloth lay suspended just below the serene almond eyes and the face looked Arabic, veiled, secretive. Then the cloth fell away and the Madonna and child shone out, revealed, the baby nestled in the somewhat rigid folds of the mother's blue gown, with an elongated, angular face, a replica of the mother's.

She knew enough to know it was an icon. This was about all she knew about icons—that they were religious images, often painted on wood or ivory. She'd had an impression of them as gaudy, somehow, but this was a beautiful thing, with the remote, cool beauty of the past. She admired the stylized serenity of the faces, the dull gold halos, the classical drape of the robes.

She carefully put the icon on the table and drew from the trunk the next thing, a knapsack. This ancient pea-green rucksack felt brittle, as if it might fall apart in her hands, and sure enough, when she began to undo one of the buckles that held it closed, the metal fell away from the fabric. The stitches had rotted completely. Inside the rucksack were several black suede pouches—stained by mold—with silky drawstrings, and one oddly shaped wooden box that reminded Nicola of a container the Shakers might have made. The suede was stiff and dry and she had some trouble getting the first pouch open. When she did, she spilled out a necklace of graduated amber beads. It looked quite ordinary until she held it up to the light; the beads seemed to catch the light in a wonderful way, as if some delicate swirl of motion was trapped inside each one. Two other pouches contained brooches—one cameo and a large piece of what Nicola thought might be lapis lazuli in the shape of an elephant. The blue elephant-shaped stone was surrounded by discolored silver filigree.

She handled these wonders in a dazed, entranced way, as if she were dreaming. It occurred to her that they might be valuable, and she felt a little thrill in her throat but she pushed it down. *Probably not*, she told herself. She put the little blue elephant on the coffee table next to the cameo, and began to struggle with the clasp of the oddly shaped box.

Finally its hinged top yielded. She lifted the lid and her eyes widened involuntarily and her hand flew up to her mouth. Inside the box, against a black crushed velvet bed marred with the residue of white mold, lay an impossibly bright red jeweled egg. She lifted it out and held it up to the light from the window. Some intricacy of design lay beneath the surface so that the enamel seemed to be composed of innumerable facets, like fish scales, overlapping each other. Around the middle of the egg stretched a band of white gold, flanked on either side by lacelike scallops of yellow gold. There was an elaborate jeweled clasp, which she unlatched.

The egg opened, and from inside it she lifted out an enameled pink rosebud. The petals, outlined in gold, were also hinged and she drew them apart. Inside the rosebud was a crown of brilliant red and white stones. *Rubies?* Nicola wondered. *Diamonds?* Suspended from the crown was an egg-shaped, faceted stone that sparkled in the light.

She just stared at the egg for a long time, immobilized. Russia, she thought. The tsar. Fabergé egg. *Probably not*, she told herself. A copy, an imitation egg. She couldn't tell cut glass from diamonds, silver plate from sterling, costume jewelry from the real thing. The egg seemed to glow, as if it were an energy source. She put it back together and took it apart, playing with it, almost like a toy. It was so ingenious, and so beautiful. She put it back together once more; putting the crown back into the rosebud, closing the petals and replacing the rosebud into the egg. Then she slid the egg back into its bed of crushed velvet and closed the wooden box.

A loud thump at the front door startled her and she jumped up and ran to it. But when she pushed it open, there was no one there. And then she saw it: a little brown bird, a sparrow, lying on the drop cloth that covered the flagstone stoop. At first she thought it was bleeding, because its feathers were touched with red, but then she realized it was paint; the poor little thing had flown right into her front door.

"Oh no!" she said out loud.

"Are you all right, Nicola?" called her neighbor, Alice Orkney, who was out weeding her flower bed.

"A bird flew into my door."

"Bill!" Alice called. "Come here. Nicola's got a dead bird."

She watched Bill and Alice, their gray heads inclined slightly toward each other as they walked her way. Nicola quietly rapped the door jamb three times—to dispel bad luck. She wasn't sure if there was a superstition about birds flying into your door, but a bird in the house was certainly bad.

Alice twittered like a bird herself: "Poor thing . . . oh my goodness . . . is it dead . . . ?"

"I think the best thing to do is to leave it," Bill Orkney advised. "It might just be stunned." He stood there, smoking his pipe, his arms crossed. He looked perfectly comfortable, as if he might stand there forever, advising women about injured wildlife.

"What if we leave it here and a cat comes along? Poor little thing."

"I think Bill is right," Nicola said. "I'll come back and check on it in a few minutes." There was some half-absorbed folk wisdom about birds—Nicola couldn't remember. You couldn't touch bird eggs, she knew that. The tainting smell of the human would get on them; their mother would refuse to return to the nest.

The wind lifted Nicola's hair away from her face and even ruffled the soft down on the bird's breast. Peering close to the little bird, Nicola thought she could detect a tremor—the bird's heart-beat—but it was impossible to be sure. She returned, subdued, to the trunk.

There was a large paperboard box, about the size of a hatbox, filled with letters and photographs, and another photograph album, and she spent an hour looking through the photographs, fascinated. Her impression of her parents, no longer confined to that one wedding picture, expanded with each new image.

Among all the faces in the photograph, there were only two others, besides her parents, that she recognized: those of the Goulds—Aunt Marga and Uncle Arthur. Aunt Marga was her mother's aunt and it had been she and Uncle Arthur who had brought Nicola to the United States. Several times, Aunt Hillary and Uncle Brian had taken her to visit the Goulds in New York City. The last visit, when she was about five years old, was the only one she remembered.

She remembered the apartment in New York City—well, not the apartment exactly, but the trash in the streets, the crowds, having to walk up four flights of stairs. What made the visit really memorable was that somewhere in New Jersey, she'd opened the back door of the car and gone swinging out over the rushing pavement. Uncle Brian had pulled the car to a stop and got out and spanked her right there in view of all the passing cars. The humiliation stayed with her all the way back to Washington. And the trip became a family fable, resurrected as a warning whenever she leaned against an unlocked car door. There was a photograph commemorating the visit too—Nicola, in a sailor suit, smiling a huge, ferocious grin, eyes squeezed shut—in front of the somber-looking Aunt Marga and Uncle Arthur.

Every once in a while, Nicola had asked Aunt Hillary about these relatives. In third or fourth grade she'd become self-conscious—why didn't she have aunts and uncles and cousins? Why didn't she have grandmas and grandpas? Well, Aunt Hillary had said, she *did* have some relatives. There was Aunt Hillary's sister, Caroline, who lived in England and sent greeting cards, one for Christmas and one each for Aunt Hillary's birthday and her own. Someday, when they had enough money, they planned to go and visit England. (There never had been "enough money" and then Aunt Caroline had died.) Then Aunt Hillary would remind her about Aunt Marga and Uncle Arthur. She would drag out the photograph. When could they go and see the Goulds? Aunt Hillary would promise, vaguely: someday, when they had time.

And then, when Nicola had been in high school, going on a class trip to New York, she'd asked Aunt Hillary again about Aunt Marga and Uncle Arthur. Maybe she'd visit them, look them up. Aunt Hillary had hesitated and looked at the refrigerator, unable to look Nicola in the face, as if she were ashamed of something.

"Well," Aunt Hillary said finally, looking at her lap where her hands clasped and smoothed each other, as if she were applying hand cream. "I just couldn't tell you about this when you were younger, you know." She looked up then with an expression of regret. "But I guess you're old enough to know the truth now. They were murdered—your Aunt and Uncle, years ago. Murdered in their apartment. It was a terrible thing, such a shocking thing. I didn't want to tell you about it when you were little, when it happened." She wrung her hands some more.

"But why? Why were they murdered?" Nicola could remember her excitement, the tainted, vulturish rush.

Aunt Hillary had shrugged. "The police said it was robbery, but they didn't have a bean, really, not a bean. It scared me, to tell you the truth. I couldn't understand it."

Nicola kept looking at the photographs over and over again. As soon as she finished looking through them once, she started over. It was so comforting, this collection of images, this profusion of nostalgia. For the first time in her life, she felt anchored in history, secured.

She couldn't have explained why the photographs should seem so reassuring. Maybe because she could see herself in the faces, and every once in a while, she'd catch an expression that was just like one of Kate's. Visual echoes . . .

It was lonely though, having this trove of photographs, and these amazing things, and no one there to share it with. She wanted to call Kate but she knew Kate wouldn't be at Stan's house now. She'd be out in the fields, working. The thought of Kate in the fields "working," made her nervous and she got up and put everything back in the trunk, carefully, precisely, and carried the packing crate out to the detached garage. She walked around to the front to see how the bird was doing. She was trying to think if she

150

knew anyone who spoke Russian or Chinese. Somewhere, in all these papers, there must be clues to the people in the photographs, she thought, and maybe through these papers, she'd be able to find some of her family.

She saw that the bird was gone. It hadn't just stumbled off the stoop either, because she looked for it. Bill Orkney had been right—it had just been stunned.

CHAPTER

EIGHTEEN

Nicola finally reached Kate the next day and told her about the trunk. But Kate sounded indifferent. She wanted to talk about her success in the fields, being the best onion harvester in her row. "And I gained a pound, Mom, a whole pound."

Nicola oohed praise, and stifled an impulse to undercut Kate. She didn't say: *Don't work too hard.* She didn't say: *Maybe it's just a new scale.*

"Jesus is so cute," Kate gushed. "He's teaching me Spanish. He calls me Katarina."

Then Nicola called Charlotte Armstrong, whose beautiful old ship-captain's house in Wiscasset, furnished with equally beautiful antiques, had once been featured in *Architectural Digest.* She asked Charlotte to recommend a dealer, or someone who might appraise some antiques.

Charlotte was full of questions: What kind of things? How old? How did Nicola get them? Nicola hedged: "A long-lost uncle; they're not *that* old." She ended up with the name Angus McNab, who had a little shop in Brunswick called The Strawberry Cottage. "He's as fair as they come," Charlotte said. "And he never seems to care if you buy. Sometimes he gets depressed when he sells one of his favorites." They went on for a while; the word "lunch" floated through their conversation without ever settling to earth as an actual appointment.

The next day Nicola drove into Brunswick in a downpour and hustled into the pink cottage with her treasures. Angus McNab looked like an antique himself, white-haired, wearing Ben Franklin specs, which he took off when she entered the shop. He rubbed at his eyes and peered at her.

"May I help you?" He cocked his head to the side.

"I'm the one who called," Nicola said. "Nicola Ward."

"A pleasure." He tilted forward from the waist. "And these would be your goodies?" He angled his head toward the small leather suitcase she'd used to carry the stuff and protect it from the rain. "Let's have a look," he said genially, as he led Nicola into a back room crammed with lamps and pieces of furniture. Every surface but one—his desk—was covered with china, glassware, silver.

Nicola felt a little breathless as she passed the items from the suitcase. One by one, McNab unwrapped and placed on his desk the icon, the egg, the amber necklace, the cameo, the lapis elephant. Against the rough texture of the desk's oak, they looked even more valuable than they had before.

"Oh my," said McNab, rolling the amber beads between his fingers. "Oh my. I'll not be of much help to you here. These are too fine for me to judge, too fine by half." He held up the egg and looked at it from various angles. "You'll have to go to Boston." He paused. "Or down to New York." He nodded his head. "I think New York. I think you'd be best off going straight to Allenby's in New York.

She ended up driving to Boston and flying from there. It was the cheapest way. On the plane, she kept the small brown suitcase containing the egg and the icon and the jewelry tucked under her feet.

Once at Allenby's, she was intimidated. She whispered to the one person she was able to identify as being an employee: "I have an appointment with Robert Hastings."

"Half a tick," the girl said, in a British accent, returning to her telephone conversation. Ten minutes later, Nicola trailed along behind her and saw the surroundings rapidly change from elegant to utilitarian. They arrived eventually at a small office, as disappointing to Nicola as Bob Hastings, who was not the silver-haired, deferential scholar of antiquities Nicola had imagined but a young man with inflamed skin who seemed annoyed at the intrusion. He was writing in a notebook and didn't look up while he said, "Please sit down; I'll be with you in a moment." Finally, he put the papers aside. The crispness of his motions seemed rehearsed. Still refusing to make eye contact, he glanced at his calendar, and made a notation. At last, he looked up.

"Ye-eh-es?" he intoned. "You are Mrs. Ward, I take it."

"Yes," Nicola said too quickly, as if to dispel any doubt. "Yes. I have—I have some things for you to look at." She pulled at the suitcase's clasps and brought out the items one by one, handing them to him. First he unwrapped the cameo, and the lapis-lazuli elephant. Then he spilled out the amber necklace. He looked at them carefully and Nicola noticed the quick suspicious glance he shot her way, as if he thought she might have stolen them. When he unwrapped the icon, he scrutinized her more openly. She could feel the wheels turning in his mind; she felt he was mentally computing the cost of her clothing. She couldn't decide whether his attitude meant the stuff was fake or real. But when he opened the egg-box, he lost control of himself and his voice rose half an octave.

"But where did you get this? My God! Where did you get this?" he demanded.

"Well, my uncle," Nicola started. She stared at her feet.

"Yes! Your uncle!" His attention was almost fervent.

She told him about Brian Sunderland, the trunk that was sent to her.

"Sent to you?"

"From Shanghai. Only we weren't *there*, you see. I mean we were in the United States and the trunk was sent to Dorset."

"To Dorset." His urgent voice made her speak faster.

"And that's why we never got it. We were living in the States when the trunk was sent. It must have been a mistake—to send it to Britain."

"A mistake. Hmmmm." He looked annoyed, as if her story were unconvincing. She rushed on.

"Well, you see, then my aunt and my uncle separated, and I stayed with my aunt and . . ." Nicola felt inarticulate, adolescent. She thought it was strange that Bob Hastings should have this effect on her.

"Hmmmmm." He held the egg up to the light and shook his

154

head. "Can you wait here a moment, Mrs. Ward?" He seemed to remember something and gave her an oily smile. "Would you care for some coffee?"

"Sure. That would be nice."

"Back shortly."

He returned with two Styrofoam cups full of coffee and offered her powdered cream and sugar from a collection of individual packets in his top desk drawer. A moment later, there was a rap at the door and Bob Hastings smiled a twitchy smile, then said, "Come in."

A tall, gray-haired man with a powerful, aristocratic bearing strode through the door. Nicola found herself instantly on her feet.

"Rudolph Michalowski," he said, shaking Nicola's hand with a smooth, muscular grip.

"This is Mrs. Ward," Hastings said.

"Nice to meet you," Nicola said.

"Please," Michalowski said, motioning her back into her chair. He smelled of some pleasant, old-fashioned men's cologne, and was so groomed and polished it was possible to believe he had a valet. Authority radiated from his sharp hazel eyes, but the crow's feet around them bunched up in a friendly way when he smiled, softening his cold glance. He gestured toward the array on the desk, the things from the trunk.

"Ah," he said, almost in pain.

In the flaccid fluorescent light of Bob Hastings's office, the egg shimmered as if lit from within, an impossible strawberry red. Michalowski picked up the icon and held it to the light and studied it, shifting his head about in jerky rhythmic movements, like a bird. He angled his eyes toward the icon in ways that might reveal to him the texture of the paint, the glint of light off the gold leaf, the cracks and fissures in the surface. He reminded Nicola of an eagle, sharp-eyed, seeking prey with his exceptional vision.

Nicola shifted in her chair. The room seemed suddenly crowded and she felt overpowered by Michalowski's fierce energy. She watched him put down the icon, and pick up the egg, almost reverentially. He frowned. Her mood plummeted with his frown. At once it seemed likely that everything *was* a fake; Sunderland's ample free time and vicious personality had combined to produce a hideous joke.

She yawned. She remembered reading somewhere that in certain animals, the yawn is a sign of aggressive behavior, designed to show the teeth in a less overt way than an outright snarl. Michalowski turned from his examination and bestowed on her his beatific smile and slightly accented English.

"Mrs. Ward, I must say, I never expected this day to bring me treasures such as these and to give my old eyes their best time in years." His cold, autocratic manner was gone and Nicola's doubts melted in the glow of his smile. "If you don't mind, I'd like to learn how these things came to you." He spread his hands open like a book. "You understand that in order to appraise such potentially valuable objects, we must evaluate them, explore their history, their *provenance*, to use the proper term."

"You mean to find out if they're fakes?" she asked.

"Well, a bit more than that, actually . . . although authentication is of course *part* of our concern. We need to find out more about the origins of these treasures, who might have owned them before they came to you, that sort of thing."

"Oh," she said. "I wouldn't have any idea. I mean, who knows? That's why I'm here." She gushed out her story—about Uncle Brian, the crate. He took notes in a leather-bound notebook—the solicitor's name and address, Uncle Brian's full name and address.

"I take it the trunk contained other things as well?" Michalowski asked. His hand swept over the objects arrayed on the desk. "This is not enough to fill up a trunk. What I mean is, were there things not so obviously valuable?"

"Oh yes. It was full of papers and photographs. It was wonderful because I—I don't have much—*any* family . . . memorabilia."

"But that is wonderful news, Mrs. Ward," Michalowski cried. "Quite probably, you see, the papers will help establish how it is that these beautiful objects (his hand swept over the desk) ended up in an attic in Dorset. I don't suppose you brought the whole trunk down?"

"No."

"Well, it's horrifying that you were on your own bringing these things down to New York. I mean if they are, as you Americans say, the real McCoy, it was rather risky. Anyway, the papers will have to be fetched, or sent—*insured*—one way or the other, Mrs. Ward."

156

Nicola had a drink and a sandwich in the lounge at the airport while she waited for the shuttle. There had been hours of formalities to get through, and endless papers to sign: papers granting Allenby's the right to appraise the "items," stacks of insurance documents. Allenby's had arranged for a specialist in art insurance to provide interim coverage until the value of the items was determined. A legal adviser had to be engaged, the IRS informed of the proceedings. Inheritance taxes might apply, or gift taxes. Nicola had been a British citizen at the time the trunk had been shipped; it was possible the Brits would take a cut. Nicola felt she had started a new industry. But although she was very tired, she also felt peaceful and expansive. If Michalowski's "instincts" could be trusted—that the items were extraordinarily valuable—her financial worries would soon come to an end. She could have the luxury of worrying about "minimizing the tax bite."

The lounge tried for an upscale look and was made to resemble the sitting room of someone's house: leather-look wing chairs grouped in twos and threes around small tables. Framed hunting prints hung on the walls like the afterthoughts they usually were. Bowls full of nuts rested on the tables.

Nicola ordered another gin and tonic. A balding man with big brown eyes sat in an adjacent chair and tried to strike up a conversation.

"Here on business?" He had the accent of a Bostonian. His manicured hand plucked one peanut at a time from the dish and popped them into his mouth.

"Well . . ." Nicola stalled. She didn't want to go into the whole story. "Sort of." She avoided eye contact.

"Too bad about the Iranian thing," he said and gave a little wincing shake of his head.

Nicola nodded, but focused her eyes on her glass. She wished he would stop talking. She deflected him by yawning, looking at her watch—she really didn't want to get up, but she didn't want to talk, either.

"Want to fuck?" the man asked conversationally.

Nicola couldn't believe she'd heard him correctly. Maybe he'd said: "Want a nut?"

"Want to fuck?" he repeated.

She stood up and watched her hand brush off her skirt. Did sitting alone in a lounge and drinking two gin-and-tonics make her a justifiable target for this sort of question? She turned slowly and began to walk away.

"Want to screw?" the man shouted. "Ball? Make it? Make love? Have sex? Fool around? Want to have intercourse with me? Make whoopee?" His voice kept getting louder. A waiter passed Nicola, speeding toward the bald man. "Do it? Go all the way?"

She stepped out of the lounge into the hubbub of the waiting room. A wacko. Her heart was bouncing around in her chest. She was surprised at how upset she was by the man. Just a wacko, a wacko, she told herself. A *wacko*. And although malevolence had been absent from the man's voice, she kept seeing his googly eyes and hearing his voice: *Want to fuck? Want to fuck?*

Two days later, she was back at Allenby's with the papers from the trunk, which filled her wheeled Samsonite suitcase and made it so heavy that two of its wheels caved in. When she arrived at Allenby's, men were dispatched to help her. The suitcase was transported into Rudolf Michalowski's beautiful office on a furniture dolly.

Michalowski greeted her warmly and offered her sherry and smoked almonds. "One of my vices," he said. He raised no serious objections when she insisted that all the documents and photographs be copied and the originals sent to her. She explained that until the arrival of the trunk, she'd been a person with no *documented* family history. He said that while most of the original documents could be returned as soon as they were copied, some would have to be retained for technical analysis. "We can send you copies of those," he said, "if that's all right." Then he explained that copying the photographs, especially, would be quite costly. Allenby's would certainly advance the necessary funds, but he didn't want her to be surprised, later, at the fee. She asked him how much it would cost and he raised a calculating eyebrow.

"It would have been necessary to have copied everything in any case, you see—Allenby's itself will require more than a single copy of these papers. The real expense is in copying the photographs. It will probably be a thousand, two thousand dollars." She was shocked. "But you should not worry, my dear. This is a trivial amount." He waved it away with his hand.

She laughed. "I'm a schoolteacher, Mr. Michalowski."

His face took on a hurt look. "How many times do I have to ask you to call me Rudy? You make me feel *quite* antique."

She asked him how long the evaluation would take.

"Well, it really depends. It could be as long as six months."

She was shocked again. "Why so long?"

"We have to be quite sure of what we've got, and there are only a few individuals qualified to make the necessary studies." He extracted a leather-bound diary from the trunk and weighed it in his hand. "It's in your interests to have the . . . ummm . . . articles documented as fully as possible. For instance, there is a vast difference between a Fabergé egg and an egg in the *style* of Fabergé. Or even between an Imperial Fabergé and a Fabergé made for a less royal customer. There is a vast difference between an icon made in the fourteenth century and an icon painted later. And so on. Eventually, we may put everything up at auction, or you may choose to keep some of them. . . ." His hand rotated elegantly in the air. "There are private collectors . . . well, all this we shall see. . . ." He placed the diary back in the trunk and released the tension from the air with one of his dazzling smiles. All the creases and wrinkles in his face supported and surrounded the smile, amplifying its radiance like the corona around a light. "You will have lunch with me, Nicola?"

They ate at the Russian Tea Room, where Michalowski seemed to know everyone. Nicola felt like a bumpkin, impressed with the polished force of the people, gawking at the occasional celebrity. The waiters all said hello to Rudy and people kept stopping by to talk to him. He drank Stolichnaya and told her amusing stories about his youth as a Russian exile in Paris. He flattered her: "Everyone wants to know who you are. You really are quite wonderful-looking, you know."

Still, when she walked back to the parking garage with her purse full of receipts, she couldn't stop feeling sad, as if she were selling her birthright.

CHAPTER

Nineteen

Neil Walker rode the metro home from the Archives, where he'd spent the last few hours in the main reading room looking through passenger-arrival manifests for the port of Baltimore, 1939–1945. He'd been searching for evidence of the arrival of Karl Stokowski, the younger brother of his client, Leonard. The brothers had been separated in Warsaw in 1939. That separation had haunted Leonard Stokowski, and since his discount clothing business was flourishing, he'd set aside a fund to search for his lost sibling. The Search and Location Department of the Hebrew Immigrant Aid Society had mounted a missing-person search for Stokowski without success. The International Tracing Service for Holocaust survivors had not been able to trace Stokowski either. Walker was doing the only thing left, grunt work, plowing through non-indexed arrival records.

A group of black men in work clothes boarded the train at L'Enfant Plaza. Their appealing laughter seemed to fill up the car and they made themselves comfortable, extending their legs, resting their feet against the metal poles. Their bodies, in repose, took up as much space as possible, and their uninhibited laughter created even more space around them. Their relaxation was completely at odds with the posture of the other passengers, who sat stiffly, almost primly in their seats, insulating themselves with their books, their papers, their averted gazes.

He got out at King Street and walked the three blocks home as rapidly as possible. It would have been Diana's thirty-sixth birthday today and all day she'd been on his mind. As he'd slowly sorted out the household things, he kept discovering things of hers, and ways of doing things, that he'd known nothing about. He'd learned so many things about her only after her death. The attic was full of these surprises. A secret romantic, she'd kept all the cards he'd ever sent her, all the letters. Her practical side had been revealed when he'd had to search for their winter clothes. They were up there in the attic, carefully boxed. An index-card file showed the contents of all the boxes: C#1: Seasonal clothing, shorts and T-shirts, C#6: Seasonal clothing, hats and gloves. He was dazzled by her organization.

She'd saved buttons; she'd clipped and saved hundreds of recipes, none of which he could remember her preparing. She'd saved articles about how to thin the thighs, to shape the legs. She'd had wonderful legs; why was she worried about her legs? She'd possessed what had seemed to him a huge number of scarves and shoes.

She'd been an inveterate reader and clipper of articles about childhood development. The extent of her concern made him feel his own limitations. He didn't know enough to worry about Andy's small motor skills, the "building blocks of self-esteem," the intricacies of language development. Stray pieces of paper revealed worries he'd never known she'd had: "Call doctor about Andy's stutter." Had Andy stuttered? When?

He felt like an archaeologist.

Mrs. Bradshaw was out at the store and Andy wasn't due home from camp for a couple more hours. He made some coffee and went upstairs to play back his messages. Jim Jacobsen's message was the longest and he returned it first.

Jacobsen's secretary put him on hold and he drummed his fingers on the desk, waiting. The outside had already acquired that lush but parched look common during Washington's summers, the vegetation luxuriant but burned. It wasn't a good climate for lawns, and across the street, the Braswells' front yard, already beat up by their three kids, was browning badly. They were at the beach for the week, which Walker knew because Nancy Braswell had asked if Andy could go along. She felt guilty that her son, Tony, formerly Andy's best friend, was neglecting Andy. But Walker understood that neglect. Their friendship had centered around the physical pursuits of childhood: bike riding, basketball, soccer. Tony's few post-accident visits to Andy had been brief and nervous and not helped by Andy's sullen, self-conscious attitude. Even as Nancy Braswell offered to take Andy along to the beach, Walker could see in her eyes that she wanted to be turned down. And the thought of Andy in the beach house, while everyone else was swimming and playing volleyball . . .

"Hey, Neil, thanks for getting back to me," Jacobsen said. Walker pulled his eyes away from Ashley Braswell's Big Wheel, which seemed to be melting into the parched lawn, and looked down at his yellow legal pad. He'd been jabbing his felt-tipped pen down on the paper and there was a constellation of dots.

"How's it going, Jim?"

"How are you set for time right now? What I mean is, can you clear your desk in a week or two and devote yourself to a big one for a month or six weeks?"

"Depends on what it is. What've you got?"

"Rudolph Michalowski at the New York office—he called this morning. He was impressed with your work on the Meissner icon. Anyway, they've got a big job, and no one on deck that's really qualified to take it on—at least no one who's got the time for a few months. They like your background, and they're ready to give you a shot at it. I think they figure the worst that can happen is that one of the folks they really want for the job will do it when the time is available and they'll still be ahead because you'll have done all the groundwork—you know, the translating and so on. Got a pencil? You can still catch Michalowski if you hurry."

"What do they know about my *background?*"

"Well—*enough*—I mean, I couldn't tell them you'd been a schoolteacher for the last twenty years. They were dazzled, by the way, by your 'archival methods.' That's a direct quote. And they were impressed with your reports. Your reports *shine*, Neil, I mean, you outclass the field."

"I see."

"I'm glad you do, boy. Just in case you want to ease back a little, your report was completed in roughly one-quarter the time they expected."

"Oh."

"Now, you give Rudy a call and don't be put off by his manner. He's a little stuffy, but that's what he's paid for."

In fact, Michalowski was not stuffy. He flattered Walker about his earlier work and seemed quite excited about what he called "the Ward project."

As he described the valuables and the circumstances of their discovery, Walker automatically analyzed his voice. The rolling Russian rhythm of his speech had been smoothed and modified by early exposure to English, and, Walker guessed, French, and continual usage of both.

"We want you to do fairly much what you've done for us before—provenance studies for the articles. Presumably, the documents will provide most of the data you'll need. I suppose the actual nature of what you do will depend to an extent on what you find in those papers. There is even what seems to be a diary of sorts—which may prove the best starting point. In the meantime, here, we will be proceeding with the technical analysis—of the paper stock, the ink, the glues, all that sort of thing plus the appraisal of the *objets* themselves. What we'll send you, if you're in agreement, are copies of the documents and the photographs." He paused. "Of course, we'd like to get started as soon as possible."

Allenby's offered fifteen hundred dollars a week and, Michalowski added quickly that they would, of course, "pay all reasonable expenses."

"It sounds good," Walker said. "I should be able to start in a week or so."

"Then I'll have the Washington office prepare a contract," Michalowski said in a pleased voice. "Of course, you could come up here if you prefer. . . ."

"Is it necessary?"

"Not really." Michalowski paused. "One more thing—" He hesitated. "Absolutely no discussion with the press. We may eventually want to publicize the egg, but not until we know that it's genuine."

"I think that was in the contract for the icon work, too."

"Ah—I am forgetting. Yes. Well, we will express-mail the document package to Washington as soon as the copying is completed. The photographs will take a bit longer to copy, but we'll send them along as soon as possible."

"When can I expect the documents?"

"Oh, I should think in three or four days' time." He coughed. "Oh, one more thing. Some of the papers are in Chinese. Do you have the language?"

"No, I'm sorry."

"Will you have any difficulty subcontracting the translations?"

Walker had already taken to farming out some of his translation work and even some of the simpler genealogical tracing to GW and Georgetown graduate students. A Chinese translator shouldn't be difficult to find. "No, no problem."

"Good. *Good.* The Chinese papers seem to be largely official ones. I could arrange translation, but . . . it will be more expeditious this way. Oh, and I will send along color plates of the *objets* themselves, as soon as the technical division completes the photography. I am so pleased, Neil," Michalowski said in parting. "I'm sure you will do a wonderful job for us. If you will call me when everything arrives, please, and then whenever you wish to talk. And if there is any further way we can provide assistance, you will let me know."

"Fine," Walker said.

"Then I bid you good evening."

Just the slightest distortion of the "V" sound, Walker noticed. By the time he said good-bye, Michalowski had already hung up.

CHAPTER

TWENTY

───────────────

Walker returned from lunch a few days later to find the two boxes of documents from Allenby's waiting in his front hall. He lugged them upstairs to his office and opened them. The original clutter of letters, bills, and miscellaneous papers had been homogenized by the Xerox machine, which was too bad because there was no sense of texture to the mass of paper. The documents had been sorted into bundles which were sandwiched between two sheets of cardboard held together with crossed rubber bands. Walker began laying out the packets along the middle two shelves of his bookcase, which he kept empty and used as a kind of visible file. Scrawled on the cardboard were crude classifications: Chinese, Financial, Personal Correspondence, Important Documents, and then several stacks marked Miscellaneous. Finally, he found a stack marked Diary, and put it on his desk.

He took a heavy oaktag expansion file and a sheet of red-rimmed self-stick labels from his supply drawer, wrote WARD/DIARY on one label and stuck it to the file. He opened the spiral book in which he kept track of his projects, found the first fresh page and wrote the date in the upper-right-hand corner. He entered the time. He knew his filing system and method of keeping financial records was primitive, but it seemed to take the least time to do it that way. He removed the rubber bands and cardboard from the thick sheaf of papers and sat in the old brown corduroy chair.

The first piece of paper—what had probably been a flyleaf—read, in a fine, strong hand: *Sergei Borodin, Shanghai, 1924, Villa Medvedev*. At first Walker read slowly, more or less translating into English as he proceeded, but it was never long before his mind made the transition to another language, and gradually, the separation between the two languages blurred and his mind shifted into Russian.

It turned out not to be a diary but a memoir. Sergei Borodin's words were not a daily record; they were set down more or less at once.

My name is Sergei Borodin. I was born in Kulada, Siberia, in the year 1865. Kulada is a small city in the Altay Kray region of western Siberia, near the River Ob. I am the illegitimate child of Nicolai Shuvalov, a wealthy landowner, and Anna Borodin, a worker in his dairy and a Jew.

My father, Nicolai Shuvalov, was his own man. He must have loved my mother very much, and perhaps me as well. I was his first-born and for the first decade of my life, his wife remained barren.

I say this because a bastard's fate was seldom a happy one in Imperial Russia, and a Jew's even less so. With few exceptions, children of Jewish descent were kept isolated from "practical knowledge." At best, they might attend one of the "Jewish schools" for a few years, after which their education would be confined to religious instruction.

Even more painful was the blunt anti-Semitism of the masses, who tended to blame the Jews for the continuum of grinding poverty that was their lot. In this the masses were encouraged by the aristocracy, who found in the Jews convenient scapegoats for the economic ills of the peasants. The tsar's policies were openly repressive where Jewish people were concerned. Besides the drastic Jewish quotas imposed upon the schools and the professions, the tsar's minions established laws restricting the vast majority of Russian Jewry to the Pale of Settlement—an area of 15 Russian provinces and some parts of Poland.

Walker was beginning to wonder if the document would turn out to be a study of conditions of life for Jews in tsarist Russia. But then the text shifted to Borodin's personal story.

I tell you all this because you need to know it to understand my extraordinary story.

166

Whatever the reasons, Nicolai Shuvalov, my father, although he could give me neither his name nor any part of his estate, provided for me in a different way. In return for my admission to gymnasium in Moscow, he sold some of his lands for a hundredth of their worth. Not surprisingly, the new owner was a patron of the gymnasium. I learned of this years later when the information was spit out at me by Nicolai's shrewish wife, who was wildly jealous of any little attention paid me by my father and who hated the fact that some of his estate was lost to benefit me.

In any case, I returned to Kulada, after many years in Moscow, a physician, and a better educated man even than my father.

In 1890, after consulting a marriage-broker, I married my beloved Marthe Abramowicz.

Borodin went on to detail the joy of his marriage, the death of his father and the birth of his five children. His life proceeded in a "happy way," although his first-born child, a girl, Anna, was "simpleminded." Then he described how his half-brother, Pavel, arrived at his house one night begging him to attend to his pregnant wife. Borodin did so, but was unable to save the woman, who had been hemorrhaging for hours. The grief-stricken Pavel, "taught from birth to hate me by his mother," took his revenge the next day. While Borodin attended to an injured peasant, Pavel and other town officials arrested Borodin's wife, Marthe, and lynched her in the town square. Borodin cut her dead body down. Pinned to her blouse were the words: JEW BUTCHER'S WIFE.

Borodin longed for revenge, but knew that his five children would pay the price of any reprisal. So it was that "I and my five children fled the malevolence of my birthplace. It must have been fate," Borodin went on, "or the hand of God that guided us to the town of Ekaterinburg in the Urals."

Walker's attention intensified at the mention of Ekaterinburg, site of the assassination of the Romanov family.

As I have written before, I am a medical doctor, Moscow-trained. As I am half-Jewish, I never treated the well-born as a doctor, although often I served as their veterinarian. Perhaps it was for this reason, because they thought a veterinarian was good enough, that it was I who was called in to treat the tsar and his family when they were moved to our town.

In the town, we all came to understand that the Romanovs had been moved from Tobolsk to Ekaterinburg because the political climate was more pro-Bolshevik in the Urals. So there were fewer worries about security, about someone freeing the Imperial Family. None of us in the town knew what was going on at first—when the tsar and his family arrived. We only knew that some people had moved into the Ipatiev House and that it was heavily guarded. The Bolsheviks soon stopped calling it the Ipatiev House and began to use that grim name they invented: The House of Special Purpose.

Of course, the Romanovs' physician, Dr. Botkin, and the physician to the tsarevitch, Dr. Deverenko, had been with them, had stayed with them since the abdication, but they were both ejected from the House of Special Purpose, along with the Romanov servants, the ladies-in-waiting, the tutors.

No more such privileges for Citizen Romanov. It was said that the Bolsheviks hadn't really decided what was to be done with the Romanovs. The rumor was that there were plans to barter them to England—after all, wasn't the King of England the tsar's cousin? Also, it was understood that the Bolsheviks were reluctant to kill the Romanovs because they didn't want the world to think them barbarians.

One day, when the tsarevitch Alexei had quite a bad fall, the Bolshevik guards acceded to the tsarina's demands for medical attention and called me in. They didn't intend to be nice—I'm sure they enjoyed telling the tsarina that I was a veterinarian. (Actually, I'm a much better doctor—better-trained too—than was the "real" doctor in town. And also, I don't think things turned out quite the way the Bolsheviks planned. But I am getting ahead of myself.)

That day in late April when I first laid eyes on the tsar and his family, we could hear the heavy artillery thumping in the distance. That was the White Army, moving closer to Ekaterinburg. I was shocked at the conditions inside the house. The guards, farmers and factory-workers, armed at all times, were often drunk, I learned, and always nervous. The walls of the mansion were covered with crude graffiti, the windows whitewashed so the prisoners could not even look out. And living in these conditions was the Tsar of all the Russias!

I treated Alexei, the tsarevitch, as best I could. I learned from his mother that he suffered from hemophilia (this was a closely guarded secret), a condition which made the bruising from his fall a life-threatening occurrence. The tsar and tsarina urged me to keep silent about Alexei's affliction and of course, I agreed. I also

168

promised to seek out Dr. Deverenko, who was still in Ekaterinburg, for instructions.

Now I don't know how to explain this, even to myself, but what happened was that my heart softened toward these poor captive people and as time went by, I fell in love with them. I, Sergei Borodin, a Jew, with no reason to love the tsar, could see immediately that the Romanovs were special. Even the tsarina, whom I expected to be every bit the haughty empress, impressed me with her humility and devotion to her family.

As the days passed, Alexei's condition improved slowly. But I hid that improvement so that I could continue my visits. The food had deteriorated as the supply lines were severed by White advances. Everyone was hungry, but the Romanovs bore their hunger stoically. Each day, the White Army was rumored to be closing in, but weeks dragged on, and nothing happened.

I continued my visits and my love for the Romanovs grew. It is difficult to convey the conditions under which the Romanovs were living. The grand duchesses, two of whom had come of age under house arrest, were molested by loutish guards who insisted upon accompanying them everywhere, including to the bathroom. The tsar and tsarina were continually insulted and occasionally knocked about. For months, they told me, their jailers had pilfered their possessions. My face burned with humiliation for them, but I could do nothing without risking a ban from the house.

At night, the guards drank vodka and commanded Olga and Tatiana to play revolutionary songs on the piano: "Let's Forget the Old Regime," "You Fell as a Victim in the Struggle." The walls displayed their passive insults. On the south side of the house, near Voznesensky Street, one of the guards had sketched a crude pornographic mural depicting the tsarina in the embrace of Rasputin.

Walker couldn't read fast enough; his eyes swept along the pages; he was totally absorbed. Sergei Borodin was an able writer, telling his story in a concise, stylish prose that suddenly became overblown—absurd, even—as he described his religious conversion.

How to explain what happened next? Can I convey, with the stroke of my pen, the cataract of emotion, the turmoil of sensation that beset me? Or the clean light that pierced the cloud of confusion that had been my life?

There followed quite a bit of gushing in this vein until Borodin seemed to return to his story.

> I must explain that although a Jew by birth, I was not much of a Jew. I was not a believer or even a Jew who practiced the customs of my culture. And you must remember that doctors are the most practical of men. We repeatedly see the swift, uncaring hand of death; we see the good people die, the bad ones thrive.
>
> As a doctor, I had often seen Christians in fervent, desperate prayer, begging what seemed to me an indifferent deity to intervene on their behalf.

Borodin went on to describe how, one day, he'd come upon the tsar comforting his wife. She had just discovered the latest insult— a sketch on the bathroom wall depicting her with huge, grotesque genitalia.

> She had worn her fingers bloody trying to rub it out. The tsar calmed her and then knelt down. As he looked up toward the heavens, oblivious of me, I saw in his luminous brown eyes the eyes of the Christ, and just for that one moment (and I cannot explain this), I knew that I was looking into the eyes of Christ and I fell down on the spot and I believed.

Borodin's words went on to tell of his official conversion in the church in Ekaterinburg, a voluptuous description of his ecstasy during his first communion, and how he felt the bleakness lift from him, how for the first time in his life, he did not feel alone. Being one with the Lord made him realize how clumsy all human attempts at union were, physical intercourse "a mere flutter" compared to the power of his Christian union with God.

There was quite a bit of this and Walker was beginning to wonder about Borodin's mental stability, until he came upon the words: "and the Lord sent me a plan, in a dream." Those biblical words worried him. He was afraid he was going to read a confession from the murderer of the Romanovs. In fact, if possible, Borodin's tale was even more depressing.

> The Lord told me, in the dream, that the Reds would slay the tsar, the tsarina, and their children and that Russia would suffer a terrible torment after the deaths of the Romanovs, that millions would

170

die, but that circumstances had brought me to Ekaterinburg so that I could save the tsar's children from death.

The plan revealed to Borodin by the dream was one in which he was to substitute his own five children (similar in age and sex to the tsarevitch and the four grand duchesses) for the doomed Romanovs.

I begged the Lord not to ask for my children's deaths and he told me they would be spared. The Romanov children and myself, with the help of Lett guards, would escape. It was part of the divine plan that the tsar and the tsarina would have to die, martyrs to the future Russia. My own natural children, once the ruse was discovered, would be imprisoned, but not harmed. I was to smuggle them into the household, one by one, with the help of the Letts, and hide them until the time came. It is hard to explain how I came to know this: the Lord did not speak to me in words, but in some more direct way that I cannot describe.

Borodin confided his dream to the tsar, who apparently listened attentively but with a "sad little smile that told me he did not take me seriously." The memoir went on to explain how conditions changed on July 9, when one Captain Yurovsky took charge of things in the Ipatiev House. A new unit of guards, most of them Letts from the Baltic provinces, were seconded to the Ipatiev House from secret police (CHEKA) headquarters in the America Hotel. It was then that the tsar, in great excitement, drew Borodin aside. He had not paid attention to the plan Borodin had dreamed, he said, because the Lett guards had been critical to it and there had been no Lett guards. But now there were! Both men took this as a sign from God and began to work toward implementing the plan.

Borodin described an abrupt change under Yurovsky's command. The humiliations suddenly ceased. For the first time in months, the Romanovs were permitted to hold religious services, "in which I joyously took part." Sympathetic nuns once again were allowed to deliver fresh eggs, and milk, bread, and cheese. The tsarevitch Alexei was permitted a visit from Dr. Deverenko (whom Borodin reported was "pleased with the tsarevitch's health and . . . complimented me."). Yurovsky issued orders warning his men to treat the Romanovs with military courtesy.

Borodin began engaging the Lettish guards in conversation, one by one, hoping for a sympathetic man. He related the plan to his children.

Marga and Hester and Iraida were so thrilled and excited, I had to be quite stern with them lest they confide in their friends and give things away. I had some trouble with my son, Nicolai, a good boy, but defiant, and with Anna, who was never quite sound in her mind and had a little trouble understanding her role. At last I found two patriotic Letts, who seemed trustworthy and were willing to give their lives, if necessary, to the tsar.

The week of July 16, the town buzzed with furious excitement. Elite divisions of the White Army (Czech and Cossack) had been deployed to the north and south of the city. Partisan counter-revolutionaries had attacked the railways at night, and even the police station had come under fire. With the help of the Letts, I smuggled my children into the Ipatiev House during the commotion. I confess that I had to drug Nicolai because I didn't feel I could count on his cooperation. It weighed on my soul, but the Lord gave me the strength to do it. We hid the children in the tsarevitch's room. The children were so excited to meet each other—my children and the Romanov children, I was afraid our game would be discovered because of all their talking.

I overheard discussions in the house between the officers. They seemed to think it was impossible to evacuate the Romanovs to another location without risking their rescue by White Army units. Telegrams were flying back and forth between Ekaterinburg and Moscow. I myself heard Yurovsky send the messenger to headquarters—they should inform Moscow at once that Ekaterinburg would fall within twenty-four hours. Yurovsky urgently needed instructions.

It was time for me to act. I smuggled the Romanov children out of the house and into a peasant's cart. It took much pleading and hugging and kissing on the part of the tsar and tsarina before they could persuade their children to leave.

Walker read how Borodin and the Romanov children got away without incident.

We made a vast cocoon of furs and blankets for the tsarevitch, to minimize the chances of a bruise, and we rolled out of town on the cart, suffocating under the layers of rags and odds and ends heaped up to hide us. The children and I stayed quiet and still although every once in a while Marie, who suffered from a cold, sneezed violently. We rolled on toward Perm. Some way out of Ekaterinburg, a White Army officer, alerted by the Letts, met us and took over from the peasant who had driven us to freedom.

Borodin reckoned that the atrocities must have occurred while he and the Romanov children were still en route to Perm. When they arrived at the house that had been arranged to shelter them, he was taken aside and told that the tsar and tsarina had been assassinated. Although it was not possible to be sure that this information was true, a White soldier had ridden straight through the night with the news, arriving at the house in Perm hours before Borodin and the children. The tsar and tsarina were dead, and, also, Borodin wrote, there was "news that made my heart heave horribly in my chest—all five children also shot down by the Bolshevik monsters."

Borodin described his guilt and grief and how "my despair was such that my mind remained in a fever of grief for some time. . . ."

I grieved for my own precious children, for the tsar and tsarina, and for Russia. The Romanov children and I gave some comfort and succor to each other—they had lost their parents, and I my children—and we twined together in our grief and sorrow.

Borodin described how he and the surviving Romanovs learned "the true horror of our loved ones' end." Several messengers had come from Ekaterinburg with a story that never varied. The fact that there were not "versions" of the awful story, but "just one that was always, horribly the same" made Borodin think it must have originated from one of the Letts who was present at "the final hour," and that it must have been true.

According to the account, Captain Yurovsky assembled the royal family in the drawing room of the Ipatiev house.

Alexei (actually my Nicolai) was carried down from his bedchamber and along with the others, made to stand against the wall. I will confess that I do not understand this. Yurovsky would have seen that my children were not the Romanovs. And the children would have been frightened; it makes me ill to think of how frightened they would have been. They were grown children, practical children; they would have screamed to the rafters that they were not the Romanovs, and that fact would have been obvious from looking at them.

At any rate, the group was made to stand against the wall, facing the obscene mural of the tsarina and Rasputin. Sixteen Lettish guards were summoned, and, without a word, assumed the position of a firing squad. The children gaped, their mouths slack with horror. The tsar shouted and leapt in front of "Anastasia" (actually my Hester), who was nearest him. There was a moment of silence. The rifle bolts snapped into position. And they were all shot to pieces. In the end the gunfire went on for some time; more than forty rounds were fired. Captain Yurovsky himself administered a *coup de grâce* to the temple of each "Romanov."

If the massacre was brutally efficient, the aftermath was grisly. Yurovsky ordered the corpses decapitated, and when this had been done, the heads were placed on straw bedding in a black steamer trunk. The trunk was sealed with red wax. With an escort of Hungarian guards, Yurovsky boarded a train for Moscow.

Borodin told how he and the Romanov children were moved at night from the house in Perm to a monastery where they remained for several months, "waiting, waiting, waiting . . . waiting for help that never came." While at the monastery, Tatiana, who had been raped in the Ipatiev House by a guard, bore a child, a girl. She named the child Katarina, but "it seemed too long a name for such a tiny thing so we all called her by her nickname—Dasha."

Over the months, Borodin and the children received many visitors and were often prepared for evacuation. They were told rescue attempts had been mounted from England—several of them. And also from Germany, but so far all had failed or been discovered. As winter made travel more difficult, the ports of egress were closed to them. And eventually, the tide in the country turned against the White Army and Borodin and the children were forced to leave the monastery in Perm.

We had a long and hideous journey, broken many times because of illness: the slightest injury to the tsarevitch could delay us for weeks. The journey was made even longer by the necessity of skirting Red-controlled territory. Every step of the way, we were aided by loyalists, but still, the journey was so difficult that now, none of us speak of it. It is a miracle that any of us survived and the fact that the tsarevitch did not die during our travels is, believe me, nothing less than a testimony to divine intervention.

We eventually made our way to Vangou, a small village near Vladivostok. There were many refugees from the War there; a continual stream of White refugees were pouring into the Vladivostok region. In such a town, a town in upheaval, we were not remarkable. The children's true identity was kept quiet as it was increasingly difficult to know whom to trust.

Borodin described their life in Vangou, the quiet life of a family. He found work in the village as a physician and veterinarian. Eventually, he was pressed into service for the White Army—doctors were desperately needed to tend the wounded. And although there were those who knew the true identity of the "Borodin" children, as the White Army lost ground on all fronts, no coherent plan was made to put the rightful heirs to the throne forward. And the days of the Eastern Republic, the last White stronghold, were numbered. Everywhere, the Reds prevailed and the last remnant of the White Army sailed from Vladivostok in 1923.

I, Sergei Borodin, and the five Romanov children, sailed in that last, sad White flotilla. Word of the identity of the children must have preceded us to Shanghai, because our boat was met there by General Medvedev. One of the tsar's representatives in China, the general was stranded abroad by the Revolution. And now we live with him, still waiting.

Borodin concluded his strange document with an impassioned plea for revenge on the Bolshevik murderers and the restitution of the Romanovs, in the person of the tsarevitch Alexei, to the throne of Russia.

Walker stood the copies on end and tapped them together, then refastened the stiff cardboard and rubber bands. He ran his fingers over the pages, stunned, wondering if Rudolph Michalowski had had a chance to look at this astonishing document yet. If the memoir could be authenticated, it would mean that Nicola Ward, the client, was the great-grandchild of the tsar, a Romanov!

He slid the diary into the accordion file, thinking that his knowledge of the last days of the Romanovs was pretty sketchy: he'd need to read some books about it right away. Wasn't there an old woman in the South who claimed to be Anastasia? South Carolina? He couldn't remember.

He stood up and stretched his legs. While a playful, speculative part of his mind turned over the exciting possibilities raised by the diary, a stricter, stodgy sector waited patiently for the raptures of speculation to cease. And when he got tired of thinking how much fun it would be if the Allenby client turned out to be a living Romanov, that pragmatic, down-to-earth part of his mind weighed in with its judgment of the memoir: it's a *fraud*.

He spoke to Michalowski the next day.

"I had to restrain myself from calling you, once I'd read the thing," the Russian said, "but I wanted you to approach it with a clean mind, unsullied by my excitement. But I am most anxious to find out what you think."

He could read the Russian's wishful thinking in his voice. "Well, it really got my attention."

Michalowski let out what Walker presumed was a chuckle. "When I was a younger man, the world was teeming with little Alexeis and Anastasias. I know the story is fantastic, but it's very well done, don't you think?"

Walker agreed.

"And, as far as I know, none of those other 'Romanovs' who surfaced did so clutching what seems to be a Fabergé Imperial egg. It would be so . . . thrilling." Michalowski couldn't quite keep the excitement out of his voice.

"Well," Walker said. "There are three things in the memoir's favor. One: it was only recently unearthed. Two: it was never exploited—as far as we know. And three: it was accompanied by what may be genuine Romanov artifacts. On the other hand, the story is hard to swallow. The photographs should be a help—I mean, if there are photographs of the Romanov children among them."

"What a fabulously clear mind you have, Mr. Walker."

"Neil."

"Yes . . . Neil." Michalowski paused. "You know, I barely glanced at those photographs before I sent them out for copying. I keep thinking—if the tsarevitch had been in the photographs, surely I would have recognized him. This is a face imprinted on the heart of every Russian exile. Of course, I haven't set foot in Russia since I was a schoolboy. But my parents were very much 'exiles,' and they saw to it that the face of the tsarevitch was to me the face of my leader. But," he sighed, "you know how it is when you are looking at someone else's old family photographs."

"You sort of glance politely."

"Just so. In any case, we should have them soon—*you* should have them soon. I'm extremely anxious to find out what the other documents are."

"How about the technical testing?"

"Just getting under way. I'll keep you well informed."

CHAPTER

TWENTY-ONE

Hobie James walked through the hallway at CIA headquarters wearing nothing but a pair of nylon running shorts and shoes and socks. His plastic ID card dangled from his neck. Once outside, and past the gate, he would clip it to his waistband, where it would not annoy him as he ran.

Ellen called him a "hyperactive adult," and she had a point. He had to keep moving or his nervous energy piled up until he just couldn't think. He had to get some kind of regular exercise or his concentration span shrunk to about a minute.

The previous year, he'd wrecked his knee in a skiing accident and was forced to abandon racquetball and tennis for a while, but he had at least recovered enough to jog. So even though the thermometer was nudging up toward 95 degrees and the humidity was oppressive and the air was rotten, he was determined to get in his three or four miles.

The guard at the gate rolled his eyes to show he thought Hobie was crazy.

He trotted off down the access road toward Dolley Madison Boulevard. Within five minutes, his knotty muscles were slick with sweat. His mind was occupied with LUCIFER.

When he brought his concentration to bear on LUCIFER, all the bits and pieces of information flooded into his brain with a compelling rush—like the electric fizz of the TV as the photons coalesced into an image. But if his brain was like a television, in the case of LUCIFER, it was tuned to a channel it did not receive.

He had a meeting later that afternoon with Director Childress, who was slated to attend a Fifty-four Committee session midweek. Childress would expect an update on LUCIFER's progress.

Hobie intended to hand him a new bunch of nonsense about his team's success in tracking down the leads provided by Ronald Peters and Boris Shokorov's San Francisco friends.

He'd been steadily feeding Childress details of an imaginary investigation based on photo identifications by Ronald Peters. In fact, Peters had been less than useless, a complete waste of time. To make it look as if Peters had done them some good, he'd arranged to get a few years chopped off the man's sentence. Lemro had almost puked at the notion of giving something for nothing until Hobie had reminded him they were buying themselves cover.

Soviet, U.S., and NATO UN staffers were the foci of the investigation. He rehearsed in his mind the buzz phrases he'd give to Childress. "It seems more and more likely that DANTE is not a single source but the coded locus of a matrix of sources." "The investigation has narrowed its focus," "concentrating on certain UN employees," "close surveillance."

Sweat began dripping down over his bushy eyebrows and he rubbed it off with the back of his hand. He wished he'd remembered to wear a headband.

As for the real LUCIFER investigation, the news was mostly bad.

The good news was that he'd eliminated Lemro and his other two assistants as suspects. He'd eliminated Lemro first and Lemro had helped in the subsequent check on the other two. Once the three of them were vetted, the available manpower had allowed the investigation to proceed at a much faster clip.

But he had to face it, the pace was still glacial.

The other bad news was that he still had a dozen suspects. Worse, all of the lesser lights had been eliminated: what was left was a clutch of extremely powerful men. *Paul Childress* was one of his suspects. He shook his head. Sweat sprayed out from his hair. The *Assistant Secretary of the Navy* was one of his goddamn suspects. One of the *Joint Chiefs* was a suspect, as were the Deputy Secretary of State, the National Security Adviser, the chief of Army Intelligence and Security Control, the Undersecretary of State for

Political Affairs, and the chief of staff at the White House. The field was rounded out by three senators and a congressman.

The other bad news was that Childress had declined to supply him with either a Centerfile clerk of his own or unrecorded blanket access to the Agency's files. Childress had insisted it was a bad "precedent" to deliberately violate the procedures that protected files from unnecessary perusal, that the procedures were vital to the secure functioning of the Agency. To allow OS to override the checkback mechanisms ("even though we know *you* wouldn't abuse the power, Hobie") might allow a future OS chief to really turn OS into something "similar to its nickname, the Gestapo." In the long run, Childress was probably right.

Hobie churned his powerful legs, charging up a good-sized hill and then reminded himself to slow down. This heat could kill you.

Even though he had C-clearance, and technically had access to anything and everything, Centerfile procedures still operated on a need-to-know basis. Some of the database was freely accessible, but the system required that many files be officially requested. This worked both ways. Since all of his suspects were C-cleared, he was glad as hell they couldn't just lay their hands on any Agency data they wanted to look over. But it worked against him too. In the case of his requesting a *flagged* file (a flag meant that someone was keeping track of who accessed the data within), an automatic set of controls kicked in.

Requested access to a flagged file was reported to the Office of Security. Never mind that Hobie himself was the head of OS. OS personnel were not exempt from security regulations. Otherwise, yet another watchdog branch would have been needed to watch over OS. It would have been like those nesting Russian dolls, except you'd never get to the end of them.

No, what happened if he requested a file and it turned out to be a *flagged* file, was that he had to supply his reason. Then the officer corresponding to the crypto on the flag (or the ranking officer, in the cases where the crypto identified an operation) would grant or deny access.

And there was no way to tell, in advance, which files were flagged. So there was no way to avoid alerting whoever had requested the flag that you were poking about in what they obviously considered their business.

180

So the whole wealth of the Agency's information base was almost unusable. Since he had C-clearance, access could also be denied or allowed by the Director, or one of the deputy directors—but with the Director on his suspect list, he obviously couldn't risk showing his hand like that.

He trotted across the street to avoid further exciting a Doberman who snarled at him from behind a pathetically inadequate picket fence. The dog lunged toward him halfheartedly a few times and then sat down panting. He looked up from between his paws, disconsolate. Hobie checked his digital watch. He'd been out fifteen minutes. Time to head back.

The Centerfile procedures were a problem, because unlike most inquiries, with LUCIFER it was critical to avoid warning the quarry. Usually, this was not the case—quite the opposite. The feeling of a net closing in was sometimes the very thing that led a suspect to do something foolish, to take an unnecessary risk, to expose himself, to abandon caution. But DANTE, whoever he was, was in a position of such power that he might, if feeling cornered, bring the walls tumbling down.

On himself, his government, his country.

Lemro came in right after Hobie finished showering off. He was carrying two mislabeled accordion files that actually contained dossiers on two of the DANTE suspects, and another, slender folder that contained the progress report of the fake investigation.

A cigarette dangling from his lip, Lemro slapped the fake report on the table. "Fitz is sick of blowing his time on this crap," he said. "It really burns him to labor away on this fairy tale."

"He'd better get used to it." Gerry Fitzgerald was the staff member who was actually writing the fake reports, interviewing Shokorov's old buddies in Brighton Beach, conducting the shadow investigation.

Lemro sighed. "Dis-in-for-ma-tion. It ain't much fun." He tapped one of the accordion files. Hobie knew it was Childress's. "Paulie's looking almost home free. Just a few more gaps to close."

"Great."

The investigation was proceeding in the most dreary way, real nuts-and-bolts gumshoe work, made twice as tedious by the need for absolute discretion.

Lemro was in the process of compiling diaries for each suspect. Once the whereabouts of each man during a certain period (they had selected calendar 1977, a particularly busy year for DANTE) was ascertained, they would begin to match up the dates with passages of information (from source DANTE to the Soviets) recovered from the decrypted cables.

The evidence would be circumstantial. But if they found that the Undersecretary of State for Political Affairs had taken a holiday in Hawaii during a period when cable traffic to Moscow showed two DANTE transmissions, they might drop the man down to the end of their list of suspects.

Lemro was concentrating on Childress's date line because if they could exonerate Childress, then they could enlist his aid and maybe obtain blanket access to Centerfile.

Getting detailed information on someone's whereabouts wasn't *hard*. There was abundant information available—credit-card records, telephone records, etc. But it all took a while. Many banks now issued dual credit cards, both in one name. Then the actual micros had to be perused to see if the husband or wife signed. Establishments also had to be checked to be sure the posting dates for credit transactions were correct (half the time, they weren't). Since the evidence was so circumstantial, they really had to nail the edges down hard. The whole thing was a colossal pain in the ass.

"How long do you think it's going to take?" Hobie said. "To close those gaps on Paul."

Lemro drew his shoulders up to his ears and screwed up his face as if he were looking into a blinding sun. "Two weeks, I don't know."

Hobie shook his head. It had taken months just to get it down to twelve suspects. Even after the dossiers were completed, they might be able to eliminate only half of the list. Then they'd have to conduct a surveillance on the most likely candidate. Whoever DANTE was, he obviously had a babysitter of some sort, some contact man. With the tiny staff Hobie had—and the necessity of using up most of Fitz's time chasing shadows for show—they could only conduct surveillance on one suspect at a time. They really didn't even have enough manpower for that.

It could be another *year* before he'd narrowed the field. When he thought of the secrets draining away from the country, when he thought of the damage being done, it made him feel almost physically ill. Think of how long it took the Army to come up with some real advance in radar equipment. Then DANTE could blow it in one day. That was just a tiny example. The access DANTE had was frightening. Hobie couldn't even contemplate it without taking a deep breath.

"Hey, boss," Lemro said. "It ain't all gloom and doom. The Orioles won again."

"Yeah," Hobie said. "How 'bout them birds."

CHAPTER
TWENTY-TWO

Neil Walker was always surprised, upon entering the elaborate Greco-Roman main reading room of the Library of Congress, at the silence within. It wasn't that people were reverential, or over-awed. The Library was open to the public and there was plenty of evidence that some of the public didn't give a damn: graffiti in the stacks, and a depressing number of Masonite boards (indicating lost books) testified to that diffidence. Sometimes a board would show that a book was out on loan, but more often, it would bear the legend: PRESUMED LOST. The Library of Congress's great virtue was its all-encompassing nature, and when a researcher came upon one of those boards, it was sickening.

But there was something about the main reading room, with its huge dome, its battered wooden card catalogs, its odd-looking people hunched over their desks—something that reduced everyone to a cloistered whisper.

Walker proceeded through the huge room toward the alcove which housed the Xerox machines and the Scorpio computers. The computers were only knowledgeable back a certain way in time: only books printed since 1965 were listed. The staff struggled to keep them up to date, and then to chip away at the centuries of books that remained to be added to the database. Still, he was after broad, contemporary knowledge. He wanted to compare Borodin's narrative to other source material describing the final days of the Romanovs. He typed in the search command for Romanov, narrowing his focus as he went, then told the computer to print out. He ripped off the short list, printed on thin shiny paper, and got up. The monitor read: *this search required 4.75 minutes. SCORPIO is a service of the Library of Congress.*

He spent the next few hours surrounded by books. He skimmed through, fascinated, looking at every photograph, reading descriptions of the assassination and its aftermath, studying the accounts of Romanov claimants. He had a permit (wangled for him by the editor of a tiny magazine that had printed an article he'd written) that allowed him to take books home. He found three that he wanted: *The Red and the White*, *The File on the Tsar*, and an account written by Alexei's tutor, Gibbes.

He read an account of the White Army investigation into the events at the Ipatiev House in *The File on the Tsar*. This fascinating and exhaustively researched book, published in 1976, contained the latest research into the massacre, although much of the text was devoted to a careful study of the would-be Anastasia, Anna Anderson—the woman who lived in the South, whom Walker had vaguely remembered.

The surprising thing was that Borodin's account was not contradicted in any major way by what he'd read so far.

When he got home, Andy was in the dining room, playing Monopoly with Mrs. Bradshaw.

"He's whipping me," Mrs. Bradshaw said, looking up at Walker with her steadfast brown eyes. "He's got two monopolies and I've only got Mediterranean and Baltic."

"Yeah, but you've got hotels."

"Big deal. You can *afford* to stay in these hotels, young man. Now if you'd just trade me Indiana for my railroad, you might be giving me a sporting chance."

"Don't listen to her, Andy. She's trying to sucker you."

"I know. This could be the first time I ever beat her."

"Don't give her an inch; she has a ferocious capitalist's heart."

Mrs. Bradshaw giggled. "I swear," she said. "A person is a little bit lucky from time to time and you ack like . . ."

Andy and Neil laughed in unison. "A little bit *lucky*," Andy said. "We're talking undefeated, Mrs. Bradshaw."

"I'll give you five hundred dollars for Indiana."

This was a routine both Andy and Mrs. Bradshaw enjoyed. "Five hundred bucks! No way! *No* way."

"A thousand."

"Forget it."

"A thousand dollars." She considered inducements. "Plus, I'll make some popcorn." She licked her lips. "And lemonade. *Hand-squeezed.*"

"That's low," Walker said. Mrs. Bradshaw smiled her smug smile and pushed at the air in front of her, denying it.

"You've got to do what you've got to do," she said implacably.

"No," Andy said. "You have to come up with something better than that."

As Walker headed up the stairs, he heard Mrs. Bradshaw saying, "Been in jail *three* times, never landed on free parking. That's luck, all right, that's some kind of luck."

Mrs. Bradshaw had all the right instincts with Andy. Walker was inclined, after the accident, to let Andy win at games. He'd been unable to deal wtih Andy's poor sportsmanship, his gloom and sadness when he lost. Gradually, he'd come to see that letting Andy release his feelings of unfairness and gloom during a game was not such a bad thing, that letting Andy win all the time was patronizing. Andy had a lot more fun playing Mrs. Bradshaw, who never gave him an inch, and in fact, took advantage of him every chance she could. "When he's going to win," she said, "he's going to win for real."

Thanking his lucky stars for sending him Mrs. Bradshaw, he sank into the brown corduroy chair and went back into the world of the Romanovs.

He knew a great deal about the contemporary U.S.S.R., and he was pretty sharp about recent Soviet Bloc history—from the outbreak of World War II to the present. But going back before 1940 he was on shakier ground. He was probably as well schooled in Russian history as he was in the American variety; and his memory of the Russian civil war was about like his recollection of the American one: he could recall the highlights, but the rest of it was hazy.

Three days later, he knew much more about the last days of the Romanovs, the revolution, and the civil war. He'd also gained a passing acquaintance with some of the Romanov claimants who had surfaced in the years after that terrible night in Ekaterinburg.

When he was at the Agency, he remembered the almost comical horror that greeted the announcement by Michael Goliniewski, one of the most important defectors ever to come to them, that he in fact was the tsarevitch Alexei. Counterintelligence had been humiliated because the assertion was so strange that it destroyed the Pole's credibility—yet all of his *intelligence* information had been accurate.

Walker leaned back and looked out the window. *Borodin.* Now that he knew so much more about the historical background to Borodin's memoir, he was surprised at how well it fit in with other historical accounts. He'd also been surprised, when he'd reread it, not to find the kind of textual inconsistency common to fraudulent documents.

Ekaterinburg had fallen to the White Army only three days after the supposed assassination of all the Romanovs. Since the White victory came so quickly, investigations began on fairly fresh ground. But those investigations proved frustratingly inconclusive. White tribunals established that a number of people *were* executed in the Ipatiev House, but no bodies were ever recovered. And while mention was made of the ferocious Captain Yurovsky and the *coups de grâce*, the decapitations, and of Yurovsky's boarding the train for Moscow with his Hungarian guards and his grisly luggage, neither the captain nor that gruesome luggage was ever seen again.

At that point in the civil war, July 1917, White resources were still vast. But although no effort was spared in tracking down Yurovsky, he had vanished: it was as if he'd stepped off the edge of the earth.

As a result, the identities of the dead remained perpetually in doubt. White investigations eventually centered upon explorations at the Four Brothers mine, a few miles from the Ipatiev House. Evidence gathered there suggested that at least the tsar and the tsarina had been murdered in the Ipatiev executions. The tsarina's right index finger, her corset stays, and Nicholas's dentures, along with other Romanov belongings, were recovered from the mine shaft by investigators. Even this evidence, however, was inconclusive and disputed.

Which meant that Borodin's story remained plausible.

Superficially plausible. There were problems. So far, Walker had not found one shred of paper to show that any of the Borodins had so much as set a foot in Ekaterinburg—no receipt, letter, bill, school record, nothing. And emotionally, Walker had trouble imagining a man sacrificing his own children to save another man's children. Of course, Borodin took pains, in the memoir, to insist that he didn't think he was putting his children in danger. But that assertion was unconvincing. Certainly he was a fool if he imagined that Captain Yurovsky, entrusted with the task of guarding the Romanovs, would have done nothing upon finding the Romanov children gone, and five stooges in their place. And Borodin's tale of grief was somehow not as convincing as his factual accounting of life in the Ipatiev House—in the same way that the fervent rhapsody of the passages dealing with his religious conversion was not convincing—these passages seemed to Walker as if they'd been composed by another man.

Still, Walker knew he might be making the mistake of substituting himself for Borodin. While the notion of putting one's child at risk was repulsive and alien to him, there were enough historical examples of infanticide . . . matricide . . . fratricide, to prove that where royal blood was concerned, greed for power often displaced familial love. And why take Borodin's word for it that he was a humble physician? Perhaps he was grasping, a vulture, anxious to become the guardian of the Romanov heirs and fortunes, only too ready to sacrifice his own children to do so.

He leaned back and looked out the window. It was desolate outside; there were fewer pedestrians now than in the dead of winter. It wasn't nearly dark yet, but one of the mercury vapor lamps on Russell Road flickered on as he watched. Its sickly pinkish glow added to the ghost-town look.

A few days later, Walker opened his ledger to write the date, July 16, 1980, and stopped, his pencil poised in midair. A coincidence: July 16 was the date of the Romanov executions in Ekaterinburg.

He walked over to the bookcase, where the sorted documents were arranged on the middle shelves. A graduate student, Julie

Clover, had finished the Chinese translations the day before, and he'd sifted through them and separated those that were most promising. Also on the shelves were the "important papers" and the sorted piles of personal correspondence.

The Borodin family was slowly taking form in his imagination. He'd even started to construct a Borodin family tree—it was pinned to the bulletin board, surrounded by photographs torn from a paperback copy of *The File on the Tsar*.

The photos on his bulletin board had been taken of the Romanov children near the time of the revolution. The girls were in their teens and early twenties; only Tsarevitch Alexei still looked like a child. The Romanovs were attractive; they glanced at the photographer with mischievous grace. Most photographs taken in the nineteenth and early twentieth century were once-in-a-lifetime mementos, and most subjects were stiff, unmoving, fearful of spoiling the image. But in these snapshots, the Romanov children were relaxed, accustomed to the camera.

The photographs of Nicholas and Alexandra were more formal. The severe, unsmiling face of the tsarina always seemed to be shown in partial profile. Only a hint of melancholy around the eyes, a certain looseness about her mouth, gave a hint of the passions that drove this woman. Before his intensive reading of the past two days, Walker had had only a foggy notion of the pivotal alliance between the empress and Rasputin, the Siberian mystic. He remembered well enough how worry about her sick son led her to take up with this "holy man," whom she hoped would heal the boy. He recalled that the Russian people believed that the tsarina's liaison with Rasputin was sexual and resented the influence both Rasputin and Alexandra had on the tsar, who made some disastrous decisions at their urging. Now it was much clearer to him exactly how Rasputin had acted as a trigger for the revolutionary upheaval that ended up victimizing Alexandra's entire family. In all *his* photographs, the tsar stared straight out at the camera with such a doleful gaze it seemed to Walker he must have sensed his tragic fate.

There were several shots of Ipatiev House as well, the graceful lines of the mansion only hinted at by the roof, since the lower part of the house was obscured by a crude stockade fence. Red guards stood on the lawn, leaning on what looked like bayonets.

While most of the accounts he'd studied tallied with Borodin's, there was one major fact at variance. While the Romanovs were deprived of the company of most family retainers, Dr. Botkin actually lived in the Ipatiev House and even Dr. Deverenko was allowed to tend the ailing tsarevitch until the end.

Walker remained emotionally unconvinced that the Borodin children were the Romanovs. For one thing, the children were *never*, except in Borodin's memoir, referred to by their Romanov names of Olga, Tatiana, Marie, Anastasia, and Alexei. In every other instance, in all their school reports, in all the letters, notes, even within the family, they were called by their Borodin names: Anna, Iraida, Hester, Marga, and Nicolai.

And while impostors impersonating the tsar and tsarina had been few, the number of claimants pretending to be any of the grand duchesses and even Alexei (a more difficult matter: to be taken seriously, a claimant had to suffer from hemophilia) were numerous.

That Borodin never put the children forward had to be counted against the likelihood that his memoir was genuine. If a man such as Sergei Borodin, a man without resources, had actually substituted his own children for the tsar's, and smuggled the Romanov children out of Russia to Shanghai, wouldn't he then have claimed or at least attempted to claim their "birthright"? Wouldn't he have attempted to rally White loyalists around the children and himself? Wouldn't he—at the very least—have used the children to gain for himself a position of power within the White community? To live a life of ease and luxury?

It wasn't as if Borodin and the children fled to Shanghai and were never seen again. They lived there at least until 1941, when the trunk was sent. And instead of being celebrated as possible Romanovs, according to the documents, Sergei Borodin (a medical doctor) *opened a café* in the French Concession, a modest little place called the Café Celeste. Judging from the ledgers Borodin kept, it had been profitable, and provided the family with an adequate living, but it had certainly not allowed them to live a life of luxury, an *imperial* life.

He looked at his watch and reminded himself not to get too hung up on the Romanovs—the *Borodins* should be his focus. He had to keep in mind that it was not his job to prove the diary true or false but to establish how it was that a Fabergé egg and a valuable icon ended up in an attic in Dorset. He took a package of personal letters—these from Hester Borodin to her father, Sergei—from the stack on his shelf and began to read.

CHAPTER
TWENTY-THREE

The courier asked for Walker's signature and then handed over the carton from Allenby's. Knowing it had to contain the photographs he'd been waiting for, Walker ripped into the cardboard box in the grip of a luxuriant swirl of excitement. If they looked like the Romanovs, if they looked *anything* like the Romanovs—it would solve one of the great mysteries of the century.

He dug through the Styrofoam peanuts and lifted out a photo album bound in maroon vinyl. A sticker on its front bore a six-digit number and the words: NICOLA WARD/Michalowski. Within a minute he had flipped through the entire book of plastic-encased photographs. His lips flattened into a disappointed line.

He looked through the book again, more slowly this time. The faces in the photographs didn't look *anything* like the faces on his bulletin board. Totally different people, no question about it. Apart from the parallels in age, number, and gender, there was little similarity between the Borodin offspring and the Romanovs.

Oh, perhaps you could stretch it and say that Iraida Borodin looked like Tatiana Romanov—if you squinted, if you tried—but as for the rest, there was not even a superficial resemblance. The Borodin photographs were detailed, high-quality affairs, taken with an old-fashioned large-format camera, not blurry snapshots that might have encouraged wishful thinking.

Each page of the photo album had an index card stapled to it. The cards bore typed transcriptions, in Russian, of the captions taken from the original photographs. About half the pictures were dated. The last five photographs in the album, in full color, depicted the objects from the trunk—including the stunning red egg.

Once Walker got over his disappointment—that the Borodins were *not* the Romanovs—he looked through the photographs again with growing interest. It really was a pleasure to see the faces that went with the lives he'd been exploring through the mass of documents.

He studied one large, formal family photograph, showing Sergei Borodin and his five children. In this shot, which lacked a date, Sergei appeared to be about fifty years old and the children in their late teens and early twenties, except for the boy, Nicolai, who looked to be nine or ten. The ages of the children in this shot were roughly parallel to the ages of the Romanovs in photographs on his bulletin board, which made it particularly easy to compare the two clans.

Sergei's face had powerful features—a large mouth and nose and big, deerlike eyes, topped by a mop of curly hair. The girls were all attractive, but the boy, Nicolai, was almost beautiful.

There were four photographs of brides and grooms in the album. One showed a young Sergei and a light-haired, light-eyed wisp of a woman—Sergei's wife, Marthe. There were wedding photographs of two of Sergei's four daughters. Marga, the middle child, was photographed in traditional dress with her husband, Arthur Gould. Hester, the youngest girl, in a stylish suit and pillbox hat, stood smiling happily next to a man in German military uniform. Walker knew this sturdy-looking German, whose uniform seemed a couple of sizes too small for him, to be Ernst Roeder. There were dozens of letters about Hester's marriage to Ernst, most of them from Hester to her father, begging Sergei to realize that Ernst was just a German, not a Nazi. In the end, Sergei had relented in his disapproval, but shortly after that, Hester's letters had stopped.

Then there was a photograph of Katarina "Dasha" Borodin, Sergei's granddaughter, with her British husband, Tony Sunderland. They were a good-looking couple. Somehow, Walker had pictured Dasha as a swarthy Siberian girl with heavy eyebrows, but in fact she was a beautiful young woman with delicate, slightly oriental features. According to the marriage certificate in the trunk, Dasha had really been born in Vangou, not in the monastery near

Perm as Borodin had claimed in his faked memoir. She and Tony Sunderland had been married in Shanghai in 1938. The memoir had claimed that Dasha's mother had been raped by a guard in the House of Special Purpose in Ekaterinburg. Possibly, the rape claim, if not the locale, was true. There was no record that Iraida Borodin, Dasha's mother, had ever been married. He added the dates of Marga's and Hester's marriages to his Borodin family tree.

There was one other photograph in the batch that particularly interested Walker because it was the last one, chronologically, found in the trunk. It was taken in 1940; the trunk was sent in 1941. This was a fine, eight-by-ten print, showing a much older Sergei Borodin. The notation read: *Grandfather's 75th*. Walker guessed that Dasha herself had taken the photograph. For one thing, she wasn't in it, and the inscription "Grandfather's 75th" suggested she had written its caption. For another thing, among the papers in the trunk were tuition receipts and grade reports from the Shanghai College of Commercial Arts. Dasha had studied graphic design, printing procedures, accounting, and *photography*. Shortly after their marriage, she and her husband Tony had opened a printing shop and photo studio called the Zeitgeist Grafix, on Bubbling Well Road in Shanghai.

The photograph of Sergei's seventy-fifth birthday party was dated November 1940. Walker glanced over to the Borodin family tree and saw that indeed Sergei was born in 1865—the dates matched up.

In the picture, the white-haired Sergei was leaning over a birthday cake, the cake itself nearly obscured by a forest of candles. The photographer had caught the flames angled to the side from the force of Sergei's breath, but only two had actually been extinguished and showed plumes of smoke. The handsome young man looming over Sergei's left shoulder was Tony Sunderland. His pursed mouth and puffy cheeks showed that he was helping Sergei blow out the candles. The woman at the extreme left of the photograph, looking childishly happy, pressed her hands together in delight. This was Anna, the eldest of the Borodin children. None of Sergei's other children were present.

Walker checked his family tree. By the date of this party, at least two of Sergei's children were dead: Iraida, Dasha's mother, who had died of meningitis in 1930, and Nicolai, who was mur-

194

dered in what seemed to have been a gambling fight, in 1938. (There were many documents dealing with Nicolai's death—court proceedings, transcripts of testimony, sketches of the street outside the hotel where Nicolai had been stabbed by an American seaman named Offerdahl. From the evidence in the trunk, Nicolai, apparently a morphine addict and probably a homosexual, had been in trouble with the law most of his short life.)

As for Sergei's other children, Hester had gone to Germany with her husband, Ernst Roeder. But the last letter from her (ominously postmarked from Dresden) had reached the family in Shanghai in 1937. Marga Borodin and her husband, Arthur Gould, had moved to New York in 1940; the return address was Avenue C, in Manhattan. He wondered if the Goulds had continued to live in the States, and if they were still alive.

So of Sergei's five children, by 1940, two were dead, two others had left Shanghai with their husbands. Only Anna remained with her father. Walker looked at the birthday photograph again. There were six other people in it besides Sergei and Anna and Tony Sunderland and one of them looked very familiar to him.

This man, at the extreme right of the photograph, was not smiling or laughing like the others. Instead he wore a worried, preoccupied look as if someone had just given him bad news. Walker couldn't shake the feeling that he'd seen the man before—the man had a distinctive face with a dime-sized birthmark on his cheek. But the more he tried to put a name to the face, the more nebulous the memory seemed. Probably he was thinking of a movie star, an athlete, some public face. He closed the book.

One thing was settled: the memoir was false. The excellent quality of the photographs removed any doubt. These Borodin faces wouldn't survive the simplest police identikit comparison.

He called Michalowski.

"So," Michalowski said in a regretful tone, "you have seen how little our Borodins resemble the Imperial Family. Of course, I didn't *really* think it would be otherwise."

"I had my secret hopes, too."

"Yes, well, it was a nice fantasy. . . ." Michalowski's voice trailed away. "For a week or so, I had interesting dreams. . . ."

"I don't know whether it would be of any help," Walker said, "but I do know some . . . experts . . . who could make a professional physical comparison . . . earlobes, that kind of thing. If you want that for the client . . ."

"The client . . . well," Michalowski sighed. "I didn't . . . I never mentioned this memoir to her, let alone what it said. Ostensibly she doesn't read Russian, you see. And if the memoir had been cooked, I thought she might try to bring it to our attention." He sighed. "When the whole study is completed, we might tell her about the memoir, but until then, I think it's best to leave it. We did, incidentally, check out her story and at least on a superficial level, it seems quite genuine. I called the uncle's solicitor; everything seems to have happened just as she said.

"We thought possibly the trunk had been salted away in the attic a couple of years ago, and then 'discovered.' But it seems not. It appears on two different inventories of the house taken by her uncle's staff, where it is described as 'Shanghai Trunk.' One was done in about 1950 and the other just a few years ago. It really looks like the trunk was just sitting there for forty years."

"So Mrs. Ward wasn't in touch with this uncle?"

"No contact at all since she was a child. At some point he and his wife split up and Mrs. Ward went with her aunt. The uncle went home to Dorset and never set foot out of his house again. A bit of a recluse, apparently."

"Would you mind if I called her? In case she has some papers or information that might help?"

"Oh, by all means. I thought I'd given you her address and phone. No?"

"I don't think so."

"Hold on a minute. Let me get her file."

He wrote down the address as Michalowski read:

Nicola Sunderland Ward
11 Willow Street
Bath, Maine 04530
207–884–5252

"I didn't know she was from Maine; I thought she was a Bostonian."

"Oh no. Lived there most of her life."

"We have a cabin up there—not all that far from Bath." In fact,

196

Bath was about fifteen miles from the cabin, the closest town of any size; it was where they did their shopping.

"I'm a city dweller," Michalowski said. "The country makes me quite nervous. I stay right in town for the weekends, which are quite pleasant, actually, since everyone else is out in the Hamptons or up to the Vineyard, or someplace. Can you hold on one minute?" Walker heard him speaking to someone else and then he came back on the line. "Look, Neil, I've got to go. You just carry on. The diary doesn't really make any difference. In all likelihood, Borodin was a schemer of some sort and he cooked up this hoax of a memoir with some notion and then the plan fell through, or he got cold feet, whatever. The other papers may still tell you how he got hold of the egg. Or have you been through them all?"

"Most, and there's nothing yet. How's the technical analysis going?"

"So far, everything seems quite genuine. And the egg is an *Imperial* Easter egg—I mean the tests aren't done yet, but it's an Imperial egg or a copy of an Imperial egg."

"What does that mean?"

"About half a million dollars." Michalowski laughed. "An Imperial egg was one that was made for one of the tsars—Nicholas or his father. Fabergé did make others for lesser mortals."

The two men agreed to talk in a week.

Walker drummed his fingers on the table. Concluding that the memoir was false solved one puzzle but created another. Without the memoir's implied explanation for Sergei Borodin's possession of the valuable objects, he still had to figure out how they had fallen into Borodin's hands.

If it had turned out that the egg was not Imperial, that would be one indication that possibly Borodin had invented the memoir to make the articles more valuable—relics of the massacred Romanovs. If it turned out that the objects seemed to be all known possessions of the Romanovs, he had to take a different tack. Maybe Borodin had bought the things from some Romanov servant or crony—or even from one of the men who had guarded the Romanovs during their period of house arrest. Maybe he would find out that Sergei Borodin was an old Shanghai con man.

He felt he needed to know more about the historical conditions in Shanghai at the time the Borodins lived there. And more about Borodin's relationship with General Ivan Medvedev (if he existed), the man with whom the Borodin clan had lived at the beginning of their stay in Shanghai. The phone rang.

It was Mike Hale calling to see if Andy could go swimming with him at the Yates Center in Georgetown.

"It's fine with me," Walker said. "But he's not home yet. I'll tell him to call you."

Andy, of course, wanted to go. He always made excuses about going swimming with his father, but he'd do anything for Mike.

Hale came by to pick him up at seven, driving his Porsche because Andy was car crazy and thrilled to ride in it. "We're going to swim about eight hundred laps and then we're going to eat some burgers at Clyde's," Hale said, giving a little salute. He tossed the keys to Andy. "You drive, okay?"

Andy got that sheepish look on his face and then adopted Hale's bantering tone. "Not tonight," he said, tossing the keys back. "I'm not in the mood."

CHAPTER
TWENTY-FOUR

Kate's return and the constant worry about her had begun to wear Nicola down. She felt suffused with a poisonous lethargy. Once in a while, she'd recognize the dangerous nature of that lassitude and rouse herself for a flurry of activity. She'd throw herself into some task with phony energy—cleaning out the drawers, polishing the floor, embarking on a run, a walk, a rowing expedition.

But each time, the energy spent exhausted her and she lapsed back into her fatigue gratefully, almost sinfully; it encased her in its faded comfort like an old robe. She stayed in bed a lot, dozing intermittently, reading trashy books. Only lurid plots could hold her attention. Only the most violent emotions could keep her eyes open. She had no patience with subtlety or wit. She even read romances, books she'd always scorned. She found their sameness soothing: the trite plots, the happy-ever-after endings pleased her. She didn't need surprises. She also became addicted to several soap operas and devoted her afternoons to them. The characters' lives, tumultuous as they were, seemed more viable than her own. On weekends, without the company of the soaps, she was lonely. At all times, she had the feeling she was operating at a slight remove from herself.

Kate had returned from New Mexico looking better, and for a few days, she and Nicola enjoyed being together, but soon it was clear that the separation had raised some combativeness between them. Nicola tried to cast it as a step forward, and maybe it was, but she was beginning to see that she and Kate were a destructive combination, like a binary explosive. Even as Nicola thought of the word "binary," she felt a distance from it and her teachy voice spoke in her head: binary: two-part. Bi. Two.

Kate had withdrawn; that was what had happened. It was a re-play of puberty, going back in time to when she was twelve or thirteen, with all the simmering resentment of that phase. Nicola had the hopeful thought that maybe the hormones were kicking back in. Whatever it was, Kate didn't really want to talk to her anymore. She gave simple, teenage answers, answers that meant *don't bother me*. Nicola felt like an interrogator.

Today, to please Kate, Nicola had taken her shopping at the big mall in Portland, even though it was hideously crowded with sum-mer people. When they were finished, Nicola wanted to stop and visit Mrs. Cutter, the old lady who lived next to them in town, but Kate scorned the idea: "I don't want to go see her, Mom, it'll be boring."

"This woman used to play Go Fish with you for hours when you were little. You think Go Fish isn't *boring?*"

"Mom, I'm *tired*, okay?"

"*No it isn't okay*," Nicola said with unexpected vehemence. "Don't you think you owe something back to people who have been kind to you?"

Kate said nothing.

"Don't you?" Nothing. Nicola knew she should stop but she couldn't shut up. "Answer me when I talk to you," she said, as if Kate were a young child. "I feel like I'm talking to a wall."

"*Okay*," Kate said.

"I think you owe her a visit now and then," Nicola heard her-self say in a disgustingly satisfied voice. "It's the least you can do."

"Shut up," Kate said in a dangerous, deranged, voice. "Shut up shut up shut up."

Once they got home, Kate marched into her room and Nicola didn't see her for the rest of the day, although once, coming in from the deck, she caught a glance of Kate's robe disappearing around the corner.

They didn't see much of each other anyway.

Nicola got up at dawn and went to bed at eight or nine. Kate slept until two or three. They met at dinner, which Kate did not

200

eat. Still, when Nicola straightened up the kitchen in the morning, waiting for the coffee to be ready, she swept up little piles of crumbs where Kate had stood and eaten in the night. It was in this way, and because quantities of food were missing that she knew Kate was eating at all.

Each day, Nicola would be gripped at least once by a cold, heart-gripping spasm of fear. When Kate hadn't appeared by noon, and she never did, Nicola would think: Kate's dead. She's *dead*. She'd creep into the guest-room closet and put her ear against the wall. It was a thin wall, its opposite side next to Kate's bed. Sometimes she could detect the steady ryhthm of Kate's breathing, and she'd crawl out of the closet—relieved, but somehow feeling ashamed. Sometimes, she couldn't hear Kate at all and then the fear would increase. She imagined what she'd do if Kate didn't appear by evening. She'd hurl her body against the door, burst in. . . . Kate would be there in her bed, still. . . .

The fear, in fact, produced her only bursts of energy. But even these episodes of terror were diminishing. Even the fear was fading into the blank lethargy that had become the dominant mood of her days.

That night Nicola sat out on the deck for a long time. The stars glittered coolly in the deep black sky as she sat there drinking brandy and water, thinking, recognizing her maudlin mood but unable to lift herself from it. So, she thought, a relationship that started when a helpless infant had been laid on her belly and she'd fallen in love with such a heady lurch that just to look at Kate's tiny, perfect fingernails made her almost cry had come to this—two people caught up in such a tangle that one of them resorted to the prisoner's last pathetic weapon against his captor: "You can't make me eat. You can't make me *live*." Nicola poured some more brandy in the glass. She looked at the lights across the water.

With every sip of brandy, she got more unhappy and more pleased with her unhappiness at the same time. Indulgent tears ran out of her eyes. Suddenly, she stood up, wobbling a little. Stan used to kid her out of these moods; even if she didn't want to cheer up, he wouldn't give up until he'd turned her mood around. Stan, Stan, she couldn't think about him either. What was it about her that drove people to such extremes?

She flicked on the floodlights that shone down on the water. Her fingers hit the switch with a quick, paranoid touch. She'd installed the lights herself and could never quite believe that she'd done it correctly. Electricity remained an almost magical force to her, and although the lights had been functioning perfectly for over a year, she still expected a paralyzing shock when she turned them on, a rebuke from the power of the universe: *Nicola, you fucked up.*

She walked with exaggerated care down the ramp to the float at the bottom. It wasn't high tide, the ramp wasn't that steep, but she wasn't sure how drunk she was. Sitting down and hugging her knees, she looked into the water, waiting for the schools of fish, attracted by the floodlights, to appear. She could always misplace her gloom for short periods of time, watching the fish, intrigued by their sheer numbers, the visual thrill of their rapid and totally co-ordinated shifts of direction.

She watched them for a minute, but this time they failed to distract her. She resented the sure instinct that seemed to guide them—while she herself was so unsure of what to do. She fought off a momentary impulse to jump in and make them scatter.

CHAPTER

TWENTY-FIVE

Neil Walker's desk at the Library of Congress was covered with a spread of unusual papers—pages from the 1939 Shanghai census, gossip columns from the *New China Mail*, the passenger lists of nine vessels (out of dozens) known to have arrived in Shanghai in May of 1923, the date the memoir gave for Borodin's arrival. That had to be close to their true arrival date because there were documents from the trunk that placed the Borodins in Shanghai by July 1923.

He'd spent the previous day at the Archives, and was now in the Library of Congress, checking data. He hoped to get through these passenger manifests before it was time to quit for the day and take Andy to the Orioles game. His mind wandered as he scanned the handwritten lists for the name Borodin.

They'd have to arrive early at Griffith Stadium, the earlier the better. Andy could go short distances on his crutches but still had to stop and rest a lot. His arms were very strong now, but the crutches chafed them, and walking was tedious. Andy couldn't feel his feet touching the ground, and lacking the feedback his nervous system normally would have provided, he had to look at each spot where he planned to put his foot, then put it there, then go on.

Walker had arranged for seats that presented the fewest obstacles, but even so, getting to them would be an ordeal. No wonder disabled people lobbied for full access. Even with good ramps and lifts, every outing with Andy required planning and extra time. It was easy to say forget it and stay at home, which was just what Andy would rather do. He remained painfully self-conscious.

Walker's reverie stopped because some attentive fraction of his mind caught on the word "Borodin." He'd gone right by it, even though it was the *only* thing he was looking for; he'd gotten caught up in the rhythm of reading the names. He looked back and found it: Borodin, Sergei. It was the embarkation list for the Japanese vessel *Kodama Maru*, which sailed from Vladivostok in April of 1923. Borodin was listed as ship's doctor. The names of his children, and also of his grandchild, Katarina, followed his own. Walker slapped his desk in triumph, which earned him a glare from his neighbor, a woman with wispy red hair. He'd seen her in here many times. As far as he could tell from the accumulation of books on her desk, she was studying tartan patterns.

He hurried over to the machine to copy the embarkation list. He'd been incredibly lucky to find Borodin's name so quickly, in the first day of searching. He rode the Metro home in a state of elation only to be brought down by Andy's newest assertion that he didn't feel well enough to go to the baseball game.

"But, *Dad*, I don't feel good. I really don't."

Andy tried, but he couldn't destroy Walker's cheerfulness or make him deviate from the plan.

"I know. But I really think what's making you feel bad is that you don't like people staring at you. You may not like people staring at you, but you can't just stay inside until you get better. It might take a long time. So, where do you want to eat dinner? At the ball park? Or on the way?"

"I really don't feel good," Andy said in a desperate voice. "I mean *really*, not because I'm . . . just . . ."

"Well, you don't have to feel all that great to go to a ball game."

"Great. What if I barf all over the place?"

Walker shrugged.

"What if I barf *on* someone?"

"I'll take my chances."

Andy seemed to know that his father wasn't going to change his mind. They were reaching a place, well established before the accident, where a tone in Walker's voice established a limit. In pre-accident days, Andy had known instinctively when his father would bend and when he wouldn't, but their sense of each other's reactions had been destroyed by the tragedy.

Andy wasn't quite ready to give up on sicking out of the ball game. He took a more subtle approach. "Well, I guess you're right, Dad. I guess I really don't want to go. But you know why?"

"Because you're self-conscious."

"No. Because I'm sad. Because today for the first time, I thought: but what if I don't get better?" He looked up at his father. "What if, Dad? What if I don't get better?"

Walker turned away. He never allowed himself to think about this—that Andy would never get better—except in some secret recess of his mind. But he could see that Andy didn't really think it either. It was just a con.

"Well, if you're not going to get better, then you'd better get used to it—going out, I mean. Because I'm not letting you stay in your room for the rest of your life. Look . . . if people stare at you, that's their problem, isn't it?"

Andy shrugged.

The Orioles won and Andy didn't insist on suffering all night to spite his father, so they had a good time. Walker drove home in a good mood, Andy sleeping in the seat next to him.

Having the arrival date of Borodin's ship, the *Kodama Maru*, as a starting point, made it much simpler for Walker to locate other records about the Borodins. At the Library of Congress, he obtained annual records from the tsarist consulate in Shanghai; he easily found Borodin's name. Sergei had registered on June 2, 1923, declaring his birthplace as Kulada, Siberia, his occupation as pharmacist and medical doctor, and his temporary address as the Villa Medvedev on the Avenue du Roi in the French Concession.

By now, Walker had done enough reading to have formed a vague picture of life in Shanghai during the twenties and thirties. Enough of a picture to know that the French Concession, despite its name, was inhabited largely by White Russian émigrés, refugees from the revolution. Most of them were poor and lived by selling off their valuables one by one. Medvedev might have been in Shanghai longer, might not have been a refugee: "Villa Medvedev" had a settled sound to it.

He finished up at the library for the day. When he returned

home, he still had an hour or so before Andy got back. He found himself looking through the Borodin photographs again. The one of old Sergei's birthday party had been nagging him ever since he'd first seen it—the irritating familiarity of the man with the birthmark. When he looked at it this time, there was something about the man's beaky nose, the birthmark, and the cleft chin that made the proper connection in his brain, and instantly, he recognized the face.

It was the face of Vassily Zamatin, an Agency colleague, an adviser in the Soviet Bloc division. He hadn't recognized Zamatin at first because the photograph was forty years old and it showed a man in his early twenties, a young man with luxuriant black hair and a precisely trimmed mustache. The Val Zamatin Walker knew was clean-shaven and also entirely, completely, billiard-ball bald. But when he put his finger over Zamatin's hair in the photograph, there was no mistaking Val's distinctive features—the nose, the chin, the birthmark. He never would have made the connection without the visual clue of the birthmark.

It could be a very lucky coincidence. Maybe Val Zamatin would be able to *tell* him how Sergei Borodin came to have a Fabergé egg. At least Val would know more about the Borodins. They must have been friends—probably he'd been a friend of Tony's or Dasha's— they would have been roughly the same age. It seemed reasonable that Zamatin was a close friend of the family, or else he wouldn't have been at the birthday party.

Walker looked up Zamatin's number and called it. Zamatin's secretary, Dottie Singer, answered in her thick Southern accent. Silly men—mostly Northerners—at the Agency mistook the slowness of her speech for lack of mental agility, but Walker knew what a valuable asset Zamatin had in Dottie Singer.

"Dottie, it's Neil Walker."

"Why Nee-yull. How *are* you?" Suddenly, she remembered, and a new sincerity came into her voice. "And your *son?*" The way she said it, son had two vowel sounds.

He gave his stock answer about how everything took time.

"I guess I *told* you not to hesitate to *call* me if I can do anything for you. I really *mean* it—babysittin', whatever. You do *call* me, Neil Walker, if I can *help.*" She paused. "I heard you went into business for yourself, is that true?"

"Yeah, and it's okay, I kind of like it."

"I sure do miss you round here. Well, what can I do you for?"

Walker smiled. Val Zamatin had adopted that peculiar locution and it sounded so odd in his accented English. "Val there? I need to talk to him."

"No sir. No sir, he surely isn't here. I'm sorry, Neil. He's in *Sardinia*." The way she said it, it sounded as remote as Jupiter. "At least he's on his way. He just left for vacation, Neil."

"How long will he be gone?"

"Two weeks." She sounded heartbroken. "I'm *sorry*."

"Can I reach him by telephone?"

"He's going sailing."

Walker knew there was a way Dottie could reach Zamatin, but he also knew she wouldn't do it short of a flat-out emergency.

"Tell him I called."

"I surely will. And you take care of yourself, Neil Walker," she said in her fervent voice.

"Thanks, Dottie, you too."

Two weeks. Val Zamatin wouldn't be much help after all: in two weeks, he hoped to have the whole thing wrapped up. He rummaged through the things on his desk to find Nicola Ward's telephone. So far, he'd been unable to reach her.

It finally occurred to him that she might have a cabin on the water. Most of his neighbors in Maine weren't from out of state. They were natives, from Bath or Brunswick, who had summer cottages on the shore. He called information—the Down East accent of the operator made him smile—and was happy to be proved right. Nicola Ward had two telephone numbers. He called the second one and this time, she answered.

She said she had virtually no family papers. What she had was in town—death certificates for her parents, who had died, she said, in prison camp during World War II, and her adoption papers. She promised to send copies.

He asked her if the Goulds were still living in New York and she told him they'd been murdered in a robbery years before. She told him that as far as she knew, she had no living relatives except for her daughter, that she was hoping the papers in the trunk might lead her to some family.

He regretted that he hadn't found any yet. Then he mentioned that he had a summer place not far from hers—on Spruce Point—and that he hoped to get up to Maine for a week later in the summer. She invited him to drop in for a visit if he did.

CHAPTER
TWENTY-SIX

Washington, D.C.

When Hobie James called to see if he wanted to have lunch, Walker agreed immediately. The two of them were old racquetball friends. Until the accident, they'd played together a couple of times a month. Just when they'd started playing again, Hobie had wrecked his knee skiing.

Walker had seen Hobie in January (Hobie in a full leg cast, following knee surgery), but that meeting had been a formal one. The Office of Security had requested an interview with Walker about his debriefing of the defector Boris Shokorov. A few days earlier, Shokorov had been discovered dead in his apartment in San Francisco. It was standard operating procedure for OS to investigate any defector's death. Walker remembered thinking that it was a sign that Shokorov's death was considered both suspicious *and* important that Hobie was the one heading up the investigating team. Hobie's gee-whiz exterior might fool some people, but Walker knew that he brought to investigation the same relentless hustle that made him tough at racquetball. He would never give up, never acknowledge defeat.

Walker remembered telling Hobie what he could recall about the interrogation of the Russian—the only thing that stood out in his mind were some speech anomalies, Ukrainian locutions that had bothered him a little at the time. But the irregularities had been both explainable and explained, not enough to prompt a deeper level of interrogation. He'd recalled how he'd tried to trap Shokorov and got no glimmer of response.

This time, their lunch was purely social; it had been so long since they'd seen each other that their friendship was in danger of crumbling from neglect.

Hobie had suggested Shezan, and as Walker descended the flight of stairs to the dining room, he saw that it was an inspired choice. After the pulverizing heat outside, the room was refreshing: the glint of chrome, the linear furniture, the pink tablecloths, the lack of windows—a cool, stylish cave. Hobie was drinking a Perrier. He jumped up when he saw Walker coming and gave him a vigorous handshake.

"Hey, you're looking good, Hobie."

"Does that mean I get dessert?" His sputtering little laugh burbled out of him. They both sat down. "And how are you? And Andy?"

"Doing okay. We're hoping to get up to Maine in a week or two."

"I'm lucky if I get outside the beltway these days. I'm back on the roads, jogging. I may yet return to dominate you on the courts."

"That's great, Hobie. It went well?"

"It looks good." Hobie held up his crossed fingers. "I'm still on restriction for another month. No pivoting."

"How's the book coming?"

"I got a little bit done when I was laid up with the knee but I'd have to say it's still going slowly."

The waiter arrived and they ordered drinks. Hobie told him stories about Civil War spies—anecdotes that he planned someday to incorporate into his "big" book. For years, Hobie had been feeding data into his IBM for the grand work he planned to complete when he retired: *A Short History of Espionage.* In the meantime, he regularly turned out small, impeccable, scholarly works on the subject of intelligence. The most recent example was *Jedburg Units in Belgium, 1943–44.*

In the course of their lunch, Walker told him a little about the work he was doing, the provenance study for Allenby's.

"The antique people? Really? So what's that like?"

"It's a lot like genealogy except that instead of tracing a person's life, you trace a *thing's* life. Hey—" Walker remembered that he'd brought along the photograph of Sergei Borodin's birthday party, which he thought would amuse Hobie because Hobie and Val Zamatin were friends. "I've got something to show you." He leaned over and flipped open his attaché case and removed the picture. "I wanted to see if you'd recognize a mutual friend."

Hobie put his drink down and peered intently at the photograph for a few seconds, then struck himself on the head with the heel of his hand with an audible whack. "Neil, promise I can have a copy of this for my collection," he said fervently.

Walker was puzzled. "Really? I didn't think Val would merit inclusion in your collection, Hobie. You're usually very picky."

"What do you mean, *Val?* I'm not talking about Val."

"Val Zamatin." Walker moved over into the chair next to Hobie's and pointed to Zamatin's face. "Right there."

"Well, you're right. That *is* Val, isn't it? Son of a gun. But he's definitely a lesser light in this group, you realize." Hobie pointed to a man with large dramatic features. The man's arm was draped over Sergei Borodin's shoulder. "This is the Hall-of-Famer. You mean you really don't know who this is?"

Walker moved back to his own seat and shrugged. Hobie was almost bouncing with excitement. "This is *Richard Sorge*, Neil. *Richard Sorge*. Where did you *get* this?" he demanded. "Where was this photograph taken?"

"This is from the provenance thing I was telling you about. It was in an old trunk full of papers and valuable things." He explained about the trunk's long sojourn in an attic, its eventual arrival. "I was amazed to find Val in the photograph—so amazed that it took me a couple of days to realize it was him."

"From Shanghai. Hmmmmm," Hobie hummed. "Of course, Sorge was spending most of his time in Tokyo by then, but he must have periodically visited his cells in Shanghai as well. You honestly didn't know this was Richard Sorge?"

"I read a book about him once, but it was a long time ago. It was a paperback; I don't think it had photographs."

"It never ceases to amaze me how ignorant most of us are about our own history—I mean the history of espionage," Hobie said righteously.

"Weren't you surprised to see Val in here?"

211

"Not once I saw Sorge, not really. I mean Val's been with the Agency *forever* it seems, but let's not forget he once worked for Moscow Center. And I knew he'd worked under Sorge. I took him out to dinner once and tried to pick his brain." Hobie laughed. "But he really didn't want to talk about it, and I could understand why. In fact, it couldn't have been much after this photograph was taken that Val defected—he defected to the Nazis first, of course. He came to us later, after the war was over. You didn't know that?"

"No, not really—I knew he once worked for the Russians; I guess I knew he was with Gehlen. I never really thought about it." Walker was thinking he ought to pick *Hobie's* brain a little.

If Richard Sorge was at Sergei Borodin's birthday party, maybe that meant the old man was involved in the Sorge ring; maybe that would explain how he ended up with the Romanov artifacts. Maybe they were fomenting some weird operation with the faked diary. "Tell me about Sorge," he said.

"Well, do you want the twenty-minute rap or the two-hour rap?" His laugh squirted out. "Just what was in this trunk, anyway?" Walker told him; Hobie was impressed. "A Fabergé egg? No shit?"

"Well," Walker said. "Pretend you don't know that. I'm not actually supposed to talk about this. Allenby's has its own worries about security. These days everyone worries about it—I think it's kind of a viral thing."

Hobie was nodding vigorously. "Not to worry, babe, lips are sealed." Walker thought Hobie James was one of the few people left in Washington who used the word "babe."

The waiter came and took their order, and Hobie happily launched into his description of Sorge's career.

"First of all, Richard Sorge was a German, not a Russian. He became a Communist in about 1916, when he was wounded while serving in the German Army. By 1925, he was a veteran Comintern agent and a citizen of the Soviet Union.

"In 1929, if I've got the date right, he was sent to China to set up an espionage network. He posed as a German journalist—and in fact he was accredited to an agricultural journal called *Grain*." Hobie chuckled.

"To make a long story short, Sorge spent three years in Shanghai setting up his apparatus after which it was decided that he should do for Tokyo what he'd managed in Shanghai.

"Richard Sorge was apparently very *simpatico*, very charming. Anyway, he arrived in Tokyo at an opportune time, during a change of ambassadors, and managed to ingratiate himself with the acting German ambassador. With that entrée, he charmed his way into the highest and most influential social circles. Within a year or two, he was the German ambassador's *best friend* and trusted, if unofficial, adviser.

"At its peak, the Sorge ring had six cells—two in Shanghai, two in Manchuria, and two in Tokyo. The ring operated from about 1930 until 1941, engaged in espionage against the Japanese (and to a lesser extent the Chinese) on behalf of the Soviet Union. And let me tell you," Hobie added, waggling his fork, "it was wildly successful."

The waiter arrived, gliding to the table as if on wheels. He delivered samosas, coriander chutney. They ate it up in what seemed like seconds.

"What kind of information was Sorge giving them in the beginning, in the Shanghai period, I mean?"

"*Everything. Anything.*" Hobie stretched his arms out, nearly delivering a blow to the waiter, who was pouring water. "He was to organize the Red Army spy network in China and report about every conceivable thing: Chinese agriculture, American military strength, whatever. He was more focused in Tokyo. I'll tell you," Hobie said, shaking his head, "in Tokyo, Sorge became such a popular social figure that when he was finally arrested, the Japanese and Germans refused at first to believe that he was a spy." Hobie clapped his hands together in delight. "They just couldn't *fathom* it." He shook his head. "They must have been so pissed. Of course, once they found the documents, the copying cameras, once the thing unraveled, they couldn't go on doubting."

"How did they get him?"

"Well, through the usual kind of mistake, something that no one could imagine. He was careless, Sorge was, a drinker, and a womanizer. You have to know that at the time, the Japanese were gearing up for war. So Tokyo was crawling with cops of various sorts—the Kempetai, the Tokko. And they were cracking down on Communism, which scared the Japanese to death. It was similar

213

to the situation in China where the entrenched conservative forces were terrified of Communists, and supported Chiang Kai-shek. In Japan, they even had a special law against Communism which allowed them to arrest leftists at will. Anyway, in one of their sweeps, the police picked up an elderly Japanese couple. The woman had Communist connections back here, in the States, in California. She also had quite a bit of American money on her and they questioned her about where all that Yankee dough came from.

"She told them it came from a man named Miyagi. Now Miyagi, you see, was one of Sorge's agents. And when the police searched Miyagi's rooms—well, you can imagine the rest. Miyagi tried to commit suicide, threw himself out of a second-story window and did manage to tear himself up some. But he recovered enough for the Kempetai to break him down and he told them everything he knew, which was plenty. By *then*, of course, the ring's most important feat had already been accomplished."

"What was that?" The waiter delivered chicken tikka, lamb biryani, cucumber raita, poori.

"Well, at first the ring's objective was vague, as I said—secure intelligence about Japanese intentions, order of battle, operations in China. Japan and Russia were supposed to be allies at the time, but of course there were all those Japanese in Manchuria—Manchukuo, as they called it—making the Russians nervous. And the Japanese controlled virtually all of China north of the Great Wall, including the long border with Russia.

Hobie ate incredibly fast. Between bites he talked on. "As the Second World War rolled on, with Germany ready to invade Russia, Sorge's operational targets narrowed to one: to learn whether the Japanese were going to pursue their . . . imperial designs . . . by pushing south"—Hobie's hand pointed to the floor—"you know, into Singapore, Indochina, Malaya, Burma . . . *that* way, *or* . . ." He stopped to shovel some raita into his mouth. His eyebrows bounced up and down. ". . . *or* would the Japanese go *north* into Russian Siberia. If Sorge could determine *for certain* that Japan didn't intend to attack Siberia, Stalin could begin to move troops from Asia to the Western Front to defend against the German attack that everyone knew was coming. If the Japanese *did* intend to attack Siberia, the Russians would have been forced to defend two fronts." He stopped eating for a moment and held

214

a forkful of rice balanced precariously in midair. "It's possible that if the Japanese *had* attacked Siberia, Hitler's invasion of Russia would have been successful—many historians believe that the Japanese decision was a fatal one for the Axis.

"Anyway, by early 1941, the Sorge ring had achieved its purpose—it transmitted the information that the Japanese would push south and not, as the Russians feared, into Siberia. The Sorge ring's intelligence about Japanese intentions ranks as one of the all-time globe-tilting feats of espionage. Eventually, the Japanese hanged Sorge. Twenty years later, he was named a hero of the Soviet Union—this was after the end of Stalinism, you know. I think they named a street after him. No, maybe it was a stamp, or they put his face on a kopeck coin . . . I'm not sure."

"Do you think the others in the photograph were part of his ring—I mean, you say Val Zamatin was, how about the rest?"

"Well"—Hobie bounced his eyebrows—"there are always more spies around than you think. Maybe if we spooks had a trade association . . ." He waved his hand over the photograph. "Do you know who the rest of these people are?"

"Some of them. I wish Val were in town. He could probably identify all the people, and tell me all about Sergei Borodin and the Sunderlands and make my job simpler."

"Where is he?"

"Sardinia, vacation, two weeks. I hope to be *done* in two weeks." He pulled his chair around toward Hobie's and identified those in the photograph he knew, beginning with Sergei Borodin.

"The birthday boy."

"Right. And this is his daughter Anna. This is Sergei's son-in-law Tony Sunderland; we know Val, of course, and now, Sorge, but the other four . . ." He shrugged.

"He's young enough to be alive," Hobie said, pointing to Sunderland.

"But he's not. He died in prison camp during the war—both he and his wife. His daughter sent me the death certificates. I just got them today."

Hobie frowned. "When was the trunk sent?"

"Nineteen forty-one."

"Must have been before Pearl Harbor. The Japanese came right in after that and all the foreigners in Shanghai—except for Germans—were interned. Do you have any more information about this Sunderland character?"

"He was a Cambridge man, had a post on the Bund in one of the big merchant firms. He married Sergei Borodin's granddaughter, Dasha."

"Okay. He's a Cambridge man married to a Russian girl—I'd say chances are excellent that he was a spook of some stripe. At the time, it was considered a noble profession of sorts, although I doubt the marriage was popular back home. What about the wife? Where is she in this picture?" He pointed to the woman next to Sorge. "Is this her?"

Walker shook his head. "I think Dasha Sunderland probably *took* the picture. She was a photographer, a commercial photographer. They had a print shop."

"Bingo!" Hobie leaned forward in the chair and rapped his spoon repeatedly on the pink tablecloth. He vibrated with excitement. "I'll bet you . . . I'll *bet* you they did papers. It wasn't . . . let's see. . . ." Hobie screwed his eyes shut and looked like a little boy. "It wasn't the *Zeitgeist* print shop, was it?"

"I think it was, I think that's right. Zeitgeist Grafix—I definitely saw that name somewhere in the papers."

"Well, that's *it!*" Hobie gulped at air like a fish. "That's it. It's well known."

The waiter glided over. "Decaf," Hobie said dismissively.

"Coffee," said Walker and then turned to Hobie. "What's well known?"

"In Shanghai. Sorge's people ran a print shop. They used it to make up papers, travel documents and so on. This is *fascinating*. This could be a *book*."

Walker laughed. At least once during every conversation, Hobie said, "This could be a *book!*" in exactly that tone.

"I'm not kidding, Neil. Not that much is known about Sorge's Shanghai period." Hobie stopped to think for a minute. "Tell you what. Why don't I run the parents' names, the ones who ran the print shop—what did you say? Sunderland? Why don't I run them through the computer at the Agency? Wait—" He held up his hand. Hobie kept a supply of three-by-five index cards with him at all times. He pulled one out and asked Walker to write down the full names. He grabbed the card back and drained his coffee.

"I'll check them out. You never know—there's a lot of ancient history in those files. Maybe we'll get lucky. Of course, in return, I'll want a copy of that photograph. Deal?"

Walker shrugged. "I'll try." He was mildly curious about Dasha and Tony Sunderland, but the person he really needed to know more about was Sergei. "Try Sergei's name, too, if you could, Sergei Borodin."

"Is it my nickel or your nickel?" Hobie asked when the waiter arrived with the check.

"My nickel," Walker said.

"Do you mind if I go? I talked so long, I'm late." Hobie was halfway to the door. "I'll call you in a day or two," he promised, wiggling his eyebrows.

CHAPTER
TWENTY-SEVEN

Walker spent the afternoon at the Archives, reading about an organization called Nightingale—a secret White organization of which General Medvedev seemed to have been an important member. By three-thirty, he was only halfway through the box of documents he'd intended to complete that day. He started yawning and then he couldn't stop; the fat man at the table behind him kept shooting him annoyed glances. Alicia, one of the clerks, walked past wheeling a wooden cart on bicycle wheels.

"Late night?" she joked.

He yawned. "Guess I'd better get a cup of coffee."

He left his desk as it was, but stopped at the free lockers outside the reading room and got his briefcase, so he'd have something to read in the cafeteria. Security was tight in the Archives. Not only did you have to sign in and out of the building, and have a researcher's card to do so, but you had to sign in and out of the reading room as well. Briefcases, books, and files were not allowed inside the reading room. He passed a small crowd waiting for the elevator and he heard someone say: "Jeez, this elevator is nicer than my living room."

He took the wide marble steps down to the cafeteria, thinking maybe the exercise would help wake him up. He bought an apple and a cup of coffee and pulled out a sheaf of papers from his briefcase. These were the documents he'd received from Nicola Ward; they had arrived in the morning mail. He'd looked at them briefly, but now he looked at them again: death notices for her parents, mailed by occupation authorities, a news clipping about the murder of her aunt and uncle, the Goulds, a naturalization certificate, and some old correspondence between Hillary Sunderland and the British Home Office.

Nicola Ward had included a note saying: "Not much, but all I've got. Please do call if you make it up to Maine this summer—we'd love to meet you. Nicola Ward."

He pulled out his much-scrawled-on Borodin family tree, filled in the death dates for Tony Sunderland and Dasha Borodin and took another bite of the apple.

"Neil!" said a voice, and he looked up to see Ebenezer Lang, the king of the fifth floor—Modern Military Records. Lang had a thin face, with fine features and a perpetually startled look. His thick eyebrows had an unusual central peak—like tiny roofs over his eyes. "I haven't seen you in an age. How *are* you?"

"Hey, Eb," Neil said with pleasure. "Sit down. I'll buy you a yogurt."

Walker replenished his coffee and bought Eb a container of yogurt—this was the major component of Eb's diet. Eb Lang was a compulsive reader, whose eyes automatically fixed on any printed material within eyeshot. Walker knew Eb must have been one of those children who compulsively read cereal boxes. Within a minute of sitting down, he was spooning cherry yogurt into his mouth and peering across the table to read Walker's papers.

"What's this you've got, Neil? Is this from my shop? I haven't seen you up on five lately."

He picked up the death notification for Anthony Sunderland. "No, Eb. A client sent me this."

"Fushun Camp," Lang said. "Fushun Camp. You know there was a big story about that camp not long ago, don't you? You've heard about it?"

"No," Walker said. "I never heard of it before. I just got this in the mail today."

"Holy cow, Neil." Lang was so excited, he sprayed Neil with tiny particles of yogurt. "I can put you in touch with the reporters who worked on this if you want."

Lang was so excitable, and such an eager beaver, Walker didn't have the heart to tell him that the death notice was peripheral to his real work. "Sure, Eb," he said. "Appreciate it."

"Well, I wouldn't be so *blasé* about it," Lang said in a huffy voice that was so uncharacteristic, Walker stared at him.

"What do you mean?"

"What I mean is that there were horrible atrocities, and *we* covered it up. I mean all this stuff about Unit 731—it was a big story in Japan and in the U.K., but it didn't even make the front page here. I mean, can you figure it? Some old Nazi gets tracked down in Paraguay and everyone goes wild but here a sidekick of MacArthur admits we knew the Japanese tortured and experimented on *U.S. citizens* and no one gets excited. I mean, how do you figure it?"

"What are you talking about, Eb? Backtrack a little, you've lost me."

"That's what I *mean*—no one *knows* about this stuff."

"You want to tell me about it?"

"People should know about this, they really should. You come on up, I'll show you."

Walker followed Lang up to his incredibly cluttered office. He noticed for the first time that Lang was wearing bedroom slippers.

Lang showed him the press clippings. From the *New York Times: MacArthur aide admits U.S. covered up Japan germ-war POW tests.* From the *Washington Post: American POWs tortured in WW II Horror Camp. Cover-up of Germ War Project Alleged. Pact With Japan Hid Results of Germ War Tests on POWs.*

Walker read the horrible lead of the *Post* article:

During World War II, the Japanese experimentally killed about 3,000 humans, including American prisoners of war, with biological weapons and the U.S. military establishment made a secret arrangement with the Japanese to hide the experiments, according to an article in the current issue of the Bulletin of the Atomic Scientists.

The details were even more shocking. POWs were deliberately infected with diseases, such as smallpox, anthrax, and plague. The diseases were then allowed to progress unchecked until Japanese doctors ordered the victims slaughtered and autopsied. Eight thousand slides, prepared from these autopsies, became the property of the U.S. government after the war, apparently in some trade-off which allowed the staff of the camps in question to gain immunity from war-crimes charges.

Other atrocities were listed in the *Bulletin of the Atomic Scientists* story, which was written by John Powell, based on information obtained through the Freedom of Information Act. Prisoners were apparently irradiated, pumped full of horse blood, and dissected while alive.

Walker looked up. "I can't believe this. This should be a *huge* story. I don't know how I missed it."

Lang shrugged sorrowfully. "You missed it because it *wasn't* a huge story. It's the kind of thing Americans don't want to know—especially about WW II (Lang pronounced this *double-yoo double-yoo* two) where we were supposed to be the good guys. You don't want to know your government was making deals with guys who were using human beings as guinea pigs—so your government could *use* that valuable information. But I would say that if you know some people who died at Fushun, chances are, they didn't die in their sleep."

"The death certificates listed T.B."

Lang's eyebrows disappeared under his shock of hair. "Yeah. Well in Germany, about five million people died of 'T.B.' It was a popular disease."

"I'd be curious to find out what *exactly* happened to the Sunderlands." Neil tapped his attaché case. "You think there's any way to find out?"

Lang tilted back in his chair and looked at the ceiling.

An hour later, Walker was in the reading room looking through the second of eight green boxes. The boxes had already been screened for reporters working on the Japanese War Crimes story for any possible Privacy Act violations. Walker shook his head, wondering how this story had escaped his attention. According to the *New York Times* story by Aaron Epstein, there had been a bestselling Japanese book about the atrocities, *The Devil's Gluttony*, and a British television documentary as well, not to mention a broadcast on ABC's "20/20."

In the first box, there was a list of prisoners, who were given numbers by which they were subsequently identified. It took him about an hour to find the prisoner numbers of Katarina and Anthony Sunderland. It took another couple of hours to find the Sunderlands' numbers listed among participants in a study to determine the effects of cold on the human body. Subjects were repeatedly submersed in cold water and then forced to stand nude in freezing weather. Water temperature, air temperature, and body fat caliper readings were meticulously recorded. One of the reports dryly noted that the human beings in the study huddled together in clumps, seeking to combine their body heat. It was thought that this might interfere with test results, so the subjects were then separated. Vital signs were taken during all of the testing periods, and recovery rates noted: meticulous records of how long it took for body temperature to return to normal, how cold it had to be before frostbite affected extremities; the clinical indications of hypothermia were noted. There was a notation about prisoners attempting to dig holes in the earth in the experimental areas. Walker searched the results sheets for the numbers assigned to Dasha Sunderland and Tony Sunderland. Anthony Sunderland died 16 October 1944, and Katarina Sunderland nearly six months later, on 12 April 1945. Among the conclusions drawn, it was noted by researchers that women's superior body fat percentage was responsible for longer survival in exposure situations.

Walker meticulously restored the material and returned it to the central desk. Despite the clinical language of the reports, it was impossible to dislodge the images of naked human beings submerged in water and staked out in yards in the cold while guards took blood-pressure readings. They were denied even the company and warmth of other frozen bodies. It was impossible for him to stop thinking of Dasha Sunderland—the pretty young woman from the photographs—clawing into the frozen earth with her bare hands, trying to dig a shelter. He turned the boxes in silently, and left the Archives without a word to anyone.

CHAPTER
TWENTY-EIGHT

Hobie James removed the collection of index cards from his pocket and sat down at his desk. It was his habit to accomplish tasks in a strictly prioritized fashion. Difficult or unpleasant tasks, as well as those which were overdue or had time deadlines, had to precede tasks about which he felt neutral, which had to precede tasks he enjoyed.

First he read a few pages of newly translated cables that crypt-analysts believed originated with Source DANTE. Then he had a short meeting with Lemro and Bailey, who presented the latest work they'd done on the Childress investigation. Fitz was headed out to San Francisco to continue his shadow pursuit of leads. Of course there was always the possibility that he would turn up something of actual use.

At eleven, he chaired another meeting about the investigation of a wife-swapping ring that involved two officers from Counterin-telligence. Then he made a phone call to his doctor, and fielded one from the Director of Operations. He had lunch with Barney Sistring of NATO Intelligence, and then spent the afternoon beating his head against the DANTE dossier, going over ground he'd been over many times before, looking for a pattern, an inadvertent clue. The process by which he studied a case was mysterious to him. He read over the same information many, many times, in a kind of reverie, waiting for it to cohere into meaning, waiting for revelation. Sometimes, it never came.

At ten minutes to five, he called in his secretary. He dictated two letters to her and also directed her to fill out a requisition to Centerfile: to run a trace on the names Katarina Borodin Sunderland (aka "Dasha" Sunderland), Anthony (Tony) Sunderland, and Sergei Borodin.

"Do you need this today?" Cathleen asked in a resigned voice. "And the letters, too?"

"No, no, there's no rush. Tomorrow will do."

That was on Thursday. He spent the weekend with his computer, a system so powerful and so expensive, he tended to hide its existence from all but his closest friends. Lately, he'd been logging in data—for his book—about certain OSS operations in Italy that had recently been pried loose from classified status through the Freedom of Information Act.

It wasn't until Tuesday that his secretary returned the memo about Dasha and Tony Sunderland. His original three-by-five card was stapled to the front of the file folder.

When he opened the folder, there were two surprises waiting for him. One was that two of the names *were* listed, which meant that files existed for both Dasha and Tony Sunderland. The second was that the files were *flagged:* ROMEO. He was stunned.

Since he didn't have access to the crypto ROMEO, of course, he was denied access to the files.

He flipped the file shut and shifted uneasily in his chair. Shit. His fingertips tapped a rhythm against his desktop. He'd stumbled over Agency regulations before—and had been warned sternly not to make "recreational" use of the files.

He knew that the clerk in Centerfile was bound by procedure. Shortly, Hobie would be called in by one of his colleagues—one of his *subordinates,* and have to explain his reasons for requesting the flagged files. It would be embarrassing all around. He would have to say that he'd just been "browsing." Maybe he could work out a little bit of a dodge by explaining that he'd been doing a favor for Neil Walker. Because of Neil's tragedy, it wouldn't look *so* bad.

He flipped through his Rolodex, then dialed Walker's number.

"Hey, Hobie. I was just going to call you to see if you got anywhere with those names."

"I stepped in some shit here, Neil." He told Walker about the flagged files. Then he paused. "Do you mind—hell, you'll tell me if you do, right? Do you mind if I tell OS I was doing a favor for you, checking on those files?"

"Well, there's no question about it. You *were* doing me a favor."

"Sometimes they think I'm a bit of a loose cannon—but if I explain that I was"—he hesitated—"that I was doing a favor for *you*, I think that might . . . help."

Walker understood the implication. What Hobie meant was that everyone still felt sorry for him.

"Well, what the hell, Hobie, whatever you want."

"It's weird, though, isn't it Neil? I mean these files are history, *ancient* history. They're thirty years old, for Christ's sake. And they're *flagged?* You could have knocked me over when I saw that."

"Maybe no one ever got around to removing the flags."

"No, it's nothing like that. When they computerized the files back in the sixties, they pruned like crazy. All flagged files had to be grounded by updated request. There was a lot of old filing flagged to guys that were dead and buried, or worse, gone to the private sector. That was the reason for the housecleaning in the first place."

"So someone saw to it that those files stayed flagged. That is interesting."

"At least as of ten years or so ago, in the late sixties, early seventies. We can safely say that as of that time, someone still wanted to keep tabs on anyone interested in Tony and Katarina Sunderland. The old man, Sergei Borodin—there was nothing on him."

"I have to say, Hobe, that I have no idea what this means," Walker said.

"Didn't you tell me the Sunderlands died in the forties?"

"Definitely. In fact, since I saw you, I found out exactly how they died. They died in Fushun Camp near Mukden. Remember that story a while ago about the Japanese doing medical experiments on POWs?"

"Oh yeah, I read about that. Weren't there even some survivors of the Bataan death march in that camp? That's an ugly story. Maybe that has something to do with the flags." Hobie sucked in some air. "On the other hand, if they *died*, it makes the flags even more mysterious. I don't know, you could try and get at it through the Freedom of Information Act. Maybe it's some kind of filing error."

"Yeah," Walker said. "Maybe I will." Actually, he knew he wouldn't bother. By the time the FOIA request was processed, he'd be long done with the study.

"Neil." Hobie hesitated. When he did speak, his voice was sheepish. "Can I still have a copy of the photograph?"

"I'll check with the client, but I can't imagine she'd mind."

"Thanks, babe."

"I'll be in touch."

Rudolph Michalowski always enjoyed walking through Allenby's public showrooms—so like the rooms of a prosperous private museum. The sparkle of crystal, the faint smell of furniture polish, the beautiful interplay of color and texture from the paintings, the oriental rugs, the porcelain—all this seldom failed to restore his mood following what was often a brutal trip from his apartment on the Upper East Side. In the summer, the city could flatten you: the streets were choked with bad air and worse tempers. And he wondered if they were just more visible lately or were there more deranged people on the streets, more homeless? On his way to work, he was often hustled for spare change—which he gave, occasionally, although he hesitated to ponder the uses to which it was put.

His secretary, Eleanor, looked up when he came in and then hurriedly hung up the telephone. She always seemed to be in a hurry, as if he'd nearly caught her at something. She was plain-looking, except for a big, wet-looking mouth, and extremely timid.

"Morning, Mr. Michalowski." There was a slurpy, liquid quality to her voice, as if it were filtered through saliva.

"Good morning, Eleanor," he said warmly. He angled his head to the side. "I like your dress." As usual, when complimented, she lowered her eyes and looked embarrassed just to be acknowledged. She was so painfully self-conscious, he knew she would prefer to be treated like a bit of furniture, inanimate, but his manners wouldn't allow him to ignore her. He stepped past her into his office, and sat down at his desk. He was a man who liked a clean desk and there was nothing to mar the expanse of cherrywood but his telephone, his In and Out baskets, and several letters waiting for his elaborate signature. He got those out of the way and then turned to the items of real interest.

Mentally, he'd set aside the first part of the morning to deal with the Ward objects and he sifted through the pile that filled his In basket to see what pertained to that case. There were just two things: Neil Walker's weekly memorandum and the latest progress report from the Technical Analysis Division. He read the latter first.

The full spectrograph analysis of the paint from the icon had come in and he looked it over. No anomalous colors or dyes had been revealed so far by spectrographic techniques, no telltale solvents turned up by chemical analysis. There was no underlying pentimento on the ivory, no traces of acid baths or chemical aging treatments. Tests were proceeding on the ivory itself. Michalowski pulled out a form and filled it in, requesting certain further tests on the paint—specifically on the gilt of the halos.

As far as the technical analysis of the egg was concerned, so far, so good. The *en plein* opalescent enameling on the egg itself, and also on the rosebud inside, would have required firing successive layers of transparent and opaque enamels at temperatures in excess of 700 Centigrade. It was considered doubtful that modern craftsmen could duplicate the exacting feat of fusing the layers successfully, an especially difficult procedure on rounded surfaces. It just wasn't done any longer; no one bothered. It seemed to him that it would have been more likely for a potential forger to pick a different style egg—one of the later, elaborate, jewel-encrusted eggs—not only would it be showier, but much easier to fake.

The value of Fabergé's work stemmed as much from the exquisite workmanship as it did from the materials. Even the most jewel-laden and elaborate of the Imperial eggs—the Lily of the Valley Egg, or the Mosaic Egg—were not fabulous in terms of materials but by virtue of their craftsmanship. Michalowski remembered reading in one of Snowman's books that the "surprise" inside the Coronation Egg, a tiny golden replica of Nicholas and Alexandra's

228

coronation coach, had required fifteen months of one assistant's time. On the Ward egg, the guilloché engraving under the enamel would in itself have been possible to duplicate, as would the gold-work. The relatively large fields of plain, unadorned enamel, the "simplest" parts of the egg, would have been the hardest to fake.

The egg had been definitely identified as "The Rosebud Egg," the first egg given by Nicholas II to Alexandra, in continuation of an Easter custom begun by his father. The Rosebud Egg was supposedly created in 1895 and the marks on this egg were consistent with that date.

It was one of the few Imperial eggs that had no base or pedestal. The jeweler's marks were found inside the shell. It bore the crossed anchors and scepter of St. Petersburg, and the number 56, which was the zolotnik number, indicating the percentage of pure gold in the alloy (this corresponded to the Western percentage system of 14-carat gold). The old St. Petersburg gold mark had been abandoned in 1899 and replaced by the standardized *kokoshnik*, a woman's profile in oval. Many of the eggs were dated according to variations in the zolotnik notation. Fabergé's name, in Cyrillic, appeared, along with the initials of Michael Perchin, Fabergé's work-master in St. Petersburg from 1886 until his death in 1903. The marks were, as they should have been, flush with the metal—in other words, the marks had been made in the metal before the object had been crafted and not afterward. Michalowski had seen any number of *objets* falsely stamped with Fabergé's famous Cyrillic characters, easily detected by a casual examination of the metal.

The Rosebud Egg had been lost since the revolution. However, photographs of it—albeit black and white ones—did exist and copies were included in today's progress report. This was both fortunate and unfortunate. Certainly the egg resembled in every respect the photographs of it; by the same token, it was not possible to entirely disregard the possibility that the photographs had served as models for a forger. Examination of the stones, a search for fixatives—superglue was sometimes found in jewels pretending to be a century or so old, a horrible short cut—would continue. Tech would also analyze the box which had contained the egg, a beautiful piece in its own right. The report pointed out, citing Snowman, that Carl Fabergé had a workshop in Moscow, employing fifteen workers, solely to construct boxes for his *objets*. Most of the boxes were made of polished white holly wood; the craftsmanship was of a high quality. Michalowski shared the Tech Division's opinion that a forger would be unlikely to go to the trouble of creating a fine holly-wood box—a demanding exercise in carpentry. Tech would pursue an investigation of the hinges and so on, to see if they were consistent with extant Fabergé boxes.

Unless Walker came up with evidence to the contrary, it appeared more likely each day that the egg from the Dorset trunk was genuine. If it could be established with reasonable cetainty that the Dorset egg was *the* Rosebud Egg, its sale would be an important and extremely lucrative event—for Nicola Ward, for Allenby's, and . . . for Rudolph Michalowski. Already, despite the clamp on publicity, feelers had arrived from museums and from private collectors. The egg might bring three quarters of a million dollars at auction, possibly more.

Michalowski slit the manila envelope containing Neil Walker's memo with a jade letter knife, and settled back into his chair. Walker was really a find, a workhorse. In the end, though, the credit for his research effort would probably go to a better-known name in the field, who would rework Walker's efforts—and no doubt make some useful additions to it. In the meantime, since Walker was new to the business, he included interesting details that would have been left out by most researchers. What's more, his reports were models of clarity and very well written. Today's memo was five typewritten pages; footnotes were appended.

MEMO #7 / 9 AUGUST 1980
RE: GENERAL IVAN MEDVEDEV

Borodin's (false) memoir states that the ship, *Kodama Maru*, which bore himself and the "Romanov children" from Vladivostok to Shanghai, was met upon its arrival by one General Ivan Medvedev. There is no reason to take Borodin at his word that Medvedev met the ship at the docks, but records at the tsarist (unrecognized) consulate do show that when Sergei Borodin registered there, his address was listed as the Villa Medvedev, Avenue du Roi, in the French Concession. Incidentally, Sergei stated that his occupation was "pharmacist and medical doctor."

In any case, it seemed worthwhile to look into the background of Ivan Medvedev. He was appointed the tsar's personal representative to the provinces of Kiangsu and Fukien in 1912. He resided in Shanghai, in the French Concession, in a large dwelling built for him in 1913 on Avenue du Roi.

I began my research thinking that perhaps Borodin and Medvedev had come to know each other when Borodin performed duties as a medical officer in the White Army, but although this seemed a likely premise, it turned out not to have been true. As far as can be determined, Medvedev's active military service ended before the civil war. He was a commander in the Russian Army during World War I, and had been severely wounded serving under Brusilov in the Galician offensive of 1916. His injuries included a bayonet wound to the throat which damaged his vocal chords and left him unable to speak above a whisper.

In the gossip columns of the *New China Mail* and the *Shanghai Evening Post* and *Mercury*, he was nicknamed "The Whispering General," or sometimes, "The Whispering Russian." One cartoon portrayed him imperiously speaking to a much shorter person forced to stand on tiptoes to hear the pearls of wisdom dropping from Medvedev's mouth.

Michalowski stopped reading. This material would really flesh out the catalog; this was great stuff. He rolled his knuckles across the desk as if rolling out dice, an unconscious gesture he often performed when he was excited and happy. He read on.

By the time of the tsar's assassination and the subsequent Russian diaspora to the East (an estimated 125,000 Russians emigrated to China between 1918 and 1922) Medvedev was a firmly entrenched and powerful member of Shanghai society. He belonged to a welter of White organizations and was the unofficial commander of French Concession's Russian Volunteer Detachment (composed of displaced Cossacks) which worked for the municipal police force. Medvedev traveled frequently to the city of Harbin, in Manchuria (called Manchukuo at that time) and also to Mukden.

In Mukden, Medvedev stayed in the elaborate French château of the famous "Tiger of Manchuria," Chang Tso-lin. Chang was one of the warlords who had seized power in China following the disintegration of Manchu dynastic rule in 1911. The "Tiger" controlled much of Manchuria and commanded an army of 250,000 men that included a corps of four thousand Russian troops known as the Dolov detachment, commanded by Medvedev's good friend, the popular Imperial commander Boris Dolov. Thousands of other

Russians were employed by Chang in his government, particularly in the police. Chang was famous for driving an armor-plated 1921 Packard mounted with water-cooled machine guns and stuffed with bodyguards. More important, Chang was well-known for other "Western" tastes, including an extensive art collection and a vast wine cellar. It is certainly possible that Medvedev could have secured the articles in question through Chang, who purchased large quantities of valuables from the streams of fleeing Russians traveling through Manchuria.

Indeed, Michalowski thought, the Fabergé egg would not have been particularly valuable at that time. The Bolsheviks sold off a great deal of "decadent, Imperialist" art in the twenties and thirties, and Fabergé's confections were considered trifles, trinkets, presented as examples of Imperial frivolity and decadence. In the mid-thirties, Christie's had held a sale of Fabergé objects and the Imperial eggs had gone for less than a hundred pounds each. In the twenties, from a desperate fleeing White Russian in, say, Manchuria, one could imagine an Imperial egg going for fifty dollars, maybe even less.

Ivan Medvedev also traveled frequently to Harbin, in Manchuria—an interesting city at that time. Harbin had had a substantial Russian population since the late 1800s because it served as the hub of the Russian-owned-and-operated Chinese Eastern Railway. There were numerous Bolsheviks in Harbin, vying with the Whites for control of the rail system.

Once Russian émigrés lost the extraterritorial rights granted other foreign nationals in China (1920), many of Harbin's Russian residents took Soviet passports, merely as a convenience. They were known as "radishes" (red outside, white inside), but Harbin was also stuffed with Comintern spies, phony radishes who were red through and through and doing their best to infiltrate White political and paramilitary groups.

As John Stephan points out in his excellent book, *The Russian Fascists*, Harbin was "an emporium of contraband" seized by the Bolsheviks during the revolution. "Art objects, furs, and jewelry . . . found their way across Siberia to Harbin for sale." Stephan tells of a Russian princess who happened upon her mother's tea set displayed in a store window. Medvedev could easily have purchased the icon, the necklace, and the egg in Harbin during this period.

Medvedev belonged to several fascist groups, including the Brotherhood of Russian Truth, and the shadowy, supersecret organization called Nightingale, a kind of White Russian PLO, which engaged in espionage and terrorist acts, continually plotting against the Bolshevik "interlopers." Founded in 1918, the aim of Nightingale was quite simply to reverse the Russian revolution of 1917. Initially, the group appeared to command no fewer than three White divisions (1917–1919) in the Urals, but diminishing support for its operations reduced the organization to sporadic acts of terror and intrigue. In 1938, the apparat was saved from dissolution by the patronage of ideologues in the Nazi SS *Ahnenerbe*, the occultist bureau of the Third Reich. After a brief resurgence at the outset of World War II, Nightingale finally dissolved in 1943.

During the time when Sergei Borodin and his brood arrived in China, Medvedev was a famous character in Shanghai and also in Harbin. I have barely touched the surface of the newspaper material about Medvedev; he seems to have appeared almost daily in the gossip columns of both English and Russian language dailies. Not only was he connected to a great many White organizations, but he had some disturbing habits. He was bisexual and an opium addict, but his most famous penchant was an insistence on drinking nothing but human milk, which he believed preserved his youth and vigor. Human milk was not unknown as a beverage in certain Shanghai restaurants at that time, but Medvedev carried it a bit further. Espousing the belief that human milk combated the aging process, Medvedev reportedly worried that precious vitamins were lost in storage. During the last few years of his life, he was accompanied everywhere by two wet nurses, from whom he would suckle whenever a "wave of feebleness" threatened to engulf him.

Sensational, Michalowski thought. He paused and buzzed Eleanor. He asked her to bring some tea. He leaned back in his chair to rest his eyes. *Nightingale.* He'd heard the name plenty of times—always in whispers—when he was a very young man living with his parents in Paris. Until the day they died, his parents believed that one day they would be restored to their proper place in the society of their native St. Petersburg (they never got used to calling it Petrograd, as it was renamed following the declaration of war against Germany in 1914—to get rid of the German "burg" ending—and certainly never referred to it as Leningrad). Although they both spoke excellent French and adequate German and English, they lived in an encapsulated Russian world in Paris. Their friends, without exception, were Russians. They lived in that curious suspension of the exile—the past was important, as was the future, when things would be restored to the proper order—but the present was insubstantial and illusory.

They spent ridiculous amounts of their money on food, wine, tickets to the symphony, never relinquishing that aspect of their "standard of living." His mother was laughed at by the Parisian shopkeepers for her haughty aristocratic bearing, her imperious way of speaking to them. Still, his parents had managed to educate him at the Sorbonne, and something of their passion for Russian culture had blossomed in him; he obtained a degree in art history with a specialization in Russian art.

Eleanor arrived with the tea, which she placed on his desk with a kind of bashful grace, as if she were disturbing him. He thanked her and turned back to Walker's report.

Whatever the reasons for Medvedev's patronage of Borodin and his children, they were lucky to have his protection. Once the Chinese excluded White Russians from the extraterritorial privileges enjoyed by other foreigners in Shanghai, Russian émigrés were often beaten in the streets, exactly like the Chinese coolies who shared their unprivileged status. Although there were a few wealthy Russians in Shanghai, men like Medvedev, most refugees were poor and lived in the ghetto of Hongkew, certainly the likely destination for Sergei Borodin and his children were it not for Medvedev's protection. Medvedev's reasons for extending that protection remain fuzzy, although there is still a great deal of archival material available for study. Possibly, Medvedev was planning to put forward one or more of the Borodin children as a claimant to the Russian throne, either as a rallying point to collect money or even as part of a serious attempt to challenge the Bolsheviks.

With all the normal successors of Nicholas murdered by the Bolsheviks, there was no clear rule to determine the legal order of succession. This divided the ranks of exiled Russians and undermined and fragmented counterrevolutionary efforts. Facing the debilitating factionalism caused by arguments about the succession, White leaders must have yearned for a Romanov, a survivor of Ekaterinburg, to rally and unite their forces.

Really, Walker was tremendous, Michalowski thought. He himself had personal memories of the bitter dispute about the succes-

234

sion to the throne. It was almost funny now, after all these years of Bolshevik rule, to think of the limitless energy his parents and their friends had poured out deciding which Imperial pretender deserved their allegiance. An idea began to form in his mind: maybe they would publish a small booklet to accompany the auction of the Ward objects. He read on.

Borodin and his children lived at the Villa Medvedev in great secrecy for a year and a half. Some rumors about Medvedev's "mysterious guests" were printed in the Shanghai newspapers. One interesting item: a banquet was thrown for Medvedev at the Palace Hotel in the summer of 1923. Most of the socialites of the city and the powerbrokers of the Shanghai *Bund* turned up to thank the General for his generosity in making the unheard-of donation of 25,000 pounds sterling to the city's Hospital for Children. From the dais, Medvedev publicly gave "thanks to the glory of God for prayers that were recently answered."

But Medvedev died in 1924, of typhus, his plans for the Borodins, if any, unfulfilled. Shortly after that time, Sergei Borodin and his children moved to the house on the Rue Père and Sergei opened the Café Celeste.

Michalowski scanned the footnotes and replaced the report in its folder. He agreed with the drift of Walker's speculation. It seemed likely that Medvedev was the source of the valuable objects and had plans for one or more of the Borodin children to masquerade as a Romanov survivor, although how he'd planned to explain the discrepancy in appearance was open to question.

He checked the time and had Eleanor put a call through to Neil Walker.

"Excellent work on the report, Neil, really first rate."

"Thank you—I'm enjoying it."

"And I do agree with you. I think the Medvedev angle is quite probably the correct one, although I can't imagine Borodin being allowed to retain possession of these things after Medvedev's death. Unless—"

"I've thought about that. It's possible that knowledge of the existence of the valuables was extremely limited and they . . . you know, Nightingale . . . tripped over their own security procedures. It happens . . ." Walker paused. "Who knows? I'd just be speculating."

"I understand what you're getting at."

"That's why today we have oversight committees," Walker said.

"*Oversight*—what a wonderful, godlike notion."

Walker made a Russian word out of it, and managed a pun.

Michalowski cackled in appreciation, and then gave Walker a brief update on the technical analysis. "Everything looks good so far."

"Can I ask you a question?" Walker said suddenly. "I—I'd like to take a week off. "Would that be possible? I've promised my son a week's vacation before school starts again."

"But certainly," Michalowski said. "We can certainly spare you for a week. You don't know perhaps that the other people who were considered for the work you are doing were not available for months. A week is no problem at all. We've got a long way to go before we're ready for presentation. Tests are going to require at least another month and we won't even think about an auction until winter."

"I appreciate it."

"I think here in the art world, we are operating at a pace very much slower than you are used to. Your reports are excellent. Believe me, you are *weeks* ahead of where I thought you would be. When will you go?"

"In a few days." Walker paused, settling it in his head. "In a week." He was already looking forward to announcing the departure date to Andy.

"If I could just have the telephone number where you'll be. I don't like to be totally out of touch."

"Actually, we don't have a phone up there, but our neighbor takes messages and I return calls." Walker flipped through his Rolodex, and gave Michalowski the name and phone number of his neighbor, Cal Tuttle.

"Of course, I won't be disturbing you unless it is important. Do you think it'll be possible to find out anything more about the Borodins in Shanghai? Were there any rumors about them?"

"That's the direction I'm heading."

"Give me a call before you leave on holiday, but don't worry about getting a memo out before you go; it can wait."

Walker felt relieved, glad Michalowski didn't object to the time off. The trip was going to happen anyway, because he'd promised

Andy, but he was enjoying the investigation and didn't want to jeopardize future work.

He got up to make some coffee. Andy had been spending more and more time playing video games on his computer and Walker hoped that being in Maine might lure him out of his introspection, might bring them closer together. Most of the activities that occupied them in Maine—rowing, sailing, swimming, fishing—were arm-related, so Andy's disability wouldn't make them impossible. And it wouldn't be hard to carry Andy down to the water. He had a superstitious fear of making permanent adjustments to Andy's disability—like building ramps.

CHAPTER
THIRTY

Hobie James squared his trim shoulders and walked confidently into the room where he was to be interrogated by Gerard Knowles. Knowles had a fleshy face and a habit of tugging on his pendulous earlobes when he was nervous. He was tugging now, but he let go briefly to stand up and shake Hobie's hand. Knowles was in the ticklish position of having to interrogate a superior. It was a situation that arose only on those rare occasions when someone in the upper echelon of the CIA's Office of Security was stupid enough to violate the security procedures OS itself was set up to enforce.

Of course, Hobie reminded himself, there was nothing inherently wrong with requesting access to files that had been flagged. There were good reasons for wanting access to files, in which case access would be granted on a need-to-know basis—providing a "higher authority" determined that no operations or operatives would be compromised. He wouldn't be in trouble right now if he'd had a good reason for looking at those files.

Still, it was hard—impossible, really—to believe that there was an ongoing investigation involving Dasha and Tony Sunderland. He thought the most likely explanation was the simplest—that the flags had been put on the files decades ago and been missed in the ensuing bouts of housecleaning. He settled into his chair.

Because he himself had organized the protocol for conducting interviews such as the one he was about to be subjected to, Hobie was well prepared for Knowles's questions. He also knew that his answers were being tape-recorded and that later they would be routinely scanned by the Psychological Stress Evaluator for "stress blocks," a form of wireless lie detection. Knowles seemed the more nervous one as they ran through the set banter and the series of prepared questions—designed to be unstressful.

Knowles slogged through the old bit about Washington being a hardship assignment, a "putrid swamp infested with insects," as one early British diplomat had put it. His listless voice repeated the words like a bored kid reciting the pledge. Knowles had a bluish mole on his left cheek which wiggled as he talked. They ran through some establishing questions about Hobie's age, his license-plate number, the color of the walls in his living room, that kind of thing. Without warning, they arrived at the real questions.

"What was your reason for requesting the files on Dasha and Anthony Sunderland?"

"I was afraid you might ask that," Hobie joked.

Knowles produced a slight smile and tugged his ear. Hobie sighed and allowed a laconic chuckle to drift out of his mouth.

"You know about my hobby, Knowles? About the book I'm working on?"

Knowles nodded. "Yes, sir."

"Hobie, all right?"

Knowles nodded again. Hobie focused on the bluish mole as it dipped and rose on the field of Knowles's flesh.

"Well," he began. "I was having lunch the other day with Neil Walker—a former officer, you know, in Soviet Bloc." He leaned forward in a confidential way. "His wife was killed a year or so ago in a car accident, and his son was severely injured—you know, there was some paralysis." Hobie waved this information away as if it were not important, although he had not mentioned it without purpose. "Anyway, for whatever reasons, Walker left the Agency and set up shop as a genealogist, which was his specialty." He stopped suddenly and frowned, looking at the ceiling. "Anyway, he was conducting an investigation—a *genealogical* investigation, you know, and . . . well, he became interested in these people, the Sunderlands. He knew that they were involved in espionage in Shanghai back in the thirties—and this is what interested *me*—they worked for the famous Soviet spy Richard Sorge. And I just thought, you know, what the heck—I'd take a peek at the files and just *see.* I was kind of interested myself and, well . . ." He spread his hands wide on his lap and smiled. He tried for a sheepish grin.

"You mean that you did it as a favor for Mr. Walker?"

Hobie James nodded. He tried for a chagrined look.

"I'm sorry, Mr. James, but you must respond verbally."

"*I'm* sorry. Yes. It was a favor for him and frankly I just didn't see the harm in it. After all"—he stopped and looked at Knowles as if the two of them were the last reasonable men in the world—"this stuff is laughably dated. I think the flag must be some kind of foul-up. Still—I'm not saying what I did wasn't wrong; I made a mistake." Hobie James allowed himself to lapse into a repentant silence.

Knowles tugged at his ear. "This is just routine," he said, almost to himself. "I'm sure. . . ." He shrugged at Hobie, who rose from his chair and shook Knowles's hand. Hobie thought that unless the man behind the crypto ROMEO, the man who had flagged the Sunderlands' file, turned out to be a really heavy hitter, this would be the end of his problem with the flagged files.

"You ever get that mole checked, Knowles?" he asked. Knowles's hand flew to his cheek and obscured the pigmented flesh.

"No," Knowles said in a weak voice, "I've always had it."

"I'd get that checked if I were you. That's not a good color, you know." And then James did something which reminded him of just how nervous interrogation can make you. He said, "*Ciao,*" a word that had not crossed his lips in years.

240

THIRTY-ONE

Nicola was taking advantage of one of her bouts of energy to tackle a massive chore that she'd been putting off for years—to clean out the garage at Willow Street. Tomorrow was the city's annual Trash Day, when citizens could get rid of major garbage without arranging a special pickup. As she drove through town, Nicola saw that the sidewalks were already lined with junk: derelict appliances, shabby couches, mattresses with huge, horrible stains, TV trays, TV stands, TVs, outboard motors stripped of useful parts, cracked aquariums, three-legged chairs.

Her garage was so stuffed with things, it was getting hard to shut the door. Some of the junk had probably been in there since Stan was a boy—ancient bicycles, studded snow tires for cars junked twenty years before. Her goal was that this winter, for the first time ever, she'd be able to park the car in the garage—which would save her ten freezing minutes of scraping in the morning.

James Mackenzie was coming over to help carry the heavy things. He was meeting them at the house. She turned up Washington Street. She'd dragged Kate along, too, over protests that she didn't feel well. If Kate could pick goddamned onions (she hadn't put it this way) in the beating New Mexican sun, she could help drag trash out to the curb.

James Mac was already there, lounging up against his TransAm. He wore sweat shorts and a cutoff top that revealed the full splendor of his abdominal muscles.

"You're going to owe me for this, Nicola," he said, standing up. "I looked in there. There are some really humongous spider-webs. I mean big mothers."

"I know it. They've been evolving without disturbance for decades."

Someone said, "Let's get to work."

It was hard just to get the old wooden doors open. They didn't quite clear. They gouged ruts in the grass as James Mac forced them apart.

Just seeing the amount of junk in the garage made Nicola want to give up.

"We'll make two piles," James said in an efficient tone, "one for stuff you want to keep, one for stuff you want to toss. I advise you to be very strict."

A couple of hours later, they surveyed the line of trash that stretched nearly the length of her property line. "Do yourself a favor," James Mac said. "Go through the keeper pile and weed it out again."

They approached the things Nicola wanted to save. "For instance, do you really need this stuff?" He put his foot on the wooden packing crate that had contained the trunk from Shanghai.

"Oh, that. I thought I might make something out of it."

"Yeah, like what?"

She shrugged. "A coffee table?" He looked at her and then at Kate.

"What do you think, Katie? Do the Wards need another coffee table?" Kate shook her head and giggled.

"He's right, Mom. It's this kind of thinking that got us here." She waved her hand toward the curb.

"Let's drag it out," James said. Halfway up the driveway, going around the keep pile, he gashed his leg on a nail. "Injury!" he shouted. "I need medical attention." Nicola peered at where the protruding nail had gouged his leg.

"That was a forty-year-old nail from Shanghai," Nicola said. "When was your last tetanus shot?"

"I'm cool."

They reached the curb and added the crate to the collection of junk. On the way back down the driveway, Kate stopped and picked something up. It was a folded sheaf of papers, about fifteen

242

pages thick. When she unfolded it, Nicola could see the Cyrillic characters.

"It must have been stuck in the slats of that crate," Nicola said.

"Give me a Band-Aid," James said. "I'm bleeding."

"Let's go in," Nicola said. She took the sheaf of papers from Kate. "Remind me to send this down to Mr. Michalowski."

"What's the word on your treasures, anyway?" James asked.

"They try not to get me too excited, in case everything turns out to be fake, but so far, so good."

"Good," James said, wincing as Kate cleaned his cut. "I need wealthy friends."

Thirty-Two

Washington, D.C.

Neil Walker was at his desk in the main reading room of the Library of Congress, poring over some records from Eastern Siberia. He wasn't having much luck.

He went up into the stacks. The tight, drab stairways and cramped aisles reminded him of being below deck on a military ship. But instead of being damp, the air was kept hot and dry to prevent mildew and mold. After a couple of wrong turns, he found the section he was looking for. He was after anything that had to do with the village of Vangou, near Vladivostok, where Borodin seemed to have lived after Kulada and until the family moved to Shanghai in the spring of 1923. He couldn't find any records concerning Vangou, nothing at *all*, which was unusual. He went looking for Ernie Heighway, who was a young archivist assigned to the Library's Russian section. Heighway looked something like a mouse, a resemblance made more intense by the way he seemed to burrow into the stacks and locate documents and books almost by his sense of smell. Within ten minutes he'd pulled out three document boxes containing Red Army reports.

"I saw something about Vangou in there somewhere," Heighway drawled. "I'd swear to it."

It took Walker two hours to find it—a Red Army report about an incident that took place in the winter of 1923. Most of Vangou's inhabitants had been killed in an artillery bombardment, and *all* of

244

its buildings had burned to the ground. The deliberate obliteration of the town provoked atrocity charges by both Reds *and* Whites and eventually led to an investigation by the Bolsheviks. But the investigation failed. The Reds made nebulous charges against "White terrorist factions," but they did not succeed in learning the cause of the slaughter. The loss of records would make it tough to find out anything about the Borodins' stay in Vangou. Walker was disappointed.

He stood up. The air was stifling and he was starting to get a headache. He went to the cafeteria on the top floor of the Madison building to take a break and have lunch. The place was crammed with tourists—Germans and Scandinavians by the look of them. When in the museums and public buildings of Washington, Walker often felt he'd been transported to another part of the country. The absence of black people was strange; it depressed him.

While he sipped his coffee, he thought about the trip to Maine and his mixed feelings about it. It would be the first time since Diana's death that he and Andy would really be alone, without the distractions of Andy's school, his own work . . . and without Mrs. Bradshaw. He was worried about how it would go, and worried about the fact that all of Diana's clothing and personal belongings, which he'd packed away here, before Andy got out of the hospital, would still be there in the cabin. They'd have to go through the trauma of sorting through her things, being reminded of their loss by the bathrobe she'd never wear again, the sand dollars she'd collected, all that. He hoped it would be therapeutic for Andy and not just painful.

It was part of his routine to call his answering machine at lunch, and after he left the cafeteria, he made the call, holding the remote device up to the handset and waiting for the machine to gear up. This process always made him feel stupid and conspicuous.

There was only one message—from Mike Hale: "Hey Neil. It's Mike. Give me a call, I've got an idea."

When he got home, Walker returned Mike Hale's call.

"Hey, *Neil*, thanks for getting back to me. Hold on." Walker waited while Hale disengaged himself from another one of his many telephone lines. "Neil, sorry. I had a guy on the other line wanted to know if I could lend him a tank, you know for a *movie*. I said, come on, go to the Army, they need the publicity. A *tank*,

245

sure. I keep a fleet of spares in the south pasture. Anyway, reason I called—can you and Andrew come out tomorrow and go tubing with me? I need a day off. Bad. I'm approaching meltdown out here."

"Tubing?"

"Yeah, you ride down the Rappahannock on inner tubes. It's a lot of fun."

"Well," Walker began. "I don't know, you know Andy can't—"

"Come *on*, he'll love it. We'll put a lifejacket on him, we'll tie all the tubes together—we'll take a picnic and float it along with us."

"What the hell," Walker said. "Why not?" Tubing on the Rappahannock might be just the right thing—good preparation for sailing on the Atlantic. They made arrangements to meet at the diner in Warrenton. Hale had a mansion in horsey Middleburg, but he also had what he called his "cabin" near Warrenton, a place Walker had never seen.

"I keep my tubes at the cabin," Hale said. "It's closer to the river."

Walker worked hard the rest of the day, taking time out only to eat dinner with Andy. Andy got home from his special camp for the physically disabled at about five. When Walker was home, he watched for the yellow van-type school bus to stop outside. He began to worry if it was even five minutes late. Then he'd watch as Andy painfully made his way from the curb to the door. It seemed to take forever and every thirty seconds or so, he had the urge to run outside and carry Andy in. He succeeded in deflecting the impulse, holding his breath as Andy maneuvered up the stairs. He could so easily fall; he could so easily miss his footing and topple over, especially while he teetered on the threshold, balancing as he opened the door. Walker sat rock still waiting for the scrape of Andy's feet in the hall.

They'd agreed that even though Walker was working at home, his "work time" was to be respected and he was not to be disturbed. Andy didn't have any trouble living by this rule but Walker sometimes couldn't resist rushing downstairs when Andy got home. Today he called down from the study in a tone that tried to be casual: "Hey, Andy, how'd it go today?"

Andy answered in his deliberate, spiritless monotone: "Okay."

CHAPTER

THIRTY-THREE

The tubing trip turned out to be an ideal outing for Andy. When he was floating in the tube, strong legs didn't matter, and even out of the tubes, in shallow water, buoyant, he was able to shift around easily, walking on his hands. They drifted along on the smooth brown surface of the river. There were long, sunny stretches when the sun beating on the black rubber of the tubes produced a smell so specific it spun Walker back to his childhood; he remembered swimming with his brothers in the pond out back, diving in and out of the tubes. The black rubber got hot enough to scorch your skin. Drifting down the Rappahannock, they had water fights whenever the tubes got too hot. Then there were stretches where it was shady, where the river was overhung by trees; branches arched over them, trailing their tips in the water. Walker watched Andy reach up and let his fingers play through the leaves. A fourth tube, holding a cooler full of food, beer, and Coke, floated with them. Tethered together, the four tubes spun lazily in the current.

"Dad," Andy had said as Walker carried him to the riverside at their launching point. "Doesn't it . . . I mean, don't the tubes look like a funny molecule?"

"You're right." It was such an apt comparison, Walker felt a surge of pride. "They do. That's exactly what they look like."

"How does the kid know about molecules?" Hale asked, gesturing to the sky. "I'm completely sure I didn't know anything about molecules until I was at least—how old are you, kid?"

"Eleven."

"Until I was at *least*—" Hale paused and faked a puzzled look. "At *least* eleven and a quarter . . . maybe even eleven and a half."

They tied up for lunch around noon. Walker was lying back, looking up through the canopy of branches to the cloud-mottled sky, listening to the slosh of water against the tubes. He had that summer-day feeling, the whole day banked up behind him, as if it might last forever. Hale was joking with Andy. Their easy camaraderie reminded him how much tension there was in his own relationship with his son. He never shook the feeling that he was pressuring Andy, no matter what he did. Even when they laughed and joked together, there was a guarded quality, an unnatural cautiousness about each other's feelings. He picked a leaf off the branch and set it free; he watched the current carry it downstream.

A jeep met them a couple of miles farther downriver, and once the tubes were secured to it, they drove back to get the other cars from the launch point and then went on toward Hale's cabin. Walker followed Hale's old Blazer down a rutty dirt road.

"You having fun, Andy?"

Andy flashed him a reassuring toothpaste-ad smile. The cabin came into sight. The property was surrounded by an efficient-looking chain-link fence topped with triple strings of barbed wire. An electronic gate swung open in response to some invisible signal from Hale and they drove up toward it.

A rustic lodge incongruously furnished in hi-tech, the place had a sinister air about it that was only partially dispelled by the friendliness of Hale's housekeeper, Mrs. Garcia. Within minutes she produced a spectacular tray of snacks and a round of drinks.

The cabin was sited in such a dense grove of trees that it was almost dark inside. Track lighting illuminated the interior but failed to lift the gloom, throwing menacing shadows off the angular furniture. On the plus side, as far as Andy was concerned, there was a computer and a vast supply of Atari games. Andy shot down aliens while Hale and Walker talked.

"Tell me more about this project you're working on," Hale said. "Another provenance study?"

"A Fabergé egg."

"Really."

"Well, probably. It looks more and more like it's the real thing.

I'll tell you a story though; you'll enjoy this. There was a picture of this old man's birthday party—the old man who sent the trunk the stuff was in—and guess who was in the picture?"

"Who?"

"Val Zamatin."

"No kidding."

"*With* hair. And so I showed it to Hobie James—we were having lunch."

"How's Hobie? Still sleuthing along?"

"Hobie would call you on that, Mike. A sleuth and a spook are not the same thing, not the same at all."

"Well, if we're going to be strict."

He told Hale about Richard Sorge being in the photograph, and how Hobie James had looked in the agency files for the Sunderlands and found their files flagged. "I mean these people have been dead for thirty-five years. Thirty-five years. And their files are *flagged?* Does that make sense to you? It's a hassle for Hobie, too—he got caught, you know, got the old wrist slapped. But who would have figured . . ."

"Don't go away. I'm going for another beer. You want one?"

"Sure."

Walker joined Andy at the computer for a minute but Andy was absorbed, uncommunicative. When Walker tousled his hair, Andy shrugged his hands off and said, "Dad, you made me get killed."

Hale came back in with more drinks. "Hey, Andy, can I have a turn?"

"Sure." Hale got killed almost instantly. "Oh no, Andy, he got me, he got me—I'm deeply sorry."

"It's okay."

"Kid's got a heart of gold," Hale said. "So what was the flag?" Hale asked. "Or shouldn't I ask."

"ROMEO. Mean anything?"

"Nope. Romeo, Romeo . . . *nothing*." He tapped his temple.

Walker shrugged. "It's not important; I was just curious."

"Maybe I can find out. Want to give it a whirl?" Hale asked. "That is, if Andy will excuse us for a minute."

But Andy had fallen asleep, joystick in hand. "He still gets tired easily," Walker said and immediately regretted it. It sounded like he was apologizing. He picked up Andy and moved him to the sofa.

"We're going downstairs for a while, Mrs. G.," Hale yelled. "Keep an eye on the *niño*, okay?"

Walker followed Hale through a hall and down a short flight of stairs into a library. He wondered out loud how Hale was going to find out something like that—who a crypto belonged to.

"I've got my sources—even in the Agency, I've got my sources. It worked out more or less the way I thought it would. Officially, I'm still shunned by the Agency, but now that some of the top faces have changed, we have a (Hale made quote marks in the air) 'business relationship.' After all, I'm a real timesaver for them, sometimes. If they need some equipment quickly, if they don't want to bother setting up a dummy corporation—say it's a one-shot deal—they come to me. But as for cryptos, I just thought I'd run that through the computer.

"Information, coin of the realm, you know. The company has its profiles; I've got mine. They've got their computers; I've got mine. Hell, *I'm* even in my own computer: HALE, MICHAEL, the whole sordid story. My weaknesses, my strengths, my *curriculum vitae*. Unpredictable: that's a weakness and a strength. Amoral. Fond of his own celebrity. Easily impressed by other celebrities. That's right: my own computer calls me a starfucker. Abuses alcohol, occasionally drugs, specifically cocaine. High organizational ability, delegates responsibility well. Sexually repressed, but promiscuous typical 'macho' type. That's me: an organized, amoral, promiscuous, repressed, drunken, coked-up starfucker."

Walker watched as Hale removed two books from the bookcase and pressed a lever. The wall slid open and Walker gave a startled laugh. "Don't laugh," Hale said, "it's not polite."

"I was just . . . surprised."

"It's a little James Bond, I know."

They descended another short flight of concrete steps and went into a room hidden behind another false wall. Hale flicked on some fluorescent lights. The room was full of files, computers, telephones, utilitarian desks. Hale laughed in an embarrassed way and said in a radio voice: "And this is command central."

"I see."

"The thing to remember is that this was my first house. I hardly use it anymore, but at the time, I *wanted* all these gadgets. I built this right after I left 'government employment.' I'm surprised no one locked me up, then; I was one paranoid dude. I think you were the only one I trusted. I didn't even trust myself."

He started ticking off features on his fingers. "There's a wine cellar here, canned food for a year, rotated regularly, two separate water supplies, a well-stocked sick bay, oil tanks, various generating systems, a security system that's, well, amazing. The architect who designed the place warned me that no one would be able to stand living here for long—fortress mentality, I think that's what he called it. But at the time, I wanted to be able to withstand anything, even a nuclear attack. At the time, I wanted my own private Mount Weather."

Mount Weather, the supersecret CIA installation in Virginia, the "retreat headquarters" to which the government was to repair in case of nuclear war, was not far from Warrenton. Once, Walker had participated in the clean-up operations—during his Minuteman days—following the crash of a commercial airliner less than a mile from the Mount Weather installation.

He watched Hale fiddle with the computer. Hale kept banging on keys and the computer kept beeping at him. "Want to know the truth?" Hale asked. "I'm faking it here. I don't really know what the fuck I'm doing. Freddy—my computer man—tells me my intelligence is strictly intuitive. Being irrational, I can't 'think' like a computer, which is strictly logical. I always forget the commands, the paths, all that basic stuff. I do know how to call up the people files, though."

"Why don't you punch in Val Zamatin."

"You got it."

Walker watched the cursor blink and then the green characters appear on the screen.

ZAMATIN, VASSILY ANDREEVICH
BORN: SMOLENSK, 1915

There were no real surprises in Zamatin's dossier, but Walker knew relatively little about him, so he read with interest.

"Holy shit," Hale said. "Look at *this*." It was a printout of Zamatin's financial holdings. Some quick arithmetic showed that the Russian's personal fortune totaled nearly a million dollars. Zamatin appeared to have come by it honestly, through clever investments in Washington real estate and some smart moves on the stock market.

"Who would have thought Val would have that kind of dough?" Hale said.

"You've got this kind of shit on everyone?" Walker was amazed.

"No, you kidding?"

"I mean players."

"Well, yeah, *players*, most of them, yeah."

"This is scary as shit."

"Well, you like to deal from a position of strength, you know."

Details of Zamatin's life continued to scroll onto the screen as Hale hit the Page Down key. "What is this guy? An eagle scout? This guy's so smooth, nothing stuck to him in sixty years?"

Walker shrugged. "Is that the focus? Dirt?"

"We call it angles."

Even Zamatin's sex life seemed to be above reproach. After the death of his wife, Lisa, Zamatin remained alone for three years and then began seeing a fifty-year-old Arlington librarian named Moira Cummings, who shared his taste for opera, golf, and ballet. Under weaknesses, the computer listed: NONE EXPLOITABLE. The computer went on to assign Zamatin a high "loyalty quotient," a number Hale took exception to by pounding his fist on the desk.

"Can you believe that? Look at that astronomical loyalty quotient. This guy was a defector, after all, a goddamned traitor."

The computer finished up Zamatin's file by printing out several cross references to West German intelligence files.

"That's it?" Walker asked, disappointed.

"That's it."

"Damn. I really wanted to know more about his early days—his early career. Did you know he was part of the Sorge ring?"

Hale shrugged. "That's so long ago."

"I'd like to know when he *left* Sorge, when he crossed over—and *why*, if possible. And how he came to work for the Germans."

"Well, the West German files, you know, the Gehlen stuff, that's in another archive. I didn't bother with it when I set up the database here. I mean, the stuff is ancient history—there aren't many of those old players left in action, you know?"

"That's exactly why I find those flags Hobie tripped over so weird."

"Well, I can get the German files for you, or Freddy can anyway. I'll get a little Zamatin dossier together for you. Have it for you by the time you come back from Maine."

"Yeah?"

"Count on it. Right now I'm going to call Freddy and see if he can tell me how to find ROMEO."

Hale called, turned on the speakerphone and then sat down in front of the monitor and followed Freddy's directions exactly. Freddy snapped his gum in between spurts of rattled-off instructions, but no matter what Hale typed in, the screen informed him of failure. INVALID COMMAND. FILE DOES NOT EXIST. INCORRECT PATH.

"I'm not getting anywhere, Fred."

"Well, what we've got here is a direct read from the Agency databank, so—"

"Forget you heard that, Neil."

"Well, you know, the Agency never bothered logging in some of their older files," Freddy said. "Deliberate foot-dragging. That way, if someone asks for something—say a Freedom of Information request—the Agency gets to charge a small fortune for the physical search. Either that or the requester has to jump through hoops to get the fees waived. All that helps to slow down the march of information. But if Mike is following my instructions correctly, what we're finding out is that no one has accessed the ROMEO archive in twenty years—if they had, see, it would have been logged into the databank."

"So what you're saying is that we come up empty-handed."

"Yep."

"Thanks, Fred." Hale hung up. "Most of these computer types make me feel like an idiot," Hale said. "But Freddy's a good man. His only apparent sin is that he wears string ties."

They fooled around on the computer for a while longer, Hale calling up exotic files to show off.

"How about me?" Walker asked. "If you're in there, does that mean I am too?"

"I betcha you are." Hale punched a number of buttons and Walker's file scrolled up. He stood behind Hale and read. It was interesting, and kind of amusing, until they reached the category of VULNERABILITIES in his psychological profile. The video display terminal blandly informed him that his wife, DIANA WALKER, NEE HOLT had two affairs during his Minuteman days.

"Shit," Hale said. "Want me to turn it off? Shit."

"I might as well. . . ." His voice stopped. He felt a convulsive shift in his head, a sickening relocation of his memories: It made him dizzy; he swayed on his feet. He read the glowing green letters. "Stuart Mayfield," he heard himself say, after reading a paragraph noting a yearlong affair Diana had. His voice sounded adolescent, amazed. "Shit, I never even heard of him." Another, briefer fling was described. "Frank Hannigan," he said, in a loud, clear voice, as if he were calling roll. "How the fuck could Diana make it with Frank Hannigan? He's an asshole."

"Yeah, well," Hale said. Something about the way he said it made Walker know that Hale had known about Diana's affairs. He wheeled on him.

"You *knew*. You motherfucker. You knew and you didn't fucking tell me."

"Yeah, well, you didn't need that information at the time. You were running out of room, man, and you had more room with the lie than you had with the truth."

"How could you know that and not fucking tell me!"

"You still don't get it, do you?" Hale said. He turned off the computer and fixed Walker with his eyes. "You still don't know what kind of shape you were in? You still don't know why you popped off in Rabat. You were a fucking mess a long time before that, man. You want to know why? You want to know why I didn't tell you?" His voice had been getting louder and louder and now it fell away to a whisper. "If I'd have told you, you would have killed her, you know that? You would have flat fucking killed her."

The mood at dinner was edgy. Andy sensed that something was wrong and made some touching attempts to cheer up Mrs. Garcia, who had worked hard to prepare a Mexican feast.

"Aren't these enchiladas great, Dad? Mrs. Garcia, these are so great."

Walker kept seeing the green letters: DIANA WALKER, NEE HOLT, STUART MAYFIELD, FRANK HANNIGAN.

"Normally, he loves Mexican food, Mrs. Garcia; he must be sick."

Hale bantered halfheartedly with Andy; eventually, dinner staggered to an end. When they left, Hale gave Andy a gift—a small, hand-held computer football game. All the way home in the car, the little electronic beeps of the game irritated Walker. The arithmetic was on his mind, not just the betrayal. It was simple, it was inescapable: Andy was not necessarily his son. Somewhere near Chantilly, the annoying noise of the game seemed to penetrate to the very center of his brain.

"Turn that goddamned thing off before I throw it out the window!"

"Why are you in such a bad mood?"

For one reprehensible second, Walker was tempted to tell him the truth.

THIRTY-FOUR

Mrs. Bradshaw sailed out to the taxicab, her large hand in the air delaying its departure. "I almost forgot," she said, and pushed a little bundle of comic books through the window. "I got these for you, Andrew. Now, you take care of each other, you hear? I'm going to miss you."

"I wish you could come," Andy said.

"And don't you go forgetting that lobster you promised to bring back."

"I won't."

They boarded the plane early, along with the mothers and infants, the aged, the infirm. An emaciated woman whom they'd seen earlier was moved from a motorized wheelchair covered with FULL ACCESS bumper stickers into a regular chair. She gave Andy a jaunty wave as they rolled up the ramp, but Andy pretended not to see her. He didn't like to think of himself as part of her club, the permanently disabled.

Without people on board, the plane looked alarmingly small, no more than a metal lozenge with an upholstered interior. Andy had never been a carefree flier, but during takeoff his squeezed-shut eyes, his rigid jaw showed the new strength of his fear. Walker put his hand on his son's arm to reassure him, but Andy was inside his fear; he didn't even seem to feel the hand. Perhaps he'd made some deal with the future: *if I don't move, everything will be all right.* It made Walker sad. It was unfair that a child should be scared like that, to know he can die. As a boy, he himself had been not so much brave but fearless, reckless. Fear had cheated his son of that freedom.

Driving from the Portland airport to the cabin, an hour's ride, Andy hailed each landmark according to a routine established before he could even talk. "There's the big Indian!" "The shacks, we're not far now." "There's the frog rock!" Andy coated his voice with enthusiasm, but at each consecutive landmark, it rang more and more false. Walker heard Diana in Andy's voice. She'd identified these features as notable punctuations, used these landmarks to build a crescendo of excitement at the end of the long drive. They crossed the bridge on Berry's Mill Road, over the tidal New Meadows River. "Look," Andy said, still following the routine, "it's low tide." His voice seemed incredibly slow, as if it barely had the velocity to break the sound barrier.

The arrival at the cottage was much worse than Walker thought. It was as if the place belonged to Diana—with few traces of his and Andy's existence. Of course, when he thought about it, it made sense. He and Andy had spent most of their time outside, fishing, sailing, rowing, while Diana had been inside, reading the books that were everywhere, doing needlepoint or crewel work. There was the "existential" sampler she'd brought from Alexandria, the one that read: MAYBE I WILL AND MAYBE I WON'T. WHAT IF I DO AND WHAT IF I DON'T. Here was the antique table they'd found on one of their expeditions; he could remember it, tied to the top of the car, then out in the yard while she refinished it. An image of her came to him: scraping mushy varnish off, wearing yellow rubber gloves, warning a six-year-old Andy about the dangers of the stripping solution.

He went around turning things on, noticing the dust, the cobwebs, the mouse droppings. A two-year accumulation because they'd never made it last year, because . . . He threw the switch for the electricity, connected the pump. The water gushed out, rusty brown and he let it run until it cleared. He asked Andy to set the clocks and opened a can of Dinty Moore stew for dinner.

He banged the plates onto the table, thinking about Diana's affairs. The names rushed into his head: *Stuart Mayfield, Frank Hannigan.* It was so unlucky that he'd found out, so fucking unlucky. Nothing good could come from knowing she'd cheated on him. Only doubt and a feeling of betrayal so powerful he wanted to take back part of the grief he'd felt. Cheated on, cuckolded *from the grave.* He gave a nasty laugh as he dished up the stew. Andy said: "What's funny?" with a worried look.

"Nothing."

"What's the matter, Dad?"

"Nothing."

"You don't have to bite my head off." It was Diana's expression, said in exactly her self-righteous tone.

The stew looked like dog food. He stabbed a piece of meat.

"I'm tired," he said lamely. It was the best he could do.

"Well, we made it," Andy said, continuing to sound just like his mother. There was something not quite perfect about the way Diana pronounced the "l" sound, and Andy had inherited or copied it, some looseness, some lack of contact between the tongue and the palate. "Well, here we are."

Later, he helped Andy to bed and then sat in the living room reading *Newsweek.* But the walls of the cabin were thin, just the thickness of the boards, and he heard Andy's muffled weeping. When he went in, he saw that Andy was hiding under the covers. He put his hand on his son's quilt covered back: "I miss her too, my man, I miss her too."

Andy struggled free of the quilts and flailed at his father's comforting hand. "You don't! You don't! I saw you in there, packing her stuff away, putting all her stuff in a box. You want to forget her. You want to get *over* it—like it's being sick." His wheezing voice was almost unintelligible. "But I don't *want* to get over it. I don't *want* to forget her and I won't. I will *never ever ever forget.* Never."

"I don't want you to forget her, Andy; and I don't ever want to forget her either."

"Then why are you getting rid of everything that was hers? I want her stuff around. That's all that's left." He'd begun to sob.

He tried to put his arms around Andy, but Andy made it clear that he wouldn't allow that; he was intent on their being adversaries.

"I'm not, Andy, I'm not. It's hard enough trying not to think of her every second; I don't need reminders. She's in my head."

258

"Well, I do. I DO! I don't want to forget. That's when I'm happy—when I'm sad, when I'm thinking about Mom. That's when I'm happiest."

"You're happiest when you're saddest?" He knew he shouldn't fall back on this, but he heard himself say: "Mom wouldn't want that. Do you think Mom would want that?"

"You don't know! You don't know what Mom would want. You're not like Mom at all."

Andy's therapist had suggested once that it might be good if Walker lost control a little, if he cried, if he showed that the grief wasn't Andy's private possession, that they were in it together. He moved from the bed, and stood up. He leaned against the wall, face to it, hands wide to the side, as if he were about to be frisked. The air between the wall and his face seemed incredibly hot, as if he were standing too close to a fire. He relaxed his grip on his feelings just a little, but even that was too much. It was as if he'd stepped into a reality of pain and rage that some mechanism of his mind had been keeping from him. It made his head hurt and he knocked it hard, *very* hard against the wall; for a few seconds, he saw pulsating silver dots and his sense of balance was gone. His hands went up to hide his face and a gigantic sob drew his breath in a gasp.

It was just habit that was keeping him upright; he'd almost hit his head against the wall hard enough to knock himself out. When he saw the blank look of fear on Andy's face, and the rigid, defensive pose of his body, he knew that letting Andy see his grief was a mistake. No matter what the therapist said, what Andy needed more than anything was to know that life went on, that his father wasn't going to abandon him too—die, or flip out or be anything other than totally reliable.

He thought about Rabat.

He made a joke about walking into a wall and pretended nothing much had happened. "I'm not very good at talking about this, Andy," he said, covering.

Andy visibly relaxed and some of his hostility returned. "Can I go to sleep now?" he demanded.

They spent Wednesday getting things together—shopping for groceries and putting the sailboat, a seventeen-foot O'Day Day-sailor, in the water. They wouldn't bother putting the dock in for just a week. Their neighbor Cal Tuttle, father of Walker's boyhood friend Billy, who had been killed in Vietnam, had offered to let them use his dock. Walker had gratefully accepted.

When the water was high enough, Walker and Rusty O'Keefe, the lobsterman who also tended the launching ramp, floated the boat into the water. Walker sailed to the mooring in front of the cabin slowly; there was almost no wind. Cal Tuttle and Andy were on the dock, fishing with drop lines. "We'll just give it another twenty minutes," Cal said. "Then I'll drive you back over to pick up your car. By th' way—had a telephone call for you—foreign-sounding fellow—Mr. . . . em . . . Mikowski?"

"Michalowski?"

"Yah, well, whatever. Number's in there by the phone. He'd like for you to call him back."

"Mind if I do?"

There was a little pause. "He did specify you could call collect. Also, first you got to check—I'm on an eight-party line and the Bartells have three teenagers."

It was not a good connection, and they had to talk over ghost voices on the line and bursts of static. Walker kept hearing a woman's detached, eerie laughter. Michalowski told him that Nicola Ward had found another document; apparently it had been wedged into the packing crate that had contained the trunk. "Since you're up there anyway, I thought you might want to see what it is. Take her out to lunch on us. I asked her to send me a copy for the file, but maybe you can do that for her."

Walker agreed. Then a barrage of static set in and they said good-bye.

He called Nicola Ward but got a busy signal. Outside, Cal and Andy had given up on fishing and were stowing their gear. Cal drove them back to Langan's Cove to pick up their car.

Afterward, he went back in with Cal to call Nicola Ward.

"Why, I know Nicola," Tuttle said. "She was married to Stanley Ward until he left her and ran off to California. The Wards have lived here since creation and then Stanley takes off like that. Mrs. Ward teaches school over to Thomas Point. You say hello for me."

He promised he would.

CHAPTER

THIRTY-FIVE

Even as he was flying over the Atlantic Ocean, Vassily Zamatin was forgetting what Sardinia was like. That was the trouble with holidays, he thought. He always expected a transition period to exist, a time when he still felt relaxed and soothed by his trip, restored, his "batteries recharged," as Dottie put it, but it never seemed to work that way. As soon as he began the return journey, it was as if he'd never left.

Already it was a struggle to hold in his mind the sensual impact of the Italian island: the saltwater smell, the texture of the sand, the taste of the food he'd eaten. Already he was forgetting the spectacular mountains, the olive trees, the lemon groves, the sound of Italian voices. His mind was done with Sardinia; it had turned to unfinished projects at the Agency, to phone calls he needed to make, to the household tasks that would have accumulated during his absence.

The next day, at the office, he presented Dottie with a finely carved music box that played the Surprise Symphony, and immediately set to work on the mass of papers that had engulfed his In basket and filled two other wire file baskets stacked behind it.

It was almost noon, almost time to break for lunch, when he got to the folder containing a report from Centerfile informing him that access had been requested to some files flagged to his crypto, ROMEO. He looked at the yellow slip and saw that the requested files were the dossiers on Tony and Dasha Sunderland. If Dottie had come in at that moment, she might have thought he was suffering a coronary because he actually pressed his right hand, spread wide, up against his chest, as if it could suppress the irregular beat of his heart. He removed his hand to turn the page, to read the routine Office of Security report on the requested access to flagged files, and was shocked, for the second time, to see the name Hobart James listed as the requester. He repeated the name, moving his lips but not producing any sound. Hobie James. Hobie James. Why?

He shouldn't have to deal with this. He only had five months to go until retirement; he didn't feel like dealing with this. First the DANTE investigation and now this. It was unfair. He composed himself, annoyed with that surge of self-pity and read on.

Hobart James told his inquisitor, Gerald Knowles, that the reason he'd requested access to the files was that he was doing a favor for a friend. Neil Walker, friend and ex-Agency colleague, had run across the names of Dasha and Anthony Sunderland in the course of a genealogical study he was conducting. Walker had thought the pair might have espionage connections, and in view of Walker's recent tragedy, Hobart James hadn't seen "the harm" in "taking a look."

Zamatin let a sigh ease out between his lips. At least he could feel safe that Hobie would be unable to find out who the crypto ROMEO was assigned to. Basic Agency security procedures (and the protection of virtually all its agents and operations) depended on the absolute sanctity of cryptonym assignment. Beyond the simple secret, top-secret, Q-clearance, C-clearance classifications, most really sensitive material was accessed by cryptonym on a strictly need-to-know basis. Naturally, the assignment and retrieval system of cryptos was based on fabulously complex computer procedures, those procedures themselves controlled by random changing codes and protected further by various traps to snare and even identify the unauthorized. After already running afoul of procedure by requesting files without a sound reason for doing so, Hobie would hardly risk unauthorized rummaging through cryptonym assignment data.

There was a form attached to the OS report, asking for Zamatin's disposition. Since Hobie James hadn't been seeking access to the files for Agency purposes, the normal option, to grant access, had already been crossed out by Knowles. Zamatin's other choices were to request a further inquiry by OS, or to let matters stand as

262

they were. He ticked off the NO ACTION box and put the file into his Out basket. It was certainly not a matter he wished to pursue formally.

Another long sigh escaped his lips. He remembered well when the flags were first attached to the Sunderlands' files. And still, after forty years, he could easily summon to mind a mental image of the beautiful Dasha and her earnest, charming husband, Tony. He sighed again, a deep, weary sound. He couldn't believe those flags had finally been tripped after all this time.

Neil Walker. He buzzed Dottie and asked her to get Neil Walker on the telephone. He'd received a telephone call *from* Neil Walker while he'd been away; it was on his list of calls to return. But Dottie buzzed to say that she had Walker's housekeeper on the other line. "You know Mr. Walker called when *you* were on vacation and now *he's* on vacation. Would you like to leave a message? Or get the number where he is?" Zamatin hesitated. It wouldn't look right for him to call Walker while the man was on vacation; it would look too eager. "No," he told Dottie, "never mind. Just tell her I was returning his call. Then see if you can get me Hobie James."

He'd have to have lunch with Hobie, easy enough to arrange since they were friends. He'd find some way to turn their conversation to Neil Walker and hope that Hobie would take it from there, and solve the mystery of Walker's interest in Dasha and Tony Sunderland.

"I have Mr. James on the line," Dottie said.

"Hello, Hobie."

"Hey," said Hobie James in his buoyant voice. "I heard you were away, Val. *Sardinia*. How was it?"

"You certainly can't keep a secret around here. It was delightful; I have a secret passion for islands, you know."

"I didn't know. I'm sure that says something about your character."

"Oh, I don't think so." Zamatin laughed. "Now I'm calling because I have a not-so-secret passion for sushi, which I could not find on Sardinia. I was hoping I could talk you into lunch."

"Name the day."

"How about . . . tomorrow? Not to make a bad pun, but I have more than just a yen. . . ."

Hobie groaned at the pun. "Sure. I can make it tomorrow—just tell me where and when."

"How about Matuba, in Arlington, at one?"

"Great. I look forward to it."

When he hung up, Zamatin thought about the pun—it reminded him that he didn't even *think* in Russian anymore—instead, he made puns in English. Perhaps this was the key to assimilation—one's sense of humor seemed to him enmeshed in language.

He leaned back in his chair and looked at the ceiling. Images of Dasha and Tony swam into his head. He wondered what he'd do if it happened today—if Center ordered him to betray a string of comrades today as they had back then in Shanghai—he wondered if he'd do it. He thought maybe not.

When he was first sent from Moscow to Shanghai to take command of the Lotus cell of Sorge's spy network, he'd been thrilled. The previous commander had contracted severe malaria and Zamatin had felt flattered to have been selected. He'd been so naive.

It was ironic that in the end the Sorge ring's very success doomed it. Once the ring learned that Japan was going to push south, and not into Russia, its espionage operation in the east was unnecessary to Moscow; it would serve little purpose in the European war that Russia would now have to fight. Moscow's new priority in espionage was to penetrate the Nazi Intelligence apparat (Foreign Armies East of the Wehrmacht) masterminded by Reinhard Gehlen. And Moscow saw a functional way to do so—by sacrificing the obsolete Sorge network.

And he, Val Zamatin, was the instrument of that sacrifice. He was told exactly how to do it. He approached a certain Nazi Intelligence official in Shanghai. When he made contact with this man, he bought him several drinks and in the course of the evening told him that he had no faith in the Russian cause, that he was certain the Nazis would emerge triumphant at the war's end. He, Vassily Zamatin, was prepared to expose the most important spy ring in the East in return for three things. He'd pretended to be quite drunk himself—even today he could recall the way he'd held up his left hand and tugged on his fingers for emphasis.

His first demand was a job—he wanted a continuing relationship with Wehrmacht intelligence. The second was a sum of money

264

deposited in a Zurich bank. The third was that his sick mother, who needed an operation on her eyes unavailable in Moscow, be brought to Zurich and given that operation.

Negotiations took about three weeks, but in the end the Nazis accepted Zamatin's deal, in effect embracing a double agent. The exposure of Sorge and Miyagi had rocked the diplomatic and business communities in Tokyo and Shanghai. Zamatin's bona fides were proven, so far as the Nazis were concerned, by the scope of his betrayal—over forty persons were arrested in the mop-up.

Shortly after the deal was struck, and before the ring was exposed, Zamatin left Shanghai for Zurich. He'd been in Zurich only a few days when the news began to surface—the spy ring shattered, everyone arrested. He'd gone on a terrible drunk, a monumental bender. Even though his mind accepted that the end justified the means, that his act was for the overall good—in his soul he felt like a traitor. Nothing could eliminate his sense of guilt—he lived with it still.

General Reinhard Gehlen, the chief of the Wehrmacht's 12th Branch, which handled all intelligence pertaining to the East, had impressed Zamatin more than any other superior he'd worked under. The man was sharp, energetic, relentlessly thorough. The intelligence he fed to Hitler was correct and would have been invaluable except that it was so often ignored. Gehlen's correct warnings and Gehlen's correct estimates of Soviet troop strength did not help Germany's cause because the Fuehrer preferred his astrologists, his occult soothsayers, his fire-and-ice theories. Gehlen was nearly driven insane—that Hitler should base tactical decisions on notions that the Aryan flame of Nazism would melt the ice of Russia, rather than on Gehlen's carefully collected data.

But if Hitler couldn't see which way the wind was blowing in 1945, Reinhard Gehlen could—and he took his entire team, which by then, of course, included Zamatin, to the Alps, hoping to work out a separate deal with the Allies. He surrendered not to the Army, but specifically to the OSS. He'd carried with him to the Alps a complete set of microfilmed records of his unit's files—a treasure trove for Allied Intelligence and his main bargaining chip. He offered his records and his apparat to the Allies in return for immunity from prosecution and a continuing role as spymaster.

Allied officials were beginning to see that the next worldwide conflict would be with the Soviet Union, and Gehlen's offer was accepted. The OSS took under its protection Reinhard Gehlen and his apparat—his network of agents within the Soviet Union and the Balkan states—and, not least, his files. It also took under its wing Vassily Zamatin.

And so it was that Zamatin came to work for his new employers, the Americans—although for a while he continued to work directly under Gehlen. First he was assigned to OSS Frankfurt, then to the compound at Pullach, near Munich. At Pullach, Zamatin's duties included recruiting agents in Displaced Persons camps—agents who would work in the Ukraine, Poland, Czechoslovakia, spying for the United States against the Soviets. There were some serious attempts to revive decimated anti-Soviet partisan groups in these areas. Vassily Zamatin did what he could, and actually it was quite a bit, to see that U.S. attempts to recruit anti-Soviet agents were doomed to failure.

Zamatin had a long and distinguished career working for U.S. Intelligence. In 1946, the United Sates, which, unlike the Soviet Union or Great Britain, had never maintained a permanent intelligence service (what use are spies in peacetime?) finally created, out of the shreds of the OSS what was ultimately called the Central Intelligence Agency. In 1947, Vassily Zamatin was transferred from Pullach, Germany, to Washington, D.C., where he became part of the Soviet Bloc Division of the fledgling CIA. And so it was that from the beginning the CIA was compromised by a well-placed double agent.

And now, in 1980, that well-placed agent was looking forward to his gold watch, his farewell dinner, his well-earned retirement. He was looking forward to his CIA pension, to the income from his wise capitalist investments. He was looking forward to giving up the game at last. And he didn't want ghosts from the past—Dasha and Tony Sunderland—interfering with his plans.

THIRTY-SIX

Nicola Ward answered on the first ring. When Walker explained Michalowski's suggestion that he come and look at the document she'd found, she suggested the next afternoon.

He and Andy had planned a sail, so they settled on Friday. He suggested lunch, but she said she'd rather not drive into town, and they agreed to have coffee at her place. She began to give him lengthy and complicated directions about how to reach her cabin. He wrote them down carefully, but then she said, "You know, it's a whole lot closer by water." She described how her cabin looked from the water. It was right at the mouth of the cove, a natural gray cedar cabin with green-painted trim. She described the dock. "The dinghy is tied up to the dock with the name SAUCER painted on it."

"About three-thirty?" It was a time he selected to minimize Andy's problems with docks and ramps. Their boating activities would be more or less controlled by the tide.

"We'll look for you then," she said, "by land or by sea."

"Cal Tuttle said to say hello. He's my neighbor."

Her voice was animated. "Tell him Kate and I say hello back. Good night."

He and Andy went back next door and built a fire in the wood stove and played a few games of Mastermind. It had been a good day, and after Andy went to bed Walker stood on the deck watching the boats bob in the gentle chop until the mosquitoes drove him in. The boats swung around in the current, and he liked hearing the faint sounds they made as the water slapped their hulls and the wind rattled their halyards. A big boat was making its way past the point—he heard the low hum of its engine and saw the green running lights. The bell buoy near the spindle marker almost a mile away across the water was audible too, ringing in rhythm with the waves.

The next day the breeze was stiff, and they enjoyed their teamwork as they tacked out from the cabin. Andy worked the jib better than ever and Walker complimented him on it.

"You haven't forgotten a thing. We're *moving*."

"Well, you know, my arms are stronger now, Dad. Not only that, but I do more things with them—you know, they're *better*."

"I guess you're right. Look at that—a seal." Andy watched for the seal to surface and it did, almost next to them. Andy laughed and the seal dived under again.

"Mr. Tuttle says there's lots of seals this year."

"That's good; that probably means lots of fish."

On the run back in, Andy went to the back of the boat and set out a line for mackerel, even though they usually didn't bite once the tide had turned.

Walker lay back, suffused with contentment—listening to the hiss of water under them, the clacking of gulls passing overhead, watching the concentrated pleasure on Andy's face as he let out the trolling line. Then Andy had a strike that nearly yanked him off his feet and managed to reel in five good-sized mackerel at once without losing a single one.

"God, Dad, *five!*" Andy said. He was so excited and happy that for a moment he forgot and said, "Five at once! Wait till I tell Mom!"

Mom. The word hung there between them, heavy, immovable. Walker said, "Mom would be really amazed, Andy."

"Yeah," Andy said, removing the last fish from the hook and flipping it into the bucket. "She'd be amazed." His voice was subdued, sober.

"You know," Walker started, you know . . . I know it seems to you that I'm trying to forget Mom, that I don't miss her as much as you do." Andy wouldn't look at him. "But . . ." He couldn't find the right words, but he kept trying. "When you were in the hospital, I well, sometimes I couldn't stand it, I was so sad. You were struggling to stay alive and get better and I tried to keep myself from being a basket case for your sake, but I—"

"Sometimes," Andy interrupted, "I think it was my fault and I can't get that thought out of my mind and it . . . it drives me so crazy to have that thought in my head."

"Why do you think it's your fault?"

"Because"—Andy struggled for composure—"because . . . Mom wouldn't have driven up there except for me. She would have waited for you."

Walker put his hand on Andy's arm, and this time Andy seemed to sag into him a little instead of stiffening away from the contact. "I can't stop feeling guilty either because I keep thinking if I hadn't gone . . . you know . . . to Finland—I keep thinking if I was there, in the car, it wouldn't have happened."

A motorboat with a bunch of kids wearing orange lifejackets passed them. The kids waved and Andy waved back.

"You know what I really think?" Walker said. "I think feeling guilty is a way of trying to make ourselves responsible for what was purely an accident. And I think it's because feeling responsible seems better—I mean, if something is your *fault*, that's better than having things just *happen* to you."

"Maybe you're right. Maybe if you didn't feel like it was your fault or something, you'd just lay there and go 'Okay, now what?' And you'd just wait there, you know, like a blob."

As Walker tied up, he felt the trip had already accomplished a lot—just forcing the two of them together, forcing them to talk. Some positive feeling might be able to develop between them, to replace the tension, the carefulness that had been stifling their relationship.

He carried Andy up to the cabin and went back to clean the fish. They'd invited Cal Tuttle to dinner.

"You going to try a mackerel tonight, Andrew?" Cal asked as they sat down to the table.

"Yuck, are you kidding? Pass me the hot dogs." There was a pause. "Please."

269

When it was time for Cal Tuttle to go home, Neil went with him. Outside, in the dark, Cal seemed old to him for the first time. He was hesitant; his eyesight couldn't cope with the darkness. He moved slowly and carefully, making sure of where he put his feet.

Thirty-Seven

Arlington, Virginia

Matuba was an unpretentious restaurant in Arlington, known for its good fresh sushi. It shared the block with a Korean Tae Kwon Do school and a Vietnamese grocery; across the street was a Thai restaurant. This Oriental monopoly was interrupted only by St. Coletta's Thrift Shop.

As Val Zamatin walked by St. Coletta's, his eyes met those of the manager, who was in the display window holding a large, grotesque doll by the hair. The man gave Zamatin a rueful smile. A row of the huge, ugly identical dolls festooned the window, their plastic faces staring out. One eye of each was fixed in a grotesque, lewd wink; mammoth orange freckles disfigured their porcine cheeks. The dolls looked new, donated to St. Coletta's. And no wonder.

Zamatin turned from the shabby street into Matuba's and into an oasis of elegant order. The waiting area was separated from the restaurant proper by shoji screens. A black lacquered bench was provided; a window shelf was full of combed gray pebbles, a bonsai in one corner. He wondered if the spare elegance of Japanese culture was the result of the premium their crowded islands placed on space, or if it proceeded from the austere nature of Zen. . . . But then he spotted Hobie James gesturing to him from a table in the back. Hobie was drinking a Sapporo.

"Hey, Val." The two men shook hands. "You're looking well. I usually come back from vacation frazzled; it takes me a couple of weeks of working to get back into shape."

"I kept thinking—this is my *last* vacation; soon I'll be retired and the concept of the vacation will be gone from my life." Zamatin gave Hobie a smile that had a tinge of sadness in it.

Hobie had the wiry fit look of the serious runner, but his baby face—which looked even more infantile because he was nearly bald—didn't seem to belong to his angular body. He brushed his hand over his little tuft of red hair and lifted his glass in a semi-salute and said, "I can't *wait* to retire—personally, I can't wait."

Zamatin shrugged. "You have your book."

"Hell, there's always consulting—if you can't handle that much leisure."

Zamatin shrugged again. He was cultivating a slightly depressed look so that Hobie would feel compelled to cheer him up. "I need some wasabi, some yellowtail, some—"

"Hey, darlin'," Hobie said to the kimono-clad waitress. "Can you take our order?" She bowed slightly and giggled. "I'm in love," Hobie said. "Go ahead, Val, your choice."

Zamatin rattled off his order, which was specific and extensive. "And two more Sapporos, or Kirins, or whatever is coldest."

"So," Hobie said, draping his arm over the chair next to him, "what do you think of the circus in Teheran?"

"The blame will probably come to us," Zamatin said, "faulty intelligence or something."

"Well, there probably was some 'faulty intelligence.' Count on it. That's the problem with public perception—they see the intelligence community as some monolith, whereas it seems to me—well, less like a *community*, even, than a collection of fiefdoms. And which way we go depends on which warlord has the ear of the king."

"But it's *Agency* funding that will suffer," Zamatin said, wondering how he was going to turn the conversation toward Shanghai, toward Neil Walker. "CIA is the most *visible*." He paused. "I wonder how the president feels about his human rights initiative in Iran now that we have the spectacle of people being hung in public."

"Surprised. I think the man has a tremendous capacity for being

272

surprised." Hobie cocked his head. "Of course, that's probably to his credit."

Hobie shifted in his chair. The waitress brought two bowls of miso and their beers, and a little while later two boards of sushi glistening with fish and rice. A small pyramid of pink, translucent slices of pickled ginger was heaped on each board, along with a healthy smear of chartreuse wasabi horseradish. "Hey, darling, do they play golf in Japan?" Hobie asked the waitress. She giggled.

"Some," she said. "Yeh."

"No kidding?" Hobie said.

"You keep talking," Zamatin suggested. "I cannot wait any longer." He lifted a piece of tekka-maki with his chopsticks, delicately picked up a single slice of ginger, rubbed it into the wasabi, dipped the whole thing into his soy sauce, and popped it into his mouth. The explosion of horseradish was almost orgasmic.

"Two bald men," Hobie said, shaking his head, "eating raw fish. Who would have thought?" They both laughed. He popped a bite into his mouth. Hobie ate incredibly fast, as if it were unnecessary for him to chew. "Hey hey *hey*—I saw a picture of you the other day *with* hair."

"Oh . . ." Zamatin was not fully paying attention. He'd lost his hair early, starting in his late twenties. "That would be quite an antique. Where was that?"

"You were even better-looking with hair, Val—I hate to say it. I like to think the smooth look is *more* attractive, but—"

"Where was this—this artifact?" Zamatin said. He forced himself to relax but already he had a light, spongy feeling in his chest and the sushi tasted like nothing at all.

"Neil Walker," Hobie said between bites. "I was having lunch with him the other day. He had it. He promised to get me a copy, for my collection, you know, maybe even for the book. Hey, speaking of the book—I'd like to pick your brains about that. I knew you were acquainted with Richard Sorge—I knew you were *associated* but I didn't know you were *friends*." Hobie's voice was reverential. "I didn't know you went to *birthday* parties with the guy."

The plunging sensation within Zamatin deepened. He felt hollowed out, almost out of breath. The worst had happened. In a way he felt almost peaceful.

273

"Whose birthday was it?" he heard himself ask, but he was stalling, obscuring his agitation. He already knew the answer. He'd only been photographed at *one* birthday party with Richard Sorge and he remembered it perfectly. He listened to himself say, "I went to lots of birthday parties."

"It was an old man—let's see, what did Neil say? Borodin? Does that ring a bell?"

"Ah yes." Zamatin pretended to search his memory for the first name to go with the surname. "Sergei . . . it was Sergei Borodin. We used his café in Shanghai as a meeting place. His granddaughter . . . she . . . ah . . . she worked with us." He tapped his chopsticks on his dipping plate. "I wonder what ever happened to her. I left, you know, I was out of Shanghai by the time things fell apart there. I was lucky."

Hobie inhaled a piece of California roll. "How did you end up? Getting out, I mean."

"Well," Zamatin sighed. Was it possible Hobie didn't know his story? He thought not. Hobie was just being polite. "Well," he said again, "this is still kind of personal—and I am still feeling bad about this even now." He studied his fingernails. He had told this particular set of lies so often, it had the ring of truth to him now. Even to his own ear, it sounded convincing. He ran through the story about his mother being ill. He looked at the ceiling for a moment, as if seeking to compose himself. "And . . . and she wasn't going to get any help in Moscow. We were from an aristocratic background and, well, you know . . . you Americans don't understand class hatred . . . once that particular beast is unchained . . ." He shook his head and had a sip of beer.

He told Hobie James about how he'd made a deal with the Nazis, although he didn't elaborate. "Not that I was a Nazi, you know, but they were the only customers interested in Russian spies at that time." He laughed.

"What was *that* like, working for the Nazis?"

He was ready to talk about that, a subject that posed no threat. "It wasn't so different from working for Moscow. For one thing, I wasn't a Bolshevik, so it wasn't as if I was abandoning my . . . faith, you know. And I was quite young—at an age when saving your parent seems like a tremendous thing. Also you don't tend to plan ahead that much at that age. If I had . . . I don't know what

I was thinking would happen—after the war I would join my mother in Zurich and become a banker or something? I just was going along day by day." He laughed and shook his head.

"Working for Gehlen—well, most of the Germans were not Nazis, just as I wasn't a Bolshevik. We operated like a think tank. A lot of the Germans thought their Fuehrer was more than slightly cuckoo—including Gehlen. They were professional—their attitude was very businesslike and that's the way I tried to be, too."

A woman behind him laughed—a high-pitched whinny, and he heard her companion say, "I told you, I told you." He looked up at Hobie James, who had devoured his plate of sushi and was now fishing single grains of rice out of his dipping plate with his chopsticks. Zamatin wanted to turn the conversation back to Neil Walker. "I wish you'd tell me how is it that Neil Walker came to have this ancient picture of me. Of this, I am really curious."

Hobie leaned back in his chair. "I know Neil wanted to talk to you—he was hoping you could help him. He thought he'd be all done by the time you got back. Hell, he probably is all done. I don't think he'd mind if I told you about it." He signaled to the waitress. "How about some tea, darlin'? Val?"

"Coffee."

"The picture turned up in a trunk old Borodin shipped outa Shanghai in the late thirties. It was addressed to his grandchild, and to make a long story short, she got it forty years late. You know, she was a baby when it was sent, and she got it in the middle of her midlife crisis." Hobie laughed. "Anyway, there were some things in the trunk that are worth money—some jewelry, that kind of thing."

"I see."

"Neil's doing a provenance study for one of those auction outfits."

"It must be—I remember this baby! What was her name?" He took a sip of coffee. Dasha had always wept when her child was mentioned, and when he'd lived in Shanghai, he'd had the impression the baby had been stillborn or died in infancy. Her grief had seemed too profound to allow for inquiries. Later, he'd learned the truth—that she had sent her baby from Shanghai shortly before his own arrival.

"I don't recall," Hobie said, and then the waitress came with the check. Hobie tried to grab it, but Zamatin made the waitress give it to him. "My turn," he said. "Tell Neil I'm happy to help—if he still needs it. When does he come back—do you know?"

"I think it's just a week. He should be back this weekend." Hobie's eyes did a quick flick to his watch. "Shit, for someone who eats too fast, it always seems to take longer than I expect." He immediately stood up. "I'm gone. Thanks, Val." Zamatin watched him rush out the door.

CHAPTER
THIRTY-EIGHT

Zamatin took the rest of the afternoon off. He went directly home from Matuba, called Dottie, and told her not to expect him back, then poured himself a stiff bourbon, and took it out back to his deck. He stretched out on the redwood chaise and sloshed the whiskey around in his mouth. The smoky taste soothed him and deepened his contemplative mood, and he sat there in the dappled shade of the big oak tree thinking about that damn photograph Dasha had taken and how much trouble and aggravation it had caused. He set his drink down on the glass-topped wrought-iron table and somehow was not surprised a few seconds later when an acorn fell directly into it. He fished it out and lobbed it toward the rose garden. He was remembering Shanghai, remembering the day the photograph was taken.

He'd had no sense, at the time, that there was anything fateful about the day—except that Sorge himself was in town, and that was unusual—Zamatin had only met the man on one other occasion.

He could recall his own sweaty anticipation as he'd dressed for the party. He'd been as nervous as a teenager, checking his appearance in the mirror—twice—before setting out. He wanted Sorge to have a good impression.

Dasha was a girl who loved celebrations: she seized on any excuse to have a party. She'd invited every member of the Lotus cell plus about a dozen other people. And so, the back room at the Celeste was covered with banners she'd run off in the print shop—HAPPY BIRTHDAY SERGEI emblazoned everywhere. She'd fixed a cluster of balloons and ribbons to the ceiling. She'd even dressed up—Zamatin was used to seeing her in her dingy print-shop clothes—in a red sequined dress. He'd always thought of Dasha as attractive, but for the first time she provoked in him a sharp twist of desire; he wondered if she took lovers.

Crazy Anna, Sergei's oldest daughter, had obviously spent the week cooking because one long table was covered with food, and Anna stood blushing, shifting from foot to foot, both embarrassed and thrilled by the frequent compliments about her culinary skills. "Ya," she would reply, to each compliment, and then look at the floor.

Sergei was standing in the corner when Zamatin arrived, drinking vodka with an unfamiliar man with a huge mustache. Sorge kept flirting with Dasha shamelessly, and several times during the evening, Zamatin saw her physically remove his hand from her bottom. She was embarrassed and angry, but she obviously didn't want to make a scene. Tony Sunderland, too, was clearly annoyed by Sorge's behavior but restrained his anger.

After all, Sorge was their leader—he'd started coming to the Café Celeste when he'd been a newcomer to Shanghai and he'd made it his unofficial headquarters. Eventually, he'd recruited Dasha Borodin—it was Sorge himself who'd insisted she attend classes to learn printing and photography. And long before Dasha had married Tony Sunderland, Sorge had recruited the idealistic young Brit as well.

But there was no question that the great Sorge was getting on Tony's nerves that night, and the drunker Sorge became, the worse it got and it almost reached the point where Tony Sunderland looked likely to lose his composure and deliver a punch or two.

Zamatin remembered young Dante catching his eye and raising his eyebrows at one of Sorge's particularly lewd remarks. Maybe to get out of Sorge's way, to keep busy and establish some distance from him, Dasha dragged out her camera and began snapping pictures. Sorge was distracted enough to shift his amorous impulses toward a girl named Lily and the two of them sat on the couch—Lily on Sorge's lap.

"Give him a kiss then, Lily," Dasha encouraged, and photographed the ensuing clinch.

Zamatin stood in the corner, appalled. He'd been warned before he was sent to Shanghai that the tradecraft of the Sorge ring was sloppy, but he couldn't believe Dasha was actually taking photographs. He firmly believed the credo "no postcards, no photographs, no souvenirs."

And then matters became worse. Crazy Anna trundled in, carrying the birthday cake, her goofy grin even stranger than usual, and Sorge himself summoned the entire Lotus cell to the table. They toasted Sergei's health and Sergei, illuminated by the blaze of candles on his cake, blew mightily at it, spraying saliva in the process. The flashbulbs partially blinded Zamatin and ghost explosions flickered annoyingly in his eyes. Anna was dishing up the cake; Dasha was taking a photo of Sorge and Lily, who were stuffing cake into each other's mouths. Sergei was pouring champagne. Tony Sunderland and Dante were attempting a Russian dance. Zamatin stepped back.

In his mind's eye, he could already imagine the photograph of the group being extracted from a manila envelope in a court of law. He could imagine the grease pencil mark around his own face.

You don't take pictures of a spy ring! An idea came to him—how to destroy the film without making a scene. He called Dasha over.

"We don't have any pictures of you, Dasha!"

"Oh well—" she said in English, and gave him a sweet, happy smile. "It's not matter."

"I'll take a picture of you with your grandfather."

Sergei had come over to where Tony and Dante were attempting their Russian folk dance and was providing drunken supervision.

"Yes!" Sergei agreed, "and then I will dance." Sorge was telling stories—still sitting with Lily on his lap. Zamatin heard a raucous jolt of laughter.

Sergei draped his arm around Dasha and they posed for him. "One more!" he insisted. And then, pretending to have trouble advancing the film, he opened the camera and exposed its innards to the light.

"Oh! What are you doing?" Dasha demanded. She rushed toward him and took the camera from him and closed it.

"I'm sorry," he protested. "What a clumsy idiot I am—God, Dasha, I'm so sorry."

But then Tony called to her: "Dasha! Come and dance, come on."

"It's all right," she said to Zamatin, and put her hand on his arm, briefly. "Coming!" she called to Tony. And Zamatin watched as she put the camera in a cupboard and went to dance. He was content that the photographs had been destroyed. He felt quite good about it, congratulating himself that he'd saved them all from a potential weapon against them.

Of course, although he was quite expert in the use of a camera he hadn't known much about film. He'd had limited training in camera work and his instructors had been quite adamant that film should only be changed in subdued light; it was this explicit warning that had made him think opening a camera would expose the film inside. He learned later, after Dasha and Tony and the rest were already in prison, that he'd only managed to destroy a few frames of film— and not the ones he'd have chosen to ruin. To wreck all the film, it was necessary to pull it out.

He left Shanghai, about two months later, after the deal with the Nazis was struck but just before the Japanese moved in on the members of the ring.

He was in the rickshaw, heading for the station, when the desk boy ran out with that day's mail. The desk boy (actually, the man had been at least forty) was named Tung and he was one of the cheeriest persons Zamatin had ever encountered in his life. He came running out to the rickshaw, two letters and a large manila envelope in his hand. "Master, master. Mail!" he'd yelled, nodding his big head up and down. Tung always took great delight in handing one one's mail, as if each letter must contain the most wonderful news. Zamatin had succumbed to a sentimental gesture and gave Tung a Maria Theresa dollar, a great fortune for a Chinese. This so astounded Tung that tears came into his eyes.

It had given Zamatin a terrible, queasy feeling to draw out of the envelope Dasha's photograph, to look at the faces and know that soon all these people would be arrested. It must have been quite some time before she'd gotten around to developing the roll of film from the birthday party. He guessed she'd run off this extra print for him because he'd seemed so upset about ruining the film.

He could still remember it now, turning the photograph over as the rickshaw bumped past Bubbling Well Road, and reading Dasha's familiar scrawl: *See—you look so handsome, Val! And you didn't spoil the film after all. Love, Dasha.*

His trip to Zurich had been without incident. Once there he went to the rooms arranged for him by the Nazis, in a pension on the Limmatquai. He was to wait there for his handler from the Wehrmacht, Albert Mann, to make contact. While he stayed in his rooms, sick with anxiety, waiting, the news rose to the surface like scum on soup—the Soviet spy ring in Japan and China broken, dozens arrested. The Japanese could hardly believe that Sorge was a spy, but true to his reputation as an incautious man, Sorge's rooms were stuffed with clandestine paraphernalia and littered with compromising documents.

Zamatin stayed in his room at the Pension Lucerne for two more days—perhaps the longest two days of his life. It was hard for him to imagine feeling more alone and isolated than he had those two long days, and still the Wehrmacht failed to make contact. He tortured himself with thoughts that betraying the Sorge apparat was all for nothing, that the Wehrmacht had somehow changed its mind, that he would be arrested. And he kept thinking about his comrades in Shanghai and how they would *know* the identity of their betrayer because of the timing and secretive nature of his departure. He couldn't decide whether it was the betrayal itself or the fact that the Lotus cell members would know that he was their Judas that bothered him more. He wished there was some way to let them know that he was acting on orders.

But maybe it would have been worse for them to know that they'd been betrayed on orders from Center—even though, like himself, they accepted the maxim that the end justified the means. To know that the cause they'd believed in and worked for and risked their lives for could expend them so ruthlessly . . . that would be hard knowledge. It was hard knowledge for him.

He became obsessed with the photograph. He could barely stand to slide it out of its manila jacket, to confront the images of those he had betrayed, but he couldn't keep from doing it, either. Their very smiles were painful, accusations. . . .

As many as fifty times in those two days, some compulsion made him pull his suitcase out from under the bed and unearth the manila envelope from beneath its shield of soiled clothing. And his eyes would fasten on the photograph. He felt compelled to look at them, the smiling, doomed faces of his comrades, even though it gave him a queasy feeling in his chest. He looked at them and he thought: all arrested, all betrayed by him. Only young Dante was safe. Only Dante.

After two days locked in his room at the Pension Lucerne, he'd spent the next two entire days drunk. Those two drunken days were lost to him forever. He woke up on a bench near the Grossmünster Church wearing a tie but no shirt and shoes but no socks. Most disturbing of all, he'd somehow lost his underclothes. He tried not to think about those two days, but occasionally, frightening vignettes would loom up in his mind: a drunken confession to a bartender who seemed bored with his story and disgusted with his tears; and worse, fuzzy images that suggested to him that he had engaged in some baroque, masochistic sexual activity. . . .

But his two-day bender had accomplished something; it had blunted the worst of his guilty brooding. When he returned to the Pension Lucerne, determined to stop agonizing, he found that at last, there were messages from Albert Mann. Before he responded to those messages, he went to his room and pulled out the manila envelope one last time. Without removing the photograph from it, he destroyed it—tearing it into shreds and then burning the result in the fireplace.

Of course, the photograph posed no danger to him. He destroyed it for two reasons: the main one was to rid himself of the compulsion to look at it; the other was because Dante was in it.

Center had gone to some trouble to place Dante in the United States. Although his value at the moment was only latent—his *potential* value was enormous. The boy was really something special. And because of Dante's presence in the photograph, Zamatin considered alerting Moscow to suggest that searches be conducted at both Dasha's print shop and Sergei's house. He was sure Dasha had printed several copies—certainly one for Sergei, maybe one for herself. But his procedure for making contact with Center was both untested and complicated. And he was afraid Center would think him foolish to worry about Dante—who after all, might never be of any value to them. And even if Dante did become important to Center, it wouldn't be for a long time.

In the grate of the Pension Lucerne, Zamatin watched the shreds of the photograph blacken and curl. Some of the large pieces retained their shape even when burnt, and he pulverized them to fine ash.

Zamatin got up from the redwood chaise on his deck and took his bourbon glass inside and rinsed it out. He was restless and drove to the club to see if he could squeeze in a round of golf. But he just couldn't keep his mind off Dasha's photograph, and it was clear by the third hole, he was going to have a lousy game. He couldn't stop thinking about Dante.

Of course, Dante was just a boy when that photograph was taken—seventeen, just seventeen. He looked quite different now. There was the ear job, for one thing. And now he wore those heavy glasses, which obscured his features.

In Dasha's photograph, Dante was smiling. He'd been seeing a lot of that smile lately. Just today, Dante had been pictured in the Style section of the *Post*, smiling that same smile as he escorted his glamorous new wife to some function at the Kennedy Center. Zamatin lined up a fifteen-foot putt and missed it, wide. Dante had gone further than anyone had ever thought he would—further than they had permitted themselves to dream. . . .

CHAPTER

THIRTY-NINE

Arlington, Virginia

Dante walked through the Pentagon corridor with a general whose uniform was covered with the gold frill called scrambled eggs. He'd never understood the aspect of the military mind that allowed middle-aged men to wear gaudy uniforms. It was this as much as anything that made him distrust their ability to make sensible decisions, outside of strictly tactical ones. There was something about the whole military mind set that was dangerously narrow.

The man next to him was saying, "You know what I mean?" He hadn't been listening so he turned the full beam of his attention on the general and said, "Exactly. I know exactly what you mean."

He said good-bye to the general and stepped outside. It was like stepping into a furnace but the heat wasn't the worst thing. There was a flat, repellent quality to the light that made him edgy. The huge expanse of the Pentagon lot stretched away from him, the rows and rows of cars quivering in the waves of heat distortion. His car and driver waited at the curb and he got into the back seat, grateful for the air-conditioning.

His driver's name was Cody. He liked Cody. Cody looked ready for anything, combat ready. He'd been highly trained in terrorist avoidance tactics, of course, and he drove with total concentration, alert to the smallest nuance in the flow of traffic.

"Where to?" Cody said.

"White House."

Dante was lunching with the president, a briefing session about the latest developments in Afghanistan and Teheran.

Cody nosed the car toward the exit, toward Shirley Highway. They got stuck in traffic near the Treasury Department, where the road was being repaired. A bored-looking black man in a Day-Glo vest held up an orange flag. Tourists were pouring out of the doorway across the street, where the free half-hour tours of the Treasury Department were held, demonstrating the process of printing currency. Some of the tourists were clutching pencils attached to thin plastic tubes that held shredded money.

"You want some toot?" Cody asked.

"Sure."

"The air is shitty today; it might help clear your head."

Cody had introduced him to cocaine a couple of years ago. He'd been shocked at first at Cody's temerity, but Cody had shrugged it off. "It's just white powder, you know. I know it's illegal, but that's just the law."

"Aren't you afraid I'll have you arrested? Don't you worry about the law?"

"Not much. Like driving for you. I can go a hundred miles an hour with you in the car and the law won't do anything, right? The way I see it, the law depends."

"What about getting fired?" Dante had been intrigued by Cody's frame of reference. "Don't you think that's the kind of suggestion that might get you fired? And what if we had an accident with that kind of shit in the car?"

"You would just blame it on me."

"I should fire you," Dante had said. "You must be crazy."

Cody had shrugged. "Go ahead. But you'll have to get yourself a new driver."

He'd been excited. He'd watched Cody pulverize the powder and delicately separate it into lines. He did it on the back of the small clipboard that held his trip log. He watched Cody inhale two of the white lines, delicately, precisely. Cody passed the clipboard into the back seat. Dante hesitated one more time before trying it. "What's it like? What's it going to do to me?"

"Clears your mind," Cody said with a shrug. "That's all." Dante bent over the clipboard with the rolled-up dollar bill.

The flag man now gestured to Cody, who gave him a little salute and went forward. They passed another clutch of tourists strung up the sidewalk, trying to make it in for one of the tours of the White House. The tourists looked puzzled and hot but patient, as if they could wait there forever if they had to. He and Cody did a couple of lines in the White House lot; he needed a little boost for his talk with the president. A lot was happening these days, most of it bad, and the president was depressed. He was a man with good intentions and that was most of his problem: he took everything too personally. He actually felt responsible. Anxiety tended to paralyze him, make him fearful and unsure of himself.

That was where Dante thought he differed from most people, in his relationship with anxiety. Where most people reacted against it, shrinking away from it, he rolled with it. It powered him along.

He'd been introduced to it young, of course. And very early in his life, he'd developed what they called "good nerves." He'd laid the whole thing out in his biography: *Man of the Seventies*. He still got a kick out of that book. One shelf in his office was devoted to it—the American version and the fifteen or so translations. The whole story was there to inspire the reader: the escape from Vienna before the Nazis absorbed Austria, the stay in the ghetto in Shanghai, where his father eked out a living as a saccharine trader, the lucky trip to the United States, the frustrating years studying accounting, working nights and weekends at the dry-cleaning establishment. Then the brilliant academic career at Harvard, the sensitive government consultantships, the editorship of the influential quarterly—the gradual but unstoppable ascent to power.

But readers of *Man of the Seventies* were not privy to the one fact that turned his myriad accomplishments inside out, the fact that his allegiance was not to the United States (despite what the *Times* had characterized as his "moving tribute to his adopted country" in the book's foreword) but to the Soviet Union.

Richard Sorge had recruited him when he was fourteen years old. He was a talented artist and he contributed to the family income by sketching advertisements and doing cartoons for the *Shanghai Evening Post and Mercury*. It was these cartoons that first caught Sorge's attention. Sorge had been an exciting, charismatic man, and Dante still remembered the first time they'd met—and Sorge's flattering consternation at learning that the daring *Mercury* cartoonist was only a teenager. In no time at all, Sorge had recruited him. Of course, because of Vienna, he'd been ripe for the taking.

His father had been smart enough to get them out, but virtually all of their relatives and friends remained trapped in Vienna. And what a Vienna! Once the last restraints had been removed, he could only imagine how the city must have embraced anti-Semitism. He'd heard later that it was much worse for Jews in Vienna than it was in Berlin. Even before they left, they'd already endured a huge change in status. They'd already felt set apart, wary, uncertain if their own social institutions would protect and defend them. Gigantic swastikas decorated the city and mobs of Nazi youths in their white knee socks terrorized the weak and the vulnerable. The slogan *Ein Volk, Ein Reich, Ein Fuehrer* was shouted— in crowds, in the dark—and scrawled on walls.

In one fast year, young Dante had seen his family go from being well-off, upper-middle-class Viennese citizens, to being impoverished, stateless refugees in Shanghai. His father, the owner of several factories in Vienna, sold candles and saccharin in Shanghai— first as a simple peddler and later as a trader. And the news that came to them from Vienna was very bad indeed, and kept getting worse.

So he was more than ready to be recruited by Sorge, to swear his allegiance to Communism. Communism seemed to him pure and luminous, a system without the malice and nationalism that spawned the horrors of Fascism. Communism seemed to him the only possible salvation of the world.

Within a few months, he had become Sorge's protégé. The two of them loved to have long ideological and political discussions when Sorge was in Shanghai, usually late at night, often at the Café Celeste.

And Dante had loved his work for the Lotus cell, delivering documents and coded messages to strangers. He rode his bike all over Shanghai, played in the orchestra, drew cartoons, had long, nourishing political discussions late into the night in the back room at the Celeste. He couldn't imagine a more exciting life in a more exciting city.

It was Sorge who insisted on his promotion, charging Zamatin (who was the cell's new commander) with bringing him to the at-

287

tention of Comintern Intelligence Headquarters. Sorge was excited about Dante's prospects. His recommendation was that Center ought to assist Dante's parents in leaving Shanghai for the United States, where Dante could be placed as a deep penetration agent.

Several months after the proposal was made, Dante and his parents *were* assisted in leaving Shanghai. Of course, his parents never knew *why*, exactly—they thought it was about time they had some good luck.

Once in the United States, Dante had been told he could expect to be given help in furthering his education, would be coached in career decisions, but would have no immediate intelligence duties. He would be the kind of agent known as a *sleeper*. He was to attempt nothing on his own. In time he would be contacted; the contact would use his code name.

He'd languished in New York for two years, worried that he'd been forgotten, but not wanting to violate his instructions. Finally, the call came—he almost fainted when the long-awaited name DANTE was spoken. His heart leapt against his ribs and he had to strain to keep from telling his parents. And at last, in 1943, he'd entered Harvard (with the help of his patron, Alexander Heller), a twenty-four-year-old freshman with a full scholarship. In 1946, he had officially embraced his new country, becoming a naturalized citizen.

And in 1947, Val Zamatin had been transferred from West Germany to Washington, D.C. Since Alexander Heller, who'd been serving as his case officer, was increasingly crippled by arthritis, it was considered appropriate that Zamatin replace him.

Dante sighed. He was tired of the little Russian. Being a double agent had made Zamatin cautious and boring. Now that Zamatin was going to retire, Dante would finally have a chance to make the contacts, to do all that spooky stuff again. It was a prospect that pleased him, a kind of second adolescence.

He went into the Oval Office. The president's chief of staff looked a little pouchy under the eyes and the president himself looked as if he wanted to be somewhere else.

The president smiled wearily. Their eyes almost met, but the president's eyes never quite achieved focus anymore. He looked like a man who had seen something so horrible he was never going to look closely at anything again.

Dante rubbed his hands together. "What'll it be first, gentlemen, Kabul or Teheran?"

"Let's talk about Atlanta instead," the president said. It wasn't that funny, but everyone laughed loudly.

CHAPTER

FORTY

Val Zamatin drove into the rough off the fifteenth tee, producing a choked gurgle from Barney Halloway, his partner for the round. "Jeez*us*," Barney gushed. "Happy hunting, know what I mean? You're never going to find that ball." Just to prove Barney wrong, Zamatin resolved that he *would* find the ball—if it took all day. He tramped through the brush, cursing, looking down to discover that his pants legs were studded with the bristly "hitchhiker" seeds of a plant. He couldn't get the damned photograph off his mind. The only thing that threatened his own exposure—the only thing that had *ever* really threatened his exposure, was Dante. Not Dante *per se*, but the efforts he made to protect Dante. He took his club and swacked some grass aside and there, miraculously, was his ball.

"Hoo!" said Barney Halloway when he emerged from the rough. "Look at your pants."

While Barney attempted to blast his way out of a sand trap— only his head was visible to Zamatin—Zamatin stood with his foot up on his golf cart, picking seeds from his pants leg.

He was remembering the second time Dasha's photograph had appeared in his life. It was in 1947, shortly after his arrival in Washington. Dante, who showed a stupendous knack for being involved with the right mentor at the right time, was working at that time as an assistant to Eugene Bennett, the Harvard professor. The dapper Bennett, famous for his dandified dress and his collection of walking sticks, was a member of the team charged with drawing up the charter for the Central Intelligence Agency.

290

Dante and his new case officer, Zamatin, had not yet established a routine for getting in touch with one another, and Dante had approached Zamatin, rather awkwardly, at a cocktail party in Georgetown, saying in an intense voice, "We've got to talk."

They took up a position distant from the food or any attractive women, Dante changing the subject rather obviously whenever anyone came near.

What he wanted to tell Zamatin was that he'd been at a family dinner with two old friends of his parents from Shanghai—the Goulds. They'd gotten to talking and reminiscing about Shanghai and the Goulds had pulled out an old photo album. Dante was just going through the motions of looking at it until he confronted a photograph of himself with Richard Sorge's arm draped around him. "In fact, you were in it too, Val. It was taken at the Celeste, at old Sergei's party—right before I left. Remember that? Do you think it matters? The Goulds don't *know* anyone."

Zamatin had reported this conversation to Center. This was back in the days when he had actual meetings with people. That was very rare now. Only once in the past five years had he spoken a word to anyone from Center.

Moscow did think the existence of the photograph constituted a security risk. They requested whatever information he could supply about the Goulds and the rest of the Borodin family. He gave them what he had: a rudimentary family tree constructed from memory and the address and places of employment of the Goulds, which he got from Dante.

Shortly after that, he and Dante met for the first of their chess games—which they'd decided would serve as cover for regular meetings. Zamatin had preferred golfing as a cover—it provided ideal surroundings—but Dante refused, swearing that he thought golf was the most boring game in the world.

At their first game of chess, Zamatin beat Dante in twelve moves, but Dante was too excited to care—excited by the speed and violence of events that had followed his report of the photograph to Zamatin. "My parents called and told me—the Goulds were murdered! The place was a mess—the police suspected robbery." Zamatin could still remember the perverse excitement on Dante's face.

He had not added to that excitement by telling Dante that the Gould double homicide was not the full extent of Moscow's action in the case of the photograph. Of Sergei Borodin's five children, all were dead by 1947 except Anna, the eldest, who was discovered by Center still living in Shanghai, in a mental institution. It was found that Anna was still technically a citizen of the Soviet Union and she was transferred without fuss to a Stalingrad loony bin. Zamatin couldn't believe they'd bothered. But Center wasn't taking chances. Dante had become quite the little asset.

About that time, Zamatin had also learned of the eventual fate of Dasha and Tony Sunderland. But his contact from Center corrected him when he said that that was "the end of the Borodins."

"Dasha had a child," the man said, studying his fingernails. "Sent over here to the United States in 1939."

"No!" Zamatin had shouted. "Dasha had no children. She had a baby but it was dead, or something. Stillborn."

"A girl," the man said in his unpleasant, bored voice. "Nicola. She was sent to the United States to stay wth Sunderland's brother. But we don't know where she is now."

"What's happened to the brother?"

"He's back in Dorset." The man pulled a white handkerchief from his pocket and blotted his forehead. "Ga-ga apparently."

Zamatin remembered being glad that Center hadn't pursued the child or the uncle. He'd been surprised by the brutal way Center had eliminated the Goulds, and was reluctant to think that an innocent *child* might come to harm on the remote chance that there was some old photograph lying around. It occurred to him that he'd changed—thinking of children as "innocent." As a young man, he'd been dogmatic, a true believer. There were no innocents; every person on earth was a combatant in the struggle.

As a final precaution in the matter of the Sorge/Dante photograph, Center had directed Zamatin to construct a kind of safety net. He'd requested an interview with the just formed Office of Security. He could still remember the interview and the wispy man who'd conducted it, although it had taken place in 1947. The man's name popped into his head—George Armbruster. He had a vivid recollection of shaking hands with Armbruster. In the middle of the handshake he'd realized that Armbruster had a only a thumb, the rest of his fingers were little nubs. Zamatin had reflexively pulled his hand away, and through the rest of the interview, felt ashamed and embarrassed. He wondered at the time if Armbruster had been chosen specifically for his deformity—to put people at a disadvantage.

In response to Zamatin's fears that some of the Lotus cell members might come after their betrayer, Armbruster agreed that an attempt should be made to find out what had happened to all of them. He made a note to himself to that effect and then said in his whispery voice that files would be started for Dasha and Tony Sunderland, for Lily, for Wing Ho, for all the members of the Lotus cell. A flag, assigned to Zamatin's own crypto, ROMEO, would be attached to each file. "It's a way we've developed to keep our ships from running into icebergs," Armbruster had confided with a smile.

"Oh?" Zamatin said. He pretended to be puzzled because he could see that Armbruster was very pleased with this system he'd invented, and wanted to elaborate.

Armbruster leaned back, his protruding front teeth and wispy mustache giving him a rabbity appearance. He stroked his deformed hand as if it were a piece of sculpture. "Yes, well, to keep operations from crisscrossing in destructive ways. It seemed quite possible to us that some double agent being run by Counterintelligence might easily be mistaken for the real thing, and no *end* of trouble might ensue. This way (he gestured toward his notes with his ruined hand), any activity within the agency that involves these names will come immediately to your attention. And you will be alerted to any interest in these folks that comes to the notice of the Agency. We'll set up these flags, and that's really all we can reasonably do—just wait and see if anyone trips them."

"Val?" brayed Barney Halloway. "Earth to Val."

"Sorry, Barney."

"Talk about being a million miles away. Your shot."

He had the closer lie but he three-putted the seventeenth. Barney Halloway used a lot of body English on his own effort: "Get in there, ball, get in there, get in there." His ball wobbled on the lip of the hole and curled in.

When they'd finished the round and were headed into the clubhouse, Barney said, "I don't think I've ever beat you before, Val. Buy you a drink?"

"You never beat me before?"

"No sir!"

Suddenly, Zamatin couldn't stand the thought of having a drink with Barney Halloway. "I'll take a raincheck," he said, attempting a smile. He glanced at his watch, and shook his head. "But since you beat me, I'll buy."

"*Deal*," Barney nodded. "That's a deal."

Zamatin opened the doors of the BMW, to let it air out for a minute and then put his clubs in the trunk. He'd been toying all day with the idea of *not* informing Center about the photograph Hobie James had shown him at lunch. But he'd decided he'd better. It was just terrible luck that Hobie James had happened to see that photograph of Dante with Sorge.

On the way home, he stopped in at a Giant supermarket to use the pay phone. He glanced at his watch. It was almost six. It would take him about an hour and a half to encode a message. Since meetings were set to take place three hours after he called, if he called right now, the meeting would be set for five of nine. That was no good for him—unless he begged off dinner with Moira.

The scheduled meet site for today was the National Gallery's cafeteria. Although the Smithsonian museums stayed open until nine in the summer, it would be cutting it awfully close. Besides, he didn't want to cancel dinner with Moira. This was a peacekeeping dinner. Moira was possessive and was harboring resentful feelings that he'd gone to Sardinia without her. "I just want to be with you," she'd said, in hurt tones. "I can't understand why you don't feel the same way."

And he couldn't explain to her that the psychological pressures of keeping two Vassily Zamatins rolling—each with its different set of lies and compromises—made occasional periods of solitude absolutely necessary to him.

Tomorrow's meet site was the zoo, at the panda house. If he called right now and pushed one button in for a meet tomorrow, the specified three hour time lag would mean that the meet would have to be set for nine. Too late. He thought about it; he could be at the zoo at six-thirty. He could even meet Moira there afterward. He tossed the quarter into the air and turned away from the telephone booth. He'd have to call tomorrow at three-thirty—a nuisance, but it couldn't be helped.

A tall black man in a Giant Food uniform, seeing Zamatin turn from the telephone without making a call, chuckled and said in his rich baritone voice: "A lady, am I right? You were going to call a lady but you changed your mind."

Zamatin nodded with a you-guessed-right grin.

"I always say if you have to think about it, don' *do* it," the man went on in his chuckling, good-natured voice.

"I'm sure you're right," Zamatin said, giving a little wave.

"Hey, you take care now. It all be turnin' out all right. You see."

Zamatin got into his car. I hope so, he thought. I hope it'll all turn out all right.

CHAPTER

FORTY-ONE

There were schools of fish in the mouth of the cove, fleeing unseen predators, churning up the water. Nicola sat drinking her coffee, watching through the picture window.

The radio was on, a talk show. A man with a liquid baritone voice was interviewing a member of the Charles Manson Family. The names poured into her head: Squeaky, Sadie, Linda Kasabian, Tex. A horrifying, pivotal turn of events for the children of the sixties. Flower children gone amok, up to their elbows in blood. Stylized, malevolent death. And as with Nazism, the public fascination, unrelenting, greedy for detail. Nicola had never trusted her own morbid interest. It felt voyeuristic; the fascination with evil seemed evil itself.

The voice on the radio reprised the murders and trial, then began to run through the whereabouts of various Manson family members—a sort of cutthroats' "Where Are They Now?" It all seemed wrong, picking the bones of the dead. Her disapproval conquered her interest and she flicked the knob off before she could hear which family member was speaking, or what the woman was going to say.

In the bathroom, she caught a glimpse of herself in the mirror that Kate had recently hung on the back of the door. Mirrors had proliferated, during Kate's illness—it seemed she constantly needed to observe her image. For reassurance? For pleasure? Nicola herself looked dingy—dressed in gray sweat pants and sweatshirt, her hair stringy, her face dull. The house was a mess, too. And all of a sudden it occurred to her that this was the day that Neil Walker, the man from Allenby's, was coming over to get the document she'd found in the packing crate. She should make an effort to get herself together.

She felt a little panicked. There was so much to do. She had to clean the house, she had to shop, she had to take a shower. Luckily, he wasn't coming until three-thirty. The best thing would be to clean up the house first.

Despite the noise of the vacuum cleaner, Kate didn't get up. Nicola would wait until she was ready to leave and then wake her. She made a shopping list in her head as she jumped into the shower. She'd need beer, some Coke, maybe some white wine—something to offer the man—as well as regular groceries. While she soaped her body, she tried to remember the last time they'd had a guest. It alarmed her to think how long ago it was—months. She shaved her legs. She woke Kate and drove to the shopping center, energized.

First she went into Shaw's. She bought some cheese, water biscuits, a baguette, some chips, beer, Coke. As she wheeled the cart out, she decided that the mental sloth had to come to an end too.

She went into Bookland to buy some good books, some *real* books. She and Kate would start a summer reading program. Or, forget Kate. Kate would feel patronized. She would start her own summer reading program: one good book a week. She'd given a summer reading list to the fifth-graders and asked them to read a book a week. She ought to be able to do as well.

She picked out three paperbacks: Don DeLillo's *Running Dog,* Scott Spencer's *Endless Love,* and Norman Mailer's *The Executioner's Song.* She'd read all the authors before and she knew these would be good books. She couldn't bring herself to buy any hardcovers, but she checked out the remainders table in the middle of the store. There she found a copy of *Man of the Seventies.* It had been on the bestseller list for about a year and she'd always meant to read it. She also found a hardcover copy of *Ragtime,* which she'd somehow never read.

She drove back to the cabin with her books and snack food, in a good mood, full of resolve.

Andy was rowing the dinghy and doing it surprisingly well. Walker sat in the stern and admired the smooth, strong strokes. Only occasionally did Andy falter and splash water, or veer too far in one direction. They spotted Nicola Ward's cabin easily. It was one of the big old ones, right on the water. None of these places perched on the shoreline could have been built now—the new law required structures to be a hundred yards back from the high-tide mark.

Walker saw a woman come out on the deck while Andy tied up the dinghy—she gave a little halfhearted wave. He stooped to pick up Andy (they had finally developed the least awkward way of doing this—half fireman's carry, half piggyback) but Andy shook his head. The ramp had a sturdy handrail and Andy inched up it, standing. Walker carried the metal crutches.

The woman approached them, hesitated, and then stepped back, opening the door.

"Come on in, I'm Nicola Ward."

Walker was startled by the woman's appearance. She was very pretty, stylishly dressed in a denim dress with a carefully twisted scarf as a belt. But what surprised him was her uncanny resemblance to her mother, Dasha. It was a shock to come face to face with an image that had previously existed only in two dimensions.

He introduced himself and Andy.

He liked the way she immediately turned to Andy and spoke to him directly rather than through his father: "Would you like to watch television or—actually, there's not much on." She frowned. "Would you like to read some comics? How about a Coke?"

Andy shrugged. "Sure."

Then she turned to Walker. "Can I get you some coffee? A beer? A Coke?"

Walker wondered why she was so nervous. "I'll take a beer."

She hesitated. "Excuse me."

She settled Andy on the couch with a Coke, a basket of potato chips, and a huge stack of comics. "I'm the one that rowed over here," Andy volunteered.

"You're kidding," Nicola said admiringly. "You must be very strong."

Andy executed an "it-was-nothing" shrug, and Walker felt a little surge of pleasure in this new, nonchalant Andy.

She brought a beer for him and sat down across from him with a cup of coffee.

"Well," he started, but stopped because a skeletal young woman had entered the room. She looked almost unreal, impossibly thin, attenuated like a Giacometti sculpture.

"Oh!" Nicola jumped up, nervously pushing at her hair. "This is my daughter, Kate."

Walker took the bony hand. "Neil Walker." He gestured toward Andy. "And this is my son, Andy."

"Hi," said Andy.

"Would you like to go for a motorboat ride?" Kate asked Andy.

"Um—" Andy threw his eyes toward his father but then looked back at the girl. "Sure. But . . . um . . . you know, I can't . . . um . . . you know, really *walk*."

"Can you get down to the float?"

Andy shrugged. "Well, I got up it." Walker liked this practical exchange.

"I can bring the boat in to the float—there's plenty of water. We can troll out to the Basin and back. Go see the ospreys."

"I caught five mackerel the other day."

"Maybe you'll catch one for me. I haven't had any luck this year."

"Well, how about it, Dad?"

Walker felt very uneasy. So much could go wrong on a boat ride and the girl looked anything but strong and capable. But he was highly sensitized to Andy's feelings—almost always—and he could tell when Andy wanted him to provide an excuse. He wasn't getting that feeling now.

"Sure. But you can't stay out too long. Want some help down the ramp?"

"No."

They stood on the deck. As soon as their damaged children were out of earshot, Nicola Ward said, "Don't worry. She's very skilled at operating the motorboat. She's grown up on the water."

"Andy was in an accident," he said in a flat voice. "They hope the damage isn't permanent." He stood up and she followed him out to the deck. The girl, Kate, was already in the dinghy, rowing briskly toward a blue and white Starcraft. Despite her shocking, emaciated body, her motions seemed strong and capable. "His mother was driving the car," Walker heard himself saying, volunteering information that he usually kept back. "She was killed instantly."

Nicola murmured something shocked and sympathetic. They watched Andy slowly make his way down the ramp. Walker saw that the girl easily handled the big Evinrude outboard, tilting it and lowering it into the water. Within two minutes she had the boat idling at the dock. "She certainly seems to know what she's doing," he remarked, and then held his breath while Andy negotiated a tricky pivot to get himself on board.

"You mean especially for someone who looks like she's terminally ill," Nicola said with a nervous laugh. "I saw the way you looked at her. No, don't worry—everybody looks at her like that. She thinks they're admiring her." She laughed again, a beat-up laugh. "She's an anorexic—in other words, she's starving herself— we hope not to death. They call it an 'eating disorder.'" Her voice had an ironic, resigned tone that made any reply not only unnecessary but almost impossible. They both waved as the boat curved away from the dock. Walker followed the narrowing white vee of its wake until the boat disappeared behind the point. "I don't know why I'm telling you all this," she said. "You're practically a perfect stranger." She smiled, not at him, but at the cliché.

"If you wonder why I keep staring at you," he said, not really in reply, "it's because I can't get over how much you look like your mother. You don't seem like a stranger at all." He thought that she must be nearly twenty years older than the woman in the photograph, but only the most delicate lines around her eyes and mouth showed the accumulated years of smiling and talking. And he found the soft texture of her eyelids touching, almost sexy. He looked at her too long again, and she looked away. Her hands tapped nervously on the railing of the deck.

"The photographs," she started. "It was so wonderful to see all those photographs! I'm an orphan, and—"

"I know."

Her hand came up to her face and hid her mouth. "I forget that you must know quite a bit about me—it's a little weird. Do you— I mean, would you like some more coffee?"

He held up the can of Bud. "I'll take another beer."

Her hand flew up to her face again. "That's right, *I'm* having

300

coffee. I'm a little"—she shook her head—"a little scattered. Do you want to come in? I mean, or do you want to sit out here."

"Well, the mosquitoes—" He laughed. "I'm trying very hard not to scratch my ankles to shreds."

"It's been a wet summer. I can't remember when they've been so bad." He followed her around to the side of the deck. She had an athletic, fluid walk; she slid the screen door aside.

They sat at the table in front of a big bay window. "I was so excited," she said in her smoky voice, "getting that trunk full of letters and photographs after so many years of having *nothing*, I mean I had one picture of my mother and father, that was it. . . ."

He remembered sitting in the Archives and reading the clinical details of her parents' horrible deaths. The image of Dasha Sunderland staked out in a yard came into his head. There was no reason for this woman to know about that. He said it must have been an amazing moment to find the jewels and the egg.

"It was kind of funny. I was *giddy*—I mean, it was *fantastic*, but, I don't know. . . ." She looked out the window. "Good luck makes me nervous. I always feel like I might be getting set up." She looked up at him. "You know?"

"Yeah, I know the feeling. When things are going too well, I feel like I'm riding for a fall."

"That's it," she said. "It's too bad to feel that way—it's a guarded reaction. It takes the fun out of things sometimes."

His eyes met hers and she looked away. "But you don't get blindsided."

"Exactly. Anyway, as soon as I found these"—her hand stirred the air—"treasures, it was like I couldn't wait to get them out of the house. I was afraid I'd lose them or something, I don't know. I took them down to Allenby's right away, I mean immediately. And I keep expecting to hear that they're fakes or that there's some complicated legal reason I can't have them."

"Well, I don't know that much about it, but so far, I can tell you that they don't seem to be fakes."

"I—" she started. But then the thought seemed to desert her. He heard a woodpecker outside making a pock-pock-pock sound. "But the papers and things," she finally said. "That was like an answered prayer. I mean, I always felt—well, I don't know, kind of like adopted children must feel or other orphans—that I was missing

301

some link to the past, that I *had* no past. And so seeing the photograph albums from the trunk, seeing *my family*—it was, you know . . ." Her voice trailed away and she smiled her appealing, girlish smile. "It was great," she concluded in a wistful voice. Her voice—the throaty rasp combined with the Down East accent—was wonderful.

"You might be interested in—you don't speak Russian do you?" He knew she didn't.

"Oh no," she laughed. "Not me. I never got past college French."

"Well then, you'll be interested in reading some of the papers from the trunk—I mean my translations."

"Mr. Michalowski . . . uh, *Rudy*, he keeps wanting me to call him Rudy but I can't seem to do it. Anyway, he promised me that I could have them, eventually."

"He's probably waiting until the whole thing is done. I wonder—" He wanted to tell her about Borodin's diary, but he thought Michalowski wouldn't approve.

"What?" She pushed her fingers into her hair, and combed them through.

He had a feeling that had been missing from his life for a long time, an almost flirtatious desire to entertain her, to engage her. "Well, I'm probably not supposed to tell you about this yet," he began in a conspiratorial tone, and then hesitated. His eyes caught hers.

She sat straight up and put her hands on the table. "What?"

"Do you remember seeing a leather-bound book in the papers, a kind of diary?"

"Yes, I remember that. I wondered what it was."

"It's a diary written by your great-grandfather—now we don't know exactly *why* he did this—but it was a *faked* diary and in it he insisted that, well . . . if what he said was true, let's just say that you would have been the great-granddaughter of the tsar."

A laugh spurted out of her. "What?"

"It's a great story, really—it just doesn't happen to be true. Do you want to hear it?"

"Of course."

In a smooth storyteller's style borrowed from one of the tapes Andy had been so fond of when he stayed in the hospital, he told her of Sergei's religious conversion, of the monastery near Perm, of the Villa Medvedev in Shanghai.

302

"My opinion is that the general put Sergei up to it," he told her in conclusion.

"But how do you know it wasn't true? I mean I'd hate to let go of a romantic notion like being a long-lost Romanov without a little scrap."

"Well, I got the documents before I got the photographs. And I don't know how to break it to you, but—not one of the five Borodins in question—and I mean your grandmother, and your, I guess they'd be your great-aunts and -uncles—not one of them looks a bit like any of the Romanovs."

"Well, if you're going to go by appearances."

"I can't get over how much you look like your mother."

She smiled and then looked embarrassed. "Oh!" she said and jumped up from the table. "I almost forgot the reason you're here—the papers we found. I'll be right back." She picked a file folder off the top of the refrigerator and set it on the table. "Kate found them, really. We were dragging the packing crate—you know, the one the trunk was in—out with the trash. This must have been stuck in there somewhere. Of course, I have no idea if it's anything important. Probably not."

CHAPTER
FORTY-TWO

He took the papers from her and unfolded them. The first page
had only one line of Cyrillic writing on it.

"See this," Walker said, pointing to the single underscored line
of writing at the top of the front page. "It says 'The True Story of
Sergei Borodin.' This might be very important."

She asked him to read some of it if it wasn't too difficult. "I
mean, do you need dictionaries and things?"

"I can read it, but I can't promise it will be as exciting as the
false story of Sergei Borodin."

He began translating out loud, haltingly at first until he became
accustomed again to the way Sergei Borodin formed his letters.
There was no doubt that both memoirs were written by the same
hand.

"Only after our good friend Li hammered the packing crate
around the trunk did I realize that inside was the old diary I wrote
for General Medvedev. It's now too late to take the crate apart—
Li is already gone and when he returns, it will be time to take the
crate to Dasha and Tony at the shipping office. Anna and I have
pried off one board and we'll wedge these pages in there. Because
if this trunk does reach you, my little Nicola, I don't wish for you
to believe the lies in that old diary. It is right too, that you should
know something of us, your family. The Japanese will be here in
Shanghai any day now and we don't know what will become of
us. I know your kind Uncle Brian and Aunt Hillary will preserve

these things for you until you are older, and can understand. So I will take this little time to tell you some history of our family.

"I am Sergei Borodin, your great-grandfather. I was born in a small town in Siberia, near the Altay Kray mountains. My mother, Anna Borodin, was a worker in the dairy of a large estate. My father was the owner of that estate, Nicolai Shuvalov. I was the illegitimate product of their love."

It covered the same early ground as the false memoir and Walker said as much to Nicola.

"My mother died when I was a child, and my father came to her funeral. My relatives were afraid of him, but he was a kind man and even after my mother's death, continued to show an interest in me. My father's wife, Irina, was childless for a long time. Understandably perhaps, she hated me from the start. When I was about ten years old, she had her only child, Pavel, my half-brother. After this son was born, she hated me even more. She hated my father to show me any affection and she hated for him to squander money on my care and education. She taught her son Pavel to despise me, never relenting in her efforts to fuel his jealousy and hate."

Borodin detailed his education and his return to Kulada as a physician.

"I delivered babies to the poor and calves and foals to the rich. In 1890, I married my beloved Marthe Abramowicz, who came to me from Warsaw. The lady in the next village arranged the marriage. 'It is time you got married, Sergei,' she told me. And she was right.

"But Marthe was just a child when she came to me—a terrified child. She wept for a year out of homesickness and fear. She could not understand me—a Jew ignorant of the customs of his own people. But slowly we came to love each other and our first child, Anna, was born in 1896. Marthe was a slender girl and she had a long and difficult labor, but both she and little Anna seemed to come out of it fine and healthy, although within two years, we knew that poor Anna was not quite right in her head. She was dreamy and slow to learn but she had a sweet disposition."

Borodin told of the births of his children "all of them smart and quick," and how he and his wife argued about the naming of the youngest, and only boy. Borodin wished to name the boy Nicolai, to honor his father, "Nicolai Shuvalov who had always behaved so honorably to me." But his wife insisted custom forbade the naming of a child after a living relative. In hindsight, Borodin conceded that his wife might have been right.

"Perhaps some of a child's strength is lost when he must share his name with a living person, although I don't really believe that superstition. For whatever reason, most likely because he was youngest, Nicolai was always spoiled, and willful. But his name, oh his name only made my father's wife hate us all the more. She thought the name had been given to curry favor, to wheedle more worldly goods from my father, and daily she fed this venom to her son, Pavel."

Borodin told how his father died when little Nicolai was only one year old, leaving the family for the first time without a protector. Naturally, the father's estates passed on to his legitimate son, Pavel.

"My father set aside for me only one excellent horse. I could not even attend his funeral, and I worried for my family's future. I even considered moving, but it is not so easy to be moving with five children. Besides, Pavel's life was going well—he, too, was married and had two little children—and since we seldom saw each other, I did nothing."

Borodin noted that Pavel, nurtured by his mother's jealousy and taunted all his life about his "Jewish relatives," became an official in the Sviaschennaia Druzhina, a secret league of Russian nobles that stirred up pogroms against the Jews.

One night when Nicolai was still "a very small boy," Pavel came to Sergei's cottage with an urgent plea. His wife was in painful labor and the family physician was falling down drunk. "He begged me for my help and I could not refuse." But when Borodin arrived, he found that Pavel's wife had been hemorrhaging for a long time. He saved the baby, but there was nothing he could do for the woman.

"This is still the same as the false memoir," Walker said. "Only more detailed."

"The next day, Pavel had his revenge on me. While I was seeing to a peasant thrown from a horse, Pavel and some other members of the Druzhina arrested Marthe and lynched her next to the church. When I cut her down, I saw pinned to her white blouse a sign that said: JEW BUTCHER'S WIFE."

Walker looked up from his reading. The light coming in the window was bright; the aqueous glare hurt his eyes. "I'm sorry."

Nicola stood up and pulled a cord, and let down some rattan blinds. "I didn't even know I was Jewish. I didn't even know that." Her voice was careful, under control.

"Do you want me to stop reading?"

"No," she said emphatically, "I mean, if you don't mind."

Borodin told how his desire for revenge was tempered by his knowledge that exacting it would cost not just his own life, but the lives of his children as well. He packed the family up and they set out on a long journey. After detailing some of the trip's hardships, Borodin concluded that "I did not feel safe from my anger until the entire width of Siberia lay between me and Pavel." The family settled in Vangou, a small village near Vladivostok, and lived there for many years. "Now this is different," Walker said. "In the false memoir, they went to Ekaterinburg and *then* to Vangou."

The area around Vangou was at that time, Borodin pointed out, occupied by Japanese soldiers and also by Americans. Walker's eyes skipped ahead and he read Borodin's account of how his daughter, Iraida, was raped in 1917 by a Japanese soldier.

"But that was my grandmother!" Nicola said.

"Maybe I really should stop," Walker offered. "This is kind of personal."

"No, don't stop now." Her hand touched her face. "It explains the eyes," she said. "Stan always said I had 'chink' eyes."

Walker returned to translating. Borodin told of the civil war and the changes it brought to him and his family. At first the war had little effect but eventually he was impressed into the White Army to labor as a medic.

"At first this idea was repugnant to me. I had no sympathy with the White Army's cause. Was it not the tsar who instigated the anti-Semitic military Soyus Ruskago Naroda? Was it not a Romanov who promulgated the anti-Semitic Protocols of the Elders of

Zion? Was it not the Romanovs who sent Jews to live beyond the Pale of Settlement? No, I was not a friend of the Romanovs or the Whites, but still, the Eastern Republic, where we lived, was now totally White territory. And sick and wounded are all needy of attention, no matter their politics. So I tended the sick and wounded of the White Army."

With the Reds victorious, Borodin had to flee Vladivostok with the White Army, or else face execution as a counterrevolutionary.

"A kind of ragtag flotilla was organized, to carry off the defeated and discouraged shreds of the White Army. I envisioned that traveling conditions would be grim at best, and I secured a spot on one ship, the *Kodama Maru*."

Walker broke off reading and looked up: "Yes!" he said triumphantly. "The *Kodama Maru*. I found his name on the ship's manifest!" Nicola Ward looked puzzled, unable to share his researcher's pleasure in seeing the tedious hours he'd spent poring over logs and manifests validated. "Never mind," he said. "You had to be there." She managed a laugh.

"I secured a spot on the *Kodama Maru* as ship's doctor. The flotilla had a tragic air to it. The passengers, including myself and my family, were stateless. Some were ill, many were crippled by wounds suffered in the war. Conditions aboard the ships were horrendous—food, water, and sleeping space were scarce. Sanitation was almost nonexistent—people were shitting and pissing on the open deck—and the worst of it was that none of us knew if any country would accept us.

"I did what I could to protect my family. I commandeered the ship's library as a sickroom for patients requiring quarantine. In fact, there had been cholera in Vladivostok and it was feared that an outbreak aboard ship would doom most of the passengers. I used that fear to establish my family—my five children and my granddaughter, little Dasha—in relative comfort and safety.

"I am not sure exactly how the rumors got started but I can guess. The first thing that happened was that my Nicolai actually did fall ill. I didn't diagnose it properly at the time, but he was suffering from the onset of a tubercular condition that would weaken him for the rest of his life. No one on the ship—they were terrified of cholera—came near the quarantined room. But then three days out, one of the girl relented to Nicolai's demand for fresh air and opened the portholes. It was Marga who told me about the men peering in. I was so cross with her—she couldn't understand why. I just didn't want anyone to see these healthy children of mine living in the relative comfort of the library.

"But some seamen did. And the seamen saw—well, they *saw* four healthy young women and a much younger male, a boy—this last one rather sickly. No doubt they were questioned about the appearance of the five in 'quarantine.' The women? Two were pretty, one a bit fat, the other indifferent-looking. Did they have an imperious look? Oh yes, I can imagine the seamen saying, quite imperious.

"Rumors start just like that, out of nothing, and it's easy to imagine how this one, once rolling, took over the imagination of the ship. I began to hear the rumors myself after just one day. A cavalry captain with a badly wounded arm had a faded newspaper photograph hidden in his tunic. It showed a pretty girl seated at a piano. Was she one of them? The seamen couldn't be sure. The captain asked them to look more closely, reminding them that the photograph was a few years old. Sensing the answer the captain wanted to hear, the seamen must have agreed. 'Yes,' I can imagine one of them deciding, the woman in the photograph was definitely one of the women in the quarantine room. No doubt about it.

"After two days, the ship buzzed with the news—that the Romanov children were aboard, incognito. The three seamen became shipboard celebrities. With repetition, their tales became embellished. They'd spoken with Anastasia; they'd been sworn to secrecy by the ailing tsarevitch; they'd kissed the hand of the beautiful Marie.

"I was asked about the rumors but my denials were only winked at and taken as indirect confirmation of the story's truth. Without being asked, the ship's purser sent the officers' daily ration of fresh fruit to the library.

"The rumor, by the time we anchored in Shanghai, had acquired the force of fate. It had spread to the other ships in the flotilla. Some of these ships stopped also in Shanghai, others went on to the Philippines. The rumor had also preceded our own ship to Shanghai, because at the docks, we were met by General Ivan Medvedev, who was part of the White-Government-in-Exile, and a member of Nightingale."

"Yes," Walker said, looking up from his reading. "I had guessed that Nightingale had something to do with it."

"But what is Nightingale?"

He explained that it was a secret White organization which worked to overthrow the Bolsheviks and restore White rule—Romanov rule—to Russia. "This is fantastic. Now we're finding out the truth."

Nicola got up. Her foot was asleep. "Do you want another beer?"

He asked for coffee, and when she came back, he went on.

"I could read the disappointment on Medvedev's face when he came to the library and looked at my children. I suppose he hadn't really *believed* the rumors, but he had *hoped*. One look at my Anna, my Iraida, my Marga, my Hester, my poor sick Nicolai—and he knew immediately that he was not looking at the Romanovs. While my children weren't peasants, neither were they aristocrats, and apart from their number and gender, they didn't resemble the Romanovs in any way. Then too, there was Dasha, Iraida's half-Japanese baby. I saw the general look at her with distaste in his eyes.

"Nevertheless, the general took us under his wing. I guess he thought something might still be gained by perpetuating the rumor. He made a deal with me—and you will understand that I was in no position to turn him down. In return for my writing a false memoir, and allowing him to tutor my children, he would give us his hospitality and protection.

"All that summer, I worked on the 'memoir'—it is inside this trunk and you can read it for yourself. The general helped with the details of this fantastic document, spending hours with me each day. We spent that summer—the children and I—living in seclusion at the Villa Medvedev. As I labored on my 'diary,' the children were tutored in French, English, the Christian religion, the social graces. They were shown photographs of relatives, of places they had been, of palaces where they had lived. Nicolai recovered some of his strength, lying on a hammock strung through a gazebo.

"One night, the general called the children and myself into his drawing room and showed us some valuables—an icon, a beautiful Fabergé egg, some jewelry, some marbles from Timor that had been playthings of the tsarevitch. These things had been collected—I suspect by Nightingale—to support the story Medvedev was concocting. The children were made to memorize the occasion of their mother receiving the pieces of jewelry and the Easter when she had been given the egg.

"Of course, all this time I was worrying. The general, with his ruined whispering voice and his two disgusting wet nurses that went everywhere with him, was a frightening figure. I knew we must break free of him. More and more he concentrated his tutoring and attention on Iraida, who most resembled her Romanovian counterpart, Tatiana. This made me worry very much about what he planned for the rest of us. When I allowed myself to think about it, which was not often, it seemed likely to me that the rest of us would be killed, Iraida blackmailed. Medvedev would use her little Dasha as an incentive to see that she did everything he asked. He might then present her, as the 'last Romanov' to Shanghai. I was trying to plan our escape when the general fell ill.

"What he had contracted was—unmistakably—typhus. The likelihood of his dying was a double-edged sword. We enjoyed ease—actual luxury—at the Villa Medvedev and yet, we were still penniless. He had kept us isolated and although recent secret forays of mine had located a few friends, those were without resources.

"The general got sicker by the day and his fever remained high. I knew now that only a miracle would save him. And so, I robbed him. I searched his private rooms for the jewels and the egg and I found them. Then I went through his papers and tried to eliminate every connection between Medvedev and myself and my family. All along I had known that this was a dangerous charade for us and that sooner or later, the children would become the objects of violent attention. Now I saw my chance. I asked one of Medvedev's servants to show me where to sell something valuable— offering him a generous consideration—and I sold one pair of the tsarina's earrings to a Chinese.

"When the general died, I was ready. Hours after his funeral, I moved the family to a house I'd rented on the Rue Père in the French Concession. Though I was fearful that Medvedev's associates in the Nightingale would come to retrieve the relics they'd assembled, or worse, to find the family whose pretensions these things were meant to support—nothing happened. After a year or so, I found the courage to sell one more necklace and we opened a little café—the Celeste. And that is how we have made our living in Shanghai."

Borodin related how the rumor about his children eventually abated, lost in a flurry of other "last Romanovs" and he talked about how the children adjusted to the change once they left Medvedev's villa. "Nicolai," Borodin stated, "continued to tell strangers, at times, that his name was Alexei. The girls were older and understood the danger."

Borodin went on to express his fears for the future. He made it obvious that he himself expected to die and his fears were for the living.

"My daughter Anna, my firstborn, is mentally unsound. I fear for her, once I am gone. Friends have promised to look after her but I cannot trust that they will have the kindness not to lose patience with her. It is because she will never be able to keep track of documents and things that I send all these papers to your father's house in England where they will eventually find their way to you. There are rumors that the Japanese will requisition this house and we cannot count on any of our belongings being safe.

"It broke Dasha's heart to send her little baby away, but now I can see how wise she was to send you to safety. The only peace I find in my heart is that you are safe and that my daughter Marga married Arthur Gould, who was clever enough to take her to America where this war will not come to harm her. Soon, the war will come to Shanghai and Russians with no passports cannot expect an easy time of it."

He closed with an outpouring of thanks to Hillary and Brian Sunderland for their generosity in taking care of his great-grandchild and a plea to continue that care "if the worst happens, and none of us survive the war." He urged them to sell the "tsarist trinkets" in the trunk "although they won't bring much and I have sold the best of them." He begged Hillary and Brian to take Nicola to visit her Aunt Marga in New York City. And he closed:

"And if in later years, my precious Nicola, you should read this letter, please know that you were this old man's joy and hope and I love you very much.
Sergei Borodin
11 Rue Père
Shanghai, China
November 5, 1941"

Nicola Ward kept her head down because there were tears in her eyes. Ever since the discovery of the trunk, she had been expecting her rediscovered past to comfort her, to somehow steady

312

her. She'd thought that just the *fact* of all the trunk's papers, photographs, the written evidence of her history, would make her feel anchored, safe. She'd expected—once her life was defined by a past—that she'd feel less afloat, less alone in the world. But here was knowledge of the most personal sort, and still it didn't take away her sense of isolation. She felt sad for her grandfather, a brave man with a lot of tragedy in his life, who'd ended his days in an alien country, his children, except one, dead or gone. He was as alone then as she was now.

Neil Walker looked at her sympathetically; he touched her arm. His hand made her want to sink in to his touch, to be consoled, to have his capable arms around her. Not that she could believe any more that someone could protect her, but she wanted a moment's illusion.

But her reticence wouldn't allow it. She shook her hair back from her face. She swallowed hard and gave a little sniff that pulled the tears back inside. His wide-set eyes seemed calm and nonjudgmental and she wanted to explain to him how isolated she felt. Suddenly she was annoyed with herself. What was she whining about? His wife had been killed, his son badly injured; she couldn't imagine herself telling him why she was sad. "I'm like this," she said instead. "I cry in movies too. Kate can't stand it."

The moment she said Kate's name, a rush of worry flushed through her. Neil Walker stood up as well, with a concerned look on his face and together, silently, they walked toward the deck. The progress of time was palpably marked by the sharp angle of the ramp down to the dock. The tide was almost low now; the kids had been gone a long time.

"They should have been back by now," she said.

Walker was on an instant guilt trip. *Was I out of my mind? To send him off with a complete stranger? A complete stranger who was obviously seriously ill? What could I have been thinking?*

"I lost track of the time," Nicola said. "Maybe they had engine trouble. Maybe they sheared a pin." Nicola had heard the phrase "sheared a pin" offered up dozens of times as a likely reason for a late boat. She offered it to Neil Walker, but he didn't seem to hear her. The distant whine of an outboard claimed her attention and she held up her finger to her mouth. She had learned to distinguish their motor's whine from that of others.

"No," she said. "That doesn't sound like them." Then she rushed to reassure him, listing all the other things that could have gone wrong. "Why don't you row out past the island?" she suggested, to give him something to do to divert him from his worry. "Maybe they had engine trouble and they're rowing back."

The explanation turned out to be even more innocuous than that. Distracted by their success (they'd caught thirty mackerel)—Kate and Andy had simply forgotten the time. They had the selfish concentration of the young and hadn't yet developed the branching of consciousness that would have permitted them to remember, even while reeling in fish after fish, that their parents would be worried, that they were expected back.

Before Walker cleared the island, he saw the blue and white Starcraft bearing down on him. He signaled to Kate, and she slowed and circled and finally cut the engine. As they shouted back and forth between boats, Walker's relieved anger dissolved. Andy was flushed with pleasure, holding up a big white bucket full of fish, exaggerating its weight with his grimacing effort to lift it.

"It's half full, Dad. Really!"

By the time Walker reached the motorboat's mooring, Andy was already tying up the dinghy at the float. The three of them spent the next half hour down there, swatting at mosquitoes, cleaning the mackerel in an assembly line (Neil scaled, Andy beheaded, and Kate gutted). The dock ramp was very steep, but Andy managed to climb up it. Nicola insisted that they stay for dinner and they did, eating some of the fish, listening to Andy and Kate retell fish stories.

"I hooked a bluefish," Andy said for the fifth time. "He was huge. I almost got him in but he bit off the line."

"I'll have to put steel leaders on," Kate said. "I heard rumors that the blues were in but this is the first real evidence."

Nicola poured some wine. It was nice to have guests. "Would you like some more milk?" she asked Andy.

"Yes," he said. "Please."

It was nice to ask a question like "Would you like some more milk?" simply. To ask such a question of Kate was tricky, a complex interaction, a question of stresses and counterstresses, of shifting meaning, of intent.

Walker leaned back in his chair and laughed at Kate's description of once falling down, while water skiing, into a school of porpoises.

Nicola thought it was nice to have a man in the room, to hear a man's laugh. Nice, nice, nice. Kate made a gesture with her fork and then pushed the food around on her plate.

"You know that package that fell out of the crate?" Nicola said. "Mr. Walker translated it for me while you were out in the boat." She turned to Walker. "I wish I'd tape-recorded it—I mean it's a great story, Kate, it's fascinating. It's our . . . our family history."

"I'll make a written translation for you," Walker said.

"Wonderful," Nicola said in a passionate voice.

"Hey, yeah, that'll be great," Kate said without conviction.

"No, *really*," Nicola said. "It's fascinating."

"*Okay*," Kate said. "I believe you."

"At one point," Walker said to Kate, "we thought you were heirs of the Romanovs'."

Kate put her hand on her bony chest as if about to salute the flag. "Us? You mean the Russian guys—the king?"

"The tsar," Nicola corrected.

Walker said: "But it was all part of an elaborate hoax."

Kate still seemed uninterested; Walker determined that he'd get her attention. "The truth is even more exciting in a way—I mean about your grandparents."

"What do you mean?" Nicola asked.

"They were spies," Walker said. "Russian spies."

Kate turned toward her mother. "I thought your father was British."

Nicola said: "He was."

"I mean spies for the Russians," Walker said. "*Soviet* spies. And they helped win the Second World War for the allies—I mean, you could say that. Their spy ring was very important."

He told them about it while Nicola made coffee. He finally succeeded in winning Kate's attention.

"And then they died, right, Mom? In prison camp? Right?"

"Yes," Nicola said. She raised the blinds. The sun had fallen below the horizon; the clouds were pink. The back-lit pine trees looked black. "Red sky at night, sailor's delight," she said.

"Dad," Andy said, yawning. "I'm real tired."

Nicola decided it was too dark for them to row home. "The mosquitoes will kill you. I'll drive you around to the cabin."

"I'll tow your dinghy over in the morning," Kate promised. "Maybe we can even go out for another trip."

"No more mackerel," Nicola said, laughing. "The freezer is packed."

"Maybe we'll try bottom fishing out by Lumbo Ledge," Kate said in a teasing voice. "Mom loves flounder."

"Well," Nicola said, "flounder . . . flounder are a different kettle of fish."

"Mom, that's bad." She turned to Andy and Walker: "She can't help herself. This is what happens when you hang around fifth-graders most of your life. No offense, Andy."

CHAPTER

FORTY-THREE

Washington, D.C.

Vassily Zamatin walked down Connecticut Avenue, crossed the street, and strolled toward the zoo. He was headed for the panda house. That morning, in the *Post*, he'd read a story about a Nicaraguan man found living in a shanty in the zoo—in a "wooded area, near the horned animals." Now a crowd had gathered near the zoo entrance. The bodies shifted momentarily and through the gap, Zamatin glimpsed cables and TV cameras, lights. A black man in a suit was doing a stand-up for the evening news near the big freestanding concrete letters that spelled ZOO.

Zamatin had to smile at the thought of a man living undetected on the grounds of the zoo for eighteen months. It was right out of a children's story; the wilderness within the city, the secret hideout, life among the beasts.

The man had become nocturnal. Zamatin imagined him roaming the zoo at night, sharing his neighborhood with wildebeests, antelopes, dik-diks. Then during the day when thousands of people would arrive, he'd retire to his hut. When it was night, a city night that never got truly dark, there were again only himself and the animals.

Newspaper photographs showed the well-camouflaged hut, the tidy stacks of firewood and kindling, the furnishings scavenged from sidewalks before trash pickup. Social welfare agencies had stepped in, of course, to "manage the case," and Zamatin could imagine the man now in a sterile room lit by fluorescent light. . . .

He stopped at an information kiosk to pick up a zoo map. Pretending to look at it, he took from his pocket the four onionskin sheets he'd encoded the night before, arranged them inside the map, then curled it into a baton. He tapped his leg with it.

The cement was imprinted with various colored animal tracks to help visitors find their way to specific zoological domains. He followed the big blue bear prints to the panda house.

Visitors descended a few steps into a kind of subterranean viewing area—open to the air at either end—where huge glass windows formed one wall of the pandas' indoor quarters. Eager spectators craned into the two vast enclosures at the immobile bears, Ling Ling and Hsing Hsing.

Mating season was the only time the two were allowed to be together—otherwise they tended to maul each other. During the annual "mating window," the sexual problems of the duo were reported daily in the local media, often directly after items of global importance. It lent a surreal quality to certain broadcasts: an item about the Camp David accords or a report on a major natural catastrophe might be followed by the news that "Ling Ling rebuffed Hsing Hsing's advances."

Today, the pandas seemed comatose, as interesting as large black and white fur pillows. Still, parents lifted their children up: "See. See, Adam. That's a *panda*." "Where?" "See. *There*."

Just then there was an explosion not four feet from Zamatin, a concussive blast intensified by the cavelike observation area. The crowd convulsed in reaction, a quick reflexive jerk away from the sound. "A balloon!" someone yelled and the crowd immediately relaxed, although several children began to cry.

Zamatin walked out of the panda house and followed the path up to the refreshment stand located right above it, on its roof. Hot dogs and beer were served there and a clutch of customers waited in a queue. He spotted his contact easily. It was hot and the man carried his jacket draped over his arm, which exposed even more of the signal tie to Zamatin's view. In any other town, Zamatin might have felt conspicuous in a suit and tie at the zoo, but although most of the crowd wore T-shirts and Nikes, there were several men and women in business suits. Washington took itself seriously. Despite Carter's blue jeans and cardigans, it was a formal, almost stuffy city.

Zamatin watched his contact balance a beer, a hot dog heaped with sauerkraut, the jacket, a copy of the *Washingtonian*, and, of course, the curled-up map of the zoo. The man walked very carefully indeed toward one of the concrete picnic tables. Zamatin stayed in line behind a Hispanic family, and the man, having put the food down but still holding his camera and his map of the zoo, headed back toward him.

"Excuse me," the man said in accentless English. "Can I just get through to get a napkin?" Zamatin moved aside and in that instant, as the man stepped by him to reach the napkins, the pass was made, a seamless transaction. Zamatin held the new, curled map in his hand, feeling the heat on it from the other man's hand. He stuffed it into his pocket.

The refreshment stand, a strictly outdoor affair, had a good view of the pandas' huge exercise yards. Zamatin drank his beer looking out that way, over the stands of bamboo.

He was thinking about the information he'd just handed to his contact, information that he'd encoded last night. It included a description and short history of Dasha's photograph, and everything Zamatin knew about how Neil Walker came to possess it. He'd provided Walker's address, telephone number, and the fact that Walker had a live-in housekeeper. He'd noted that Walker was on vacation in Maine and given the date of his expected return. He'd included a short summation of Walker's career, reminding Center of his part in the Boris Shokorov debriefing.

Occasionally he offered Center his recommendations about intelligence he reported, but this time he hadn't. Obviously the photograph had some potential to expose Dante.

He did caution that if steps were to be taken, there were a lot of loose ends which would require attention. Besides Walker, Nicola Ward might have a copy of the photograph; Allenby's certainly would have retained copies of all the documents it had supplied to Walker. And Hobie James had *seen* the photograph and been promised a copy, although Zamatin thought it unlikely that he had it yet, or would get it, until Walker returned from vacation.

In closing, Zamatin speculated that the greatest danger to Dante was presented by Walker and (should he obtain a copy of the photo) by James. They hadn't recognized Dante yet, but both were professionals, schooled to be observant. They would understand the implications of his presence in the photograph, and not least of all, they were in the position to do something with the information.

The printed yellow bird tracks on the sidewalk, and the sign of the crested grebe led Zamatin toward the huge, enclosed bird cage, where he'd promised to meet Moira. They walked around the zoo together, then ate dinner at Omega in Adams Morgan before driving back to his place.

"Now you can have your way with me," Moira suggested in a totally uncharacteristic way, as she settled into the couch, fidgeting, crossing and recrossing her legs. She'd been worried by his solo trip to Sardinia. He guessed she'd been reading articles: "How to Keep Your Man." He found it touching to watch her now. She struggled with her natural reserve, and reached over to touch his thigh. Although her tentative, shy touch was certainly not sexual, her determination to please him made it obvious that he must make love to her. She would consider anything else a rejection. When it was over, they returned to the couch and watched the late news.

Some footage of street fighting in Kabul was replaced by the anchorwoman's face. Then Dante's face swam into view. "Administration spokesman," intoned the anchorwoman, reverently pronouncing Dante's name, "responded this afternoon to the most recent developments in Afghanistan."

Zamatin sighed. Dante had risen so high, was so visible, that he wasn't sure what would happen if he were exposed. It would cause global tremors, would in itself upset the balance of power.

Dante made a joke and smiled his famous dimpled smile. Zamatin jumped up and flipped the channel.

"Val!" Moira complained. "Don't you care about what's going on in Afghanistan?"

"No," he answered truthfully. "I don't."

CHAPTER

FORTY-FOUR

Maine

With Andy's help, Walker made pancakes for breakfast and then Andy tried his luck casting from the deck. Twice, his hook got caught in the oak tree but he was able to free it himself. Walker continued cleaning up the breakfast dishes, a time-consuming procedure that involved heating water, pouring it in basins, washing, dipping.

"Didn't you catch enough fish yesterday?" a voice asked.

"Oh, hi!" Andy said with genuine pleasure in his voice. When Walker looked outside he saw that the voice belonged to Kate Ward—who had towed their dinghy back as promised. Andy offered her some hot chocolate and Walker put the kettle on. Ordinarily he would have stepped into the conversation and tried to "help" Andy—acting as a buffer, for instance, explaining for Andy why he couldn't do something, or being friendly on Andy's behalf when Andy was acting sullen—but he could see that Andy and Kate Ward had forged an unlikely friendship during their boat trip.

"Would you play Monopoly with me?" Andy asked. Walker stopped himself from intervening and making excuses, like "She probably doesn't want to." He often did things like that, as if he could somehow spare his son rejection. "Dad always cheats and lets me win," Andy said. "I don't think he really likes to play."

Kate struck Walker as too old to want to play games with Andy, but then, Andy was always making friends with surprising people.

"I'm very very hard to beat at Monopoly," Kate warned.

"So am I," Andy said fervently. "Mrs. Bradshaw—she's our housekeeper—she usually beats me, but she is *super* lucky."

"What do you mean, *usually*," Walker said. "The woman is *undefeated*."

Kate chose the shoe.

"That was always my mother's favorite piece," Andy said, without emotion.

"She was smart then, because it's the luckiest piece," Kate said.

The game was close, but even with the luckiest piece, two hours later, Kate lost the long, seesaw battle to Andy, refusing to give in until she was totally bankrupt and every piece of property was mortgaged.

"Good game," Andy said, tilting the board and sliding the plastic houses into the box. "Maybe I'll beat Mrs. Bradshaw next time. Maybe I've turned the corner."

At about the same time Andy Walker completed the construction of hotels on Indiana, Illinois, and Kentucky avenues, Lavinia Bradshaw was closing the front door of the Walker house in Alexandria. She'd finished the laundry and ironing, and was going to catch a bus to the Landmark Shopping Center, where she wanted to buy some underwear at Sears, Roebuck. Then she planned to treat herself to lunch at the cafeteria.

The bus stop was only three blocks from the house and she'd covered two of them when the thought occurred to her that she'd left the iron plugged in. Her steps slowed as she tried to convince herself that it wasn't true—reviewing in her head the act of pulling the plug out of the socket. But that hopeful image wouldn't take, and the notion of the iron charring the ironing board, and a smoldering ash catching on the curtain, and the house burning down— all because she was too *lazy* to go back and check what she was too *old* to remember—became impossible to dispel from her mind and she knew she wouldn't enjoy her shopping trip unless she went back and made sure about that iron.

She walked up the brick front steps, making a mental note to herself to water the two concrete flower tubs blooming with wilted impatiens when she got back from Sears. She unlocked the front door. She was annoyed with her faulty memory and was muttering to herself, "I bet I *did* unplug it. I just bet I did," as she stepped toward the stairs.

It was then that she smelled the aftershave lotion, and started to turn. The flattened edge of a large hand swept in front of her eyes—half uppercut, half backstroke. Lavinia's last, painless impression was of a flash of light as the bridge of her nose went crashing into her brain. She was dead before her knees hit the floor.

Nicola stood now on the deck outside her cottage, watching Kate tie up the motorboat.

A spider web, jeweled with raindrops, dangled from the top railing, swaying slightly in the breeze, but not releasing any of its water. Nicola wondered where the spider was—probably up under the railing—and her hand jerked away.

"What'd you do?" Nicola asked.

"Played Monopoly with Andy," Kate said. "He won—I must be losing my touch."

"I thought you might bring them back; I mean I thought they might come over for a visit."

"You like him, don't you," Kate teased.

"Who? Andy? Yes, he seems like a nice boy."

"No, not *Andy*. Andy's father."

"He's all right."

"Hmmmm," Kate said. "Okay."

Joe Fayva, who had the cabin next to theirs, waved from his boat as he started it up; they waved back.

"Let's go blueberry picking," Kate suggested. Nicola was surprised. Kate's energy level was rising. Yesterday, she'd surprised Nicola by offering to take the boy for the boat ride, and today, by taking the dinghy back. Maybe befriending the boy would be good for Kate. Maybe a relationship with a child, especially a handicapped one, made her feel strong, responsible.

"We'll get soaking wet," Nicola warned.

"And munched up by mosquitoes," Kate added. "I'll get the bug stuff if you'll get the pans."

Nicola got small pans from the kitchen cupboard—it wasn't a great blueberry year—and after slathering their arms with Ben's pungent insect repellent, they set off up the road.

FORTY-FIVE

Bob Hastings sat in his utilitarian office deep in the interior of Allenby's Antiques, grateful, for once, for the lack of windows. His boss, Rudolph Michalowski, was not expected in until the afternoon, a happy coincidence, because Bob Hastings was nursing a thumping hangover. He was supposed to be typing up entries for a catalog to accompany a very boring sale of French provincial furniture scheduled for October. This was the kind of work he was given when there was nothing else for him to do—tedious work that hardly required the "eye for quality" for which he had been hired.

Nor did it draw on any of his knowledge or make use of any of the training he'd been put through. It was secretarial work, and his resentment, fueled by the pain in his head—the typewriter bell was enough to make him wince—became so great he had to stop typing. He put his feet up on the desk, brooding, listing worries in his head.

He combed his fingers through his hair. Three or four hairs came away in his hands. Seeing them there sickened him. There was now no doubt at all that, like his father before him, he was going bald. No matter how much he looked in the mirror and rearranged his hair so that the deep vees receding from his temples were less obvious, he could no longer pretend that Significant Hair Loss was not occurring.

And two weeks ago some hillbillies had moved into the apartment next to his. They cooked terrible, greasy-smelling things and played country music too loud. The stairway was beginning to smell like beer and urine. And yet he knew he'd have trouble finding another place as nice for the money.

And, worst of all, definitely winning the bad-news sweepstakes, Deedee Stallings, his girlfriend, had informed him that past weekend (while they were waiting for a taxi—she hadn't even waited for privacy) that she had herpes, so he'd taken to retreating to the bathroom at least twenty times a day and minutely inspecting his penis for telltale bumps.

His buzzer sounded and he picked it up, already preparing an excuse for not having the catalog work done. But it was Debbie, from reception, and he relaxed. She announced that a Mr. Chatterjee wanted to see him—"He specifically asked for you, Bob"— about a piece of old jewelry. "I tried to put him off, love," Debbie said, "but he's really . . . well . . . insistent."

Normally they didn't take walk-in appraisals. A referral of some sort was necessary, except for a few times each year when they scheduled a free appraisal day—an all-comers kind of thing. Since it would give him an excuse to postpone typing, he agreed to see the man.

"C'n you come out and fetch him?" Debbie wheedled. She'd never have asked this of Michalowski or Worthington, or any of the . . . "*Please?*"

"Oh, all right," he agreed in an annoyed voice.

"Thanks."

Bob Hastings sensed immediately that there was something strange about the client, Mr. Chatterjee—apart from his being Pakistani. Chatterjee tumbled out a respectable old Celtic cross, stingily jeweled with some tiny rubies, but he seemed uninterested in what Bob Hastings had to say about it. And Hastings—who'd been trotting out his knowledge in order to impress the man—suddently stopped talking about the cross and asked the question that popped into his mind.

"May I ask how you got my name?"

"Plees?"

"Do we have a friend in common?"

"Ah." A deep, settling-in ah. Chatterjee pulled a packet of British cigarettes from his pocket and offered one to Bob Hastings,

who shook his head no. "Plees, you don't mind?" Chatterjee asked.
"No."

Chatterjee lit the cigarette and then appeared to study his fingernails. He looked up. "You are acquainted, I believe, with a man named . . . um . . . Petter Denning?"

Hastings frowned, which made his head hurt more.

"Ummm . . . he is a journalist fellow," Chatterjee elaborated.

Then Hastings remembered. Denning was a reporter, a freelancer he'd met at a party. Nice guy—he'd mentioned the *Voice, New York*. Deedee brought up the Fabergé egg, and he'd ended up telling this Denning guy about it. The next day he'd been worried—if the guy wrote a piece about it, Michalowski would fire him for sure. But as time went on and nothing happened, he'd stopped worrying. The guy wasn't a gossip columnist. He couldn't write a piece about a two-minute conversation at a party. "Yes," he said stiffly. "I remember Peter Denning. What of it?"

"Plees—I am a friend of his. He mentioned . . . ah . . . some . . . eh . . . valuables found in a trunk."

"Yes?" Warily. This guy didn't seem like a reporter.

"Plees—ah . . . I have actually a proposition to make to you," Chatterjee began, a bit breathlessly. And then he came out with it—offering a bribe, three hundred dollars, for whatever information Bob Hastings could provide about the clients who had brought in "these . . . ah . . . Russian treasures."

Bob Hastings was about to say "no way," but he didn't. "What exactly is it you want?"

Chatterjee beamed and lit a second cigarette. "Plees—we are interested in the name of the client and his address. We are interested in . . . ah . . . approaching . . . this person before publicity drives up the price of the eh . . . articles. My principal is a collector, you see."

Hastings thought about it. Allenby's would handle the sale anyway; he'd seen Nicola Ward sign the authorizations. He didn't see how it could hurt to give this guy an address. "Well, yes, I guess I could . . . do that."

"Excellent, excellent." Chatterjee pulled a billfold from his inside breast pocket and peeled off the notes. "Can you get the information right now or . . . should we met . . . ah . . . meet later at a place of your choice?"

Bob Hastings thought for a moment. He thought the file room would be less crowded at lunchtime. He named a bar on Second Avenue.

But Chatterjee wasn't done. He cradled the billfold and tapped it once. "Plees—my principal would be prepared to pay even more . . . ahh . . . another five hundred dollars . . . emmm . . . that would be in addition to the other sum, of course," Chatterjee paused to let the amount register. "Emm, for the file."

"I can't do that," Hastings said. He could smell Chatterjee's sweat. It was making his stomach turn. He wanted the man out of his office.

"Plees—is . . . of course, we don't ask you to *steal* the files, emm . . . just to make . . . emm . . . photocopies."

"I can't do that," Hastings said, a bit sadly.

Chatterjee waved the thought away, disturbing the cloud of cigarette smoke that hung in front of him. "It is up to you. If you change your mind, I will have . . . ah . . . the funds with me . . . when we meet later."

"You don't get it," Hastings said. "It's a huge file—boxes and boxes of papers and photographs—I can't possibly photocopy all that." Suddenly, he hated the thought of meeting this smooth little creep in a bar. "Look, wait here a minute and I'll get the name and address right now." When he stood up, his head throbbed.

"Ahhhh. I will be waiting here, yes?"

Hastings walked carefully toward the filing room. He was anxious, rehearsing his pretext if anyone challenged him while he was looking for the file, but, in fact, no one even looked at him.

Neil Walker headed back toward the cabin with an armful of kindling he'd gathered from the woods. The cabin wasn't insulated, so they had a fire most mornings to take the chill out of the air. He liked to keep the woodbox filled.

On his way back in, he saw the note taped to the door, with Cal Tuttle's spidery handwriting on it. *Mike Hale called. Please call back.*

When he returned the call, Hale's news was that he'd found out the identity of ROMEO. "Guess who? Everybody's favorite Russian," he said in a Don Pardo voice. "Val Zamatin."

Walker had figured Hale was bragging when he'd said he could find out who or what the crypto ROMEO was assigned to. Cryptos were sacrosanct, protected, he'd always been told, by state-of-the-art security measures. He was so shocked that it took a minute for Hale's information to settle into his head.

"You still there?" Hale said.

"Val," Walker finally managed. "So it's Val."

"Surprised?"

"I don't know. It's interesting."

"Makes perfect sense," Hale said. "I mean the flags make sense once you know that it was Zamatin who cashed in the Sorge net to the Nazis and the Japs."

"You think he was tracking the cell members."

"*Exactamente, señor.* He wanted to know if they were after his ass."

"Thanks for chasing that down."

"Sorry it ain't more helpful. When are you rolling back into town anyway?"

"Three days."

"Save me some time on the weekend. I got Andy a present—a go-cart that I bought from a guy over in Centerville who was moving to the city. But don't tell him; let me surprise him."

"He'll be your slave for life."

"Well, *hasta luego*. Bring me a lobster."

The operator called back, as he had asked her to, with time and charges and Walker pulled his wallet out, rounded off the amount and gave it to Cal Tuttle, who kept looking at his watch, surreptitiously, every minute or so, as if he couldn't believe anybody would talk that much, long distance.

"You gonna be around today?" Tuttle asked, pocketing the money.

"Most of it."

"Trying to get that old stump out with the come-along. C'you give me a hand?"

"No problem. How about right now?"

"Sounds good."

"I like this one," Kate said, "I think you should try it." She held out a simple white dress with a dropped waist and a scoop neck. "You look good in white."

"Don't you think it's too young for me?"

"You think you have to look dowdy now that you're forty? Come on, it's going to look great on you."

Nicola followed Kate back through the crowded store toward the dressing room. People tended to make way for Kate.

Neil Walker had invited her out to dinner that night—and asked if Kate would mind staying with Andy. Kate had insisted that she buy a new dress. Vicarious shopping, Nicola thought.

They'd been in town for four hours now. Kate seemed tireless, but she herself was exhausted and she hoped the white dress would do.

When she tried it on, she was amazed by how perfectly it fit, how wonderful she looked in it. She turned to one side and then the other, enjoying that rare occurrence of finding something that was made for her, that seemed to transform her. She stared at the mirror for another minute, admiring herself.

She stepped out into the store, to show Kate, in case she was making a violent error of judgment. There was evidence, hanging unworn in her closet, of mistakes—an unwearable red suit, a frightening pink dress. She should throw them away, but she couldn't. Every once in a while, she'd try on these disasters, thinking she might once again see the allure that had made her buy them.

"Oh, Mom, it's so great," Kate said when Nicola stepped out wearing the white dress. "It's perfect—didn't I tell you? It's completely perfect."

"You have a good eye, sweetie. I mean—I feel a little like Maria in *West Side Story*." She pulled the skirt wide, curtsying and sang a few bars of "I Feel Pretty." She giggled. A woman with a sailboat appliqué on her skirt said, "Are you about finished?"

She took the dress off almost reluctantly and charged it on her credit card. She hoped the charge would clear. She knew the card was almost up to the limit from the trip to New York—but it went through. She and Kate had to stop at the big house to pick up the mail and water the plants. She wanted to hurry through the chores at the big house so they could get out to the cabin with plenty of time to spare. She wanted to take a shower, take her time getting ready. She wanted to . . . *primp*. She hadn't been out with a man in more than a year.

· ·

Back on Willow Street she was just finishing up when there was a knock on the front door.

"Read your meter, ma'am?" Nicola showed the man to the basement door in a distracted way. A little while later the man came back out.

"Thank you, ma'am," he said politely. "Bye now."

Nicola watered the plants that were too big to make the annual move down to the cabin and she thought about mowing the lawn. But it was too hot and she decided it could wait. She really wanted to get down to the cabin and take her time getting ready. Kate had even offered to give her a manicure.

"We'd better take off right now if we want to miss the Iron Works traffic," Kate said.

"I'm ready," Nicola said. "Oh, wait, I need my white shoes."

She ran back in to get her shoes. She thought she smelled gas. But when she checked the stove, none of the burners were turned on.

"I can't wait to get into the shower," she told Kate.

"It's hot today," Kate said. "And if *I* think it's hot, we know it's really bad."

PART THREE

INFERNO

_____

August, 1980

CHAPTER

FORTY-SIX

The plan was for Nicola to drive Kate to the Walkers' cabin; Nicola and Walker would leave from there. When they got to the door, Andy's voice called: "Come in," before they had a chance to knock.

"Hi!" he said to Kate, looking at the shopping bags she was carrying. "What's that?"

"Just some stuff I thought you might like," Kate said.

"Hi," Walker said, to Nicola.

She admired the cabin—the old knotty-pine walls, the fine half ship mounted above the fieldstone fireplace. Andy explained its history. "It was Dad's grandfather who bought the land—from Mr. Tuttle's father. Do you know that I've come here every summer since I was born?" He stopped suddenly. "Except last year," he said evenly. "When I was in the hospital."

"He used to hide when it was time to go back," Walker chuckled.

"Someday I'm going to live here," Andy said.

"I brought you my comic collection," Kate said.

"*Thanks*," Andy said.

"But right now, I'm ready for another game of Monopoly. I want my revenge."

"Well," Walker said. "I guess we're not needed here." There was a slightly false tone to his voice, a sitcom nonchalance. "I'm embarrassed," he said to Nicola, "but I'm almost out of gas—can we go in your car?"

"No, I'm sorry," Nicola deadpanned. "Of *course*."

"Have fun," Kate said.

"Bye, Dad."

"Don't stay up too late."

The moment they got into the car, the enclosed space seemed to constrain their ease with each other. The air inside the car seemed dense and Nicola felt edgy. The heavy air seemed to press against her skin.

She felt like turning on the radio but she didn't. They rolled smoothly along the dark road. She flicked on the turn signal; it ticked loudly. She turned from Meadowbrook onto Berry's Mill Road.

Walker hadn't said a word since they'd gotten into the car and she couldn't think of anything to say either. She cleared her throat as if about to speak, and there was an expectant pause, but still, she said nothing.

"I like your dress," he said abruptly. "I—this is—I mean, I haven't been 'out' with anyone since Diana . . ."

"Do you think Andy minds? I mean—"

"He didn't seem to . . . uh . . . *notice*."

"Well," she said brightly, "where are we going?"

"I was leaving that to you."

"It's a good thing I spoke up because I was leaving it to you." She laughed nervously. "We might have ended up in Caribou."

"Kate's very nice to Andy; he's crazy about her."

"She's always loved kids. She wanted a baby brother in the worst way, when she was little. But Stan didn't want—" Her voice stopped as she negotiated a turn. She picked up again without finishing her thought. "All the kids from the neighborhood were always in our house. They played these elaborate games up on the third floor, pretending to be one huge family of *orphans*. They liked that idea, depending on each other." They rolled up the approach ramp to the Carlton Bridge. "Well, anyway," she said.

If Nicola hadn't been driving she might have looked back over her shoulder toward her house. She liked it the way it looked from the bridge, nestled into the town. And she liked the way the town looked, crouched on the bank of the river, with its steeples and widow's walks poking up above the houses. But she was heading away from town, and paying attention to traffic, and so she didn't look back.

She looked over at Walker, a quick glance. A good-looking man, but he didn't seem to care about that, which was a change. Jack Alaric, the last man she dated, had been something of a narcissist. Sometimes he'd stop to look at their reflection and she'd always think he was admiring them as a couple until she realized his focus was narrower, that he was really just checking himself out. She thought that people didn't really see themselves as they looked; everyone had a flawed self-image. Mirrors reversed you. Photographs froze you. Kate was a case in point. The mirror somehow didn't convey anything close to the truth to her. She shook off the thought of Kate.

"I think we'll go to Le Garage," she said suddenly.

"I thought it was *my* car that was out of gas."

Her good-natured laugh burbled up and she touched his arm. "Not *the* garage, *Le Garage*." This time she exaggerated the French pronounciation.

"Imaginative name." He started to stretch his hand out along the seat back, expansive, but then retrieved it.

"I think it really was," she said.

"What," he asked, puzzled. "Imaginative?"

Her giggle spurted out again and again she touched his arm, as if to physically include him in her amusement. "No," she said, "a garage. It really was a garage."

When she touched his arm this time, something swerved inside of her; it was as if the internal structure of her body rearranged itself slightly. A trigger was pulled, blood rose to her head, flushed her extremities. Without any warning, she felt a surge of desire. It surprised her, but, it shouldn't have; it had been a year. More than a year.

And from the moment she touched him, from that moment on, everything she said and did, no matter how proper or neutral its veneer, became different, seductive, purposeful.

She wasn't sure she could do it: make him like her, make him want her. As a teenager she'd been good at making boys fall for her. It had been a little frightening, the ease of her feminine power. All she had to do was look at a boy in a certain way, smile at him in a certain way, laugh a particular laugh. There was a way she'd

335

had of focusing her attention so perfectly as to exclude the rest of the world from his vision. Then she'd plant the seed, tell one of her friends, "Tell so-and-so I like him." And soon, he'd be her new boyfriend. She was a "good" girl, she never did "it," although everything short of intercourse she considered permissible.

And then, after years of having all the boys "smitten" with her (as Aunt Hillary had put it), she'd married Stan—Safe Stan, Security Stan. Who now was a Lamb of God. And had hair down to his ass and a son named Jesus. She giggled. The laugh took on a life of its own.

Neil Walker was looking at her as if he'd made an error in judgment. "I'm sorry," she managed. "I was thinking about Stan—my ex-husband."

"Pretty funny guy, I guess."

She tried to talk over her giggles. "No, I was just thinking that when we got married, he was . . . he was the straightest, the *safest* person—and then when he hit his 'midlife crisis'—don't you hate that phrase? I don't like to believe that, you know, that people get to schedule a 'midlife' crisis. Anyway Stan, you know, Stan was really . . . well . . . really buttoned-down, you know. And he ended up running away and joining a commune in New Mexico." She started laughing again, but got it back under control. "He spends his days cultivating corn with Stone Age implements and has a baby son named Hay-zooz."

"I guess you never know," Walker said in a neutral voice.

"His wife *weaves* his clothes. He looks like he's been upholstered." She started laughing again. "I'm sorry. It's not really funny; it's only recently that I've found anything about it remotely amusing." She rubbed tears away from the corners of her eyes. She felt guilty for a moment: using Stan to amuse another man. To seduce another man. She relaxed into her seat. "It probably sounds kind of bitchy, like I'm making fun of him."

"Well," he said. "There is an ironic tone there. But it does sort of sound like the sixties struck back at you."

"How long are you staying?" she asked lightly.

"Only a couple more days." He tapped his fingers on the dashboard a few times. "I wish we could stay longer." His arm did finally stretch out along the back of her seat, but didn't quite touch her. Nicola felt the tension in that inch between their flesh.

She inhaled sharply, which produced a deep swoony feeling between her legs. A couple of days, Nicola thought. Perfect. A fling, she thought. That's what they call it. Let's have a fling.

It seemed to Nicola that the dinner took forever; she ate everything unconsciously, without tasting it. The room was pretty and crowded, but even the murmuring swells of conversation seemed to rise and fall in sensuous waves. The bubbles of laughter ascended to the roof and popped and washed back over them in giddy splashes.

"Do you care for anything else?" asked the waitress.

"An afterdinner drink?" Walker suggested.

"I have a weakness for cognac," she admitted.

When the snifters arrived, he asked the waitress to bring the check and paid it, so that they could have their cognac on the terrace. When Walker pulled her chair out and touched her arm, she felt almost weak with desire. Her palms began to sweat and she clutched her cognac tightly, following him outside. The terrace had been crowded with diners earlier, but now there were vacant tables where they could sit and look out over the river. Two ruined clipper ships constituted the famous view—they'd been stuck there, in a sandbar, for sixty years.

"I remember," she said, pointing to the closest ship, which leaned on its side with its deck tilted toward the shore, "I remember when I was little, people used to go out there and tear off pieces for firewood until someone fell through the deck and . . ." Her voice was quavery, watery; she barely had the presence to finish the sentence. "And . . . and broke his leg."

"It's a beautiful night," he tried, but then his voice trailed away. He was kneading her hand in a distracted way. The rhythm of his touch stirred her and a tiny moan came out of her mouth. She clamped her legs together—between them it felt moist and sticky— but that pressure only increased her desire. Blood thudded in her ears.

"It's nice that the kids get along so well," she began but then he leaned over and kissed her. And the kiss was so passionate, so far from being appropriate in a public place that the minute their mouths separated, they stood up and literally ran out of the restaurant.

Nicola hardly had enough dexterity to fit the key into the ignition and start the car. Walker was rubbing his hand hard along her right thigh and her thighs were sliding open and her pelvis rocked forward in a way that allowed her clitoris to make contact with the seat. She was breathing heavily and each intake of breath sent a plume of sensation straight down between her legs.

"Wait," she said, forcing her eyes open, forcing herself to sit up. People were wandering out of the restaurant, walking by. She heard someone say, "I shouldn't have had that cake but I couldn't help it."

Couldn't help it, couldn't help it, couldn't help it. She drove across the bridge over the Sheepscot River to a little road on the other side—it led to a pottery store that had probably failed because it was too far off the main road. It was boarded up now, and for sale. Nicola pulled into the tiny parking lot behind it.

As soon as the ignition was turned off, they came together, making intricate and automatic adjustments to allow for the removal of obstructive clothing. None of this was easy inside a Subaru, and although Nicola had visions of public shame, they ended up getting out of the car. The bud of her clitoris felt swollen with blood, huge, throbbing. Their urgency was such that they never even got as far as lying down and Nicola received him standing up, braced against the cold metal of the car. Her knees went wobbly and she leaned heavily back against the car and she heard a sound like an animal's grunt come out of her mouth and then very quickly came the soft powerful explosion of her orgasm and she lost contact with the world for a moment in its sweet rush. Then she felt him come, too, and the walls of her vagina squeeze at his cock, as if to suck out every last drop of semen.

When it was over, they were both a little bit too surprised to say anything and they just stood there for a minute, holding each other up. And then, in the next second, she felt ridiculous standing there, bare-assed, in the moonlight, and he must have too. They broke apart, and he pulled his pants up from around his ankles and she pulled her dress down from where it had been bunched up around her waist. The car looked disheveled too, one of its open doors allowing a spill of light to fall in tawdry illumination of Nicola's underpants and pantyhouse where they lay on the ground. She started to put on her underpants but the crotch was too wet so she just used them to wipe herself off. She considered tossing them into the woods, but the thought of some tourist coming upon them and thinking of them as a particularly repellent form of litter stopped her. She stuffed them under the seat.

"I guess we should get back," she said. Her voice sounded strange, clumsy, as if she'd just learned the language. She was thinking, *I didn't have my diaphragm in.*

"Yes," Walker said, sounding relieved, "I guess so."

They drove silently for a few miles. She was thinking that she didn't trust herself. Lately she'd been thinking about being forty, about how she would soon be too old to have a baby. She wasn't sure if it was her body or her mind that had allowed her to "forget" about not having her diaphragm in. Or what it meant.

"I'm not usually like this," she heard herself say.

"Oh," Walker said, with an easy laugh, "me either. I mean . . . the last time I made love in a car . . . actually, *on* a car."

"It's a first for me," Nicola said. "I wasn't that kind of girl." She laughed, a giddy, nervous gush. There was something adolescent about the way she sounded, about the way she *felt*. Even the recklessness of risking pregnancy was a teenager's act, leaving the future to chance.

CHAPTER

FORTY-SEVEN

They crossed back over the Sheepscot and ten miles later, the Kennebec. To their left, the Iron Works rattled with activity—the lobster shift. Lights were strung along the two guided-missile frigates in the water, and lights shone out from the massive building. The bright points of welders' torches winked here and there and a dull thudding sound was audible behind the occasional sharp clang. The crane looming above the yard was such a giant that a red light flashed from its top to warn aircraft.

On the opposite side, the lights of Bath were sprinkled along the edge of the river and then back up the hill, duplicating themselves in the black water. The town looked luminous, beautiful, and there was nothing to break that peaceful impression.

Nicola turned off on Berry's Mill Road, driving automatically, the twists and turns imprinted in her brain. "Sure is a pretty night," she said inanely. She wanted to keep talking because she didn't want to acknowledge that it was happening again. A band of warmth across her thighs, which she opened as far as she could, given that she was driving. She hoped the air against her bare skin would cool her off but instead it seemed to inflame her and once again the very rhythm of her breathing became erotic, and she struggled to keep her eyes from closing on each exhalation of breath.

This time, she didn't approve of herself. This time, it was lust, not relief, not release. She squeezed her legs together and told herself to stop it, but she'd been chaste for so long, there was no stopping her body. Her body wanted more and it wasn't interested in decent intervals. She turned down Birch Point Road and when she shifted gears, allowed the pinky of her hand to trail along Neil Walker's thigh. Just this slight contact produced a shuddering thrill within the envelope of warmth that encased her and her thighs spread apart automatically.

And then his mouth was on her ear and she heard him say, "Oh baby," in a voice that seemed to be coming from the inside of her head and then his hand was under her skirt and his finger inside her and she let the steering wheel go for a second and closed her eyes. The car swerved; she heard a whimpering sound come out of her mouth.

"Up here," he said in a thick voice, "there's a place. Here." It wasn't much of a place, just a shoulder, where a car could get off the road if it met another one. They got out but didn't make it far. They lay down on the grass, right next to the tires, on the side of the car away from the road.

Nicola welcomed his weight on top of her. She wanted him to grind into her until she . . . until she was carried away by his thrusts. But he was more imaginative than that—he kept maneuvering her, even when she protested because she thought nothing could possibly improve the feeling she was having—he kept on repositioning, stopping to fondle, to suck, not listening to her feeble protests—until finally their bodies reached the equivalent of critical mass and it was impossible to make any movement at all without sending them both over the edge. "Don't move," he said but even speaking was too erotic, too much movement and as his final thrusts began she dissolved into the luxuriant rapture, the long spasm of pleasure. They lay there for a while, quiescent, tired.

When she opened her eyes, she felt for a moment a powerful integration with the world around her—the forest, the swaying tops of the trees, the glittery scatter of stars, the spiny explosions of the pine boughs, even the cool glint of moonlight on the car—she felt connected to these things in an intimate absolute way. The sky was spectacular, brilliant points of individual stars strewn against the translucent folds and swirls of the Milky Way. The pine needles felt springy, resilient under her, the cool dark air against her skin delicious.

But as soon as she moved, the mood shattered. The pine needles poked her and scratched her. She was cold, her flesh standing out in sharp points like a plucked chicken's—a disheveled, half-naked woman lying next to a car. A woman who, for the second time in an hour, had just fucked a near stranger. On the ground. Was she out of her mind? Anyone could have driven along, either time . . . indecent exposure . . . public nuisance . . . how would that be?

And no diaphragm.

"We'd better go," she said. But when they stood up, they came together for a moment and she put her head against his shoulder, and he embraced her lightly.

"Nicola," he said, "I just want to—"

"No, don't," she said, nervously. "It's better not to talk." She wasn't sure what it was she didn't want him to say. A long way from them, she could hear a foghorn moaning. They drove back to the cabin in silence. When he got out of the car, he came around to open her door but she shook her head no. He leaned down to kiss her and she let him, but it was a mistake because she wanted him again, flesh into flesh; she couldn't get enough of him and the force of her lust, the compulsive greed of it, unnerved her. It was like being rolled over in a huge wave at the beach: she was out of her element, out of breath, exhausted.

He stood back from the car, his weight on one leg, his hand pushing his sandy hair back off his forehead. "Hey," he said. Their eyes collided and she looked away. "See you tomorrow," he said. "Okay?" Tears were pressing into the corners of her eyes. She was embarrassed. She didn't trust herself to speak so she nodded. "We'll go sailing," he said, "okay?" She nodded her head some more but he seemed to be waiting for verbal agreement.

"Great," she managed to say. It sounded as though her mouth were full of water.

He hesitated for a second. "You okay?" he said.

"Yeah," she said. He squeezed her hand and went into the cottage.

As he turned away, tears began to slide down her cheeks. She struggled to control herself for Kate. She could hardly explain that she was crying because she'd just had the best fuck of her life. That she was weeping because she was overwhelmed. Don't exaggerate, she told herself. Don't make too much of it. Don't.

But also, she was ashamed of herself; she felt out of control. She wiped her cheeks on the back of her hand and turned on the ignition. She heard Kate say, "Bye." And then the slap of the screen door.

She turned on the radio; she wanted distraction. "Hi, Mom! Did you have a good time?" She could feel Kate's scrutiny in the car. An odd role reversal: Kate the suspicious mother, Nicola the wayward girl. "It's *late*," Kate went on in an edgy voice. "What did you *do* all that time?"

"Well," she began shakily. "I did have a good time." She launched into a detailed description of the food they ate, but then began to feel guilty because she was pandering to Kate's food obsession. "He's a retired spy," she said, changing the subject. "Did you know that? He used to work for the CIA."

Still, when they got out of the car, Kate behind her, Kate said, "Mom! What's this all over your dress?" She pinched it between her fingers. "God, it's pitch. *Your new dress*. You'll never get it out."

"We took a walk," Nicola said lamely. "I must have leaned up against a tree."

She opened the door and flicked on the light.

"God, it's in your hair too. You'll have to cut it out."

Nicola was initially relieved when this conversation was interrupted by a knock at the door. It was their neighbor, Joe Fayva, standing there in his bathrobe and slippers. His gray hair stuck up in points on one side where his pillow had flattened it. He looked at his feet.

"Come in," she said.

"No, no, no, no," he said, shifting his weight from one foot to the other. "What it is, is that Chief Herlihy been callin' you all night long an' when he can't get you, see, he calls me." He looked up sadly, then resumed looking at his feet. "The chief, see, he knows I live right next door. Anyway—I'm awful sorry here, but seems that your house up to town burned down." He looked up, helpless.

"What?" she said. "*What?*"

"It's a turrible thing." He shook his head.

"But it can't be true!" Nicola said, looking at Kate. In the same way that the living occasionally talk of a dead person—"I can't believe it! I just saw him yesterday!"—believing the evidence of their senses, believing their memory over a bare recitation of unsupported fact—in that same way, Nicola spoke of her house. "But we were just there today. Just *today*."

"Chief said you might want to call him," Joe Fayva mumbled. He stuck out his hand which held a tiny crumpled piece of paper. "Here's the number."

"Do you want to come in?" Kate asked.

He shook his head. "It's a shame," he said. "I'm awful sorry."

Nicola stumbled toward the phone. Chief Herlihy expressed his sympathy and recited technical details. "Must have started around three forty-five, four," he said in his booming voice. "There was an explosion. We sent three units out but the ones from West Bath and Woolwich and Brunswick—which might have helped, got stuck in that damn Iron Works traffic."

"*But I was just there, then*," Nicola said in an electric voice. "I mean I just left then, around three. *And it was fine*, I mean, *fine*. How bad is it?"

"You alone?"

"No," she said sharply. "Why?"

"It's . . . it's . . . I'm sorry but it's just . . . gone. I don't know what caused it but according to witnesses, the house just went up like a rocket." He paused for a moment. "And you know, these old ones, when they go they just . . . they just *go*. Nuthin's even standing—just your porch. Who's your insurance man?"

"John Blake."

"Give John a call. And I'm sorry, Nicola. I really am sorry."

Numbly, Nicola looked up John Blake's home phone number. A female voice answered, suspiciously: "Who *is* this? Do you know what time it is?"

"This is Nicola Ward. My house . . . my house burned down," she said apologetically. She couldn't believe she was saying that; she couldn't believe it was true.

John Blake's sleepy voice came on the line. "Calm down," he suggested automatically before she said anything at all. "Are you by yourself?"

"No—Kate's here."

"I want the both of you to sit down, have a drink or take a tranquilizer or something and then call me in the morning, all

344

right? There's nothing to be done tonight. I know you're covered, so don't worry about that—I know we've kept your coverage up to date. Okay? Call me first thing in the morning? Okay?"

"Yes," she said dully. "In the morning." She hung up and looked at Kate. "God," she said, "what are we going to do?"

Kate held her hand. "Poor Mom." Nicola began to shake. "Sit right there," Kate said, pointing her finger at Nicola. "I'll be right back." She came back with a blanket and some white pills and a glass of water.

"What are these?"

"They gave them to me once—they're tranquilizers."

"I don't want to be . . . tranquil." Nicola started laughing. It sounded horrible, like a monkey gibbering.

"Swallow them," Kate ordered. "Come on."

CHAPTER

FORTY-EIGHT

In her dream, she was trying to get out the door, but Kate was barring her way and no matter what she said, Kate wouldn't move. Finally she tried to physically move Kate aside but Kate's hand came up and slapped her. Nicola sat straight up in bed rubbing her cheek. She'd had a nightmare.

The pain in her cheek, the burning sensation—was that self-inflicted? Dream pain?

It was dead black in the room and totally silent. She found herself mistrusting her memory. Had she dreamed her house had burned down? Dreamed of making love to Neil Walker? Everything seemed phantasmagorical, illusory. Her cheek hurt from a dreamed slap. She groped for the light switch and sat up, blinking. She found her purse, her keys, stumbled out toward the car. Still in her nightgown, she drove toward town. She was almost convinced that she would turn the corner onto Willow Street and the house would be sitting there, fine, so that when she did turn the corner to confront the blackened wreckage, she felt nauseated. She stopped on the street in front of it. The area was cordoned off with poles. Stretched between the poles, bright orange plastic tape dipped and swayed in the night breeze. There were printed signs to warn away the curious.

By order of.
Danger.
No trespassing.

She pushed the car door open and stuck her head out and vomited. It didn't make her feel better. When she looked back at the house, her stomach turned again—the dead house was frightening and disgusting; it was like coming upon a raccoon or possum, squashed on the road, casually eviscerated by the whirl of a tire. The fire had destroyed . . . everything. All of her things. All of the things accumulated over a lifetime. All the little drawings Kate had made, the Mother's Day cards, the paint-by-number Christmas presents, the pressed flowers, the misspelled Valentine's Day cards. And the photographs of herself as a child, and Aunt Hillary, and even Stan, and the slides of Kate at her birthday party, and in her Halloween costumes, and the furniture made by Stan's grandfather, and all of it, every bit of it.

Nicola swung the car into a U-turn and drove back. She got the irrational feeling that the cabin would be burnt up, too, and she drove faster and faster.

The house was all lit up. Kate was waiting, worried.

"Mom. Why didn't you wake me up? Are you all right?"

Nicola broke down, then, sitting down on the couch, her composure disintegrating into huge convulsive sobs. Liquid poured out of her eyes, her nose ran; she felt Kate's hand on her back. She tasted saltwater in the back of her throat, as if she'd been swimming. She curled her fists into tight balls and pinched her face together and said, without opening her teeth: "What are we going to do? What are we going to do?"

Kate comforted her. "We'll be all right. Come on, Mom, we'll be all *right.*"

"We won't be," Nicola insisted. "You're not all right anyway. God. *God.* I can't do this."

Kate maintained a grim composure. "We *will* be all right, Mom. Don't you see that I'm better, that I'm getting better?"

"Nooooooo," Nicola moaned, shaking her head. "I don't see that."

Kate sighed. "I'm going to be all right," Kate said decisively. "*We're* going to be all right. You'll see. It's very sad about the house, it's *very* sad, but it's just a house. It's not the end of the world."

"All our things," Nicola moaned. "Everything."

Kate brought her a brandy and a smaller one for herself. "I love you, Mom. Come on, come on: it'll be all right." Nicola wandered outside to the deck and flicked on the lights. The water looked black, evil; she flicked them off. Kate stood next to her for a while. They didn't speak. When she finished the brandy, Kate brought her another one.

"I'm all right now," Nicola said. "Thanks. Go to bed, honey; you'd better get some sleep."

"Are you sure, Mom? Are you sure you're okay?"

"Ummmhmmm. You go on Katie. You look wiped out."

As soon as she heard Kate's door close, she walked down the ramp, in the dark, to the float. She listened to the water slapping against shore. The bay was dark except for one light up by Birch Point. It wasn't Neil Walker's cottage, though. His was dark. Her shoulders slumped; she felt the weight of the night air pressing down upon her. She felt weak, ineffectual. She was getting weaker. At least Kate was keeping her composure. Kate was getting stronger.

She drained the brandy. She'd never been able to take care of anyone: Aunt Hillary, Stan, Kate. She'd always blown it. They died, they left, they starved themselves. She couldn't even take care of any *thing*—the house. How could the fire have started?

She had probably left something on—the teakettle, the iron. She had probably destroyed the house over some detail like that. Because she was in a hurry to get home and polish her nails. Shave her legs. A sob caught in her throat and her eyes blurred with tears. Where would they live now? What would they do? She stumbled back inside to bed. Around dawn, when the birds began to wake up, she finally collapsed into sleep, exhausted beyond further worry.

CHAPTER

FORTY-NINE

Neil Walker was drinking his first cup of coffee of the day, thinking about Nicola Ward, wondering if it really was something special with her or if it was just that it had been such a long time.

He'd felt strongly attracted to her when they met. But he'd been living with her mother's photograph pinned to his bulletin board. And she looked so much like Dasha—it set up a kind of false . . . closeness or something.

Still he was—what?—grateful. It was certainly good that it had happened at last. He'd been celibate so long that breaking his celibacy had begun to take on heavy, symbolic weight. This was perfect. He did find her physically compelling and it had happened without him thinking about it, without complications. He'd be leaving in a few days so it would be a self-limiting affair, which was good. He wasn't ready for anything more.

He'd like to see her again—alone. Maybe tonight, maybe after their sail. At that thought, his already energetic, happy mood bumped up one more notch. He rapped his fingers on the table and poured milk into Andy's Rice Chex, humming tunelessly.

"You're in a good mood," Andy said.

"Hey, I'm on vacation. Hot chocolate?"

"Yeah, okay."

Walker tossed another log into the kitchen woodstove and stirred a packet of instant hot chocolate into boiling water.

"I asked Mrs. Ward and Kate to come sailing with us today."

"You did? Good—let's sail out past Flag. Can we?"

349

"Well—" he started, but there was a rap on the aluminum frame of the screen door. "Cal," he said, looking over, surprised.

Cal Tuttle was standing there with a sheet of paper in his hand. "Saw your fire," he said. "Knew you were up." He shook the paper. "You got a phone call. Important, the man said. Here's the number."

Walker frowned. Who would call so early? Maybe it was Hale again. "Sorry you keep getting bothered with my telephone calls, Cal. Do you mind if I call back right now?"

"Shoo. Said you would."

Detective Shepler, Cal had scrawled on the paper in his wispy handwriting, City of Alexandria Police Department. Walker dialed, frowning, guessing that his house had been burglarized. There'd been a rash of break-ins in the neighborhood. He was just beginning to wonder why Mrs. Bradshaw herself wouldn't have called to tell him, when Shepler came on the line.

Shepler had a good-ol'-boy voice, a voice that had picked up its vowels somewhere south of Virginia. He guessed Georgia—closer to Savannah than Atlanta. "Mr. Walker," Shepler began, "I'm afraid I have some . . . ah . . . verrah unhappy news for you. Our understanding is that you are the owner and occupant of a house on . . . ah . . . South View Terrace."

"That's right."

"And that you were the employer of a"—he paused—"Mrs. Lavinia Bradshaw; is that information correct?"

Walker stood up straight and pressed the telephone into his ear: "What's happened? What's wrong?"

"I'm afraid Miz Bradshaw has been killed."

"What? *What?*"

"I'm sorry, Mr. Walkuh. I know it's a terrible shock to get this kind of news over the telephone. Let me give you the bigger picture here. To be more precise, Miz Bradshaw was . . . *murdered.*" The word had a horrible, primitive sound to Walker's ear, a word like a malignant club. "In your house, in your foyer," Shepler went on. He pronounced the "r" at the end of foyer.

"How?" he said. "How did it happen?"

"Officially, she was struck with a blunt instrument, although no weapon was found. She'd been dead for forty-eight hours when her sister came looking for her and found the body."

Walker couldn't think of anything to say.

"We had a hell of a time locating you, Mr. Walker. No one seemed to know exactly where you were or how to reach you. I got to add," Shepler said, "that your house is pretty mussed up, and while we are not *officially* assumin' anything yet, it seems likely that poor Mizzus Bradshaw stumbled into a robbery-in-progress. Things probably been taken, but of course we don't know what all was *here*. One of our best chances of tracing this crime is through the sale of the stolen objects so it would help the investigation if you could return as soon as possible."

"Of course. I'll arrange to come back right away."

"How soon do you think we might be talking about?"

"I'm here with my son; I'll have to find . . ."

"I know you prolly can't think straight. Let me give you some telephone numbers and the case number and so on—and you give a call when you know when you'll be arriving. Ah . . . they done dusting your house and so on, but you may—now this is up to you, but you may want to arrange . . . ah . . . other quarters for a few days."

"I don't know."

"I am sorry, Mr. Walker."

Walker hung up, thinking about Andy and about how he would take this.

"Trouble?" Cal Tuttle asked.

Walker's eyes shut and for a moment he felt totally exhausted, almost asleep on his feet. He pulled them open with an effort and looked at Cal. "Our housekeeper was murdered—*in* our house."

"Jesus H. Christ," Cal Tuttle said, and shook his head. It was the first time Walker had ever heard him swear.

He asked Cal not to say anything to Andy. "It's going to be hard on him—he—they were friends, you know. "I've got to make a few more calls."

"How about if I go see Andy?"

"Thanks Cal, yes."

Walker stood there for a minute, thinking about what to do. He couldn't take Andy back to the house; that was for sure. He thought of Hale. Mike would probably be glad to have Andy stay for a while.

But Hale wasn't "in." Walker left an urgent message, folded up the paper with the numbers Detective Shepler had given him and stuffed it into his pocket.

Back at the cottage, he found Cal washing the dishes and Andy furiously doing leg lifts. Kate Ward was there also, encouraging Andy and counting for him.

"Eighty-seven, you're awesome, eighty-eight, keep going, eighty-nine." When Andy reached one hundred he collapsed.

"One hundred!" Kate Ward said and shook Andy's limp hand. She stood up and looked at Walker.

"Hi," she said, casting her eyes down to a spot on the floor. "I came over because I—because we can't go sailing today."

"Well, that's okay. You didn't have to—"

"The thing is, our house burned down," she said, matter-of-factly. "Not the cabin!—the one in town. It burned down last night."

Andy's jaw dropped in a cartoonish way. "Your house burned *down*," he said in a borrowed Disneyesque voice. "Your house really burned *down*."

Andy seemed to be mimicking some spunky kid on a television show. Walker saw how television, by continually exposing its audience to life-and-death situations, provided models for reaction to those events. It seemed to him a bad thing. It meant that nothing, no event, however extraordinary, had not already "happened."

"Is your mother all right?" he asked Kate. "How did it happen?"

"No," Kate said, biting her lower lip. "And we don't know how it happened. Of course we keep saying how lucky it was that we weren't *there*. . . . But Mom . . . Mom's not . . . uh . . . taking it well." She gave him a look as though she didn't want to be alone in this anymore. "I thought maybe . . . maybe you could come over." She looked up and met his eyes. He agreed immediately.

In the motorboat, as they bounced over the choppy water, weak alarms were beginning to make themselves heard in the back of his head. As a CIA officer he'd been *professionally* suspicious, and had established a vigilant mental warning system that responded to any tiny deviation from the expected run of things. Although the network of warning sensors had deteriorated, their connections frayed, it still was there. He'd learned early and learned well that almost *any* coincidence was worth another look.

A homicide at his house. Probable burglary.

And Nicola Ward's house burned down.

On consecutive days.

While he was working, indirectly, for Nicola Ward.

He never did believe in coincidence.

Nicola lay on the couch, staring at the ceiling. The ceiling was made of acoustical tile, pocked and veined to resemble—what?—marble? She wondered why anyone would want to make ceiling material look like marble. She imagined the ceiling as actual marble—an oppressive mass, waiting to fall.

She had to get up and put the phone back on the hook and make some calls. She had to, but she couldn't get herself to move. She had to call John Blake, Stan. She should call Stan. It was *his* ancestral home. Was. *Was.* Tears pricked her eyes. Then she heard voices and footsteps on the ramp and she sat up.

She realized immediately what Kate had done—gone to get Neil Walker—she heard his voice. She jumped up and ran into her bedroom. She was a mess, completely disheveled. Still in her nightgown! With white athletic socks on her feet. And her hair! Her hair was still full of telltale pine pitch, still sticking straight out from the back of her head. She didn't want Neil Walker to see her like this. She wanted him only to see her at her best; she wanted to be perfect. She ran into the bathroom, intending to take a quick shower. But even as her hand turned the shower knob clockwise, turning the water on, some opposing muscles, operating independently, began to turn it the other way, off.

She couldn't be taking showers. She couldn't believe she was worrying about how she looked. Her house had just burned down.

Burned *down.*

Nicola Ward looked ten years older this morning, Walker thought. And yet there was something about the way she looked that made her even more desirable than she'd been last night in her elegant white dress. The bruised smudges under her eyes, the raggedy chenille robe, the way her hair stuck out—she looked as though she'd just gotten out of bed. It made him want to get back into bed with her.

"Uh—hi," she said. She tried a smile, which didn't make it. "I . . ." She shrugged. "I—uh—guess Kate told you what . . . what happened." She hugged the robe around her. Her smoky voice was even rougher around the edges than usual. "I—uh—don't quite know what to do." Her voice was just a whisper at the end of the sentence and he saw her features compress as if she was going to cry. She hid her face in one spread-out hand.

"How can I help?" he asked.

She took her hand away from her face. "I'm sorry. I keep telling myself it's just a house, that it's 'lucky' Kate and I weren't in there, you know, but . . . I just . . ."

"What can I do?" He put his hand on her shoulder and she sagged into him briefly. He looked at her and he saw in her face the same thing he felt, desire, but it was so inappropriate she pulled away from him abruptly and tore her eyes away from his.

"Would you care for some coffee?" Kate said in a waitress voice.

"I've got to make these calls," Nicola said to no one in particular and drifted over toward the telephone. It was a green wall phone, next to the door. She kept messing up the dialing and pushing the receiver down with a bang, on the edge of hysteria. Walker took her a cup of coffee and set it on the counter near her. She smiled at him quickly.

She spent a long time on hold and then she seemed to be answering questions about her lawnmower and the location of various flammable liquids. He heard her say: "I doubt it. He lives in New Mexico." She mentioned a visit by the gas man. Hectic red spots came up in her cheeks and Walker could see how angry she was. "My house never burned down before," she said. "I wouldn't know what was routine." She hung up.

She rubbed the back of her hand over her eyebrows. Her elbow was resting on the washing machine and she was propping up her head with the back of her hand. Her fists were clenched. "I think," she said in a weak, amazed voice, "they think I burned down my house."

She was dialing again. She looked over at Walker, with a brief shimmer of liquid in her eyes. "I wonder what the insurance man will say."

John Blake sounded nervous and embarrassed. "Nicola," he said, clearing his throat. "I was just going to call you."

"Oh. Please apologize to your wife—I didn't mean to wake her last night, I—"

"Nicola, I have to tell you that the company has decided to investigate the fire." He said this very rapidly as if the meaning might be lost in the speed of its telling. "The fire department will conduct an investigation also but as an interested party, the company does its own investigation. A man's already been assigned; he'll be arriving at the site later this afternoon. I'm sorry—"

"What? What are you saying?"

He made an exasperated sound. "Apparently the fire didn't quite look right. Arson has not been . . . ruled out. I don't mean to suggest that you—"

"Arson?" Nicola said. Her voice was too tired to demonstrate the outrage she felt. "*Arson?* They think I'd burn down my own house?"

"No one's saying that," he said quickly. He paused. "It's known that your financial situation . . . that your daughter was ill . . . um . . . I don't mean to suggest anything by this but it's also known that—that you . . . that you went to see Betty Kincaid at Coastal Realty, that you tried to rent the place and failed. I probably shouldn't tell you all this," he finished in an amazed voice.

"John! I thought you were *my* insurance man, I mean I thought— and it . . . you . . . ."

"You know we don't just show up at the door with a check, Nicola, the way it is on television. I mean with the ruins still smoldering in the background. There's always *some* form of investigation."

"My house just burned down," she said in a voice an octave higher than her normal one. "With just about everything I own in it and all you can talk about is . . . is how we have to have an investigation." Her voice went whiny on the word "investigation" and she stopped to take a deep breath. "Where's your . . . your *fireside* manner? I don't believe this. What do you do if someone's in a car wreck? Administer a breathalyzer test? Check his maintenance records? I mean—isn't that police work? Aren't you supposed to help *me*?"

"Nicola, I just want you to be informed. It's just something we have to get through, part of the procedure. I'm just pointing out how it *looks*—it doesn't mean—"

"I don't believe this. *I don't believe it.*"

"Calm down."

She hung up.

"Well," she said, turning toward Walker with a brittle look in her eyes.

He touched her arm.

"Are you all right, Mom?" Kate said. "What's happening?"

She laughed. "They think I set the house on fire—they think that's . . . possible. It exploded, they said. It didn't look right."

"*I'll* tell them you didn't," Kate said in an outraged voice. "Those *jerks*."

"It's just kind of adding insult to injury," Nicola said in a shaky voice.

Walker pulled her toward the door. "Come outside with me for a minute."

She looked at him, puzzled, but followed him out to the deck. They stood there for a moment, watching a gray sea below a gray sky. The mist obscured the horizon. A bank of dark clouds with a skirt of rain was moving toward them, closing fast.

"I don't want to alarm you," he started.

"Oh," she said, running her index finger restlessly over a knot in the wood of the railing, "I won't be easy to alarm right now. It's been quite a little day."

He slid his arm around her shoulder and she leaned into him, but stiffly, without relaxing. "My housekeeper was murdered in my house back in Virginia," he said in an almost listless voice. "And my house was ransacked."

She stiffened even more. "What?"

"It happened two days ago, but I just got the call this morning. Please don't say anything—I'm trying to figure out how to break it to Andy. She was, you know, a sort of mother figure," he muttered.

"God, the poor kid," she said. "I'm sorry."

"What I'm trying to say," Walker went on in an insistent voice, "is that I don't like the way things look. I've got a bad feeling. If we'd just met and we didn't have anything to do with each other, I wouldn't make anything of these two incidents but bad luck. As it is . . . I don't really know how to say this. Look, I want you to be careful. I want you to lock your doors, be suspicious of strangers, and tell me if *anything*—I don't care how trivial—seems unusual."

"Do you mean you think someone did burn down my house?"

"Let's just say I think it's possible."

"But *why?* Why would anyone want to do that?"

"I don't know. Maybe Allenby's leaked a copy of the false diary and someone thinks you're a long-lost Romanov and you're a threat to someone." He frowned and shook his head. "It doesn't make sense to me. I don't know."

"Why would that make them want to burn down my house?" she insisted.

"I don't know," he said, as if her question irritated him. "I—it's just . . . too much of a coincidence. Listen, can I make some calls? I've got to find someone to take care of Andy while I go back and tell the cops what's been stolen from my house."

"Why don't you leave him with me?"

"Yeah, that's just what you need."

"No! Really—I'm serious. I'm all right now. I mean, how long are you going to be gone anyway? A day or two?"

"I was supposed to *leave* in a day or two." He put his hand over hers and squeezed it. She sagged into him slightly and he squeezed a little harder. "Let me call the airlines. I'm not even sure I'll be able to get out of here—I know it's hard this time of year." He turned away from her. "Look," he said. "Aren't you cold?"

She didn't move, just kept looking straight out to sea. "No," she said, "go ahead. Call."

Stony clouds filled the sky. A gust of wind rocked the white pine above the cabin and loosened a spatter of raindrops on her head. She watched a lobster boat pull up to the blue buoy with black dots. The boat had a similarly marked buoy jutting out from its bowsprit. The lobsterman, in his yellow foul-weather gear, hauled in the pot, tossed one lobster into his hold and then flipped some shorts overboard. He let the line feed back over the side and then headed toward Dark Cove and the next buoy.

She was trying to consider what it meant if someone had deliberately burned her house down, but it seemed so unlikely that she couldn't even focus her attention on the idea. Walker thought she should be afraid, should be careful, but she lacked the energy for fright, lacked the attention for caution. She felt nothing. She stood there for a long time, noting the complex and transient effects of the wind on the water.

CHAPTER
FIFTY

Walker called the airline and arranged the flight to D.C., then called Rudolph Michalowski. "Ah," Michalowski said. "And how is your holiday?"

"Ah well," Walker said. "It's interesting."

"Have you met Mrs. Ward?"

"Yes. That's where I am right now. And I wanted to tell you about the document she found."

"Oh yes!"

Walker began to describe Borodin's diary, but Michalowski interrupted: "I'm fascinated, but can you just hold on for one moment?" There was a brief silence and then Michalowski came back on the line. "Excuse me, Neil, but may I call you back?"

Walker was disappointed because, in fact, the Borodin diary solved all their problems and he was anxious to tell Michalowski about it. But he said, "Sure."

"I have someone here in the office. Do you have a number where you can be reached?"

"Well." Walker hesitated. "I can call *you* back."

"I'm really sorry," Michalowski said. "But you see we've had a robbery—last night—and the authorities need some more—"

Walker interrupted. "Was any of the Ward stuff taken?"

"Well, the *objets* themselves are quite safe. They are elsewhere, you know, and the security is really meticulous. But some files were disturbed and now that you mention it, the Ward file was one of them. Of course, we have it all on microfiche in the research department. But the photographs were stolen—in fact, now that I am thinking of it, we will need a set. If you could return yours when you are all finished, then we won't have to bother Mrs. Ward to recopy her originals. Just a minute." Michalowski's hand was over the phone. Walker heard some mumbling. "I really will have to call you back. The police are—"

"My house in Virginia was burglarized," Walker said. "I don't know what's missing, but it's possible that the Ward documents were stolen."

"I see," Michalowski said slowly as the implication settled into his head. "Do you really think—" He stopped and Walker could hear him speaking to someone in the room. "Look, I really must go now and talk to these gentlemen from the police. Can I call you back? Where are you?"

"How about I call you in an hour," Walker said.

He stepped out onto the deck a different person.

Nicola noticed the transformation because Walker seemed barely aware of her. His glance seemed to have a hard focus, as if he were looking for her weak spots. She started to say, "What's wrong?" but the words evaporated in her mouth. He was looking at her with the grim expression of a doctor drawing aside the next of kin to deliver some bad news.

He paused for a moment and leaned on the railing. He recognized the mental shift that had just occurred; he was thinking like a Minuteman again, a way of being in the world he thought he'd abandoned permanently when he'd staggered home from Rabat in his bloody shoes. *Arson. Murder. Two burglaries.* He looked over his shoulder toward the road.

What he saw was both more and less than what he usually saw. He didn't see the spectacular natural beauty—the huge pine trees moving in the wind, the frothy stand of ferns, the rock ledges, the misty light. What he saw was the lay of the land.

The road itself was invisible, completely screened by trees. Because of the dense forest, the house would also be invisible from the road, but visible from the ledges, and visible from the top of the driveway. He studied the woods for anything wrong. He was looking for something that shouldn't be there: a disturbance in the bushes, a glimpse of fabric, a plume of cigarette smoke. He listened,

360

too, for a rustle in the brush, a dog's bark, the rumble of an approaching car.

He led Nicola toward the big boulder to the left of the dock; she called it Big Rock. It was large enough so that four or five people could sit on it. The constant beating of the water had hollowed out small crannies in the gray stone. The small snails called periwinkles lived in these tiny tidal pools and Walker picked one off and examined its retracting foot. He nearly threw it out into the water, like a stone, but stopped and replaced it in its pool. He looked across the bay. He could see his cabin; he realized he was relieved to see that it was still there and the thought caused him to shake his head.

"What?" Nicola said.

Unconsciously, she leaned back against him and although he liked the feeling of her body against his, he shifted away from her and stood up.

"I don't mean to be an alarmist," he said, "but when I looked across, I was relieved to see my cabin still there."

She turned to face him. "What?" she said in a flat voice.

His voice was neutral, professional. "My housekeeper was murdered, my house ransacked. Your house burned up and the file on your case was stolen from Allenby's. At the risk of having you think I'm paranoid—I think we should all take a little trip. Today. Right now, actually."

"You think all this . . ." Her voice slipped. She looked dazed.

"I think the possibility that they're *not* related is almost non-existent. And I think we've both been lucky so far."

"Umm, lucky." She shrugged. "I wouldn't say *lucky* exactly covered the way I—"

He interrupted, his voice harder now, frustrated by her nonchalance. He gripped her arm hard enough to hurt and at last he saw that fear began to break through her lassitude.

"If you'd been in your house when it exploded, do you think you would have survived? Do you? I don't have the illusion that whoever broke into my house was after Mrs. Bradshaw." He tapped his foot impatiently against the rock. "I wouldn't be surprised if our cabins weren't on someone's 'Places to Visit' list. I'd lay odds that trips have been made to Town Hall, wherever they keep the deeds, that deeds have been looked at, that—" He looked up at the sky. A B-52 from Brunswick Naval Air Station, probably on reconnaissance, angled up toward its cruising altitude.

"But why?" Nicola asked. "I mean . . ." Her hands rose momentarily, clutched a ball of air and then fell to her lap. "I don't get it."

"I don't know. It may have something to do with the Romanov stuff, or even your parents—you know, the spy connection." His eyebrows angled toward each other and he shrugged. "I don't know, I really don't get it, either, but whatever it is—let's not be sitting around figuring it out while someone hits us over the head."

"Okay," she said.

"We'll just go away for a couple of days to try to figure out what's going on. I don't care where we go—somewhere we can drive."

"You mean, Bar Harbor, Camden, something like that?"

"*Anywhere.* Bar Harbor is fine, wherever. Hell, we can go ten miles down the pike to Brunswick. I'll leave that to you—but let's make a reservation, let's make sure we have someplace to sleep. Judging from the shopping centers, this is a bumper year for tourists."

She stood up, looking out at the bay. The gray clouds had solidified and it seemed likely, from the sharp gusts of wind, that it would rain any minute. "Okay, what are we going to tell the kids?"

"Sort of the truth—but"—he hesitated—"nothing to Andy about Mrs. Bradshaw yet. In fact, I'll talk to the kids while you call for reservations."

"What *about* the fire—won't they . . . think . . . I'm leaving because I'm guilty—"

"Fuck that. We'll deal with that later."

The longer he stood there, the more he wanted to get moving. His eyes scoured the hillside and the ledges and then he followed Nicola inside. He told Andy and Kate in the least threatening way that as a precaution, because the fire had him worried, and a few other things were worrying him as well, that they would be taking a little trip for a day or two.

Andy was excited. "Where?"

"What's going on?" Kate asked.

362

"The fire is part of it," he said. "The fire chief seems to think it was set and your mom is the convenient one to blame, but we know it wasn't your mom."

Kate put her hand to her mouth.

"It's not just the fire," Walker said. "Some things were stolen from our house in Alexandria—"

"In our *house?*" Andy said. "Do they know—"

"Hey, we'll talk later," Walker said. He looked out at the bay. "I want to row home before the weather gets any worse. You and I have to pack a few things while Nicola and Kate are doing the same, okay? Get your life jacket on."

"Okay!"

Walker went into the kitchen, where Nicola held the telephone to her ear. She put her hand over the receiver. "I think I found us rooms," she said, "in Ellsworth."

"We'll be back in half an hour."

"Okay." She held up one finger and spoke back into the telephone. "That's right, two nights, uh-huh, okay." She hung up. "We can drive to the top of Cadillac Mountain," she said. "I've been up there a dozen times and every single time it's been socked in with fog, but maybe we'll get lucky. They say the view is wonderful."

Walker was already thinking that the phone wasn't safe and that they wouldn't go to Ellsworth. But he'd deal with that later.

"Pack Mille Bornes," Andy yelled to Kate. "I'll pack Monopoly." The kids had a different frame of reference: they saw this as an adventure.

Walker stood in the doorway and nodded his head. "You have your papers and photographs here?" he asked Nicola. "You know, the ones from the trunk."

She looked surprised. "Yes."

"Pack those," he said in a calm, definite voice. "Okay? It's important."

"Okay."

He opened the door. "Half an hour," he said. "Be ready."

Although it still seemed possible that he would find out that his house in Alexandria was the target of an ordinary burglary (but Detective Shepler's voice came into his head: "Your house is prittah . . . messed up.") and that Nicola's fire had been caused by faulty wiring, and that Allenby's had been burgled by someone wanting a leg up in an auction fight, he was leaning toward the theory that something in the papers or photographs from Borodin's trunk was the cause of all this violence. He still couldn't figure out what it could possibly be and remained ready to back away from his theory. He watched Andy trudge down the ramp slowly, methodically. He took a quick look at the bruised sky and untied the dinghy. Maybe two days in a motel would enable him to pry something out of those papers.

The tide was going out—had it been coming in, Walker would have been in worse shape, fighting the current as well as the wind. On top of that he was rowing badly, trying to hurry and paying the price for it. His left oar kept jumping up out of the oarlock and he splashed Andy three or four times. It seemed to take forever to reach Cal Tuttle's dock. When they did, they found Tuttle sitting cross-legged on the float jigging a drop line up and down.

"Fishing for flounder?" Andy asked.

"Yeh," Cal said. "No luck so far, nothing but crabs."

Walker tied up the dinghy, adding an extra half-hitch because of the weather.

"Red tide's gone," Cal said to Andy. "Dig some steamers with me when the tide goes?" He shook his hand at the sky. "I mean if the storm goes over."

Andy looked at his father. "I can't today," he said. "Me and Dad are going on a little trip."

"Dad and I."

"That so?"

"You get going," Neil said. He shot the breeze with Cal Tuttle while Andy progressed up the ramp. He wanted Andy to hurry, but he forced himself to keep quiet. Andy turned around and yelled back over his shoulder: "We're going to Bar Harbor."

"Bah Hahboh," Cal said, shaking his head. "Once was enough for me. Too durned many people."

Andy had almost made it to the top of the ramp. "Will you keep an eye on the place while we're gone?"

"Sure enough. Hey—" Tuttle slapped at the pockets of his windbreaker. "Almost forgot. Man was here checking for termites and carpenter ants. Got your receipt for you." Tuttle finally produced a flimsy green sheet of paper from his pants pocket. "Did a good job, too, crawling all around under there. You got carpenter ants?"

Walker felt the fear roll through him, an urgency that made his heart jump against the walls of his chest. In training, he'd been taught to subdue fear (biofeedback techniques, gleaned by Agency instructors from studies on treating phobics) and he did so instantly. The fear remained only as a kind of high, rolling pain in the back of his throat. He heard his voice, heavy, compelling: "Andy! Stop!"

He watched Andy turn from the door with an annoyed, puzzled look. "Dad?"

"Don't touch the door! Come here!"

"Are you all right, Dad?"

Walker was thinking.

The gas man. Nicola had mentioned a gas man.

The termite man.

He'd ordered no inspection of his cabin. The flimsy green receipt fluttered in his hand and he looked at it. It had no business imprint; it was the kind of receipt pad you could buy at the dime store.

"What the heck?" Cal said. "What the heck's going on?"

"Can I use your phone?"

"Don't know why not, but . . ." Cal turned his attention to the drop line and resumed winding the thick green line around the square wooden frame.

Andy stood at the top of the dock, looking puzzled. Walker began to go toward him.

"What's the matter, Dad? Why shouldn't I touch the door?"

He put his hands on Andy's shoulders. "Remember *why* I told you we were going to go away? That there were some funny things going on and I thought it would be . . . safer." Andy nodded solemnly. "Well, Cal told me a man was here checking for termites and the thing is I didn't ask for a termite inspection. What I think is that—just to be on the safe side—we won't go in our house just yet. I think it might be sabotaged."

Andy looked impressed but not frightened. "You mean a *bomb?*"

The word bomb didn't mean much to Andy; it meant television explosions, *Star Wars*. But Walker was too familiar with the effects of explosion on human beings. He'd seen enough exploded bodies, enough torn flesh, enough blood. He thought of Andy's hand on the door; his heart twitched in his chest.

"It's probably nothing," he said.

"Now who in the world would want to do something like that?" Cal said. Clearly, he thought Walker was nuts, the idea of a bomb preposterous.

"Nicola Ward's house in town burned down last night," Walker said.

"The old Ward place? On Willow Street?"

Walker nodded; Cal Tuttle hugged his arms around his body.

"A bomb?" Andy asked again. "In our cabin? Really?"

"I know that I didn't order any termite inspection," Walker said. "I know that for sure."

"My Dad used to work for the CIA," Andy said proudly.

Once Walker succeeded in dislodging the teenaged Alice Preble from her conversation with her girlfriend Tina Barrett, he tried to get Nicola. Her line was busy. Then he tried Mike Hale again but he struck out there, too. He left an urgent message for Hale and said he'd call in two hours. One of Mike's assistants, Roxanne, promised she'd have Hale standing by.

He considered calling the police but dismissed the idea almost in his head. It wasn't persuasive. His fear was intuitive, based on a complex of circumstantial evidence. And anything with the police immediately. Where would the nearest bomb squad be? Portland? Even if they believed him and responded. He ran through the story would take hours; he didn't think they had the time.

He called Nicola again. Fear rose in his throat as he heard the busy signal. But what could he tell her over the phone anyway? He figured he could drive or row to her house in about fifteen minutes, maybe less.

As he hung up, a tremendous rush of wind buffeted the cabin. Any minute, he thought, it would rain.

Nicola was trying to reach Stan, to tell him about the house. Finally, she heard the phone ringing, but the connection was one-way only. She could hear Consuela saying, "What? Hello? Hello?" in her faint, querulous Spanish voice. She tried again and asked for Stan. "Is this Nicola?" Consuela said. She pronounced it with the accent on the second syllable so that it rhymed with Coca-Cola.

She was nervous, her palms sweaty. She pressed the receiver hard to her ear and then Stan came on the line: "Your house burned down," she said. The truth was out. She still thought of the house as his.

"What?" he said. "What are you saying, Nic?"

"The house on Willow Street. It burned down."

"What?"

She had to repeat it twice more before he understood her. Stan took it philosophically, the same way he reacted to all information these days—God's will was mentioned. Anyway, she felt better once he knew. She looked out the front window and saw that Neil's little dinghy was not in sight; he must have reached his dock. She started to pack.

She and Kate would share one suitcase—she asked Kate to bring in two or three days' worth of clothing and added them to the stuff she'd packed. She packed the papers and photographs in another suitcase and then she took the two bags out to the deck and went in to comb her hair and put on some lipstick. On top of the washing machine was the bag from Bookland she'd bought the first day Neil and Andy had come over, books still in it. It seemed such a long time ago that she'd bought the books, enthusiastic for her "summer reading program."

She thought she might as well take the books along. She took the bag out to the deck and put it into the light suitcase, the one full of clothes. The other one was already so heavy. Kate ran back in to get the deck of Mille Bornes cards.

"We're ready," Kate said.

"We'd better check the windows," Nicola said. "I think it's going to rain."

CHAPTER
FIFTY-ONE

Neil Walker stood in Cal Tuttle's kitchen, looking out toward the water. The sea was getting so rough, they'd have to drive to Nicola's.

"Did anyone go near the car?" he asked Cal.

"I was down on the dock most of the time the man was here."

"I'll have to check the car," Walker said.

"Do you want to take mine?" Cal offered in a pinched, reluctant voice, an offer which Walker accepted immediately. "I mean, I'll drive you over," Cal elaborated.

"Great," Walker said. "Let's go. Andy?"

It took several cranks to get Tuttle's ancient Pinto started. "Runs like a top," Cal said proudly. "Runs on a teacup of gasoline, too."

The road out from the cabin was a narrow, one-lane dirt road so narrow that in places the bushes brushed the side of the Pinto. Cal drove slowly, as indeed Walker always did; otherwise, the rocks and ruts would wreck your suspension. About two-thirds of the way out to the main road, they met a Jeep Cherokee. Cal started to back up, muttering, "Just our luck." When two cars met on the road, it was normal procedure for one of them to back up to the closest wide spot. There were several of them and Cal had just passed one.

"Do you know that Cherokee?" Walker asked. "Is it familiar?"

"Nope."

"Go around it then, go through the bushes."

Cal stopped backing up. "No sir, I'll scratch my paint."

"Do it!" Walker shouted in an amazingly loud voice, a voice so loud that the sound alone seemed to propel the car forward. The Pinto rammed through the bushes. Out of the corner of his eye, Walker saw Andy clap his hands over his ears.

By the time the Pinto lurched onto the road, Walker saw that he was right, that the Cherokee driver was reversing direction in a brutal K-turn, coming to pursue them.

The vehicles were seriously mismatched. Several times the Cherokee bumped the Pinto from the rear, its high bumper pushing directly into the body of the car, not into the bumper. But Tuttle was somehow able to hold the road.

"Sit back into your seat," Walker instructed Andy. "Brace your head hard against the back of the seat and fasten your seatbelt if there is one." Andy obeyed instantly.

"Cal, I want you to listen to me. You know the roads around here and this jerk probably doesn't, so I want you to think about how we can get loose of him. Do you know where Mrs. Ward lives?"

"Third Langan's Cove Road, right at the end." Cal's voice was high, but steady. "Did some work for Cassius Ward years ago."

Walker's mind was rattling through options. "We can't go there until we get rid of this guy, but there might be somebody after her, too, so we've got to get there soon. We only need to get rid of him for a minute. Her place is hard to see from the road."

"Ayuh."

They'd reached the main road. Cal swung to the right. As they drove along the winding, gently hilly road, the Cherokee three times overtook them and began the terrifying process of trying to nudge them off the road.

The first time, the Cherokee drew even with them, Walker told Cal to brake in that same, almost supernaturally loud voice he'd spoken in before. Andy whimpered in the back seat. When the Pinto braked, the Cherokee shot ahead, grazing along the metal flank of the Pinto with a horrible metallic screech. Cal turned the car around and the Cherokee reversed again to pursue, but Walker told Cal to make a U-turn just as the Cherokee began its turn. Before the driver could recover again, the Pinto had shot past. It didn't take long for the Cherokee to catch up, but each time it drew abreast of them, an oncoming car forced it back behind them. Walker noted that they'd passed Nicola Ward's road.

"Ayuh," Cal said. Walker saw that Cal's ears were bright cherry red. He turned the car down a dirt road Walker didn't know. The Pinto kept bottoming out, and each time it did, Cal emitted a sympathetic sound: "Ooooom. Oooh! Ouch."

They bounced down a steep, rocky hill. Ahead, it looked like a dead end—several cars parked in a wide grassy area. But he could see that there was a road beyond the parked cars—which must be Nicola's road. The two roads were joined by a rough old track. The people who lived at the end of this road obviously used the terminus as a parking area. Tuttle squeezed the Pinto between a brand-new white Saab and an old primer-patched black van. The Pinto's side-view mirror caught on the Saab's side-view mirror and then the Pinto's mirror crumpled away with a shrieking noise and they were through. The Cherokee bounced into sight behind them. Suddenly, Walker recognized some landmarks that he'd fixed in his mind the other day, when Nicola had driven Andy and him home: a clump of white birch, a pumphouse.

"Right here, turn here," he yelled to Cal a quarter-mile farther on, and they rocketed down Nicola's steep driveway. The terrain here would work in their favor. There were perhaps fifteen cabins along Nicola's road and the Cherokee driver, unless he *knew* where Nicola's was, would have to drive into each driveway before Cal's car became visible. He jumped out of the car and pushed the seat forward for Andy.

"Come on."

He could hear the sound of metal against metal in the distance: the Cherokee trying to ram its way past the Saab. The barricade of cars would only slow him down for a minute or two.

When Walker saw Nicola Ward standing there, out on the deck, with a suitcase in each hand, he felt an intense physical sensation of relief. She acknowledged him with a smile and then turned to look down at the dock where Kate was doing something with the motorboat. Even the inner cove was choppy now, full of whitecaps.

"Tell Kate to come on," he said, "forget the boat. There's a man following us. We've got to get out of here."

370

"It's true!" Andy yelled. "It's true!"

"Hello, Mrs. Ward," Cal Tuttle said in a totally normal voice. "How are you?"

"We'll go in Nicola's car," Walker said. "He'll be looking for the Pinto." He picked up the suitcases and then he leaned over the deck to yell to Kate, but the wind died down for a second and he caught the sound of an engine above it. When he turned, he spotted the flash of the red Cherokee through the trees.

"Get in the boat," he ordered in his loud voice. "Now."

He hustled everyone down the dock. Andy moved with surprising agility, almost running—stiff-legged, and hanging on to the rail, but moving faster than Walker had seen him move since the accident. The boat tossed and bucked in the heavy sea, but everyone, even Cal, got in without trouble. Walker realized he still had the suitcases in his hands and tossed them into the bow. "Go," he said to the astonished Kate, "go." He was untying the lines she just had secured. "But it's a storm," she said, "a bad storm."

"Go!"

There was a long, terrible moment when the engine wouldn't catch, but finally it did and Kate eased them away from the dock. Just as they pulled away, Walker saw the Cherokee bounce down the driveway and lurch to a stop behind Nicola's Subaru. When they were about three hundreds yards from shore, a little way from the point of the island, the man arrived on the float. Walker watched him pull the rifle up to his shoulder, sight it. He lunged for the wheel, pushing Kate out of the way. Kate said: "Hey!" Indignant.

"Get down! Everybody down!" He zigzagged in the boat in sharp swoops until finally, they passed the point of the island and he knew they couldn't be seen. He juiced up the throttle and when he finally felt they were out of range, he took an assessing look at his passengers.

Waves had been smashing into the boat, almost broadside, and everyone was soaking wet. He concentrated on driving the boat through the huge waves. The sea was growing rougher by the minute. He could see the squall line—just off Jenny's Nubble—and the black curtain of rain. He was forced to cut the speed; the sea was so rough, the boat might get swamped.

"Can I drive?" Kate said. "I'm used to it." He remembered

watching her skillfully maneuver the boat the first day he'd met Nicola Ward, when she'd taken Andy fishing.

"Do you think you can handle it better?"

She shrugged, but he insisted on an answer and she said, "Yes! Let me do it."

She eased into the driver's seat. The sea pulled ferociously at the wheel and for a second he hesitated, not sure she was strong enough to fight the force of the water. He hovered close, above her shoulder.

"Where should we go?"

"The Basin," Kate said.

"Yuh," Cal Tuttle said. "That's the best place." The Basin was the most sheltered spot in the whole bay, a nearly circular body of water with a long, narrow mouth. Under normal conditions, it was about a fifteen-minute boat ride from Nicola's, but how long it would take now, Walker couldn't guess. "It'll be tough to get through the chop in the mouth," Cal Tuttle continued. "How does she handle?" he asked Kate.

"Pretty steady. I think we can get in."

She had slowed the boat even more, because of the chop, and had angled near the shore where the waves were slightly smaller. There were dozens of cottages between where they were and the mouth of the Basin, but the waves were so powerful now, and the docks so relatively unprotected, Walker knew it would be almost impossible to make a landing. The sky darkened by the minute and ominous flashes of lightning turned the light strange and almost evil. Every other wave was now large enough to lift the propeller out of the water and each time it happened, the motor gave off a high-pitched whine.

Walker looked behind him. He saw that Nicola had her arms around Andy and was trying to shelter him from the heavy spray that kept crashing into the boat. The Basin was known to yachtsmen as a "hurricane hole," relatively calm in the most ferocious weather. If they could manage to get into it, Walker knew they'd be able to ride out the storm. He tossed the seat cushions, which doubled as flotation devices, to Nicola and Andy.

"Hang on to these," he shouted, looping his own wrist through the handles of another one.

"Dad—" Andy said.

"We'll be all right," he said although he was far from sure of that. Every wave now pummeled the boat mercilessly and broke over the sides, drenching them every twenty seconds or so. Frigid water lashed at their faces. Kate was standing up, her head poked through the unzipped canvas roof of the boat to see. She kept blinking her eyes furiously against the water. She couldn't spare a hand to wipe her face; she needed them both to hold the wheel. The bilge pumped continuously, a low counterpoint to the high snarl of the engine.

Kate was having trouble keeping their heading—the force of the water tugging so hard at the boat, skewing them first one way, and then the other, made their forward progress very slow. Cal Tuttle hunched over Kate to help with the wheel, his old cracked and gnarled hands interspaced with her skeletal white ones. At one point, Walker looked up and all he could see was water; they were in a trough between waves and even the sky was blotted out. He'd never been at sea in a storm like this and the violence of the water was terrifying. Andy and Nicola now lay right flat on the floor, Andy under Nicola, their arms clutching the life preservers.

They were almost at the narrow inlet that was the mouth of the Basin. The chop was ferocious because of the outgoing tide, but at least the swells of the waves themselves were smaller. The boat surged rapidly back and forth, buffeted by the powerful current, but finally a huge wind-driven wave pushed them through the mouth. Once they were through, they slewed sideways, dangerously close to the rocks. Then the engine stalled. Cal Tuttle desperately tried to revive it.

"Shit!" Kate Ward said. Walker heard the word quite distinctly through a kind of hole in the howling noise. The boat was out of control, bouncing back and forth with the current, coming so close to the rocks, Walker kept bracing his body for impact.

Tuttle now had a boat pole out and was pushing ineffectually against the rock cliff, trying to fend off collision. Walker added his strength to the effort, but then the pole, which was aluminum sheathed in plastic, buckled. The boat crashed into the rock. The impact made a huge shriek of noise and the boat bounced out again away from the rocks and began swirling. Walker caught Cal's helpless look. They had almost slipped back out through the neck into the open bay when another huge wave, powered by what seemed

373

now to be a gale-force wind, pushed them forward again. It was nearly strong enough to propel them past the chop, back into the Basin, but then, unbelievably rapidly, they were sucked back out into the open water.

The boat yawed and rolled dangerously as Cal Tuttle, on his belly, searched under the bow, under the seats. Walker wondered what he was looking for. Just as Cal was getting up, a wave rocked the boat and he smashed his head against a metal cleat. Walker watched, helpless; if he moved or tried to help, he knew he would only be in the way.

"Go for Tripp's, if you can, Katie," Tuttle said, finally emerging with some stubby aluminum and plastic oars. He went to the stern of the boat and asked Walker to hold his feet. He dangled himself over the back, to the right of the motor. Waves kept crashing up into his face. Using the little oars more or less as rudders, he was able to influence the direction of the boat. Walker couldn't see anything ahead of them. Time seemed to stand still.

"Do you see it, Katie?" Tuttle kept calling but she kept shouting back "No!" Walker's arms began to ache from the effort of holding Cal, and he couldn't imagine how Cal was feeling, with half his body fighting the water. Finally Kate yelled, "I see it."

"Which way?" Cal yelled.

"Hard to port," Kate screamed back.

Walker didn't know where Tripp's was or what Cal and Kate were looking for, and he didn't ask. He was sure one of the waves was going to turn them over. He turned his head to see where they were headed. It was almost impossible to see through the spray but he could make out the hunched, darker shape of land. They closed rapidly, and in between the rocks Walker spotted the stony beach that Kate was steering for. Now he remembered Billy Tuttle pointing out the little island to him once by its local name: Tripp's Island. It had another name on the charts.

They bumped up onto the rocky beach with a hard crunch, and he released Cal's feet. Cal jumped out of the boat and stood knee-deep in the water, trying to steady it. Walker stepped into the water to help. It wasn't easy holding the boat against the surging water and a couple of times it swung heavily into Walker's thighs. "Kate, put the motor up," Cal ordered, and when she had, he commanded: "Everyone out. Let's push her up onto the beach."

They heaved their shoulders against the boat's stern. It ground into the stony beach. They managed to push it only a short way, but the outgoing tide would beach it and Cal said he hoped the storm would die down by the time the tide got back in. He took the anchor line and worked the delta-shaped aluminum anchor into the mud, then stretched a long line from the bow and tied the rope to a tree on the shore. "Thank the Lord for this island," he said, "else we would have been swept out to sea."

The sky opened just then and the rain fell so heavily that instinctively they all huddled together. Kate was shaking violently. "There's a cabin here," Cal said. "In the interior of the island."

Nicola said, "The suitcases. I'm going to get the suitcases from the boat—the clothes might still be dry."

Walker went with her to the boat. She looked at its side and ran her hand over the place where they'd collided with the rocks. Cal was standing stock still, pelted by rain, his head turning from side to side. Then he stood facing the opposite direction and did the same thing.

"What are we looking for?" Andy asked.

"This way," Tuttle said, and they followed him without question. Nicola and Kate each took a suitcase and Walker carried Andy on his back. The going was tough—rocks that were treacherous and slippery and dense, chest-high huckleberry bushes. The rain pounded them unceasingly—the kind of rain that made people pull their cars to the side of the highway and wait. Cal Tuttle marched on, hesitating now and then, but never for long. Walker was miserably chilled and he worried about Andy and Kate, especially skinny little Kate. Just as he was about to suggest they rest, a cabin suddenly loomed up in front of them. It was sea green, almost camouflage-colored, and shabby. A stout, old-fashioned padlock fastened the front door.

"Damn," Cal Tuttle said. "We'll never get that off."

"I'll break a window," Walker said.

"Make sure it's leeside," Tuttle said. "We don't want the rain *inside* too."

They walked all the way around the cabin and decided to break a small side window that wasn't too far off the ground. Walker used a stick. He stood on the two suitcases and picked out the glass, throwing the larger pieces behind him, into the woods. He reached inside and unfastened the lock.

Kate found an ancient sawhorse, covered with green moss and

they dragged that over and used it to climb in. Kate went first. "There's a couch under the window," she called from inside. Walker came last, pushing the suitcases in before he levered himself through.

CHAPTER

FIFTY-TWO

It was a relief to be inside and away from the driving rain, but as soon as they stopped moving, everyone felt chilled through. Andy and Kate were trembling with cold. Cal Tuttle slapped his arms and said something about keeping moving. Nicola looked for dry clothes and blankets. The suitcases were still on the couch where Walker had pushed them through the window. Because they were so heavy, she'd packed the papers and photographs into a lightweight cloth suitcase, which she didn't remember until she opened it. The papers inside were drenched. "Wrong one," she said.

"Damn," Walker said, looking at the soggy papers. "Oh well, I guess they'll dry."

She closed the suitcase and took it off the bed and pushed it against the wall. It seemed so heavy now, she couldn't believe she'd dragged it all this way from the boat. She opened the other suitcase. This was an old hard-sided Samsonite one; the clothes inside were bone dry.

Nicola pushed her wet hair off her forehead. "Kate, Andy. Let's get into some dry clothes."

"We better see if we can find some tools to break off that padlock," Cal said. " We need to get some wood in here and start a fire."

Nicola led Kate through a cloth door to one of the bedrooms. They weren't really rooms at all but tiny partitioned areas with heavy cloth curtains for doors and seven-foot-high walls of knotty pine. She put her arms around Kate. "You were great," she said, and Kate nodded, unable to stop the violent shaking of her body. "I mean heroic," Nicola said. "I'm proud—hey, I'm even grateful."

Kate tried to smile, Her teeth chattered. "We've got to find some matches," they heard Walker say.

"Dad," Andy said. "I've got to pee."

Cal Tuttle sneezed.

"Let's get your clothes off," Nicola said. Kate couldn't get her fingers to work, and Nicola finally had to undress her. For the first time in months, she saw the full horror of Kate's emaciation. The bones of the knees protruding larger than the thigh or the calf, the huge elbows bisecting the sticklike arms. She couldn't understand how Kate could be alive with so little flesh to sustain her, but she also knew that this was an improvement, that in the last two months, Kate had put on five pounds. She rubbed Kate with a tattered terry-cloth beach robe that she took off a nail on the wall. "Oh, Kate," she said. "Oh, Katie."

Kate stuck her arms up like a little child and allowed Nicola to pull wet shirts up over her skeletal chest and then put the dry ones on: a shirt, a sweatshirt, a sweater. Still, Kate trembled and shook, her teeth chattering out of control.

"I'm so cold," Kate said. "Mom, I'm so cold."

Nicola tore the blankets off the bed and wrapped Kate up. "They'll have a fire going soon," she said. She could hear the men, the clunky sounds of wood being set on the floor. She went out to get Andy.

"They can't find any matches," Andy said in a whiny voice. He was near the Franklin stove, crumpling up newspaper and stuffing it on top of the grate.

"I'll look in a minute but first you need to get dried off."

"You too," he said.

She finally persuaded him to wear some of Kate's clothes, although he resisted. She was exasperated and almost made the kind of knee-jerk idle threat she found pathetic: "Do you want to catch pneumonia?" "Do you want to catch your death of cold?" But he relented.

"Do you need help?" she asked.

"Jeez." He was offended. She left the room while he dressed, taking the suitcase with her into the other, slightly larger "bedroom." There were two large wooden drawers built into the bottom of the bed and she tugged them open. One was full of shoes—she found some ragged children's slippers and some moth-eaten fluffy pink mules. They smelled strongly of mildew, but still would be better than nothing. There were also some huge boat shoes, a pair of hiking boots, and several pairs of the old-fashioned rubber bathing shoes Stan's parents had worn when swimming. The other drawer—sprinkled with mothballs—held blankets and some clothing obviously left behind by the cabin's absentee owners—a mammoth moth-eaten bathrobe and some colossal tattered sweaters and pants. She put them out on the bed.

It was a relief to peel off her wet clothes and put on dry ones. She carried the wet clothes into the sink, collecting Kate's and Andy's as well. Later, she would wring them out.

There was water all over the floor. Where Walker stood hammering a piece of plywood over the broken window, a pool of water had collected under his feet. There was another puddle under Cal, who was doing something with the stove pipe, fiddling with some knobs.

"There are some dry clothes in the back bedroom," she said.

"Good," Walker said distractedly. "I'm freezing."

"Fire's all ready to go," Cal said. "If we can just find some matches. There must be some here. You don't vacate an island cottage without leaving some matches behind."

"You get dressed," Nicola suggested. "I'll look." The place had been left neat and tidy. A row of kerosene lamps with trimmed wicks, their round tin metal reflectors pocked with rust, stood in a line on the kitchen counter, filled with fuel, ready for the touch of a match.

Nicola ransacked the drawers and found some candles but still no matches. Mice droppings and cobwebs were all over the counters and in the sink. The cabinets weren't true cabinets—they too had cloth "doors," suspended from long coiled springs stretched between two nails, to hide the contents. There were open shelves above the sink, holding a huge collection of free glassware—everything from tiny juice glasses to the Star Wars tumblers given out at Burger King a couple years before. Nicola tried the spigot but nothing came out. Probably, they had a way to rig up a rain barrel like some of the old cabins near hers used to. There were canisters and jars in profusion behind one of the cloth curtains. She'd found the pantry. Most of the canisters were homemade, coffee cans covered with floral-patterned contact paper. She found flour, salt, four different kinds of noodles, coffee, Red Rose tea bags. The sugar canister had been attacked by mice; they'd chewed through the plastic lid and left nothing but a layer of droppings in the bottom. Then there were the clear jars. Many of them contained nails and screws of different sizes but one of them held three books of matches.

"Matches," she said. "I found them." But it turned out their problem wasn't solved. The matches were damp—despite being packed in a glass jar—and the first few attempts failed to produce a spark.

Outside, the rain pounded down and the trees thrashed in the wind. The force of the storm was incredible; Nicola wondered if it was a hurricane.

Walker tried, and so did Cal, and then Nicola. Kate had the idea of soaking a match in kerosene and letting it dry; no one thought it would work. "Might disintegrate it," Cal Tuttle said. But when Kate scraped the match over the rough strip on the matchbook, it instantly flared into flame. In a few minutes, they had the fire going, two of the kerosene lamps lit, and were beginning to feel warmer.

There was a small cooking wood stove in the kitchen and they got that fired up as well. Nicola wandered around, looking at the stuff on the walls—which were almost half covered with things thumbtacked to them. One entire wall in the bedroom was covered with postcards, and a row of presidential cards, which ended with Richard Nixon, claimed the top of the wall in the other bedroom. There were faded posters of sailing ships, ancient calendars, a surprising poster of the Beatles in full color. Tacked to the wall near the door were two sets of instructions, handwritten in block ballpoint letters:

INSTRUCTIONS ON OPENING CAMP
INSTRUCTIONS ON CLOSING CAMP

Nicola read over the instructions for opening camp. There were directions on rigging up the water barrel, advice about replacing the storm door with a screen door, advice about how much lime to use in the outhouse, reminders to throw away any canned goods that might have been left over from the previous year, instructions on where to find the linen and blankets, detailed instructions on caring for the boats and setting out the dock once the ice was gone. There were also photographs nailed to the walls with carpet tacks and a sign, scribbled with crayon, that read ONLY FRESH EGGS SERVED HERE. The images of the photographs had faded away from exposure to the sun and apart from the faint impression of shapes of bodies, all that remained of the snapshots were captions, written in ball point on the borders. "Gerry and Gemma at Reid State Park." "Adelaide at Cadillac Mountain." These blank photographs made Nicola feel as if they were surrounded by ghosts. A yellowed newspaper photograph of a woman holding up a chocolate layer cake at what the caption identified as the St. Luke's Christmas Bazaar had curled enough to pull free of all but one of its thumbtacks and dangled from its corner.

Next to it was a five-by-seven index card. Lettered on the top was the caption: DIRECTIONS TO THE SPRING. Beneath that was a hand-drawn map and a few lines of elaboration.

Walker and Cal came out of the back bedroom looking so odd Nicola had to laugh. Walker was wearing a huge flannel shirt, and a pair of baggy gray pants hitched in with his own belt. The sleeves and the cuffs were rolled and folded and over it all was an ancient brown bathrobe. Cal Tuttle was wearing another pair of huge baggy pants, but his torso was squeezed into Nicola's gray sweatshirt, which stretched tightly over his small, distinct belly. Obviously, the owner of this cabin was a sizable man.

"It's a look," Walker said, shifting his weight from foot to foot.

"Dad," Andy said calmly, "why was that man in the car chasing us? What did we do?" No one had mentioned the circumstances that had landed them on the island; it was as if no one wanted to be the first to bring it up.

"I was going to ask that my own self," Cal said.

Neil shook his head slowly from side to side: "I wish I knew," he said. He explained to Nicola and Kate what had happened at his cottage, about the "termite inspection," and how the Cherokee was waiting for them on the road.

"He can't find us here, can he, Dad?"

"No," Walker said, "no way." But somewhere in the back of his mind, he wished they'd camouflaged the boat. From a helicopter . . . But a helicopter couldn't fly in this kind of weather.

He knew one thing: they were dealing with a professional. He remembered the man standing on the float, the way he'd pulled the rifle up to his shoulder. Walked had just caught a glimpse but it had been enough to tell him that their pursuer performed that act with a sure, professional motion. He had taken sight on them. Hunting.

"I'm hungry," Andy said.

Nicola said she would go to the spring for water. She put on a pair of jumbo black boots and made a poncho out of a green plastic garbage bag. She picked up two of the dozen glass gallon jugs lined up on the shelf near the door.

"I'll come too," Walker said, but she pointed out that although she had plenty of dry clothes, the men did not, and anyway, it couldn't be far. She took another quick look at the DIRECTIONS TO THE SPRING and went out into the rain. The path was overgrown but still discernible and she trudged along, pushing branches aside. She passed through a marshy section; huge clumps of ostrich ferns—each frond about five feet tall—gave it a prehistoric feeling.

She found the spring—a wooden cover with a handle peeked through the surrounding weeds and clumps of moss. A dozen small frogs jumped as she bent down to lift the cover. There was a screen underneath, and beneath that she could see the round outline of a concrete cistern. The water looked murky and unhealthy; algae floated on the surface. Still, she unscrewed the caps to the bottles and plunged them into the water. The spring water was so cold her hands grew numb holding the jugs under. Off to her left, a huge tree branch broke in the wind and crashed to the earth.

The rain, if possible, was falling even harder as she walked back. Still, she could tell that the light was changing, that it was late afternoon—dinnertime, maybe six o'clock. She wondered how long they'd been in the boat. It had seemed like forever, but it had probably been only an hour or so. She pushed inside.

"Now I can make some tea."

"I like tea," Andy mentioned, "but only if there's sugar."

They had tea with sugar and noodles with olive oil, salt, and pepper. Walker kept going outside every ten minutes or so.

382

"Damn," he said. "It's not letting up. I can't believe it." After dinner, they played games—Mille Bornes, pinochle, gin. Every time Neil went out—to check on the weather or to get wood—they all heard the trees thrashing, and the moan of the wind. Twice the screen door got away from him and whacked back and forth until he was able to grab it and pull it closed again.

"I think we may have to spend the night," Cal said. "The light's going and the wind's not." One branch scraped creepily against the window. The rain drummed hard on the uninsulated roof.

Finally, they settled down for the night—Nicola and Kate in one room, Neil and Andy in the other, and Cal on the couch. Nicola distributed the blankets. Walker stoked up the stove. For a while bodies readjusted themselves, and tossed and thrashed but it was amazing how quickly the movements stopped and Walker knew, from the slow rhythmic breathing, that besides himself, everyone was asleep.

He wondered if his cabin had blown up yet. There was no doubt in his mind now that it was wired and he could only hope that the detonator was a trigger of some sort and not simply a timing device. If it *was* a timing device, it would probably go off at about 2:00 A.M., a time when he and Andy would both have been asleep. Still—the waiting Cherokee meant that it probably was a different kind of trigger—just a simple booby trap attached to the door. He prayed no innocent party opened that door.

Flashes of the day's events came to him as he lay there in the dark: Detective Shepler's voice telling him Lavinia Bradshaw was murdered "in your foyer." He thought of Mrs. Bradshaw's broad smile and the way she cocked her eyebrow and tilted her head to the side to give you her "oh come on" look. A bleak sadness, the loss of her, settled drearily over him. And then a vision of Andy at the top of the ramp when Cal Tuttle was telling him about the termite man, the rush of fear in his throat. And the moment when he'd looked up from the boat and seen nothing but water. The sound the boat had made hitting the rocks. And again, the smooth motion of the man on the float, taking aim.

Nicola dreamed that she stood next to the Day-Glo orange ribbon that surrounded her charred house and shook hands with John

Blake. Squeezed his hand and blood dripped from his fingers and fell on her white shoes. The image was sharp enough to puncture her dream and she sat straight up, reaching for the light. And then she remembered where she was. The darkness was complete, impenetrable, and she sat there, unmoving, in the black, elemental island night. The darkness drove the dream right out of her mind.

She could sense Kate's body near her, hear her hushed, slow breathing, but she could see nothing. The black wind from the sea swirled and rushed outside, thrashing the trees and shaking the window frames, but she felt oddly safe and secure, held in the hand of the night. A feeling of ease and languor suffused her and she lapsed back into sleep.

CHAPTER

FIFTY-THREE

The second time Nicola woke, there was a change in the light. It was still dark, but the darkness had a brittle texture and she knew that it was dawn. She was surprised to hear that the storm had not abated. She lay there listening to the wind hurl clatters of rain into the windows until the others began to stir.

She looked through the cupboards again for things to eat. There were still a few noodles—maybe enough for one small portion each, and a jar of honey. There was flour, some crusty baking soda, a lump of rock-hard salt in one of the salt shakers, and a few rust-pocked tins of spices and herbs. She thought she might be able to make water biscuits.

Walker stuck his head out the door. "Unbelievable," he said. "This is some storm."

"We're lucky we got onto this island," Cal said, poking up the fire. "I hate to think what would have happened to us in that boat. I give Katie a lot of credit for keeping us from getting tossed over." Kate looked at her hands.

"Well, I hope we can get the motor started," she said.

"Does it do that often?" Cal asked. "Kill out on you?"

"It's getting kind of old," Kate said. "It doesn't like rain. But if you take the cover off and lift up this little thing—" She waved her words away. "I'll show you."

They had a breakfast of tea with honey, took turns at the outhouse, and tidied up the cabin. It was still raining hard but the wind had abated. They thought they'd try to leave. They made slickers out of garbage bags. Nicola packed up the clothes, sticking the wet ones into another garbage bag. She lifted the heavy suitcase with the papers but Cal insisted on carrying it, so she took the other one. Walker hitched Andy up on his back and they went toward the boat.

The rain falling on the five of them, all in their plastic bags, made a loud, rattly sound as they walked. It seemed like a short walk today, and much easier going, because they could see well enough to find the path. They emerged from the trees into the scrubby huckleberry bushes and a view of the water.

"Wait a minute," Walker said, looking out toward the sea. "This must be the wrong spot."

Cal Tuttle pushed ahead of them and walked on, toward the pebble beach. "No sir. This is where we beached her." Then Nicola saw the rope tied to the tree and the metal anchor, still buried in the pebbly sand. Cal walked along, playing the line through his fingers until he reached its end. And from that end dangled the metal bow eye that had been attached to the boat, with its two long brass bolts still fitted into their holes. But the nuts and washers secured only two rough little chunks of white fiberglass, parts of the hull. Cal stared forlornly at the device. "I'll be danged," he said. "She pulled right out; the danged bolts held but the hull give way." He coughed a deep, fruity cough, and spit. "Pardon me."

"I don't believe it," Kate said. "What are we going to do?"

"Yeah," Andy asked in an excited voice, "now what are we going to do?"

"I *could* swim to shore," Walker said tentatively. "Get some help." He guessed it was three-quarters of a mile. He was a strong swimmer, but it would be tough with the water this rough.

"You'd be crazy to try," Cal said. "Sea's not going to stay this heavy for long. There's lots of boats in this bay. I say we wait a few hours. I mean, are we in that much of a hurry?"

Walker shrugged. He shifted from foot to foot.

"This is going to satisfy all my Robinson Crusoe fantasies," Nicola said.

Walker raised an eyebrow. "Didn't know you had any."

She laughed. "It's true that they never involved wearing garbage bags."

386

"I'm hungry," Andy said.

"Well, why don't you and Kate pick some mussels," Cal said. "It's low tide and I'm hungry too."

Kate and Andy looked at each other. "I'm not eating mussels," Andy said.

"You pick, I'll eat," Cal said. "Katie, you go on up and look under the cabin. Bet you'll find a clam basket. Maybe even a clam rake—then you can pick mussels and even try to dig for some steamers. There might be a prayer of finding some steamers, since obviously no one's been living here for a couple of years."

"Okay," Kate said.

"Let's us take a little look around," Cal said. "Maybe there's a dinghy stashed here somewhere."

They took the suitcases back to the cabin. They did find an old wooden skiff, upside down, near the outhouse, under a tarpaulin covered with pine needles. They dragged it out, disturbing dozens of spiders and other bugs living under its protection. The three of them carried it to the shore, with a lot of struggle, but as soon as they pushed it in to water deep enough to float it, it sank up to its gunwales.

"This is an old-timer," Cal said, after they pulled it back out. "But it's still sound." He thought if he caulked it, it would swell up in a day or two. He went to look for some caulk. "Might as well do something while we're waiting."

"Dad!" Andy struggled toward them, crawling over the rocks. He dragged a metal mesh clam basket—full to the top with mussels, a few of the lighter-shelled steamer clams on top.

Walker said, "I'm impressed."

"There are plenty more—there are *tons.*"

The rain, which had been falling in a steady drizzle, suddenly picked up its tempo.

"Just our luck," Andy said.

Walker hitched Andy up on his back and they hurried back to the cabin. They ate mussels and water biscuits for lunch while the rain pounded on the roof. Then they raided the cabin's eclectic reading collection—old *Yankee* magazines, boating magazines, some Agatha Christie novels, and several books about carpentry. Kate was happy to read Agatha Christie, and Cal leafed through a copy of *Sail*. Andy settled down to solitaire. Nicola picked up *The ABC Murders* and put it down again. Then she remembered her "summer reading program" and the bag of books from Bookland that she'd packed in the suitcase.

She retrieved the bag from her suitcase and spilled the books out on the couch next to Walker.

He tapped Mailer's *The Executioner's Song*. "I read this," he said. "Mailer's a genius; it's great." He turned over the novels. "I don't read fiction much," he said. He picked up *Man of the Seventies*, a biography of Leo Adler, the National Security Adviser. He hefted it in his hands as if he was weighing it. "I always meant to read this but I never got around to it—do you mind?"

"Please."

They spent the afternoon reading. Nicola, immersed in Gary Gilmore's depressing world, didn't notice that the rain had stopped, but Neil did.

"I'm going to go down to the shore and try to flag down a boat," he announced.

There was a big flagpole out by the dock—which was near the pebble beach. Cal had the idea of hanging the flag there upside-down as an SOS signal. They found a flag stuck in the joists out on the screen porch, and Walker went off, accompanied by Andy.

The afternoon crawled by. Kate and Andy began a new Monopoly game. The rain started up again. Walker and Cal came in from another patrol of the beach. "Water's still really rough," Cal said. Both men had gotten soaking wet and Nicola made them change. The pickings were even slimmer now, and Neil ended up in a kind of toga made out of blankets. Cal had to settle for a pair of Bermuda shorts which hung down almost to his ankles, and another one of Nicola's shirts.

"I feel like a danged fool," Cal Tuttle said.

"Well, you look like a danged fool," Walker agreed.

"*Dad*," Andy said, "look who's talking."

The rain continued to pound down on the roof, and soon it became clear that their chances of getting off the island that day were remote.

"Maybe we ought to get started on an ark," Kate suggested.

"How about getting started on dinner?" Cal Tuttle asked. "My belly says it's time to eat."

"All we've got is more mussels, and a few clams, and some noodles."

"I'll take it," Cal said.

They ate the food greedily, quickly.

Walker got worried about Nicola's photographs, and he was right—they were wet and sticking together. He spread them out on the table out on the sun porch. "When the emulsion dried, they'd be actually *glued* to each other and then we'd have to soak them to get them apart."

Nicola helped him spread the photographs out. The scatter of faces, her mother, her father, her grandfather—confronted her calmly from the table. At first she felt comforted by these images of her long-lost family, but suddenly, her simple pleasure was rolled over by a wave of foreboding. She remembered Chief Herlihy's voice describing how her house had exploded. She remembered the man taking aim from the dock. The faces on the table belonged to dead people. As far as she knew, she and Kate were the last of the line. And it seemed as if someone was trying to kill them.

Once the natural light faded, they read by the light of the kerosene lanterns for a while, but it was hard on the eyes and soon they settled down for the night.

"Hey, I like this," Andy said. "Everybody goes to sleep when I do." Cal's coughing kept dragging Walker out of his sleep. It sounded bad.

CHAPTER

FIFTY-FOUR

As soon as she woke up, Nicola knew that the storm was over. She opened her eyes and then closed them immediately against the brightness. There was no wind and rain wasn't pounding on the roof. In fact, it was quiet enough to hear the scrabbling sound of a chipmunk running over the rooftop. She felt a little plunge of disappointment in her chest. Being stranded on this island had pleased her in some deep, unexpected way: she hadn't been kidding about the Robinson Crusoe fantasies. There was something therapeutic in forced self-reliance. And Kate. Kate ate like a normal person here. Here, where there was no food, Kate was hungry like anyone else.

She sat up and opened her eyes. Walker was standing in the doorway, the curtain pulled aside. Her eyes met his and locked to them. Ordinarily she would have averted her gaze, but there was something about the way he looked at her that held her. He smiled at her and then let his eyelids fall almost closed, slowly, of their own weight and mouthed her a kiss. There was something so erotic about that almost feminine gesture that she was instantly aroused. She slid from beneath the blankets and tiptoed out. She picked up two water jugs from the counter, and he said, in a heavy whisper that she knew was intended to reassure any light sleeper about where they were going, "I'll help you get the water."

Even inside the cabin, there was a strange, muffled quality to the light and sound and as soon as she stepped out the door, she saw why—they were completely socked in with fog. Fog so dense that wisps of it curled off the ground, shelves of it hung suspended among the trees, and when she looked up toward the sky, she saw that they were—like a piece of jewelry nesting in the cottony fluff of a gift box—surrounded, almost encased, by its whiteness. Behind it all, the sun shone; its glary, filtered light seemed stagy, artificial. She looked back at Walker, who was still wearing the chenille bedspread toga he'd put on yesterday. He looked literally fantastic, a phantasm.

They walked in silence until they were a good way from the house. It had disappeared into the fog anyway when they were only thirty yards from it. She felt his hand on her shoulder and put down the water jugs. He laced his hands up into her hair and a flush of sensation spread through her. He bent to kiss her neck. He kissed her all the way around her neck, a necklace of kisses that barely brushed her flesh, but still she squirmed under the heat of his lips, inflamed. She thought she heard him say, "Let's take our clothes off," but she wasn't entirely sure he'd spoken out loud. They undressed and hung their clothing from a branch of a tree. The cold wet air rushed against her hot skin. Steam was coming off Walker's muscular body, and off her own, and when she lay down on the path, the cool wet leaves felt silky and soothing.

And as soon as he came into her, she thought: I want to have a baby from this man. I want this to start a baby. That was such a crazy thought that there came a flurry of scolding, denying complaints into her head, but they were weak, they were nothing; they dissolved immediately under the intentions of her body. The deep arcing motions of her pelvis communicated her need to him, her urgency. She felt him try to resist, try to pull out—he would think it was too fast; he would want to prolong their pleasure—but her body refused to allow it, her body insisted, and she felt his resistance dissolve and very soon the powerful finishing strokes began. It seemed to her that inside her she was nothing but a wet pool, sucking him in, giving way to his thrusts, and a smooth tongue of rapture licked through her when he came, as if it was his semen itself that flooded her with bliss. She felt the strong absorbing spasms of her vagina suck at him after it was over, as if her body could pull a baby from him, as if she could suck from him the very spark of life.

391

"I'm sorry," he said. His voice was puzzled. "I couldn't hold off. I—"

She shook her head and put her finger on his lips and smiled at him. He rolled away from her and stood up, his slick penis still erect. She knew she would never forget the way he looked standing there like that, naked, with steam coming off his skin, in the foggy woods.

Now she felt tired, as if she'd just run a long way. She got up slowly and a little awkwardly. Walker brushed her off, picking the wet leaves from her skin and flicking them off his fingers. He ran his hands up her torso and then kissed her on the lips, very sweetly.

She felt compelled to say something as she got dressed. "I've never had an outdoor affair before," she started awkwardly. "Do you think we'll have to call it off once the weather turns chilly?"

It sounded all wrong, as if she was asking him for some kind of commitment. But he just laughed and said he thought they could handle the comfort of a bed. They walked to the spring and then back to the cabin where everyone was still sleeping. She guessed they'd been gone less than twenty minutes.

Over a breakfast of tea sweetened with honey, they talked about what they'd do when they got off the island. Nicola mentioned that the fog was thick but they all assumed it would burn off with the sun. Kate and Andy competed with each other thinking about things they wanted once were "rescued": ice cream sundaes, "thick, juicy hamburgers," movies, baths.

Walker was preoccupied with thoughts about what they should do once off the island too.

They could go to the police but he couldn't see how the police would be much help. He needed to talk to Hale—that would be the first order of business. He wandered out to the sun porch where the papers and photographs from Nicola's suitcase were arrayed around the Formica table. The photographs were beginning to dry and curl, but the stacks of Xeroxed documents, carefully placed on top of towels by Nicola, were hopelessly sodden, still too wet to risk handling. It was frustrating because he would have liked to look them over. Somewhere in those papers was a poisonous bit of information, a powerful threat to *someone*—but he remained baffled as to what it could be, about who could be threatened by these

392

old papers. He kept thinking about it over and over again, but it was the mental equivalent of looking for your keys in all the places you usually put them, over and over again, knowing they *must* be in one of those places but not finding them. Only lunatic notions— because there was nothing else—presented themselves to his mind. The files in the CIA flagged to ROMEO—could it have something to do with Dasha and Tony Sunderland's cruel deaths in Mukden? Maybe the U.S. government trying to obscure its corrupt deals with Japanese war criminals? He shook his head. That information had already been exposed in print and besides, American soldiers had perished in Mukden. CIA would hardly be concerned with a Brit and his Russian wife. Could it have something to do with the Romanovs? He just couldn't see how. It might be that Nightingale was still in existence and trying to cover up some sin of the past. That seemed absurd. He shook his head.

"Neil," Cal said, opening the door. "Let's go down and bail out that skiff and see if she's seaworthy." His voice had a rough edge to it and as they stepped outside he had a bout of heavy coughing.

When they got to the water's edge, Walker was amazed by the density of the fog—the edge of the world was about twenty yards away. The mainland was entirely invisible. He and Cal pulled the boat in, bailed it out, and relaunched it, watching it sink almost immediately again up to its oarlocks.

Cal shook his head. "It must be years and years since she's been in the water—it's taking so long for the wood to swell. I guess we'll just hope for some water traffic." Cal coughed hard. "Trouble is, nobody's going to be out in a boat in this fog. We're really socked in. But it will burn off."

"What makes you think a boat will come close enough for us to flag it down?"

Cal shrugged. "They'll see the flag or something. The blues are in—this is good fishing water."

"I'm a good swimmer," Walker said. "I think I could swim it."

"You'd get lost in this fog."

"I mean after." He waved his hand in the air.

Cal shook his head and started coughing. When the coughing stopped he said: "I know it's at least a mile, maybe a mile and a half." He cleared his throat. "When's the last time you swam a mile? And I don't mean in a pool, doing laps."

Long-distance swimming and running had been components of his Minuteman training. "A few years ago I used to do two miles."

"How many is a few?"

He thought about it. He'd quit the Minutemen after Rabat. Andy had been a baby. "Nine or ten." His answer surprised him. It hadn't seemed that long.

Cal looked at him and shook his head. "I think we'll wait for a boat."

Two hours later the fog was still almost solid and showed no signs of dissolving. The group's mood turned claustrophobic; their camaraderie began to disintegrate. Kate and Andy argued over Scrabble words. Nicola shouted at Kate for tapping her foot. Walker yelled at Andy. Cal coughed.

Nicola felt his forehead. He had a fever. Cal said, with a touch of self-pity: "I'm getting old."

Their clothes were festooned around the stoves, dangling from the rafters, hung anywhere that the air could get to them. But nothing would dry in the pervasive dampness. The sound of the foghorn, and the occasional distant drone of an airplane from the Naval Air Station, the only evidence of life beyond the island, just served to emphasize their isolation.

Kate and Andy went to the shore and yelled "Help!" into the blank white world, even though they knew it would do no good. No boats would be out in the fog. Walker went out to the sun porch over and over again, staring at Nicola's photographs, thinking. They were curling up and he weighted down the corners with stones from the collection of ocean-smoothed rocks that decorated the windowsills.

He just couldn't come up with any idea of why any of this violence should have happened. No matter which way he turned the evidence over in his mind, no answer came to him, no route of inquiry recommended itself, no clue jumped into his mind. Thinking about it just made him frustrated and edgy. It was like trying to remember a name you were not sure you had ever known.

They all went down to the beach to dig for clams and pick mussels, once the tide was low enough. They picked two baskets of mussels, more for something to do than anything else, although they'd probably eat some for lunch. Even Andy had begun to conquer his distaste although Walker noticed that he closed his eyes before popping the nubs of orange flesh into his mouth. "We're lucky the red tide isn't in," Cal pointed out at lunch. "These mussels are our bread and butter."

"Don't mention bread and butter," Kate joked.

Kate and Andy were fishing with some drop lines Walker found. Cal was lying on the couch. Nicola was putting cold compresses on his forehead.

Walker went out to the sun porch and sat in a black leatherette recliner that had been repaired with duct tape. He picked up the Adler biography from the lamp table. It seemed too heavy; his wrists seemed barely strong enough to hold it up.

After only one chapter of the thing, he already was tired of the author's pompous style. He plodded on only out of inertia. Archival work had honed his concentration, and normally he was able to read the proceedings of traffic court with rapt attention. But he was hungry, dirty, tired of being stranded and he was distracted by Nicola.

Walker was always aware of where she was in the cabin. Whenever he got a chance, he found an excuse to touch her. He wanted to get her into the woods again, but she seemed busy, absorbed, distant. His peripheral focus on her made him keep losing track of the words he was trying to read.

He flipped to the center of the book, looked at the photographs again: there was Adler as a baby, his thin father and rather fat mother in attendance. There were others of Adler as a boy and most of these with his brother, Robert, who'd died in childhood. As a teenager, Adler looked poised in front of the camera—there were three or four shots of this vintage—Adler looking calm, unselfconscious. Then there was a photograph of Adler graduating from Harvard. Adler in his office with various statesmen. Adler aboard Air Force One. Adler with his first wife and his three children. Adler with various glamorous women. Adler in the Kremlin. Adler at the Great Wall. Adler at the Wailing Wall. Adler at Camp David. He looked over at Nicola. She was sitting at the table reading. Cal was asleep. Could he ask her to take a walk? Then he heard Kate's and Andy's voices as they approached the cabin.

"Hey, Dad," Andy said, "we caught two fish."

"They're small," Kate said. "Don't get excited."

"Yeah, they're about the right size for an aquarium," Andy said, "but we'll eat them."

FIFTY-FIVE

Although Nicola and Cal had both been confident that the fog would burn off, that it couldn't possibly persist for a whole day, the afternoon began to fade into evening and they remained socked in. The sunset appeared as a pink glow wonderfully diffused by the fog.

Kate cooked the evening meal, making a seafood stew. Nicola felt a surge of vicarious pride at the compliments she received.

Nicola reviewed her worries as she washed the dishes, dunking them first into the plastic basin of soapy water, then into the clear. She knew she ought to be worrying about who had burned down her house, who had shot at them, but she could hardly believe those things had happened; it was as if she'd made them up. What she really worried about was the insurance investigator. John Blake would think she'd skipped town—that she was guilty of arson. Somehow her disappearance would wreck her claim of innocence. Her thoughts kept circling, getting nowhere. She trimmed the wicks on the kerosene lamps, filled them, and lit them all. They'd be out of kerosene tomorrow. She cooled Cal Tuttle's forehead with a towel soaked in water. Another thing to worry about. What if he got worse? Already, it was painful to listen to his hard, ripping cough.

After dinner, Walker went back to the Adler biography. It was not written in chronological order and he'd suffered through several chapters dealing with Adler's achievements—nothing but puff pieces, really, magnifying Adler's role in each situation. Now the book had retreated to Adler's past. Walker read about the comfortable life of Adler's family in Vienna, Adler's early schooling, about the Adler family's escape from Vienna to Switzerland.

When the end came for Austria, Adler's father was prepared, and the decision to leave Vienna didn't mean, as it did for most Jews living there, leaving everything—money and possessions—behind.

But the Adlers lacked the proper papers to remain in Switzerland. They joined a refugee group that managed to arrange passage to Shanghai. Once in Shanghai, they settled in Hongkew and Benjamin Adler sold wartime staples—candles, saccharin. . . .

Walker sat up straight in his chair. Shanghai. *Shanghai*. Leo Adler in Shanghai.

"Shanghai," he said out loud. He jumped up and picked up a kerosene lamp in one quick motion. He poked his head through the door and called to Nicola: "C'mere."

He prowled around the table, rifling through the damp, curling photographs, found the one he wanted and thrust it into Nicola's hands. He flipped through the book to the photograph of the teenaged Leo Adler.

"Look at this. You see who this is?" He punched his index finger into the face of the boy in the photograph of Sergei Borodin's birthday party and then at the photograph in the book. Both boys smiled the identical smile. They even wore exactly the same pair of eyeglasses. "*Leo Adler*. Our *National Security Adviser*."

"I think you're absolutely right," Nicola said. "It's the same person."

"Leo Adler is DANTE," Walker said. "Now I get it."

"I don't," Nicola said. "What are you talking about?"

"It explains everything. *Everything*."

"Not to me."

"Do you want the ten-minute explanation or the eighteen-hour briefing?" He laughed. "Seriously," he said, "I can explain."

And he did. He told her about the long-known existence of a highly placed Soviet mole—code-named DANTE. He told her about the NSA's cryptanalytic breakthrough in Soviet transmission codes. He told her about Ronald Peters, about Boris Shokorov. About Shokorov's death.

398

It all came together with shocking clarity. Hobie James was heading the reinvestigation of the DANTE matter. Zamatin must be Adler's handler, a double agent himself—it was the only thing that made sense.

"I'm sorry." She shook her head. "It still doesn't make sense to me."

"It's *supposed* to be confusing, Nicola."

"It succeeds, then."

"Do you remember when I was telling you about the Sorge network?"

"Sure." She pointed to Sorge. "That's him."

Walker pointed to the uneasy-looking face at the edge of the photograph. "See this guy? This is Val Zamatin. Vassily Zamatin. Now the story about Zamatin—and I just found this out recently—is that he was the one who informed on the Sorge ring, who identified them to the Japanese."

"And my parents!" Nicola said.

"Yes," Walker said slowly. "That's true, of course."

She stared at her clenched fists. "What happened to him?"

"What happened to him was that now, he's working for the CIA."

"What? *What?*"

"You have to remember that Sorge was a *Soviet* spy, remember, a master Soviet spy. Whoever turned him in was of course going to be quite popular with the opponents of the Soviet Union. What Val did—what he was *supposed* to have done—was to sell Sorge down the river to the Germans and the Japanese. So then, when the Germans became our allies instead of our enemies and Stalin became our enemy instead of our ally, Val made his way over here."

"So you're saying Leo Adler is a spy." She laughed. "I'm sorry but I can't believe that. I mean . . . I just can't."

He nodded. He was adding everything up in his head. He riffled through Adler's biography to find the date of Adler's departure from Shanghai. "March 1941. Exactly! He left after Zamatin got there, but before the network was destroyed." He took Nicola's head between his hands. "Now we know what is going on."

She still looked baffled. "*You* do."

"I *worked* under Val Zamatin for a while. And early in my investigation for you, I found out that the Agency had files on your parents and that they were flagged. I thought that was strange but—"

"What do you mean, 'flagged'?"

"The 'ROMEO Flag.' And Val Zamatin turned out to be RO-MEO."

She smiled and shook her head. "I'm afraid you've lost me again."

After he explained, she wanted to know why Zamatin would track her parents.

"I think in the beginning because he didn't know what happened to them." Suddenly Walker's own knowledge of her parent's horrible end flooded his senses. It seemed unbelievably patronizing of him to be keeping the knowledge from her. It seemed to him she had a right to know.

"What?" Nicola said. "Why would he flag them? I mean why not just find out?"

"It would have been tough for him to find out." Walker was thinking. Finally, he said, "Zamatin probably flagged all the members of the Sorge net. They would have known he was the one who blew the ring to the Japanese. And after the war, they'd be out on the streets again, most of them. Either that or he flagged them because he knew"—he picked up the photograph and waved it—"that this photograph existed." He stopped. "The only thing I can think of is that Hobie James—the CIA guy who's in charge of the Dante investigation—must have told Zamatin about this photograph."

"I still don't get it. Just because Adler's picture is in here, with this little group of spies, I don't see why that means anything."

"There's nothing in Adler's biography about this little social group."

"Maybe he was just there, at the café. Maybe he just happened to be there. Maybe he was just a friend of my parents."

"You're right," Walker said, "but you're wrong. I just *know*. I just know it's Adler. He's the mole. And that's the reason we're in all this shit—because he's it, he's DANTE. Because of this." He held up the photograph and shook it. "Unbelievable." He shook his head. "Leo *Adler*. Jesus Christ."

"I still don't see why the photograph is so important. I mean it doesn't prove anything."

"Because what it does is—it gives you Adler as a possibility. This is probably the only evidence that links Adler to the Sorge group.

400

But once you have suspicions about him, and a confirming source of physical evidence like this photograph, I'm betting that it won't be that hard to prove that he's DANTE. It's like knowing from the beginning who done it in an Agatha Christie book. Once you *know*, it's no problem to separate the false clues from the real clues.

"It is unbelievable, though. It's really frightening. It's bad enough *Zamatin* is a double agent. He's about to *retire*—he's about to get his gold *watch*—that's how long he's been in there leaking every goddamned thing. But *Adler*. Adler is running the arms-limitation talks! I think he's the most powerful man in government, next to the president. It's . . ." He shook his head. "Eventually, someone would have figured it out. There's got to be stuff in those cables that could only have come from Adler or his staff. But folks would have reacted like you did—*Leo Adler? No way.* Except . . ." He tapped the photograph. "This would make them think twice." His voice trailed away. He took her hand. "Listen, Nicola, there's something I know that I didn't want to tell you, but I think I should."

"About your . . . about the CIA?"

"No." He looked at the floor. He stroked her knuckles absently with his thumb. "It's about your parents. They died in a prison camp in Manchuria called Fushun." He stopped again. His voice was heavy. "It was a bad place to die."

"I knew that," she said in a puzzled voice.

"Yes," he said. "But you didn't know this."

He told her.

When he was finished, she sat very quietly with her eyes closed. "I'm glad you told me," she said, "because . . ." She struggled with her composure. "Because I always thought—why did they send me away? I could never imagine sending Kate away from me, when she was a baby. So part of me has always thought my parents abandoned me. But they were doing dangerous things, they were afraid for me. . . ." Her voice faltered and she shook her head. Her head tilted forward but she didn't touch him. "But it's so . . . horrible to think of them. . . ." Her eyes flew open. "How could people do that to other people . . . ?" Her voice trailed away.

Walker embraced her. Andy stuck his head through the door just then and said, "Yuck. Mush."

Nicola went in to check on Cal Tuttle. Walker paced the sun

porch, making plans in his head. He had to get in touch with Hobie James. Hobie would provide some protection for Andy and himself, for Nicola and Kate. But if for some reason he couldn't reach Hobie, it was essential to get the information out as soon as possible—to get the photograph to someone. Until they managed that, they remained in danger.

You could never underestimate the power of physical evidence. Hale would help.

As they began getting ready for bed, Cal started thinking out loud that maybe someone would be searching for them. They talked about that for a while. Joe Fayva—Nicola and Kate's neighbor— had been told they were going to Bar Harbor and he hadn't been home when they'd taken off in the boat. He would have noticed the boat was gone, but he probably would have assumed it went out in the storm. Cal said that his daughter called him "most every day," and certainly would have raised some kind of alarm. His car might even have been discovered at Nicola's—some empty casings from the gunman's shots might have been found as well—but on second thought, unless someone had heard those shots, they wouldn't be looking for anything like that.

"I think he was probably the type of guy that picked up after himself anyway," Walker said.

"Where do you think our boat ended up?" Andy said. "I remember once when those kids around the point forgot to tie up their boat and it floated away at night when they were running the net, you looked at your charts and you figured it out."

"Ayuh," Cal said. "The Dumfries twins."

"Yeah. You told them where it would be and it was right there."

"Would it sink?" Nicola asked.

"No, it couldn't sink all the way," Kate said. "It had too much flotation."

"Someone might have seen us going out into the storm in the boat," Kate said.

"Nah," Cal said. "Unless someone was out securing their own boat. I didn't see anybody. And no one was on the water, that's for sure." He stumbled over to the wall next to the refrigerator, where a faded chart was thumbtacked to the paneling. "Your boat went one of two places," he said. "If it broke loose when the tide was coming in, it's probably somewhere in the Basin—probably over here." He pointed to a little cove known as Light's Cove. "But if it came loose when the tide was going, it probably went up Sebasco way."

"Do you think we'll find it?" Kate asked anxiously.

"I expect someone will have tied it up and they'll eventually get around to telling the Coast Guard about it—except the Coast Guard likely's been damned busy. Lots of boats would have got loose in the storm. If it was bad enough to tear that cleat right off of your boat in here, in the bay—you can imagine what it was like down to the New Meadows—" He looked over at Neil and shook his head. "Let alone out to Small Point or Popham."

Nicola and Walker exchanged glances.

CHAPTER FIFTY-SIX

The next day there was an early mist, but nothing like the fog of the previous morning. It had been a long night. Cal, moaning and tossing with fever, had awakened them all several times. Nicola's face had a pinched, worried look. She put compresses on Cal's head and fed him cool water from the spring, but his condition was clearly deteriorating. Walker went outside to collect some wood for the kitchen fire. She followed him out. "I'm worried about Cal," she said.

"What do you think it is?"

She pushed her hair off her forehead and shook her head. "I don't know. I—I just hope he doesn't have pneumonia or something. I don't know . . . he's . . . so . . . out of it sometimes, almost delirious. His fever is high for an adult."

"I think I'll swim to the mainland after breakfast."

Suddenly, he couldn't stand the idea of being on the island another day. He didn't believe a boat would pass. They'd just be stuck on the island and he'd get weaker and weaker, less able to make the swim.

Nicola said: "Can you swim that far?"

"Sure," he said. "I wouldn't try it if I didn't think I could do it." He spoke with confidence, but he knew it would be a hard swim. He could always rest, he thought, do the backstroke, float.

After a cup of tea, Cal seemed a little better. With input from Kate and Nicola, he drew a rough map for Walker in his spidery hand—showing the landmarks on the mainland, where he should come ashore and how he could find a road, some cottages, a telephone. Kate tried bailing out the skiff one last time, but it hesitated only momentarily before sinking sedately up to its gunwales once again.

Walker took a last look at the map, trying to commit its landmarks to memory, then stood on the pebbly beach, shivering. All of them—except Cal—were standing there to watch him go.

"Well," he said, "time for my dip."

"Dad," Andy said, "be careful."

He began walking in, keeping his posture nonchalant. But the bottom was covered with sharp shells and rocks, and the cold water made gradual submersion torture anyway, so he gave a karate yell, took a deep breath, and dived.

The water took his breath away momentarily with its cold, hard grip on his chest and he came up shaking his head to clear his eyes and trying to force air into his lungs. A cheer went up from the beach and he struck out immediately in a smooth, determined crawl. The water temperature was about sixty degrees, he guessed, far colder than the water had been when he'd done his distance swimming.

But it was a relief to be off the island at last, to be doing something, to be released from worrying and thinking. He was weaker than he thought, though, and out of shape, and his stroke soon grew ragged. He inhaled water and came up choking, and had to stop, float for a while. He looked back toward the island, and he could see how far he'd traveled by the visible but tiny figures of Andy, Nicola, and Kate. He raised his hand to them, but they were too far away: he couldn't see if they acknowledged the gesture. When he looked over to the mainland to see if he was keeping his heading toward the white rock Cal had designated for a landmark, it seemed impossibly far. He rolled over on his back and considered swimming back to the island.

No, if he was going to make the swim, he'd better do it now. He breaststroked two hundred strokes, then resumed his crawl again, then floated on his back. He backstroked a hundred strokes, flipped and made sure he was heading correctly, sidestroked, breaststroked and resumed the crawl. He followed that rotation—trying to keep the muscles fresh. After a while, he couldn't manage the crawl—

lifting his head out of the water to breathe required too much effort. He rested for longer and longer periods of time, losing way sometimes to the current. Once he grabbed a Styrofoam lobster buoy and held on to it for a long time, its buoyancy helping him float and regain his wind.

If he'd had the strength, he would have tried to get it off its line, or even break off a piece, but he was weak as a baby by the time he got to it. When he finally reached the little rocky beach near the white rock, he pulled himself past the skirt of seaweed onto a ledge of the smooth white rock and lay there, exhausted. The drying seaweed made tiny cracking noises near his ear. If he'd had to swim another quarter mile, he doubted he could have made it. Inhaling hurt. He took quick, shallow breaths, wheezing like an old man. When some of the exhaustion left him, he stood up. With the first wobbly step he took, he sliced open his big toe on a barnacled rock.

And although he'd looked forward to getting out of the chilly water, the cold air on his wet skin made him feel even colder. He broke out in goosebumps, he shivered violently, and his teeth knocked together uncontrollably. He stroked the back of his spine—a trick taught in survival training—to provoke more shivering, the body's way of warming itself. He turned around and looked back at Tripp's Island, trying to orient himself. He looked around for the point Cal had noted on his map, and set off through the brush.

The terrain made his progress slow and painful. His bare feet weren't tough, and the word "tenderfoot" popped into his head with a flash of its literal meaning. Spiny juniper bushes and dense huckleberries were the predominant vegetation. The barnacle cut on his big toe hurt more with each step and he was relieved when he found the stream Cal had penciled in on the map. He walked in it for a while. The slick algae-covered rocks in the stream sent him sprawling a couple of times. The mosquitoes were bad and a few times he gave in to his irritation and swatted at them—the red smears showing that he'd got some of them too late. He'd begun to think the map had been wrong, and that he was lost and ought to retrace his steps when he heard the sound of a car's motor. The sound produced a sharp, unexpected thrill of fear. After the quiet island, after the swim, his body found the sound alarming. Panicked blood pricked the ends of his fingers and sizzled in his ears. Soon after that, he found the road.

The first cottage he passed had a dog in residence barking its displeasure with such a menacing tone that he trudged on. The next cottage was locked up tight for the summer, shades pulled. He found help in the third cottage.

The whine of a chain saw led him past the little white house into the woods behind it. A man was cutting branches off a big hemlock brought down by the storm, revving the saw between cuts. The chain saw was so loud, he had to sidestep around to where he could be seen to avoid startling the man. He caught the look on the man's red, earnest face and could almost read his mind: *What the hell? Who's this Mo Fo?*

The earsplitting whine dwindled and then stopped. "Help ya with something?" the man asked suspiciously.

"Hope so," Walker said. "Got stuck by the storm on an island near here. We've been stuck for three days—me, and some others—an old man, my son, and two women."

"Sounds like it could be fun," the man said, spitting out a good-old-boy cackle.

"Not unless you like a steady diet of mussels."

"You ain't kidding? You really been . . . what . . . *marooned?* You ain't shittin' me?"

Walker smiled a would-I-make-this-up smile. "We got caught in that storm, and—"

"That was some blow, wasn't it? And then that goddamned fog. I never—" He stopped and whapped himself on the head. "Come in, come on in, you must be freezing. I'm Lonnie Stolle." He stuck out his hand for the shake. "What island you been stuck on?"

"Neil Walker. It's called Tripp's Island."

"No shit." Stolle shook his head. "I don't believe this. Cherry ain't gonna believe this."

Once inside, Stolle fussed over him, bringing out half his wardrobe so that Walker could choose dry clothes, offering a shower, chowder, coffee. He kept saying, "You sure, man?" when Walker said he wanted to get the others first, before anything else.

He rowed Walker out to his fishing boat. Once they got going, it took only a few minutes to reach Tripp's Island. As they closed on it, Walker saw Andy on the shore standing next to Nicola. She noticed the boat first and bent over to tell Andy. Then they both waved and Andy did his best to jump up and down.

Walker went to get the suitcases—which Nicola had packed. Stolle was in a great mood, ferrying them back to his cabin. Once they got inside, he got some dry clothes for Cal and insisted on heating up cans of Snow's clam chowder, which they all ate with slurping, mouth-burning pleasure. Then he drove them back to Nicola's cabin in his rattly blue Blazer.

"We're not going to stay here," Walker said as soon as Stolle's Blazer disappeared up the driveway.

"Can we go inside and just sit *down?*" Kate whined.

"No."

"Why *not?*"

"Kate," Nicola said in a warning tone.

"Because," Walker said patiently, "we really shouldn't even be here. Your mother accidentally came into possession of a dangerous piece of information, and the people who are trying to destroy it aren't too worried about—about our well-being."

He took Kate's arm and led her up the steps to the sliding glass door. Together, they looked in. The place had been ransacked, as he'd foreseen. Every drawer in the kitchen had been emptied out, every piece of furniture turned upside down and shredded, every book tossed on the floor. Kate looked white. Andy said: "Holy cow."

"Damn it," Nicola started, but then she fell silent.

"Look, do you have a lipstick?" Walker asked. Nicola dug in her purse and produced one. Walker wrote DANGER on the sliding glass door. "I'm going to look at the cars," he said. "Wait here. Don't touch *anything*."

He checked out Nicola's Subaru very carefully, under the hood, under the chassis, in the trunk, the exhaust system, the tires. He found nothing out of the ordinary. He looked over Cal's car and it seemed all right, too.

"Cal," he said, "I think you should go to your daughter's house."

"Heck, Neil, she's got two little kids. I don't want to bring any trouble her way."

Neil looked at Nicola. "What do you think? Does he need to see a doctor, or what?"

"I'm all right," Cal said indignantly. "Touch of the grippe, that's all. Don't you go calling any doctor on me. Won't stand for it."

"Actually, his fever broke while you were gone," Nicola said. She put her palm on Cal's forehead. "It's way down. I think he's all right now."

"Well, you'd better come with us then, until we get things straightened out," Neil said.

"Can I call her, anyway? Susie, I mean? My daughter? Tell her I'm okay?"

"Sure you can, but not from here." He put his hand on the door handle of the Subaru. It was irrational, because he was trained in explosives detection, but just as he touched the metal, his heart jumped in his chest. He suggested some chores to get the rest of them away from the car—sending Kate and Cal down to Nicola's neighbor's, sending Andy with Nicola to write a warning on the other side of the house, on the picture window. He forced his nerves steady and turned the key. The engine fired and he wiped his sweaty fingers off on his pants leg. The others straggled back. From the look on Nicola's face, he knew she understood what he had just been through.

"All aboard."

"Where are we going?" Kate demanded as they bounced up the rutty road.

"To the airport," Walker said grimly. "To some motel near the airport."

"Great," Kate said. "Just great."

They ended up at the Sheraton. Kate and Andy were happy, once they got inside, to take baths and drink Coca-Cola from the soda machine. Walker tried to call Hale but couldn't get through. Cal called Susie. Somehow, Walker could tell that her relief was coupled with anger at having worried needlessly. "No need to swear," he heard Cal say. After a minute, Cal hung up. "High strung," he said. A minute later, he was on the couch, asleep. Walker made some calls.

"I'm going to make a run to McDonald's," Nicola said. "Kate, do you want to come? Andy?" She asked Walker if he wanted anything.

He was on the phone again, the receiver angled away from his head, obviously on hold. "Big Mac and large fries," he said and watched them go.

He was frustrated. Hale had been "away from the office." He'd managed to get through to the Office of Security, but only after being on hold for long, frustrating minutes. He didn't have his address book—it was in the cabin—with him, and he didn't remember Hobie's direct line, so he'd had to call the Agency's published number. He was passed around like salt at dinner, and finally, when he reached Hobie's secretary, it was only to learn that Hobie was "away from his desk."

He flicked on the television, but found only soap operas. Nicola came back, with the food. He was so hungry, he devoured it almost without chewing. He thought it was the best thing he'd ever eaten.

Nicola had also bought him some pants and a shirt that were his size to replace Stolle's clothing, which hung on him. Andy was wearing new clothes as well and Nicola had some clothes and a fish sandwich for the sleeping Cal.

A few minutes later, Walker was lying back, looking at the textured ceiling, waiting for the phone to ring. "Can we go buy a bathing suit?" Andy asked his father. "They have a pool."

"I have to wait," Walker said. "The telephone."

Nicola sighed. "I'll take him."

"I'm sorry—" Walker started but Nicola waved off his protests. Kate said: "I'll go too."

It was slow going with Andy; it was hard for him to walk in crowds. Jordan Marsh was crowded, and Nicola felt dizzy, unused to the rush and chaos. Andy found a suit right away. The ladies' suits were all gigantic for Kate, but she found one subteen suit to try. When she emerged from the dressing room, her face was set, angry. "I don't like this anymore," she said to Nicola. Her eyes looked astonished, frightened, and her face was contorted in a kind of amazed grimace. "I look horrible."

Nicola inclined her head slightly and gave a tiny nod.

"I can't go swimming like this."

"That's all right," Andy said. "You can watch me."

Mike Hale called just after Nicola and the kids left. "Hey! You already made my day, Neil."

"I always enjoy a chat with you, too," Walker said, puzzled.

"Where were you?" Hale's voice was manic, annoyed. "I mean you set up a call—I expect you to keep it. You're missing and pre-

410

sumed *dead*, buddy. Where the fuck were you?" Walker remembered the call he'd placed from Cal's; he'd been trying to see if Hale could take care of Andy for him. It seemed so long ago.

"Where I've been is in trouble."

"You're in more trouble than you know." Hale's voice sounded agitated, upbeat, nervous. *Cocaine*, Walker thought. Shit. "You're on the Trouble Hit Parade," Hale said. "You're a hot item."

Walker sat up. "What do you mean?"

"Where are you now?"

"In a motel near the Portland airport."

"You called anyone else?"

"I called the Agency, tried to get through to Hobie James at OS. I'm stuck in the middle of something major."

"Shit. Did you call straight through to James? Or through central?"

"Through central. I never got him either. Just his secretary."

"Shit." Silence. Then: "How long ago did you call Langley?"

Walker estimated a half hour, three quarters of an hour at the outside. "Why?"

"Listen, pardner, first you had the KGB looking for you, then the Agency mustered up its own little search party. We're talking heavy matters. What are you driving?"

"Nicola's car—she's—"

"The lady whose house got barbecued?"

"How—?"

"Go in to the airport and buy some tickets—real names, a little smokescreen. Then hit the long-term parking and steal a car."

Walker was already standing up, stretching the phone cord, trying to look out the window. He and Hale had been in the tightest spots together. His trust in Hale was implicit, rocklike. Hale would never overstate the case.

"I'll meet you at the Vince Lombardi Rest Area on the Jersey Turnpike," Hale went on. "In about—let's see—eight hours. Don't speed."

Hale hung up and Walker went in to wake Cal; then he packed up Nicola's bags again. They went down to the lobby and checked out. His money was still damp and limp from the days on the island. Walker kept looking around at the people in the lobby, checking out the cars in the lot. It was hard, waiting for them to come back, and he had to resist walking over to the shopping center and trying to find them just to be doing something, not waiting.

As soon as he saw Nicola turn into the motel's parking lot, he jogged out the door, Cal Tuttle trudging wearily behind him. Her eyes focused on the suitcases, puzzled.

"We've got to run," he said with a smile. "Toss me the keys for the trunk."

"But, Dad—"

Before Andy even voiced his complaint, they were rolling toward the airport. He asked Nicola if she had her credit cards.

She did. He told her what to do: buy tickets—to New York, or "wherever"—take a look at the departure log—for all of them. Real names. And then come out again. He'd pick her up in a different car.

"What do you mean, *a different car?*"

"I'm going to get a different one."

"Why? What about mine?"

"I'll explain later." A flush of fear came over her face. They arrived at the departure gate.

She had to stand in line. Everyone in the airport was impatient and everything took longer than anyone expected. Irritation hummed through the air. Nicola didn't mind standing there waiting; she tried to figure out what was happening.

She knew that this was some kind of evasive tactic. Walker was renting a car. They were going to leave this one here: the tickets would make it look as if they were flying somewhere else. She didn't fully understand everything Walker had told her about this DANTE business, but if Leo Adler was really a Soviet spy, and they were the sole repositories of that knowledge, she understood the magnitude of their danger. And it seemed they were barely staying one step ahead of their pursuers and that only good luck was responsible for their being alive right now.

Now the impatience in the room caught her, too. She scanned the board. She tried to figure out which flights were least likely to be booked solid. She couldn't get up to the agent and say: "Give me five tickets on the first plane out of here." The Delta to Boston might be full. She'd try for the flight to Burlington, Vermont. She shifted from foot to foot and flicked her American Express card back and forth against her fingertips. The line shuffled forward.

Walker parked the Subaru, leaving Cal, Kate, and Andy inside. He began walking slowly up and down the rows of cars, looking for one with an unlocked door. Eventually, he found a VW Rabbit. They'd be cramped, but he didn't want to take any more time. He cut the ignition wires with his pocket knife and made the proper connections: the Rabbit started. He drove back to the Subaru and told them all to get in back. They sat there jammed together. The suitcase containing Nicola and Kate's clothing could be left behind, but they had to take the suitcase with the papers. Luckily, it fit in the rear compartment.

He found the parking ticket, which would save him from shucking and jiving the parking attendant—or worse, driving through the gate. It was neatly clipped to the visor. The car had been there for four days. He drove to the gate. Just as the attendant was handing him his change, Andy blurted out: "Dad, did you steal this car?"

The attendant looked astonished and Neil laughed and said, "I think you've worn out that joke, Andy." And drove off.

"But, Dad, did you?"

"No, I just borrowed it."

"But, Dad—"

"Let me just get out of here, then I'll explain."

"But, Dad, you can't just—"

"*Shut up*," he heard himself say, in such a venomous tone he sensed the recoil from all three of them.

Nicola was standing outside near a lounging group of Skycaps and she slipped into the front seat of the Rabbit without a word.

CHAPTER
FIFTY-SEVEN

It was a long and tedious drive to New Jersey, made longer by Walker's insistence that they leave the turnpikes periodically, to make sure they weren't being followed. By the time they reached Massachusetts, he was confident no one was on their back. He thought all along that even if his phone call to Langley had been intercepted, they really hadn't had time to set a tail on him, but he didn't want to take any chances.

Everyone in the car had a lot of questions, of course, and though he had no answers, he told them what little he knew. He knew why the KGB was interested in them, but the Agency's interest was puzzling. Andy couldn't understand why they couldn't go to the police. Cal and, to an extent, Kate had the same impulse: go to the authorities.

Walker thought that none of them could understand how big and powerful the clandestine world was, or how it coexisted with the "real" world, a parallel but interactive universe. For one thing, they were inured to it, they took it for granted without seeing its pervasiveness. Even in ordinary life, they were continually under surveillance. Closed-circuit cameras recorded their forays into drugstores, banks, apartment buildings. Massive computers compiled data in their names, direct mail companies "profiled" them, then "targeted" them. The power company had recently requested his social security number. He'd made up a number. Why would the power company need anyone's social security number? He didn't like the thought of a computer being able to follow every line of his life, tie up every little loose strand of his existence, compile a huge, definitive dossier.

He didn't kid himself that this was not already the case.

And if they didn't see how their daily lives were the subjects of continual "intelligence gathering," how could they see that in the world of geopolitics the clandestine world beat within the apparent world like its dark pulsating heart? That for every decision made in the National Security Council, there were a dozen secret decisions made, reams of classified reports, stacks of satellite photos— that some of those decisions would implement an agenda in exact opposition to officially pursued policy. Only periodically did the crust of the apparent world rupture, and then, like a volcanic explosion spewing debris, the power of the clandestine world would reveal itself in its ashes: Alger Hiss. The Rosenbergs. Francis Gary Powers. The Bay of Pigs. Watergate.

It was dark when they arrived at the Vince Lombardi Rest Area. The pinkish mercury vapor lamps arced high above them; the huge parking area had a desolate look. They got out of the car, cramped and exhausted. Walker took the suitcase out of the trunk and they headed inside. In the parking lot, he thoughtlessly told Andy to hurry up and Andy chugged along ferociously, determined to fall, which of course he did.

The women hurried to his aid but he wouldn't let them help, insisting on getting up by himself. Getting up from falling down was one of the things Andy still had great difficulty doing and Walker yanked him up and said, "We don't have time for that now, Andrew."

He regretted it the moment he said it: it came out cruel, not matter-of-fact the way he'd intended it. Kate leapt to Andy's defense: "You're not fair! You act like if he just tries harder, everything will be all right. And then when he does try, you yell at him."

"I'm sorry."

Nicola felt proud of Kate, but she was guilty of the same flawed logic, that trying harder could overcome any obstacle. She was a sucker for triumph-over-adversity stories.

They walked past the glass cases full of Lombardi paraphernalia. Grainy, enlarged photographs of the great coach flanked the display cases. Lombardi smiled his famous gap-toothed grin. They went past the banks of vending machines selling doodads—a white plastic mouse with red eyes, tiny black and white dogs on magnets, jumping beans, folding combs—junk food, soda, cigarettes, newspapers, past the fast food counter, past the biorhythm machines, and into the restaurant.

A fuzzy-haired waitress flipped a wet rag across the counter. The mustard-colored upholstery was bilious under fluorescent tubes, which managed to cast a light that was at once weak and glary. Travelers, their eyes glazed from focusing on the road, sat quietly waiting for "refreshment," a term which seemed like a joke to Walker. It was impossible to depart a Rest Area feeling refreshed. Everyone left disappointed at the food, annoyed that it took so long, depressed that they still had "miles to go," except for kids, who loved the places.

While they waited for the hostess, he spotted Hale sitting in the back. He was wearing glasses and a billed cap with the word CATERPILLAR stitched to the crown. He got up when he saw them. Andy was excited to meet Mike in such an unusual locale and performed the introductions deftly. After they ate, Hale led them out to a tan Buick. He put the suitcase in the trunk. "Heavy," he remarked. With six of them in the car, it was still a little cozy, but a huge improvement over the Rabbit. Andy sat on the front seat, between his father and Hale.

"So," Andy said. "Where are we going?"

"Warrenton," Hale said.

"Oh *yeah?* Can we go tubing?" He turned to the back seat, to address Kate. "It is *so* fun."

"It's possible, Andy. But first, your Dad and I got to talk about some things, okay?" Hale nodded toward Walker. "So—you mind telling me what everybody's so damn excited about?"

Walker did.

Hale sat thoughtfully, listening. "But I don't understand," Walker said, when he'd finished, "why we had to leave the motel. What did you mean that the *Agency* is after me too?"

"Well, it's Val. He's working both sides of the street. Val's baked a little cake for you—strung together some cock-and-bull story, told them *you* were DANTE's control."

"That's cute."

"He's a cute guy. He knows it won't wash, but it's buying him

416

a little time. And also, it doubles his search strength, you know? I mean if he were to *find* you, I don't think we could expect to see you again. I mean, if you were debriefed, that would about wrap things up—this house of cards Val has propped up wouldn't stand for a day. But if you're not around to defend yourself"—he waved his hand in the air—"the notion of you as a double will be harder to disprove. And he can cook some papers up that make it look like you went to Moscow. I mean if you *disappear*, Val's in a lot better shape. Even if it looks like a professional hit, he's in a position to cover it.

"You know how these things are—the guy dies of exposure when it's fifty degrees out and sunny, a guy commits suicide by tying his hands and feet and blindfolding himself—never mind how he did it, hey! He was talented, a real—!"

"Mike!" Walker realized Andy was hearing this. "I think—"

Hale steamrollered on. "I mean these things happen, and investigations are conducted, but nothing conclusive ever comes up. Physical evidence generally disappears. I mean John Kennedy's *brain* went missing, along with its little bullet trails, you know?"

"Mike, I think you might have Andy a little concerned here."

Hale looked down at Andy who pretended to be nonchalant. "Hey, Andy, nothing's going to *happen* to your dad. You know that, right?"

"Just in case it does," Andy said with stunning practicality, "will you take care of me?"

Hale shot Walker a look. "You bet," he said.

"What do you mean?" Nicola asked from the back seat. "I mean about Kennedy's brain."

"Well, once someone raised the nasty specter of a possible conspiracy—you know, maybe it wasn't just Lee Harvey Oswald all by himself. . . . Eyewitness reports told of other gunmen, all that stuff. Well, they went to have another little look at Kennedy's brain. They thought maybe another forensic pathologist could examine the entrance and exit wounds. But it was gone. The brain was gone."

"How could they lose something like that?" Nicola said.

"Some folks thought it was pretty careless," Hale said.

Walker said: "What do you think we should do? I still think I should try to get to Hobie."

"Yeah, well, Hobie had better watch his ass too."

417

"I think he's good at that."

"Well, the first thing to do, before we start worrying about anyone else, is to get you all—and your photograph—out of harm's way."

They crossed the Delaware Memorial Bridge. "Where are we?" Kate asked in a sleepy voice.

"Good-bye, New Jersey," said Andy. "Hello, Delaware."

When they got through the toll booth at the Delaware Turnpike, there was a large sign that read:

INFORMATION POLICE

"Where's the fucking comma?" Hale complained.

Under the words was the time, 10:12 P.M., and the temperature, 82°F.

"So," Walker said. "What do you propose?" Andy had fallen asleep. Walker looked into the backseat. Cal was snoring gently, his head against the window. Nicola was slumped against him. Kate sat staring straight ahead, with a dazed look.

"We have a kind of summit meeting. Zamatin, Hobie James, you and me. Childress."

"How will you get them to come?"

"Oh, I think you can leave that to me. You wouldn't want to know any of my trade secrets, would you?"

Finally, fatigue overcame Walker's nervous worry, and he fell asleep. When he woke up, they were passing through Washington, D.C., rolling up New York Avenue. They passed the Hecht Company's old art deco warehouse, the arboretum, a strip of motels. The Capitol dome flashed into sight and then they went through a tunnel. Kate was excited to see the monuments, and Hale actually detoured so that they passed both the Lincoln and the Jefferson. An hour later they rolled into downtown Warrenton. Walker looked up just as they passed a butcher shop with a marquee sign that read HAM HOKES.

Hale said "Damn!" in such a crestfallen voice that Walker knew something bad had happened even though it seemed they were just cruising down the road.

"What?"

Hale did a U-Turn. "The sign in the butcher shop. It's part of my early warning system."

Walker sat up, instantly more alert. "And?"

"There's surveillance at the cabin. And I don't want anyone to know that we're here. *Damn*. And Mrs. Garcia was making me red beans and dirty rice." He tapped his fingers on the wheel. "We'll head for South of the Border."

"*Mexico*. You're kidding?"

But Hale wasn't talking about Mexico.

"How could a person not know about South of the Border? You ever see those bumper stickers in Day-Glo chartreuse with the little sleeping Mexican, his head hidden under a sombrero, propped up against some letters that read South of the Border?"

"I thought it was Mexico."

Hale laughed. "Well, you're in for a surprise." He explained that South of the Border was a motel in South Carolina just below the North Carolina line.

"Oh, I see," Walker said. "Cute."

"It's not exactly *cute*, I wouldn't call the place cute. It's its own thing." He explained that he had occasionally had meetings there. "It's sort of combination motel, shopping center, amusement park, video arcade, fireworks stand, and linen outlet."

"It'll be a change of pace from Tripp's Island," Nicola said.

"Most folks love it," Hale said.

"Can we buy some fireworks?" Andy asked.

"South Carolina," Cal Tuttle said. "Now how far would that be?"

"I'd go back to sleep, Mr. Tuttle," Mike Hale said.

"How did you find this place?" Nicola asked.

"Believe me, it's hard not to find it."

"Wake me up when you want someone to drive," Walker said, and turned toward the window.

They stopped somewhere in North Carolina. It was 4:00 A.M. Hale called and made reservations for one of the suites. The South of the Border billboards had been increasing in frequency the closer they got to it. Most of them featured visual jokes: a three-dimensional fish with a halo: HOLY MACKEREL! SOUTH OF THE BORDER; a three-dimensional hot dog: EVERYBODY'S A WEENER AT SOUTH OF THE BORDER. Andy, during the brief times when he was awake, found these signs incredibly amusing.

• •

It was almost dawn by the time they arrived at the motel, but still dark. Nicola had grown so used to the motion and the sound of the car that when they stopped she woke up to what seemed a hallucination. Despite the hour, South of the Border was totally illuminated. It was like coming upon a secret Las Vegas: every building was outlined in blinking beckoning light.

The *pièce de résistance* towered above them, a colossal Mexican constructed of steel, every girder and strut trimmed with lights. It stood astride the road, and they drove between its massive legs, looking up at the neon-rimmed exterior elevator which crawled up the center of the colossus, depositing sightseers on the brim of the sombrero, where they could gaze upon the Carolina countryside. Near the colossus was a store. A rocket covered with stars threatened to lift off from its roof; the store sign said: FORT PEDRO. FIREWORKS. Nicola felt she could use a sensory-deprivation chamber.

Within half an hour, the Presidential Suite looked like a refugee camp. Cots had been brought, extra blankets found, and they were all in their beds for the night except for Mike Hale, who spent a half hour on the telephone. Cal, Andy, and Neil shared the king-sized water bed. "I don't know about this," Cal said. "It feels downright strange."

"I think it feels cool," Andy said.

"Don't wiggle around," Cal said. "You're making me seasick."

The next morning, Hale laid down some rules—no one could leave the suite, and no one could call room service.

"We're hiding *out* here, laying *low*, keeping a low *profile*," he said in a redneck voice. "Just for a day or two. Y'all can stand it. I'm going to go get you some breakfast in just a minute."

"Can you get a Monopoly game?"

In a characteristic gesture, Hale widened his eyes and pointed his finger at Andy: "You're on. Breakfast first, though."

Privately, by the door, Hale told Walker: "A boy, excuse me, who limps, a girl who looks like a pencil, a good-looking woman, and a sneezing old man—can you think of a more conspicuous group?"

"Could you get me a toothbrush?" Cal asked. "And some Polident." He gave a fake smile. "My choppers."

"Tell you what," Hale said. "I'm going to go out—get some doughnuts, some coffee, some juice, some milk—and then, after breakfast, I'll get someone to go shopping for you." He opened the door a crack. "Make lists."

That afternoon, two taciturn young men arrived. Hale introduced them as "your babysitters, Ray Sears and Steve Bancroft." They smiled when Hale said the word "babysitters," although their smiles were reflexive, cold. They spoke very little and mostly to each other, although they nodded frequently. One was light-haired and blue-eyed and one was dark-haired and brown-eyed, but they seemed very similar to Nicola. And whenever one of them looked her way, she had the impression his focus was not normal, that his peripheral vision was working overtime. They were the kind of men who surround public figures at public appearances, the kind of men who don't miss a trick, Nicola thought.

One of them—Sears—left with the "shopping list" and the other one settled in to watch "General Hospital." Nicola noticed Kate staying in the bathroom for a long time; when she emerged, her hair was carefully combed and she'd put on makeup, and she kept sneaking glances at Bancroft.

Walker, with Hale contributing advice, wrote out a draft of a one-page statement concerning Walker's knowledge of Zamatin, Adler, and the DANTE investigation. At the end of the page was a paragraph to the effect that certain lawyers would have multiple copies of both this letter and the photograph, and instructions on disseminating same if any harm should come to any of them, including Calvin Tuttle.

Sears had long since returned with the things everyone had requested, including a stack of board games and a good-sized cassette tape player along with a couple dozen tapes.

Soon, though, everyone was bored with watching and listening, and playing games. Signs of cabin fever were apparent. They all tended to stand up a lot, and then, realizing there was nowhere to go, sit down again. They had a dinner—fetched by Sears—of tacos, beer, and Coke. Nicola finished reading *Running Dog*.

That night, she couldn't sleep. She was too aware of Walker in the next room. She kept remembering the way he looked on the island, in the fog. She tossed and turned so much that Kate said, "Mom, you're keeping me up." And then she lay rigid. *I will count to a thousand before I move.* And she did that, but it didn't help.

The next day passed in tedium. Sears went out in the morning for newspapers and breakfast. The front page carried a story about Leo Adler's attendance at a summit meeting of NATO allies where discussions were being held about the deployment of missiles in Europe. Adler smiled out from behind a forest of microphones.

In the afternoon, Steve Bancroft and Kate had an intense discussion about horses—the comparative strengths of several breeds. It seemed to be a subject they could discuss forever.

Nicola indulged a guarded hope that Kate really had turned a corner. Maybe it was being in the company of others all the time, maybe she needed that. Maybe being really hungry on the island had changed her. Maybe it had been the trip to Stan's. Something seemed to have changed. She was eating; she'd looked genuinely disgusted when she came out of the dressing room at Jordan Marsh's. Nicola wasn't going to disturb what seemed like progress by mentioning it to Kate. She caught a glimpse of Kate touching Steve Bancroft's arm when she laughed—to include him more fully in her laughter. It was a duplicate of one of her own habitual gestures.

That night, they were playing a massive Scrabble game, waiting for Sears to return with dinner. The tape recorder perched on top of the TV. Linda Rondstadt was singing "Blue Bayou." A knock came at the door. "Someone get it," Bancroft said in a distracted tone. He was holding an *N* in his hand, wiggling it back and forth in the air, considering his move. Cal Tuttle went to the door and opened it.

"Room service," said a man carrying a tray of drinks. As Cal moved aside to let the waiter into the room, Walker saw a puzzled look cross his face, and then the puzzlement turned to alarm.

"T-termite man," Cal said woodenly, his eyes growing round. Bancroft looked nonplussed.

"Wh—?" he began.

"Termite man!" Cal shouted, backing against the wall. Walker jumped to his feet as the waiter tossed his tray to the side, sending a white slush of the margaritas curling into the air. As the tray rattled down to the floor, Walker left his feet, launching himself through the air. He slammed into the waiter's midsection with a cross-body block he'd learned at twelve, playing Pop Warner football. It was a hard tackle, but the waiter gave about as much ground as a telephone pole. The heels of his flattened hands—rough, enormous hands—smashed instantly against Walker's ears, sending a white seam through his vision, as if his eyes had cracked. And then the flattened edge of the waiter's huge right hand smacked into the base of Walker's neck, sending his face flying toward the floor.

Walker gasped, rolled, and began to bleed. Eyes glazed, ears ringing, he heard Kate Ward shout, "Stop it!" And then, as the blood began to run from his nose to his mouth, Walker, trying to climb to his knees through a bank of fog and pain, could see Steve Bancroft reach, fumbling, for the Beretta he carried at the small of his back. The gun seemed to snag on his belt, while the waiter, with practiced efficiency unhurriedly fished a strange-looking weapon from the long holster under his jacket. It looked like a kid's zap gun, with its barrel covered by the fat can of the suppressor.

Walker tried to get up again, but slipped in his own blood. He saw the waiter hesitate, as if uncertain whom to shoot first, and then a decision was made and the gun was pointing at his face. The waiter smiled apologetically as his finger began to close on the trigger, and then his face came apart as the edge of the tape player slammed sideways into his temple. Walker caught a glimpse of Nicola, her hands still stretched forward in follow-through from throwing the thing.

She looked at her hands with a surprised stare. The gun discharged, cratering the floor with a sharp cracking noise, as it fell from the man's hands. Without thinking, Walker grabbed the gun, as the waiter reeled back against the wall, growling in pain. With his left hand, the waiter tried to staunch the blood spurting from his ear, even as his other arm shot out to imprison Kate's neck in the crook of his elbow.

Bancroft had his Beretta out, but was helpless to shoot.

"Jeez," the waiter said, wincing with pain. And then he snarled: "I'll snap her fucking neck . . . drop it."

Almost underfoot, Walker reached up, pointed the barrel of the gun at the waiter's balls, closed his finger on the trigger without a word, and blew a hole into his scrotum.

Kate made a quick, sharp sound like a cat in pain. The waiter dropped to the floor, spilling all over it. Cal grunted. Kate curled up on the floor in a fetal position chanting "ohmygod, ohmygod, ohmygod," in a high, thin voice, repeating the words so fast they became one continuous sound, a tense whine like wind on a wire.

He rose to his knees. The blood shifted in his head as he moved and his vision seemed to retreat to the backs of his eyes. A black blur slid across his field of vision and he felt the slosh of liquid in his nose and in his ears. There were little sounds inside his head that he didn't like hearing, tiny explosions and popping noises, strange sliding drips.

He thought he probably had a concussion because he was seeing double. Two figures of Andy lurched toward him from across the room. He swiveled on his knee, turning his back on the waiter, trying to screen the dead man, so Andy wouldn't see the full horror of it. Blood was gushing from the man's body, making an awful, burbling noise as it rushed past obstructive pieces of flesh.

Squinting made his face hurt, but removed the double vision. Andy crouched next to him and touched his shoulder. "Dad," he said, "are you all right?"

"Yes," Walker said, enunciating carefully through the blood in his mouth. He swayed on his knees and almost toppled to the side. Reaching out to steady himself on Andy, Andy shrank from his touch and he saw that the gun was still in his hand. He put it carefully on the floor.

Andy gave a little half smile and said, "Dad, I'll get you some ice, okay?" It was a direct copy of Diana's habitual response to injury.

"Good," Walker managed. He saw that Andy was already holding the square plastic ice bucket in his hand. He watched Andy step carefully over the body and open the door. There was something depressingly familiar about the expression on Andy's face and his I-can-deal-with-it manner. It made Walker think of newsreel footage of eager young Palestinians going through the routines of combat training, weapon maintenance. He knew that it was wrong to let Andy leave the room, that someone else might be outside, but there was something the matter with his brain. By the time he'd completed the thought, Andy was gone. He stood up.

The room seemed to shift two feet to the right and the black blur clouded his eyes for a second. He tore the bedspread off the closest cot with a hard yank that made tiny silver dots jump in front of his eyes. He dropped it over the dead man. Just before the fabric settled, he caught a glimpse of the man's face. The contusion on the side of his head, where the tape player had hit him, showed signs of swelling and there was a red seam of blood dripping from it and a thin line of blood coming out of his ear. Otherwise, the face looked peaceful, benign. Walker stumbled toward the bathroom. He wet a towel and pressed it to his broken nose, barely touching it. The towel came away from his face pink. Blood was also leaking from his own right ear: he thought that was a bad sign, but he couldn't remember why.

He grabbed all the towels in the bathroom and headed back toward the dead man, determined to cover him completely before Andy returned. He passed Cal Tuttle, who sat stiffly in the chair, clutching his knees. Nicola and Kate were hunched together on the couch. Bancroft was on the telephone.

"Should we call the police?" Cal Tuttle said suddenly. "Or what?" No one answered him.

There was a knock on the door, which made fear flush into Walker's throat but it was Andy, back with the ice. Andy made an ice pack from one of his T-shirts and offered it to his father. They sat on the cot together. "God, Dad," he said, "I think your nose is broken. How do they fix that?"

"Well, should we call the police?" Cal asked again, as if no one had heard him the first time. "Or what?"

"Don't worry, Cal," Walker said through the ice pack. A few moments after that, they heard Ray Sears out in the hall, whistling the Beatles' tune "Yesterday."

"Got *fried chick*-en," Sears said, turning his key. When he stepped through the door with his big bucket of chicken, nearly stumbling on the corpse, no one said a word. "Holy shit," Sears said. "Holy shit."

Nicola felt shaky. She moved with great precision, as if she'd just recovered from surgery. She could remember some things and not others. Her idea of just what had happened was chaotic and unclear. She didn't remember picking up the tape recorder or detaching its cord from the wall, which she must have done. But she did remember throwing it as hard as she could. She didn't remember the gun going off, but she clearly remembered the sharp burst of terror she'd experienced when the waiter put his arm around Kate's neck. Her mind had gone pure white with fear, as if her brain had been the site of a short circuit. And that was the last clear recollection she had. She knew Walker had killed the man.

Ray Sears organized the next few hours. She remembered a doctor coming, a gray-haired man with a prosperous belly and a thick Carolina accent. She was given an injection—tranquilizers of some sort, or a sedative. She remembered sitting absolutely still waiting for the drug to take hold, unable to relax the rigid muscles of her jaw, which was clenched together so fiercely, her face ached. Kate and Andy were sedated as well, and Neil emerged from the bathroom with a bulky bandage on his nose, looking like the Jack Nicholson character in *Chinatown*. She remembered, vaguely, sometime after the injection, moving to different rooms. Someone must have cleaned up behind them. Someone must have done something with the body. She wanted to tell everyone that the waiter's face was the same as the face of the gas man who'd come to the house on Willow Street the day it burned down. But the information seemed to lodge deep within her, and every time the thought came to her, her voice seemed unequal to the task of announcing it. And it didn't matter. The man was dead.

In fact, all the rest of the night, no one spoke of what had happened, of the dead man—although she did notice some short muttered conferences between Sears, Bancroft, and Neil Walker.

CHAPTER

FIFTY-EIGHT

The next day passed the same way the others had at the motel, and still no one spoke about the dead man. Except for Neil's bandaged face, it might never have happened. All day, Nicola was drowsy and kept nodding off; it must have been the aftereffect of the shot.

Though they were encased in their chilled room, it was still somehow apparent that outside the heat was intense. Nicola felt dull and inert. The day seemed so long that by the end of it the events of the previous night seemed tolerably distant, as if they'd happened to someone else, or years ago.

That night, she had trouble sleeping again. She wasn't thinking about the dead man, or the sound Kate made as the bullet tore into his flesh. Her mind had blocked that out and reverted to thoughts of her charred house on Willow Street. She lay there on her back with the covers pulled up to her chin, thinking about how long it would take her to put her life back together—assuming they ever left this motel room—to find a new house, to furnish it. It seemed an overwhelming task to have to replace everything that had been in the house. Paper-towel holders, colanders, two-hole punches, a calculator, a bathroom scale. She was making mental lists like this, room by room, despairing at the enormity of the task when she heard a squeak.

"Nicola," whispered Walker in his muffled, bandaged voice. "Don't scream, it's me."

He knelt down next to the bed. She was propped up on her

elbow. Walker's hand came under the cover, down through the top of her nightgown and caressed her breast. Her nipple got hard instantly. She wanted him to get in bed with her but it was impossible, and anyway, it seemed inappropriate.

His bandages scraped against her face as he kissed her. "I can't get enough of you," he whispered.

Mike Hale returned the next morning. He came through the door with a grim, disgusted look on his face. He looked like a man who'd just spotted a fly floating in his soup.

"What can I say?" he said. His tone of regret seemed forced. Walker knew he felt responsible for the waiter, for the breach of security, but he couldn't get his voice to sound as bad as he felt. He spent the next five minutes trying to find the right metaphor for how stupid he felt.

"I might as well have invited the dude down here," he said, shaking his head.

Walker wondered where the leak was, how the guy had found them.

"Yeah, well, you're not winning any IQ tests here either," Hale said, tapping his foot on the floor. "When you called me from the motel up there in Maine, I *told* you the phone wasn't secure. And then in the next sentence, I told you where to meet me. We're too old for this shit."

For the first time, Walker met his eyes. Hale's pupils looked too small; Walker thought he was looking from behind some controlled substance. Hale shifted his gaze down to his feet.

"After Ray called me the other night," Hale said, "I had a look at the guy. He was there all right, at the Vince Lombardi. The son-of-a-bitch was looking at the trophies. He even *spoke* to me, the shit. He told me all about how he'd tried out for the Baltimore Colts, about how his hamstring went out on him. He just followed us down here and we never even noticed. Hell, we never even *checked*. I hope he enjoyed the sights in D.C. Jesus."

"Who was he? Did you get a line on that?"

Hale shrugged. He seemed to notice for the first time that there were other people in the room. "My apologies," he said, bowing deeply from the waist. "I deeply regret that little intrusion the other night."

428

Walker saw that he wasn't just a little high but really popped. Nicola and Kate were packing up, sticking to the edges of the room. Cal and Andy sat there quietly. Even Sears and Bancroft were embarrassed.

"Let's *go*," Hale said in the same inappropriate, bantering tone. "Time to check out of Fort Pedro."

"Hey," Walker said. He touched Hale's arm. Hale jerked away a little, a nervous twitch.

"Go pay the bill, Ray," Hale went on. Sears turned toward the door with a look of relief on his face. "Make sure you get a receipt. This is a reimbursable expense."

"Hey," Walker said, a little louder this time. "We don't . . ." He looked at the ceiling. "How can I say this? We're not ready to joke about this yet."

Instantly, Hale's face got a white, chagrined look. His eyes checked around the room, as if he'd forgotten where he was.

"Yeah," he said, "yeah. I'm sorry, man. I'm sorry." He looked toward Andy. "I didn't get much sleep for the last couple of nights." He gestured toward Bancroft. "Uh, Steve, you better drive."

They drove out in a big blue van between the legs of the colossal Mexican. The outside of the van displayed airbrushed murals of stags surveying a rocky wilderness. The inside was plush blue velour with swivel seats and one-way windows. Andy liked it.

"Where are we going?" Cal asked. "Not that I mind. I haven't been out of Maine in years."

"Middleburg," Hale said in a neutral voice.

"What state is that in?" Cal seemed intent on small talk, as if everything was going to be normal now. "Virginia? Didn't Jackie Kennedy used to ride horses there?"

"That's it."

"Some of the finest horse country on earth," Bancroft said to Kate. Hale looked at him sharply.

They rode along in silence for about forty-five minutes. Then Nicola spoke. "Do you know who he was? I mean the waiter?"

Hale sat up straight and blinked his eyes. "His name was Allen Burgess." He shrugged and looked at Walker, "A blank. There's nothing on him anywhere."

"He was the same man who came to my house, the gas man," Nicola said.

"He got around," Walker said.

"I think he had a lot of alter egos," Hale said. The effect of the coke seemed to have worn off now. He looked a little haggard, Walker thought, but his eyes were all right.

"His gun was strange," Walker said.

"Some kind of plastic," Hale said. "Very interesting gun. That may link him up."

"Whose man do you think he was? You don't think he was Agency?"

It occurred to Nicola that life had become so strange over the last few days that this conversation seemed normal.

Hale shrugged. "Probably Moscow Center. We may never know."

"Mrs. Ward saved us," Andy said suddenly in an excited voice. "She threw a tape recorder right at his head!"

They stopped for lunch near Richmond, at a barbecue place. The sign had two pink pigs wearing top hats. When they got back in the van, Walker wanted to know about what Hale had set up in Middleburg.

"A little confab," Hale said. "A little tête-à-tête-à-tête-à-tête."

"Aren't we going to the cabin?" Andy said in a disappointed voice. "I thought we were going to Mike's cabin."

"Don't you like the big place?" Hale asked. "I'm hurt. Some people think it's real comfortable."

"Even palatial," Walker said.

"That's wrong," Andy said in an annoyed voice. "It's not like a palace. It's just a big house."

"I like that," Hale said. "A semantic discussion."

Walker turned to Nicola. "It's a kind of *nouveau* manor house, you know, the kind you see from the air in real estate advertisements."

"As a matter of fact," Hale said, "that's exactly how I bought it. I saw an aerial photograph. It's not, well, it's a little pretentious, but it's perfect for a summit meeting. That's the way I see this—a kind of summit meeting."

430

"Like Camp David?" Andy asked.

"Camp Mike."

"Camp Mich*ael*," Andy said. "I mean, they don't call it Camp Dave."

Hale pointed his finger toward Andy and widened his eyes. "You're right." A powder-blue Mercedes 350 SL passed them. The Virginia plates read: DUES PD.

"So who's coming to our summit meeting?" Walker asked.

Hale ticked the names off on his fingers: "Val Zamatin. Hobie James. Childress."

"I'm impressed."

"It wasn't easy. Hobie was intrigued, but at first Childress wouldn't give me the time of day. It took all my persuasive powers. Val was an even tougher date." In Spanish, he told Walker that he'd kidnapped Zamatin from the Bellehaven Country Club golf course.

"I hate it when they do that," Andy said, about the Spanish. He turned to Kate. "Don't you think it's rude?"

"Yes."

"Don't worry," Hale concluded in English, "he didn't mind that much. He was having a crummy round."

It was midafternoon when they pulled up in front of White Rock, as Mike Hale's estate was called. They stopped at an electronically controlled gate, flanked by old stonework columns. Hale pushed a button in the glove compartment and the gate swung open. Nicola noticed the camera scanning the entrance. They drove in, the gate reclosing silently behind them, and rolled up a winding, oak-flanked drive to the huge house.

Kate and Andy went off with Bancroft, at Hale's direction, toward the stables.

"Can't Cal come with us?" Andy asked.

"Good idea," Hale said.

"I want the grand tour," Cal said, taking Kate's arm.

Hale led Nicola and Walker into a sitting room decorated with red and blue leather wing chairs and English hunting prints on the walls. Probably it was meant to be informal, but it was hard to imagine sitting down in it. Velvet restraining ropes seemed in order

431

and costumed docents reminding you not to touch. Three men stood in the center of the room in a rough equilateral triangle. They were introduced to Nicola—Val Zamatin, Paul Childress, Hobie James.

Val Zamatin blanched when he looked at Nicola; he retreated toward a hunting print. The man named Childress was visibly surprised to see Walker and threw an angry glance at Hale.

"Hobie," Walker was saying to the wiry man with the mobile eyebrows. "How are you?"

Hobie bobbed his head and waved his hand in the air. "Hey, Neil," he said in a neutral voice. "How's it going?"

"Why is he here?" Childress asked Hale, jerking his head toward Walker as if he were a piece of furniture.

"You'll see," Hale said patiently. He moved toward a mahogany sideboard cluttered with bottles and crystal decanters. "A little liquid refreshment anyone?"

"I don't have all day," Childress said. He brushed a fleck of lint off his sleeve and adjusted his glasses.

Hale ignored him. "Neil? Nicola? A bloody Mary?"

They agreed and he began to prepare the drinks. As he squeezed the limes, Childress spoke loudly: "A little game, is that it Hale? I guess you're good at that."

"Actually, you're free to leave," Hale said. He handed Neil and Nicola their drinks and then picked up an ice cube with a pair of silver tongs and dropped it into old-fashioned glass. "Val? Bourbon, isn't it? You lost your taste for vodka as I recall."

"I might as well," Zamatin said in a soft voice. He kept looking at the door as if he were trying to spot the bathroom. "Splash of soda."

Childress remained red-faced, waiting with obvious teeth-gritting impatience.

"I'll take a beer," Hobie said, "if you have one."

When the drinks were distributed, Hale moved toward an antique campaign desk at the opposite side of the room. He withdrew the photograph from under the blotter of the desk and laid it on top of the blotter. He nodded at Walker, then addressed the room at large.

"It's been a treat," he said, closing the door softly behind him as he left the room.

432

"Look," Childress said to Walker. "Hale got us out here under false pretenses. If you think we're going to make a deal with you, you're wrong."

Nicola watched Walker turn his back on them and walk toward the desk. His walk was relaxed. When he reached the desk, he turned around to face the men. She realized he was enjoying himself.

A smile came to his mouth and he shook his head slowly. "You really bought Val's little diversionary tale."

"Everything points your way," Childress said. Hobie James looked at the floor.

Walker picked up the photograph and held it up. "Let me show you something." He inclined his head toward them slightly.

"What's that?" Childress said. With his red face and his choppy gestures, he resembled an angry child. But he moved closer to see what Walker was holding. Hobie circled in too, with careful, measured steps like a boxer. Zamatin didn't bother; he leaned against a blue leather wing chair, sipping his bourbon.

Walker let them look. "So," Childress said. "Am I supposed to be telepathic?"

"This is Val," Walker said, pointing. Childress made a perceptible twitch of recognition and flashed his eyes toward Zamatin. Pointing to the other faces, Walker identified all of the relevant ones: "Richard Sorge. And this is Nicola's great-grandfather, Sergei Borodin. This is her father, Tony Sunderland."

"So?" Childress said. He took his glasses off and polished them with a white handkerchief. He made a dismissive grimace and shook his head. "Val, Sorge," he said in a you-lose voice, "this is all ancient history, this crap. I'm getting tired of this now." He looked at his watch.

"Did you ever consider the possibility that Val never left Moscow's employ?"

Hobie said: "Um!" and his lips spread into a straight line.

Childress laughed. "Come on. Now you're really pissing up a rope."

Walker explained clearly why Moscow might have sacrificed the Sorge net, how it was possible.

Childress was not interested. "I can *imagine* almost anything. That doesn't mean it happened. I can't get a line on what you're

433

getting at. Hobie—do you have someplace lined up for interrogation? I think we'd better get going."

Suddenly, Nicola was tired. She was tired of living in strange places, tired of eating fast food, tired of adventures, tired of standing up, tired of not being at home. She went over and sat in one of the wing chairs, but she was afraid to relax, afraid she might slide off the slippery leather. When she thought of home, she thought of the cottage now. She sat up straighter, wondering about that. It meant her mind had already abandoned the old house in town; her mind had made the adjustment, but in her heart, the old house stood in its ruins, full of her charred memories.

Walker was going on about Zamatin, about Boris Shokorov, about Ronald Peters. Childress's expression had become more attentive. Hobie James stood on the balls of his feet in a ready position. Zamatin looked old all of a sudden, and uncomfortable, like a man who couldn't wait to take off his shoes.

"You couldn't have spent two *minutes* thinking about it," Walker said. He was working up to some anger now and he began to talk both louder and faster. "I'm the one who brought up Shokorov's speech anomalies. If I'm Moscow Center, that's definitely one thing I don't bring up."

"That's exactly what you'd expect us to think."

Walker picked up the photograph, almost reluctantly. "See this boy here, next to Sorge," he said. "This is Leo Adler."

"What do you mean it's Leo Adler?" Childress said. "That's impossible."

"Nicola?"

Without a word, she drew the book out of her purse. She handed it over: *Adler: Man of the Seventies*. Walker flipped it open to the photograph of the teenaged Adler.

Hobie James frowned and wound his hands together. He almost pushed Childress out of the way to get a better look at the photograph. "Leo Adler," he said and then his eyes met Walker's. "Hohohohohoho," he said, almost sadly. "So it's Leo Adler. That saves me a few more months of work."

Childress looked as though he'd stepped into another universe where there was an extra dimension, as though he wasn't sure where he was at all.

434

Nicola's heartbeat was accelerating. She kept looking over at Zamatin, who stood calmly by, watching the proceedings. He looked fit for a man his age. The phrase *in the pink* came to mind. *This is the man that turned my mother and father in*, she thought. *To the Japanese.* The thought turned over in her mind. *Who then froze them to death. In stages.*

"If you look at the cables," Walker was saying, "if you follow the DANTE data, I bet you'll see that DANTE can *only* be Leo Adler. And Val"—he gestured toward Zamatin, who was moving toward the tray of drinks—"Val has been running him."

Zamatin plopped an ice cube into his glass. He said nothing.

"But he's the National Security Council adviser. . . ." Childress sputtered. "The man is negotiating *treaties!* Nuclear weapons agreements! *Jesus Christ.*" He'd turned bright red; he looked apoplectic.

"Of course," Hobie said. He shook his head knowingly.

"You're not surprised?" Childress demanded.

"Paul," Hobie said. "Adler was one of my candidates. *You* were one of my candidates. We were just getting close to clearing you."

"What do you mean? Clearing *me?*"

"I had ten candidates and they were all in that league—you, Adler, Smythe. Whoever DANTE was, I knew it was someone with C-clearance. It's why I had to go so slowly. Once you were eliminated as a candidate, I figured you might get me some more manpower."

"What about all that crap you were feeding to me? About those guys in New York, all that stuff?"

"That's what it was, Paul, crap."

Childress shook his head slowly. "Jee-sus. Leo Adler. Jesus *Christ* on a *cross.*" He held up his finger. "You know," he said in a thoughtful voice, "when I think about it, when I *think* about it now, at all the Fifty-four Committee Meetings, when the DANTE matter was discussed, Adler always pushed the argument that DANTE was a Soviet disinformation operation, that the traffic attributed to DANTE was a plant by the Soviets, that the Soviets in fact engineered the supposed cryptanalytic code break."

Hobie had moved to the sideboard. He was picking up things with the silver tongs and dropping them: a napkin, a piece of ice, a wedge of lime. "You're right, Paul. Leo told us they were changing their code anyway," he said, "and they were just playing games with us, we were chasing our own tails. He was persuasive—some of us thought that the scenario he proposed was *possible*." He sighed. "We could imagine it. It suited us. So . . ." He clasped his hands together and then opened them like a book.

"Val?" Childress said.

Zamatin was peering at one of the English hunting prints as if it contained secret data. He turned toward them carefully.

"Yes," he said quietly. "All true." He shuffled over toward the sideboard, a strange, loose walk, as if his bones were flexible. He splashed some more bourbon into his glass. "Perhaps this is for the best."

Nicola felt her heart rev up; her face felt very hot. She hadn't said a word in the room except hello. Her voice shook when she spoke. "For the *best*. For the *best?* My parents *died* because of you."

"Dasha's daughter," Zamatin said. For a moment his face had a nostalgic look, but then it passed and he just looked very tired.

"You can't stand here saying anything's for the *best*," Nicola heard herself say. "They had a . . . they died slowly, they died horribly, and you . . ." The thought of her mother, staked out on frozen ground came into her mind and the sight of Zamatin standing there drinking bourbon enraged her. She wasn't aware that she was throwing the glass until she saw it moving through the air. A surprised look flew into Zamatin's eyes and he ducked but too late; the heavy crystal hit the top of his head. A red gouge of blood showed. He'd dropped his bourbon and the smell of whiskey rose up around them.

Zamatin was hunched up, both hands on his skull, as if he were keeping his head in place. "What is she talking about?" he muttered. "What is she saying?"

Walker was next to Nicola, his arms around her.

She began to weep. It wasn't just Zamatin she couldn't stand, she couldn't stand the way the men were talking, as if they were discussing market research for a new kind of paper towel. She needed something simpler. She didn't want to be in the room any more. She wanted to see Kate; she wanted to see Andy. She walked toward the door. "I'm . . ." she started, then she began to run.

Walker let her go. When the door closed again, he said, in a flat voice that reminded him of a bailiff's bored recital of charges: "Dasha and Tony Sunderland died in Fushun Camp in Mukden, victims of Japanese medical experiments testing the result of cold on the human body."

Blood was spilling over Zamatin's hands, dribbling down his forehead. He dabbed at it with a cocktail napkin.

"I was about to tell her how it was for me, when they ordered me to turn in the ring. You can guess how I felt about exposing my comrades. . . . Naturally, the idea was repellent to me." He looked at the napkin he'd drawn away from his wound. "But I see my own guilt is not enough, not any compensation. . . ." He swiped at his bourbon-soaked pants legs. His voice suddenly became more resolute. "But at that time, everyone should know, thousands of people were dying in Russia every day. The war was chewing people up and spitting them into mass graves. I was . . . just a young man, doing what I was told. People don't like to hear this anymore, but all the same, it is true." He was silent for a moment. A big sigh came out of him. It seemed to deflate him; he looked slightly smaller. "That was the turning point of my life; since then I have existed as an occupational schizophrenic."

Hobie James smacked his lips. His tongue rolled up under his upper lip.

Zamatin got a new napkin and dabbed at his head. "Tell me," he said, addressing Paul Childress, "what do you think happens if Leo Adler is exposed as a Soviet agent? You think you get any credit for this, for finding him out—or even me?" He shook his head slowly and then stopped, as if the motion hurt. "No. That is not the way it goes. They will think you fools. There will be another congressional committee, another agency shake-up which will do more harm than good."

"Excuse me one fucking minute," Childress interrupted. "Are you now going to tell us how to conduct our business? Amazing." He clenched and unclenched his fists. "When I think of all the operations you've compromised, of all the work you've undone, of . . . of . . ." He turned his back, his voice swallowed by his anger.

"I understand how you feel, Paul," Zamatin said.

"You do *not* understand how I feel," Childress raged.

"I'm not important," Zamatin said "Leo—do you know I still

437

call him Dante in my mind? It was his nickname, you know. Always, I am afraid of slipping with this." He rattled the ice around in his glass. "I've been thinking very hard for the past two weeks—ever since it became clear to me that my position . . . ah, that my position might be found out."

"He's been thinking," Childress repeated in a fragile voice.

Zamatin sat on the blueberry leather wing chair and crossed his legs. "I'll tell you some things about Leo," he said. "Leo is not a soldier like me. Leo is a true believer. And Leo believes that Soviet hegemony is necessary and inevitable—while I . . ." He shrugged. His hands flopped in his lap as if he wanted to raise them but was too tired. "If you analyze some of Leo's speeches, or even if you read very carefully some of the things in his books and articles—you will see how careless he is, how reckless. He actually said, and I quote: 'I believe if we resist Soviet hegemony until the year 2000, we'll have done a good job.' No one seems to notice these things he says. He seems to be the only energetic person in the current political field. And everyone is so impressed with his energy and his style that they ignore the substance of what he says and does."

"So what's your point?" Hobie James's voice had a hard edge to it now. His patience was fading.

"What I'm saying is that not everyone in Moscow is a fool. Many of them believe in détente, as I do; many of them understand that there must be the balance of power. Many are coming to realize that in Leo Adler we have a kind of monster. Leo doesn't follow instructions any longer. He makes his own policies; he makes his own decisions. He thinks he is implementing some grand design—this has been coming out more and more lately." Zamatin stood up. He looked haggard, as if he needed sleep. "I worry that he may actually be insane." He took a sip of his drink. He sounded so calm and cool, but Walker saw that his left hand helped steady his right to bring the glass to his lips. "I've seen him do some lunatic things."

"So," Childress said, "what do you propose?" He asked this question in a taunting bully's voice and Walker could see that Childress must have been an awful child.

"If you just let me finish my thoughts," Zamatin said.

Childress snapped his head to one side and shook it, as if nothing Zamatin could say was worth listening to.

"The treaty Leo has just finished negotiating is a good example. If you look at it, you'll see that the Soviets got more or less everythink they wanted and we"—Zamatin gave a little grimace of a smile—"I mean the United States, got nothing but window dressing. He bamboozles his staff, you know—by pretending to have secret knowledge about the other side. And then I think if you look closely—you will see the foreign-policy reversals you have suffered lately also can be put at Leo's feet. And that's the problem with Leo. It is not the time to punch the United States right now, while it's down. It's dangerous *for both sides*. But Leo doesn't see this. The problem with Leo is that he will let the Soviet Union get too much the upper hand and in the end this will endanger not just the United States but the Soviet Union as well. Leo is not . . ."

He leaned back and stared at the ceiling for a moment. "And so what will happen? Mr. Carter, who is a fair man even if he is a little naive—Mr. Carter will be chased from office. America will elect some flag-waver, some right-winger to restore its honor. And if America feels too bashed-around, then there's trouble, then there can be real trouble."

"But what are you saying, Val?" Hobie repeated. He cracked his knuckles like a teenager. "I mean what's your point?"

Zamatin wagged his head thoughtfully. "I'm sorry." He raised his drink. "Here's to the cold war. May it never even get lukewarm." He picked up the photograph. Walker moved toward him. He was thinking Zamatin would try to destroy it, which didn't matter—Hale had plenty of copies, sent them to the lawyer. . . .

"All the people in this photograph . . ." Zamatin said, pouring himself another bourbon. He stopped pouring, and then added some more to his glass. ". . . except Sergei and Anna—were ghosts. No—*spooks*, this is the word. Spooks, this is a wonderful word because that's what we are. Spectral. We haunt the world, like creatures from another dimension. And this is one way for two countries to do battle, just as the Olympics is another. It is a mistake for Mr. Carter to take that forum away. He does not understand. We should go on this way, fighting with athletes, fighting with ghosts. It's an honorable activity, this, in the end. We fight a shadow war, a spectral representation of a war that should never be fought. And since only ghosts are fighting, no one can be seen to win. And more importantly, no one can be seen to lose."

Neil Walker clapped, slowly and rhythmically. "Very eloquent,

Val. Very touching." He found himself moving toward Zamatin, who was now turning toward Childress, saying, "There are a couple of ways to do this, but—"

Walker found his hands on Zamatin's upper arms. "Hey," Zamatin said as Walker physically jerked him around to face him.

"Nice speech, Val. Bravo. Why is it that I can't shake the memory of this paid killer coming into my motel room with an automatic weapon pointed at my face? Excuse me if I don't find this confrontation between 'our two great countries' so comfortably *spectral*. When your fucking punks tossed my house, they *killed* my housekeeper, a good woman who didn't need to die. They tried their damned best to kill me, too, *and* my son, *and* Nicola *and* her daughter. *And* an old man who just gave us a ride somewhere. It's only after that little massacre didn't succeed that we find you talking about balance of power. Don't try to turn what is really your fucking fallback position into . . . some grandiose defense of espionage. *Jesus Christ.*" He saw the sweat spring out on Zamatin's face. "Yesterday, you weren't talking about how Adler was a danger to détente, you were doing your goddamned best . . . to keep him in there, leaking away. . . ." His voice stopped suddenly. His big hands were squeezing the knobs of the older man's shoulders. At that moment, he would have enjoyed the feeling of something giving way in Zamatin's body, of something cracking. He released his grip slowly and turned his back.

Hale had appeared in the doorway. "Get him out of here," Hale said, nodding toward Zamatin. Hobie James made a telephone call and said that a car would be coming to take Zamatin away.

Walker moved to the corner and looked out the window. He couldn't look at Zamatin anymore without thinking of Mrs. Bradshaw, without thinking of Andy with his hand on the cabin door in Maine, without thinking of the waiter's arm around Kate Ward's neck.

A little while later, a limousine pulled up the long drive; two men in dark suits got out. Zamatin walked to the limo, flanked by the two men, and Walker watched the doors shut and the limo ease up the drive. He knew Zamatin was on his way to a safe house for debriefing. Childress and Hobie James started preparing for their own departure, but Hale observed that business was not quite complete.

The four men sat down at a table in Hale's library. "First," Walker said, "because it's better than nothing, some money—maybe a half million dollars—must go to Lavinia Bradshaw's family."

Childress laughed unpleasantly. "What makes you think we have to accede to a crazy demand like that, Neil?" Childress said in a narrow voice. "You've got nothing else for us or on us. *We* didn't harm your housekeeper."

"It'd be a little awkward for me to seek redress from the KGB," Walker said.

Childress still didn't see why the Agency should accede to these demands.

Hale mentioned exposure of Adler. "We've made a little safety net," he said and gave them the details about the lawyers, and the letter and photographs that would be circulated upon a word from Walker or Hale, or any violence befalling any of them.

"But what if you have an accident! And anyway, that would be very destructive," Childress said. "Zamatin was right about that."

"It would be very destructive," Walker agreed.

"Go on," Hobie said. He'd pulled out a yellow legal pad and wrote Lavinia Bradshaw's name on it. "I assume you can supply details," he said in a tired voice.

The rest of the wish list included reparations to Nicola Ward for anything not covered by her insurance. Hale suggested that a discreet word to her insurance company would be in order. Also, a team of demolitions men was to disarm any explosive devices in their cabins and cars, and Nicola's boat was to be replaced or repaired. Cal's Pinto would require some work, too. "You understand that we're just trying to get back to where we were," Walker said. He folded his arms across his chest. He looked at Hale: "I think that about sums it up."

"Not quite," Hale said. "There's this motel bill, and I think you'll want to get that VW Rabbit from the Vince Lombardi Rest Area back to the Portland airport."

"What's that?" Hobie said. "Got a plate number?"

Walker recited it.

Hale added that he supposed Nicola and Neil and Cal and the

children would want a plane to take them back to Maine. "Right? I mean, I think the morning would be okay with them. Have a plane at the Warrenton airport in the morning. It's a little late to leave tonight."

"All right," Childress said impatiently. "If that's it."

Walker shook his head. "I guess it's too much to expect *gratitude*. I mean, we've just handed you the solution to the biggest problem the intelligence community has had for decades and you act like it's a chore helping us pick up some pieces."

"Yeah," Childress said. "Remind me to send you a thank-you note. Is that it?"

CHAPTER

FIFTY-NINE

The night was hot and humid, and the cicadas were making a racket. Hobie got into the passenger seat of Childress's Lincoln town car. The black leather upholstery radiated heat. When the doors were shut, the noise of the cicadas receded suddenly. Childress fastidiously fastened his seat belt, turned the key in the ignition, and adjusted some levers for the air-conditioner.

"Adler will have to be terminated," he said as the car swung around and they rolled down Hale's long driveway. "The sooner the better, but we can't sacrifice caution to speed. Even if it has to take some time, no scandal or doubt can attach to his death—and I mean none, not a breath, not a whisper, not a hint. It's got to be clean. We can be sure that the opposition will have a close look, and possibly NSC as well. We'll want nothing to key anyone that we knew Adler's true allegiance."

"Just a nice quiet death," Hobie said. "A tragedy: man in his prime struck down by . . . cardiac arrest, or—"

"Whatever," Childress finished for him in a grim voice. "You handle it."

"*What?* I'm not a field guy." Hobie drummed his fingers on the dash. "No way."

"Look," Childress said wearily, "who else do we want to tell about this? The fewer people—I mean, we can't have a bunch of memos and staff meetings on this. Technical Services will supply the method. They're terminally discreet." Childress laughed his nasty little-boy laugh.

Hobie was not amused. "What about my investigation? How am I going to handle my staff on the DANTE investigation?"

Childress didn't answer immediately. "I think what we'll do is use Adler's own little story. We found out that the whole DANTE shtick was a Moscow creation. There's no mole; they just wanted to throw us back in confusion, have us waste our time searching our own closets."

The two men were quiet for a moment. Then Hobie said: "What about Val? Do we know how often they met? The format? We don't want to risk warning Adler by screwing up some procedure in place."

Childress sighed. "You're right. We'll have to run some disinformation about Val. Get his car out here, smash it up, whatever. I'll leave that to you. Does he have a lot of friends?"

"A few. He has a girlfriend."

"Get him in a hospital then; keep him unconscious until the Adler matter has been taken care of."

"And then what? What about later?"

"What do you think," Childress said. It was not a question.

The next day, Hobie spent an hour in the afternoon consulting with Alan Grimes of the Technical Services Division. Grimes was a small man with leathery skin and lashless, reptilian eyes which seldom blinked. He tended to jut his head forward on his long neck. These two characteristics combined to make him resemble a turtle. His expertise was organic poisons. Of course, he had no idea of the eventual use to which that expertise would be put; Hobie had told him only what was needed, not what it was for. That information was strictly need-to-know, and besides himself, the only other person who needed to know was Philippe Marchand.

Hobie was, a little uncomfortably, listening to Grimes talk. He rejected the death cup ("Acts like snake venom, you see, separates the corpuscles from the serum") as both too common and too fast-acting. The fly agaric had the same drawback: rapidity of action and ease of detection. "People have been perishing from eating these two for centuries, so the pathology is well known. Which brings us to my favorite," he said, craning his head forward and widening his eyes slightly, "although frankly I'm really *not* well versed in fungi toxicity—fish, you know, fish are really my specialty. But this one is really a little pet. And it will suit very well for the task you describe. It's called Plato's Amanita, and while it loks rather like the Amanita Muscaria—you know, the Destroying Angel—which in turn looks rather like the common field mushroom—in terms of its toxin structure, it is very much its *own* thing. Also it's virtually untraceable. When ingested—and incidentally, it's not all that difficult to find in our own Northeast—anyway, when ingested, it produces mild, flulike symptoms twenty-four hours later. These symptoms subside rather quickly and recovery apparently ensues. One week later, death is inevitable, but almost never is the death attributed to fungi poisoning. Not only does the delayed effect tend to prevent recognition of the cause, but the toxin attacks in a novel way, which unless you know some biochemistry I will not attempt to explain to you. Let's just say that this toxin is a very interesting little guy. It produces an embolism, you see, pulmonary or cerebral." He smiled cheerfully at Hobie. "We still don't quite know how—exactly—it accomplishes this—it seems to bind . . . well, never mind." He smiled at Hobie and wrung his hands together. "Shall I . . . collect some of these little fellows for you?"

Hobie nodded and stood up.

"And the best part of all," Grimes said, "in terms of discretion is that since the death has no evidentiary pattern, and has this handy little lead time, even I won't have a clue where you use it." He smiled cheerily.

Hobie looked away.

Chandon was a chic restaurant on K Street, one of the places where high-profilers in Washington took nourishment. It had earned four "handshakes" in *Washington* magazine's latest issue rating premier sites of the power lunch. The journalists and lawyers and lobbyists who patronized the place would have been astounded and outraged to learn that Chandon, while not an Agency proprietary, was a "friendly" site, a listening post. And its popular chef, Philippe Marchand, was as highly trained in tradecraft as he was in the culinary arts. The Agency had other friendly sites in town—a disco, a couple of singles spots, a gay bar. All the places were rich sources of useful information, and all of them made money as well.

Adler was a gourmand and frequent patron of Chandon, and his arrival was effusively greeted by the maître d', who ushered him immediately into the kitchen. Adler's large head, which made him appear powerful in photographs, seemed out of proportion when one saw him in the flesh. Marchand was bent over a tray of appetizers—supervising the serving of a set menu lunch in the main dining room—and his eyes lit up when he spotted Adler.

"Leo! It's been too long!"

Marchand led Adler on a little tour of the kitchen—the two men sampled a pâté, and a salmon dish, tested some sea urchin roe. "Ah, for your lunch today, Marchand said, "I was able to find some field mushrooms to accompany the veal."

"Good?" Adler asked.

Marchand pinched his fingers into a bouquet and kissed them: "Perfection. They taste like the woods." Adler reluctantly left the kitchen for his scheduled meeting in one of Chandon's private rooms, the one known as "Soleil."

Hobie James walked uneasily through the room toward "Soleil," moving quickly, with his monkeyish stride. He'd been stuck in traffic and he was late.

As he came in, he heard Adler regaling the group with the latest hostage jokes. Hobie hadn't really needed to be here, but somehow he felt he should be.

Now that he was here, he knew he'd made an error in judgment. His anxiety was palpable: his palms were sweating, his heartbeat accelerated; a tiny whining had begun in his ears.

As soon as he sat down, his anxiety increased. The simple plan of serving Adler poisonous mushrooms suddenly seemed fraught with potential hazard. Suppose the waiter mixed up the plates? Suppose Marchand was a creature of Adler's and no one knew that? Suppose the poisoned mushrooms were served to one of the others at the table? He looked around at the men he was putting at risk. As he looked at each face, he pictured the man dead, then squeezed his eyes shut to stop this masochistic game. He knew his fears were irrational, but he couldn't shut down his imagination.

They started with tiny speckled eggshells, filled with foamy mousse of scallops, set on a nest of raddichio. This dish was far too dainty for the busy men at the table and Hobie was far too nervous to attempt handling the delicate, tiny eggshells. He picked up a roll, buttered it, and then put it back down on his bread and but-

446

ter plate. His throat felt like gravel. This grating terror was not the "heightened awareness" he imagined the field man to experience.

Larry McMillan asked him if he was all right; he admitted a touch of the flu. "I've got . . . the latest little bug." He tried to make a joke but it just made Larry McMillan look worried.

What seemed like days later, the waiter brought the main course, a veal dish *aux champignons*. After that, Hobie found himself staring at the mushrooms on Adler's plate, watching the grayish-brown slick pieces of mushroom flesh pass Adler's lips. Adler spoke to Hobie once and he pretended to be choking. Actually, he was unable to speak. What seemed like days, weeks, later, the luncheon was over. He hoped no one had noticed that he'd not eaten one morsel or drunk one drop since coming into the room.

CHAPTER

SIXTY

Maine

It had been two weeks since the Learjet had flown them back to Maine from Virginia, and they were now so immersed in what Nicola thought of as "real life" that the days on Tripp's Island and their confinement at South of the Border seemed remote and fantastic.

She'd spent the last week working at school, doing the most mundane things—cutting out letters for bulletin boards, poring over curricula, preparing attendance charts, getting her classroom ready for the opening of school. The first day was tomorrow.

It was cold in the cabin today. She had to face it: summer was over. The air had that crystalline quality unique to fall and she knew that the water, too, would be clearing, losing its light-refractive murkiness. By October, it was possible to see down to the ocean floor. Summer people had no idea of this clarity. She ground the coffee and put the kettle on, and then went outside to get some wood for the fire. She wouldn't wake Kate until the fire was going and the damp chill was out of the air.

Walker would be coming over soon with the Sunday papers; he was going to go house hunting with her that afternoon.

She and Kate couldn't stay in the cottage past October. It wasn't truly winterized; it had baseboard heating but lacked enough insulation to be tolerable in really cold weather. The pipes and plumbing had to be drained and shut off long before the ground froze to any depth. It was tempting to think they could stay the winter in the cabin—have some insulation blown into the walls, dig the ground up and wrap the pipes in heat tape. Those were all things she and Stan had planned to do. . . . But then there was the road. She'd have to get the road plowed out every time it snowed, or else trudge out to the main road and then walk back the mile in the dark. Or else buy a Jeep or a Scout that could push a plow. It would just be too hard, and she knew she'd be continually late for school.

She'd never in her life been house hunting before. She'd always imagined it would be easy to find a place. There were many For Sale signs up, and when she drove around, it seemed to her that there were plenty of nice houses available. But she hadn't realized the financial complexities involved, or how hard it was to imagine yourself living in a place completely new to you.

She still hoped to find a house to buy, but the time was so short it looked as if they'd have to rent for a while. Every time they went to see a house, she couldn't keep herself from comparing it with the one on Willow Street, and no matter how wonderful the new house was, it was always a disappointing second. The place on Willow Street had been huge, for one thing, and although it seemed crazy to buy anything nearly that big, the smaller houses seemed stingy and claustrophobic.

She'd driven down Willow Street only once, and the experience was so depressing she'd decided to avoid it in the future. Because the charred remains of the house had been dangerously unstable, the structure had been razed. All that was left was a crude mound streaked with black ashes. And so the place where she'd lived for the last nineteen years, the place Kate had lived all her life—had simply been wiped from the face of the earth.

Walker had been helping her—dealing with the insurance people, and the lawyers, and arranging the financial reparations from the Agency. He and Cal had even located the boat—near Sebasco—and taken it to Bath Fuel for repairs. But Walker had already stayed in Maine much longer than he'd planned; Andy's school started in a week and Nicola knew that soon he would leave. She'd kept this thought from cohering in her mind and now that she'd allowed it to form, she felt a rush of panic. The kettle boiled and she poured hot water into the coffee-filled filter.

They hadn't talked about it—she and Neil—about their impending separation. And she didn't know how to bring it up. Phrases formed in her mind but she couldn't imagine them coming out of her mouth.

I've been giving our relationship a lot of thought.

Just having these words in her head gave her a squirmy feeling, made her face pinch with distaste; she couldn't imagine saying that. As the kids would say: yuck.

We have something really special together.

God.

Maybe he wasn't interested in her beyond their . . . whatever it was . . . *summer of love.*

She groaned.

Maybe he was just being dutiful, waiting to see that she wouldn't crack up, so he could slip back to his life in Washington. It seemed wrong for her to be the one to bring it up. She imagined herself saying: *What about us?* She shook her head. She couldn't say that.

Their physical attraction for each other was so powerful, it had overwhelmed them both. She felt submerged by her desire. Maybe their physical bond had overpowered everything else. Maybe it made the development of an emotional relationship impossible. She shook her head: what did she know about it? What did she know about "emotional relationships"? She sighed and knocked on Kate's door. "You'd better get up. Andy and Neil will be here soon," she said softly.

"Ummhmmm," Kate answered.

Somehow, out of the chaotic events of the past few weeks, Kate had really turned a corner. Although she didn't look different yet, her attitude had radically changed. She'd registered for a couple of courses at the University of Maine in Portland and the plan was that she'd return to Bowdoin for the spring semester.

She even talked about her condition now. She'd say things like, "I'm just skin and bones." She'd rotate her arm in front of the mirror and then run her fingers up from her elbow. "God, Mom, it's so gross. How did I let myself get like this?" Nicola still felt uncomfortable when Kate talked like this. Food and Kate's weight had been taboo subjects for so long, Nicola found herself automatically changing the subject. Kate offered different theories about what had made her "see the light," as she put it. ("Maybe it was being

450

on the island, you know? There wasn't any food on the island, nothing to reject. Maybe that was it." "Maybe it was because the house burned down, you know. The past let me go. Maybe I was trying to get Dad back or something flippy like that—I mean, you know, not consciously.")

Two days ago, Kate had even made an appointment—on her own—to see a therapist in Portland. Nicola tried not to get carried away. They'd had some little reprieves before and although it seemed very different this time, she guarded her elation.

She heard Walker and Andy on the deck. They arrived without the paper. Neil shrugged and she watched his mouth curl into a smile: "Sold out. I tried to bribe the guy to give me one he'd saved for some old lady but it wasn't happening. You Yankees are so honorable."

"We'll go," Kate said. "Andy and I. We'll take the boat and go to Cundy's Harbor and get it there." They put on coats and hats and left, promising to get milk, too.

Walker came up behind her and draped his arms over her shoulders. It was an affectionate gesture that changed almost immediately from a friendly hug to a sexual overture. His hands moved to her breasts and she could feel him hardening behind her. "Hmmmmm," he said, and nuzzled her neck. Immediately, she was inflamed.

He propelled her down the hall to the bedroom, slowly, kissing the back of her neck. They rolled onto the bed. "There's a lot to be said for beds," he said.

"Ummm, that *al fresco* stuff can get a little rough in nippy weather."

He sat on the edge of the bed, untying his shoes. She kissed the back of his neck. "I got frostbite on my dick once."

"You're kidding!"

"Not from . . . uh . . . outdoor occurrences. No, this was in the days when I was heavily into physical conditioning. I ran about twenty miles that day—in ten-degree weather. I didn't notice what was happening to my . . . private parts."

"God. That's horrible. That's *scary*. What happened? I mean, obviously, you're all right."

"Well, nothing *terrible* happened. It didn't—I mean it was a mild case. It's just real sensitive to the cold—I suffer continually during the winter." He leaned back against the pillow and put his hands behind his neck, wincing. "I particularly suffer during big drops in temperature—you know, when the weather first turns cold."

"Like today?"

"*Exactly*."

"You're in pain now, I take it."

He waved the thought away. "I've gotten used to the agony over the years. Of course there is *one* sure cure known to alleviate suffering for at least forty-eight hours."

"Let me guess."

He sank back onto the pillow. "Never mind," he said chuckling. "I'm used to it. I can stand it."

"I guess it's the least I can do." Her mouth started toward its destination.

Soon they heard the whine of the outboard motor. They dressed quickly and were back out in the living room stoking the fire when Andy and Kate came through the door. Nicola and Kate fixed breakfast: bacon and eggs, blueberry muffins, fresh orange juice.

"I think Andy and I will go to the Topsham fair," Kate said, "instead of looking for houses with you." This was a generous gesture. Kate loved house hunting; it was Andy who was completely bored by it.

"There'll be horse races at the fair, Dad. Can I have some money to bet?"

He turned to Nicola. "I hate to encourage him; he's freakishly lucky."

"C'mon, Dad, a few dollars."

"Okay."

"I'm kind of lucky, too," Kate said, "but then there are all those dead tickets on the ground."

"Yeah," Andy said. "My grandpa took me once—Grandpa Del, my mom's dad." Walker watched Andy draw himself into a compact frowning imitation of Del. "Anyway, he let me bet two dollars on every race and I won *seven* races. And he points at all the tickets and says, 'Broken dreams, Andrew, you're walking on broken dreams.' "

Walker laughed. "That sounds like Del."

"Oh," Nicola said, "speaking of dreams, sort of . . . Mr. Micha-lowski called yesterday." She paused. "He said that he'd received private offers for the egg and the icon. *Sizable offers.*"

"How sizable?" Walker asked, but then he waved the question away with his hand. "Never mind." He turned to Andy. "It's considered poor manners to talk about actual figures."

"That's stupid," Andy said.

"Take my word for it, Andrew. You *never* ask how much something costs or how much someone makes."

"Is this the same reason you take price tags off birthday presents?"

"Yes."

"I never did get that. Everybody knows how much stuff costs."

Walker shrugged. He turned to Nicola. "So? What about these 'sizable offers'?"

"Michalowski still thinks we should sell at public auction—with an established floor for each piece."

"The question is," Kate said, with a glance at Andy, "will we be rich?"

Nicola paused. "Yes," she said with a nervous laugh. She rapped the table three times. "We won't exactly be rolling in money, but by our standards—"

"Will we be *sliding* in money?" Kate asked, "maybe slipping in money?"

"I'm not sure of the precise verb," Nicola said and laughed again. "The auction will be in December and we're to go to New York and stay in an insanely expensive hotel."

They spent an hour reading the papers. Nicola dutifully picked up the front page although she really wanted to get to the Real Estate section. She felt, as a teacher, that it was necessary to stay informed about current events. The lead story, the big headline, read: ADLER DEAD. "Neil, look at this," she said in a shocked voice. "Leo Adler is dead—dead of a cerebral hemorrhage. Just think—if he'd just died a couple of months ago, none of this would have happened."

"What's a cerebral hemorrhage?" Andy asked.

"A stroke," Walker said. "A blood vessel bursts in your brain."

"Oh."

Walker wondered how they'd done it. Then again, he was glad he didn't know.

• •

They went to see three houses that afternoon. The last one was in Five Islands and had a view of the old tidal power mill and another view across the bay. It had some frontage on the mill cove, and nine acres of land in all. It sat up on a granite ledge, and from the living-room window, Nicola could see the lighthouse at Parker Head; its revolving light blinked at her. After they explored the house—"It's too big," Nicola said, "but I like it"—the blue-haired real estate broker, Dolly Ardmore, led them on a flagstone path down toward the boathouse and dock. The leathery leaves of the bearberries were beginning to show purplish stains at the edges and the leaves of the staghorn sumac were tinged with crimson.

"Of course it needs a coat of paint," Dolly said as they reached the boathouse. The tide was out. The seaweed, military drab in color, lay messily on the rocks and gave the shore a scruffy look, as if the rocks and the old wooden pilings were wearing dirty skirts. "And it's lovely at high tide." Dolly seemed quite content to stand there and look at the water while they explored the boat-house. There were ancient inner tubes inside, an old wooden play-pen with beads and the letters A, B, and C strung between a metal rod, life jackets bleached a pale orange and mottled with splotches of mildew, huge rusty horseshoes, and metal spikes. There were old oars of different sizes, a toy sailboat, a pink plastic mooring and anchor line.

"Do you think I can afford it?" Nicola could imagine living in this place; she could imagine a life. She could imagine placing her white Adirondack chairs—which had survived the fire in her back-yard—out on the ledge. She could sit there and watch the sun set over the bay. She could even imagine details—walking up from the boathouse in summer, leaving wet footprints on the warm slate of the flagstone. A stand of delphiniums, their blue heads against the white of the house. Kate sunbathing on the rocks, her body recov-ered, fleshed out. Seagulls perching on the old stumpy pilings in the cove.

"What?" Neil was speaking to her. "Earth to Nicola."

"I'm sorry. I was just imagining what it would be like to live here. Actually," she looked at him, "it was easy to imagine."

"Do you want to walk over some of the land in back?"

"Sure." They rejoined Dolly. She had another appointment and locked up the house and told them they should wander around to their hearts' content.

454

"I like it very much," Nicola told her.

"I think they'd come down a little," she said.

"I have to show it to my daughter before I make a decision," Nicola said.

"Of course. I'm not very busy this time of year. Just give me a call."

She drove off in her yellow Toyota.

After they'd explored the woods and the shore, they drove home. As they crossed the bridge, Walker mentioned without preamble that he and Andy would have to leave the day after tomorrow.

Nicola felt a sudden change, as if in air pressure. She realized she'd stopped breathing. She released a breath and then lay her cheek against the cool glass of the window. They passed the old cemetery on Berry's Mill Road. The obelisk was splotched with mustard-colored lichens. A tiny American flag stood in one corner.

"I'll miss you," she said. She closed her eyes and listened to the sound the wheels made against the road. She was tired of being alone, but she could live alone. She knew that much. It wouldn't be true to say: "I can't live without you." You couldn't force it. You couldn't make someone love you or want to live with you.

"Maybe you and Kate could come down for Christmas," he said. There was something wrong with the texture of his voice, as if he were pretending to be himself.

"Maybe," she said. "Or maybe you could come up."

"I think it would be your turn." He was quiet for a moment and then warmed to his subject and began listing all the wonderful activities available in the Washington area at Christmas time. He sounded like a Chamber of Commerce booster. "We'd have a great time," he said, with the kind of fake enthusiasm that allowed her, just for a second, to dislike him. "Andy would love it," he added.

This is how it's done, she thought. This is how you disengage. This is how you get rid of someone without risking a big emotional scene. You leave a window into the future open, just ajar, just a space in which to focus dreams. And then later, when you're away, you close it.

She sighed. The tires hit the gravel; a rush of pebbles flew up under the chassis. "I'll think about it," she said.

"Good. Tomorrow Andy and I have to close up the cabin and

455

pack up and all that. Maybe we can stop by tomorrow night after dinner and say good-bye?"

"Sure," she said. "Why not?"

"And give it some serious thought—I mean Christmas." He tossed her a nervous smile.

"I'll think about it," she said. She left it at that.

That night, she sat on the toilet seat in the bathroom and saw the red stain on the crotch of her underpants. She felt a powerful mixture of regret and relief. She remembered the subjugation of her mind to the focus of her body that day on the path on Tripp's Island, their fast hard coupling in the fog. She remembered the wet leaves against her skin and the way Walker had looked, afterward, standing there naked, with the sweat steaming off his body.

It was worse this month, but she always felt this way when her period started—ambivalent. She thought men couldn't understand this—the tidal sweep of possibility each month. And now, as she looked at the little red spot on her underpants, despite her mind's disclaimer (I can't have a baby; I'm too old, I *can't*), her disappointed womb ached.

CHAPTER
SIXTY-ONE

Andy had always resisted leaving Maine. "I don't really want to go home," he said several times. Walker was working hard, cleaning the place up. Every speck of food had to be taken out—the leftovers given to Cal Tuttle—or mice would invade. The beds had to be stripped, outdoor furniture lugged inside, everything vacuumed, the toilet bowl and sink traps filled with antifreeze, their clothes packed.

Andy proceeded slowly, dawdling and delaying at every turn. He even tried a little emotional blackmail. Last week, Walker had broken the news to him about Mrs. Bradshaw, and even though that news had shaken Andy badly, he was shameless now, using it: "I'm not sure I'll be secure enough to sleep in the house, knowing Mrs. B. was murdered in there. Can I sleep in your room—at home—until I stop being frightened?" These sentences, with their un-Andy-like words—*frightened, secure*—floated through the air.

Neil turned on the vacuum and drowned Andy out. He was thinking about Nicola Ward. He felt a little bad about the way he'd just sprung it on her in the car yesterday—that he and Andy were leaving. He'd found her so compelling that, he'd realized, he'd been hanging on here in Maine, avoiding leaving because, really, he didn't want to leave her. Then he'd made a cerebral decision to go because he thought it was too soon for Andy, maybe too soon for himself, to get really serious about someone. He wasn't sure he could trust his judgment yet and he didn't want to risk making a

457

mistake that would hurt Andy too much—to let Andy get attached to someone and then . . . He didn't want to talk that shit to her though—that "it's too soon" crap. It just sounded like an excuse. He didn't want to *end* anything; he just wanted to leave it open, see what happened.

As soon as he turned off the vacuum, Andy was on his case again. "I don't see why we have to leave tomorrow. We could stay until Thursday, at least *Wednesday*. We'd still have plenty of time to get ready for school and stuff."

It was hard for Walker to understand the power of the attachment Andy felt for Maine. They'd never been there long enough for Andy to make friends with local children. He was always telling Andy that he'd probably feel the same way about any strictly summer place—that he wouldn't love Maine as much if he lived there in the winter. But Andy swore that wasn't true. "I just *feel* better here, Dad, I just *like* it." Once, when he'd been five, he'd hidden for two hours in the woods. They'd searched for him frantically—Diana nearly hysterical, certain he was dead, drowned in the bay. When they found him, with his stained fingers and face, in the blueberry patch, Diana slapped his face. It was the only time Walker could remember that she'd hit him.

Over the past few months with Andy, Walker had begun to get a feel for a child's need for repetition, and he'd planned—once they were all done with their preparations for leaving—a last-night dinner. Just the two of them would eat at the Montsweag Farm Restaurant in Woolwich. There were certain rituals to be observed, and this was one of them. They "always" (in Andy's case this meant that they had done so three times before) ate at Montsweag the night before they were to leave.

So it was at the Montsweag—where the decor was nautical, full of figureheads and ships wheels, glass display cases containing ship models, anchors, old etchings of clipper ships, framed newspaper clippings relating to disasters at sea, where the hand railing on the stairs was made of heavy rope and the restrooms were marked "Gulls" and "Buoys"—that Andy confronted his father. He got straight to the point, saying, "I want to have a serious talk with you." This was a direct echo of Diana's getting-down-to-business talks with Andy. The echo of Diana added a note of pain to the pleasure Walker felt as he beheld his son, earnestly, but not without panache, laying his cards on the table.

"I've been giving a lot of thought to our future," Andy began.

Walker raised an eyebrow but before he replied the waitress came and took their orders. Andy didn't miss a beat.

"I've reached certain conclusions."

"Oh really," Neil said in a joking way. "I'm glad."

"I'm not kidding, Dad." What Andy had concluded was that they ought to move to Maine. Now that Neil worked for himself, he could work anywhere. As for school, he was sure there were good schools here in Maine. They wouldn't constantly be reminded of Mom. He, Andy, could start over with people who didn't know him "before I got hurt and don't feel sorry for me all the time. You can't *play* with someone who feels sorry for you, you know?"

Walker pointed out the practical reasons why Andy's plan wouldn't work, including the fact that for his work, he needed the Library of Congress and the Archives.

Andy countered that he was sure Neil could do other kinds of work—translating, maybe or, "I don't know. You could get some job, couldn't you?"

"Believe me, it's not that easy."

The food came, but Andy wasn't finished talking. He went off on a different tack as Walker ate some steamed clams.

"Don't you like Mrs. Ward?"

"I like her very much. I think you know that."

"Well, do you think you're going to meet someone like Mrs. Ward every day? You're not getting any younger."

"Thanks a lot."

Andy wouldn't even smile. "You know what I mean."

"Why does this remind me of all the times you tried to make our vacation last longer?" Walker said. "I think that's what this is really about." He sensed that what he was saying was somehow unfair but the words kept coming out of his mouth. "I mean, you have to face it, Andy. Everyday life is just what it sounds like—it's every day, it's routine, and routine is good as well as bad. You think if we move, everything will be different, but it won't. I mean, our life might be a little different, sure, but *we* will still be the same." The waitress arrived with his lobster and Andy's steak. "If you're a little worried about going back, and facing the kids and all, I think that's understandable—"

"I'm not just a 'little worried about going back'—why does

459

everything always mean something else? You sound like one of the doctors at the clinic. One of the *shrinks*."

"You'll feel differently when we're back home for a while."

"Just forget it," Andy said in a loud voice.

"Andrew. Keep your voice down."

Not only did he keep it down, he refused to say another word and they drove home in silence.

"I promised Kate and Nicola we'd stop and say good-bye. That okay?"

Andy shrugged.

Despite Andy's truculence, Walker enjoyed the drive from the Montsweag to Nicola's. He'd come to know the road very well and the process of driving it was pleasurable. He touched the brake now, knowing that the paved part of the road was about to end. He slowed even more before turning down Nicola's road and maneuvered the car to the left, to avoid bottoming out on the ledge at the first curve. The air outside was cool, crisp, autumnal. He thought that in Washington, it would still be hot, summer.

When they got out of the car, he stood in Nicola's driveway for a moment.

"Look at the stars," he said to Andy and Andy, forgetting his vow of silence, said, "*Yeah*." There was a tremendous depth to the sky—the Milky Way not just a vague band of light but visibly composed of billions of separate stars.

Nicola offered him brandy and they took their drinks outside and sat on the deck, in the battered redwood chairs, facing out to sea. Walker ran his fingernail over the arm of the chair, feeling the minute ridges where the grain of the wood was raised, the fiber between the growth lines leached away by the salt air. They could hear Andy and Kate inside, playing Yahtzee at the dining-room table. "C'mon, sixes!" Andy said. "C'mon, freight trains!"

A fish jumped. The halyards of the sailboats rattled in the breeze and the boats creaked as they swung in the current.

"It's funny," Nicola said, "the feeling I've been getting lately. Although the fire wiped out all my things, you know, my entire material history—I mean except for what was in the cabin—in some ways it's not such a bad feeling."

"What do you mean?" He took a sip of brandy. The moon beat a ripply path across the cove.

"I feel . . . I don't know, unencumbered, renewed, I don't know"—she took a sip of her drink—"freed from the past. I always thought my problem was the opposite, that I didn't have much of a past, that I wasn't, I don't know, anchored in the world the way I thought other people were." She laughed. "I'm not expressing myself very well."

"You know, Andy was saying something like that at dinner." He paused. A fish jumped very close to them.

Nicola looked at him.

"Andy had an interesting idea. He doesn't think we should go back to Washington. He thinks we should stay here, live here. . . ." He hesitated, took a big gulp of brandy. It stung his throat in the nicest way. "What do you think?"

Nicola couldn't read him. At first she'd been angry and hurt—when he'd told her, so suddenly, that he and Andy were leaving. It was as if she'd offered him something—let's face it, her love—only to watch him shake his head: *no, thanks.* And all day today, she'd just been sad, just thinking how she'd miss them. But a more expansive mood had come over her, the one she'd just tried to describe to him—and she felt more able to let go.

And now Neil was asking "What do you think?"

It never seemed to her that her desires counted, that her wishes had any power over other people. *Andy* had an interesting idea, he'd said. What about him. What did he want?

Still, she did know what she wanted.

She drank her brandy down in one gulp and threw the glass as far as she could out over the water. She heard the splash and then she said, "Don't go. Stay."

He stood up and copied her gesture, downing his brandy and hurling his glass as far as he could. He knew when she said the word *stay* that it was the right thing to do. Something inside him shifted, stabilized, aligned. When he heard the splash, he imagined the glass settling slowly to the bottom. His mind felt extraordinarily light.

Author's Note

The author is obligated to the following works and would like to acknowledge her debt to them: *Carl Fabergé: Goldsmith to the Imperial Court of Russia* by A. Kenneth Snowman; *The Russian Fascists*, by John J. Stephan; *All About Shanghai: A Standard Guidebook*, a thirties guide to Shanghai, introduced by H. J. Letheridge; *Shanghai: High Lights, Low Lights and Tael Lights*, by Maurine Karns and Pat Patterson; *The File on the Tsar*, by Anthony Summers and Tom Mangold; *Target Tokyo* by Gordon W. Prange; and *Shanghai Conspiracy* by Major General Charles A. Willoughby. I am also indebted to John W. Powell, who, in *The Bulletin of the Atomic Scientist* (October 1981), first broke the incredible story about the Japanese prisoner-of-war-camp atrocities and subsequent U.S. cover-up. Most of the action in this narrative takes place in 1980 and I must apologize to Mr. Powell for my temerity in allowing my characters to read accounts of the story he unearthed before, in fact, it was published in 1981. My account of the Sunderlands' travails in "Fushun Camp" is, of course, a fiction. I should point out, also, that Fabergé's "Rosebud Egg," while indeed missing, disappeared many years after the Russian revolution; it is believed to have been seriously damaged.

My thanks to the staffs of the Library of Congress and the National Archives, with a special nod to Steve Tilley.

Except for those incidental figures, who clearly strolled across the pages of history, all the events described in this novel are invented, and all the characters, living or dead, totally imaginary.

I am grateful to my helpful readers, Joanne Bario, Scott Miller, and Devorah Zeitlin, and to my agent, Pam Bernstein. I must also thank my husband, Jim Hougan, for his encouragement and unflagging stamina in reading my many drafts. And finally, I would be seriously amiss without giving a shout of thanks to my editor, Trish Lande, for coaxing clarity from my unruly manuscript.